GW00586696

Garnet Fair

Garnet Fair

Janet Mary Tomson

PIATKUS

First published in Great Britain in 1995 by
Judy Piatkus (Publishers) Ltd of
5 Windmill Street, London W1

**The moral right of the author
has been asserted**

*A catalogue record for this book is available
from the British Library*

ISBN 0–7499–0284–1

Set in 11/12 pt Times by
Create Publishing Services Ltd, Bath, Avon
Printed and bound in Great Britain by
Biddles Ltd, Guildford & King's Lynn

For Terry, with love

Garnet fair, Ruby rich,
One an angel, one a witch,
Hair of black, eyes of green,
One a pauper, one a queen.

Part I

July 1587 – July 1588

Chapter One

The Isle of Wight was having the hottest summer she could remember. The fairground was drenched in relentless sunshine. Yet, inside her tiny, sweltering tent at the edge of the site, Mardi Appleby was at that moment oblivious to the heat and the gloom.

Sitting cross-legged on the grass, she faced her second customer of the morning. The girl was taller than she but their bent heads nearly touched as they surveyed the cards spread out between them.

'What does it say?' The speaker's voice was breathless and as she waited she twisted the rough cloth of her skirt between anxious fingers.

Mardi glanced up at her. In most ways she looked ordinary enough but a quirk of nature made her remarkable. Like the Queen, she had red hair. Like the Queen, she had a small pointed face and with a smirk Mardi guessed that, like the Queen, she too was probably a virgin.

Mardi continued to regard the cards with her shrewd black eyes. She felt a malevolent disdain for the other girl's beauty. Her own skin was honey brown from having lived in the open and her dusty black hair stuck to her cheeks. She brushed it away in irritation. It curled in thick, knotted clumps.

With deliberate slowness she picked up a card and turned it over. It was the queen of hearts and she knew that it was for her. It signified intuitiveness as well as love.

With a nod of her head she indicated to her companion to take a card. The girl handed one over, her green eyes wide with expectation.

3

What Mardi saw caused her to catch her breath, not in a dramatic way but to suspend all movement as she rapidly thought of the implications. It was a queen of clubs reversed.

'Take another.'

The girl turned another card, revealing the ace of spades, also reversed.

On seeing it, Mardi began to shake her head.

'What is it?' Alarm now showed in her customer's eyes.

Gathering her wits, she said: 'It's nothing.'

Mardi reached out and turned the next card herself. As she had known it would, the nine of clubs followed. There was so much confusion here and, although she knew it was impossible, her own destiny seemed entwined with that of the red-haired girl before her. Bereavement and heartbreak stared back at her from the cards – for one of them at least, but who?

Casting her eyes over them again, she sighed. Whatever the future held, she knew that this girl was not going to enjoy her life to the full. Unbidden came the thought: Serves her right for being beautiful.

Sweeping the pack aside, Mardi looked her in the face and said intuitively: 'You bear the Queen's name.'

'How do you know?'

The girl was gratifyingly impressed and, pleased with her success, Mardi added: 'You'll marry a man whose name begins with S.'

It was Lizzie's turn to shake her head. 'You're wrong there. I'm spoken for and his name's Will.' She began to blush. 'I expect he's here somewhere this afternoon. When he's finished his time, we'll be wed.'

Mardi shrugged, having little patience with the romantic foolery of village girls, but she asked: 'What does he do?' She needed time to calm her unease.

'He's a stonemason. He's serving under a maser at Carisbrooke Castle.' The girl hesitated. 'No one knows about our ... arrangement.' She used the last word hesitantly, looking to Mardi for sympathy. Not getting any, she reiterated: 'But we'll be wed when his time's up.'

Having caught the fortune-teller out over the identity of her lover, Lizzie visibly relaxed and handed over her groat. As she was halfway through the opening of the tent, she turned and said:

'This is the first time I've ever been to the fair. If I'm allowed, I'll come again next year. By then I'll be betrothed proper, you'll see.'

The dark girl turned her lips down in the semblance of a grin and scratched her armpit.

As soon as she was alone she gazed gravely at the cards. The brightly painted images stared impassively back at her and she sighed. Much as she would have liked it to be otherwise, she knew that what she saw was as certain as the coming-up of the sun.

Outside the tent the fairground teemed with activity. Pedlars, performers and livestock competed for the attention of revellers threading their way between the stalls. Mardi blinked and shaded her eyes, taking a moment's respite before looking for another customer.

Nearby a group of hirelings were shouting and laughing in the overloud manner of those who have consumed too much ale. As she watched, one of them caught her eye. Nudging his companion, he made some comment which set all four sniggering. She stuck her tongue out and turned back into the little tent to avoid them. A moment later the flap was pushed aside and the man who had first spotted her blundered inside, his eyes unfocused, his body swaying.

'You tell fortunes, then?' he asked.

'For a price.' She eyed him speculatively, wondering how much money he might still have.

'Yeah? How much?' He was fishing in the belt about his waist but his fingers seemed incapable of holding whatever it was he was trying to get out. Finally he extricated a halfpenny and flung it down on the grass at Mardi's feet.

'I'll tell your fortune,' he said. 'And if I'm wrong you can have that.' He poked the coin with an unsteady toe and sniggered to himself. The flap of the tent was lifted again and the man's three companions crowded in behind him.

'Here we are, lads,' their mate called. 'I'm going to tell the little tyke's fortune. She's about to get pleasured at least once.

5

The rest is up to you.' Lunging forwards, he grabbed Mardi by the shoulders and his weight sent her toppling to the ground.

Letting out a squeal, she tried to reach the flap of the tent to attract the attention of her father, who normally worked the pitch nearby. She remembered fleetingly that he had been nowhere in sight a moment ago and fear gripped her. The drunk was trying to pull up her kirtle while lying heavily over her. She screamed again as loud as she could but it seemed drowned by the hubbub of the crowd outside. At that moment real panic set in, for one of the men pushed his hand over her mouth while a third pinioned her arms to the ground.

'Get a move on,' one of them called. 'I'm bursting here.'

In her terror Mardi struggled like a demon, biting the hand that held her mouth and kicking her bare feet into any flesh that was within reach. By now, however, her ankles had been grasped in a vicelike hold and the breath was being crushed out of her by her burly assailant.

'Ain't much pleasure to be had here. She's like a skinned lamb,' he gasped, pressing her body hard into the unyielding ground.

'Dear God, no!' She twisted this way and that to avoid his drunken attempts to penetrate her. With a desperate effort she bit again into the hand that covered her mouth and screamed as if her lungs would burst.

Suddenly there was a glare of light as the flap of the tent was lifted, letting the sunlight fall directly onto her. A man was silhouetted in the entrance. The next moment he was grabbing her assailants one by one and thundering into them with his fists before throwing them aside. They put up little resistance, somehow managing to scrabble their way out of the tent and into the crowd.

Mardi, bruised and disadvantaged by the fact that her skirt was above her waist, struggled into a sitting position. Her rescuer crouched down and put an arm about her shoulder.

'Are you hurt, mistress?' The tone of his voice and the deference with which he addressed her threw her into confusion.

'No.' She was covering herself and wiping her face in her sleeve in an effort to rid herself of the taste of the drunk.

6

'There's blood on your face.' Concern showed in the young man's eyes and he gently wiped her chin.

She grinned then and said: 'It's not my blood. It belongs to the Devil's piss who –' Remembering herself, she blushed.

'Did he ...?' It was his turn to blush.

She shook her head. 'That's one thing I can thank Pa for. He's taught me how to look after myself.' She now looked directly at him and added: 'Pa prizes my maidenhead. He thinks it may come in handy one day, like a spare kerchief or a cure for warts.'

The young man sat back on his heels, looking disconcerted.

'Well, if you're not hurt ...' Standing up, he brushed the dust from his russet trousers. From her sitting position Mardi was aware of his muscular legs.

'What's your name?' She scrambled up, standing a foot shorter than he. The smell of his sweat did strange things to her and she was suddenly conscious of her dirty face and skinny, childlike body.

'Will.' He was looking down at her with candid hazel eyes. The light from outside formed a halo around his thick brown hair and when he smiled his face had a quizzical, lopsided look.

He took a step towards the flap and Mardi knew that she did not want him to go.

'What do you do?' She ran her hands over the waist of her dress, pulling the material tight so that her barely existent breasts jutted to best advantage. The young man seemed to find her action amusing.

'I'm a stonemason,' he replied, then added: 'You'd best be careful. Any man in his right mind would lose his head over a pretty woman like you.'

Mardi blushed, then, sensing that he was teasing, drew her brows angrily together. Her mouth became a fierce, defiant line. This made him grin more broadly.

With a sudden flash of realisation she said: 'You're a stone-mason at the castle.'

His eyebrows shot up in surprise. 'How the devil do you know that?'

She was back in control now. Pausing for effect, she added with great significance: 'Today you've met a woman who will change your life.'

7

Will was still grinning but there was puzzlement in his eyes. 'I know lots of things,' she continued. 'Don't you make fun of me or you may be sorry.'

His face relaxed and he said: 'Quite the little wasp, aren't you?'

She looked away and as an after thought reached up and unfastened the string tied around her neck. Hanging from it was a jagged stone formed in the rough shape of a heart. The hole in the middle had been worn by the elements and gave it a power of its own.

Holding it out she said: 'Here, I've got nothing else but this is by way of saying thank you.' When he hesitated, she continued: 'It doesn't look that special but it will protect you from harm.'

Still grinning, he took it from her and after a moment's hesitation tied it about his neck. She watched as it came to rest against the crinkly golden hairs of his chest visible beneath his open shirt.

'Well . . .' He looked awkward now, unsure of himself. Mardi concentrated hard, her black eyes on his face.

As if making up his mind, he touched her elbow and led the way out into the fairground. 'Come on,' he said.

Mardi smiled to herself with satisfaction and fell into step at his side.

For a while they wandered past the food stalls and jugglers, past the Moorish dancers and musicians. Mardi saw her father then and hastily turned in another direction. Will followed her. They stopped in front of a stall with every sort of frippery imaginable and for a heady moment she thought that he was going to buy her a brooch or some ribbon. She looked at the woman who was serving and smiled in triumph, but instead he moved on to the next stall and purchased a large mutton pie.

Holding half of it out, he said: 'Here, wrap yourself around that. You don't half need fattening up.'

She pouted at him in disappointment but her hungry stomach made her grab the pasty and gnaw her way through it.

More slowly he ate as well, glancing at her every now and then with amused eyes.

'Where do you live?' he asked.

'Anywhere. Everywhere. We travel the fairs. Pa was a

ploughman once but the farm went over to sheep. Since then we've been on the roads.'

He was nodding distractedly and started to look restless as if he wanted to get away. The knowledge filled her with panic for she still did not want him to go.

Taking the plunge, she started: 'We're leaving by barge at sunup, but tonight –' Before she could finish, her arm was grabbed and she was swung round to face her father.

'What in the Devil's name are you doing?' Taking in his daughter's bright eyes and dishevelled appearance, he looked malevolently at Will. 'What you been up to?' he demanded, thrusting his shaggy black head forwards. The light glinted on the gold ring in his earlobe and brandy fumes wafted around him. He was dressed like the poorest sort of vagabond.

'Hold on, brother.' Will straightened up and they were much of a height. 'Your little maid was in distress and I came to her aid.'

The older man grunted. Turning back to his daughter, he said: 'Well, just stop wasting time and get back to work.'

Mardi lowered her eyes. 'I've been working,' she defended herself. She looked hopefully at Will but he gave a little shrug and began to back away. She knew that the spell was broken. He was glancing about him now as if he had just remembered something or someone. But before going he turned to her father one more time.

'You've got a remarkable girl,' he said. Resting his steady gaze on her anxious face, he added: 'You could say I've just had my fortune told.'

Chapter Two

In the brief respite between making butter and collecting grasses for the floor, Lizzie Galpine sat outside her parents' cottage by the sheepwash. Eyes closed, she turned her head to soak up the mellow autumn sunshine and as she stretched her shoulders she found new areas of warmth against the crumbling cob of the cottage wall.

'Come on, our Lizzie, you call 'em out.' Her friend May's voice intruded, wheedling, persistent.

'Not now.' Lizzie clung to the daydream that absorbed her. In her mind the monarch, her own maidenhead and the Virgin Mary were mystically entwined and it made her feel essentially good. Her toes moved dreamily in the dusty soil.

'Please,' May begged.

Lizzie half opened her eyes. Her friend's moon face glistened in the heat, her stubby fingers plucking at the brittle grass.

'Oh, all right.' Reluctantly she started to recite the alphabet. She was one of the few village girls who had been sent to the Reverend Cotton at six of the clock each morning to learn her letters. As she called them out, May, face raised and eyes closed, scrabbled on the ground for a pebble.

'Got one!'

Lizzie stopped reciting. 'M. Letter M,' she announced.

May opened her eyes. 'Who does that mean?'

Lizzie shrugged. 'Martin? Michael?'

'I don't know none o' them.'

'Well, perhaps you'll marry a stranger.' Her face brightened. 'Perhaps you'll be carried off by Spaniards if they do invade.'

'Course they won't. Anyhow, they'd carry off you for sure.'

May's voice was flat, acknowledging that she would never be beautiful. 'What do you think they'd do?' she finally asked, enjoying the fantasy.

'They'd kill everyone except the young girls and lie with them over and over till they died of love.' Lizzie spoke with an authority she felt was expected of her.

'They wouldn't! That 'ud be a sin.' May's eyes shone with excitement.

'So's killing.'

They were both silent at the thought of being ravished by marauding Spaniards.

'We'd best go.' Lizzie started to get up but her friend pulled her back.

'Not yet, you do it first.'

'No. It's silly.'

''T ain't. Beth Kingswell picked a G twice and now she's spoken for by George Urry.'

'Well, it's daft.'

'Come on, it's only fun. Please.'

'Oh, come on, then.' Reluctantly closing her eyes, Lizzie let her brown fingers stray onto the grass and gabbled the alphabet until her hand closed over a stone.

'W. 'Tis Will for sure!' Wonderment showed in May's simple, wide-eyed expression.

'Don't be daft.' Lizzie flushed and her denial lacked conviction. She felt a certain relief, for the Gipsy girl's prediction still hung heavy on her mind.

She threw the pebble hard and it plopped into the stream rippling its way in front of the cottages. The geese honked and ran a few feet before resuming their nibbling at the dusty grass.

'Will's so handsome,' May sighed. 'Why don't you like him, Lizzie?'

The girl shrugged. 'He's wild.'

'He says you look like the Queen.'

'He's never seen the Queen.' Lizzie tossed her head and a strand of copper hair escaped from her cap and tumbled down, sticking to her neck. It thrilled her that he should think of her in this way but she maintained an expression of scorn.

'He's seen the Queen's likeness at the castle. Sir George has

11

her picture on the wall. Will says it's almost real.' May defended him stoutly.

Lizzie closed her eyes, faking lack of interest, but she was thinking about William Gosden. He had been working at Carisbrooke Castle now for over a year, helping to get the defences ready in case the Spaniards came.

Last harvest-time he had had special permission to come home for two days to help. The weather had been clear and hot and everyone was in the field from first dawn to dusk. Lizzie had been down with the rest, cutting and stacking, her legs scratched by the sharp stubble, her hands sore from the harsh, resistant straw.

'Cart's here,' someone had called out and she had turned to watch.

Two gentle brown oxen had waved their heads in rhythmic harmony to avoid the flies and a tall young man had stepped from behind the cart. He was stripped to the waist and his chest was brown as the earth with crinkly hairs glistening like a golden crucifix.

Lizzie had caught her breath and the strangest feeling had engulfed her. Already he was heaving loads onto the cart, the silhouette of his body bending and stretching in the sunshine.

'Come on, gal.' Her brother Jed had broken the spell, pushing her playfully, unaware of his strength.

'Ow! Don't!' she had snapped at him, overwhelmed by the feeling.

'' Tis Will come back,' Jed said, unconsciously tuning into her thoughts. She shrugged and, suddenly aware that the little ones were leaping in and out of the balk, she had turned to scold them.

At nammet-time they had sat under the great beech trees, hungrily eating their barley bread, sheep's cheese and huge apple pasties made with the first of the autumn crop. Stone jugs of ale were fetched from the bourne, where the water had kept them cool under the shelter of the reeds.

Will sat a little way away, joking with the men. When he had finished eating, he stretched and scrambled up the bank to where Lizzie and the children sat.

'Didn't hardly know you, Lizzie,' he said, sinking down beside her. 'You're grown-up. Are you eleven or twelve?'

'I'm near fifteen!' Her cheeks suffused with colour as she realised, too late, that he had been teasing her.

'You ain't wed yet, then?'

'Course not.'

'Good job, 'cause I'm coming to fetch you one of these days.'

Lizzie could not look into his face. Her heart deafened her and his hazel eyes seemed to see into her soul.

'Lost your tongue?' he teased, then, suddenly serious, added: 'Don't you forget 'cause I mean it, mind.' His hand was on her arm, a gentle pressure manacling her heart to him.

Looking down at the strong brown hand, she shook him off. He grinned before striding away to resume work. She had not seen him since.

She shied away from remembering the disappointment when he had not been at the Summer Fair. It had been her first ever visit and she had been so sure that he would be there. The Gipsy girl's prediction returned like a cold shadow and resolutely she blocked it out.

With a sigh she scrambled up and set off with May to gather the grasses for the floors. Her mother insisted upon a good store of things, slim reeds with wormwood and fleabane, fresh and pungent to keep the pests at bay.

In summer the cottage door was always open and the sour smells of winter were driven out with sweet-scented herbs. Along one wall in their downstairs room a chest holding their winter clothes and blankets was perfumed with lavender and wild roses, tightly shut against the pervading wood smoke. Its smooth, darkened lid acted as both a seat and a bed. Mam likes things nice, Lizzie mused.

She glanced at May and felt a moment of compassion, for there were eleven people living in her friend's tiny cottage. She was ashamed to admit that she did not like to go there. It had a stale-smelling earth floor, the tiniest window and one platform reached by a rickety ladder where all the girls slept. The older boys slept out in the lean-to on a plank jutting from the wall above the sheep. I'm that lucky, she thought, tugging at a silver-leaved mugwort. I'm glad there's only five of us, including Mam and Pa.

She suddenly realised that May was speaking and looked round at her.

'You wouldn't want to live nowhere else, would you?' her friend was asking.

Lizzie considered the question. 'I wouldn't mind going to London to be a court lady,' she offered.

May did not answer. Her back turned, she struggled with a stubborn sprig of wormwood.

'Pa's sending me away,' she finally blurted out.

Lizzie gazed at her. 'Where to?'

'I'm to go and be hired at the fair.'

'Oh, May!' Lizzie reached out and touched her friend's shoulder to show her concern.

'Pa says I'm costing him dear when I could be earning. You can get fifteen shillings a year.' Her eyes blinked to dissipate the threatening tears.

'Well, perhaps it'll be an adventure,' Lizzie said with an optimism she did not feel. 'Perhaps it's Fate. You'll meet that Martin or Michael and get wed.'

'No, I won't. No one'll wed me.' She started to cry.

'Course they will. Truly, May. I'll wager that you'll end up at the castle as a lady's maid.'

May shook her head, wiping her cheeks on the backs of her hands. Already a gleam of hope was calming her. Sensing her success, Lizzie added: 'I think a lord will make you his bride and you'll be Lady May and I'll have to curtsy to you.'

'Course you wouldn't.' May gave a watery smile and said: 'I wouldn't know how to behave.'

'You'd soon learn.'

May brightened as they invented more and more unlikely adventures. Sufficiently restored, she suddenly asked: 'What about you? What will you do?'

'Me? Why, nothing.' Lizzie had given no serious thought to her future. All her hopes rested in a hazy dream of life with Will and until he formally came to claim her she felt herself to be in a kind of limbo.

'Will you wait till Will comes?' May asked hopefully.

'Course not.' She tossed her head and turned away to hide her guilty cheeks. 'I'll just wait and see what is to be.'

Leah Galpine was watching through the dairy window for her daughter Lizzie. The recently installed glass still filled her with

14

wonder and the metal latch which opened and shut gave her the illusion of accomplishing a difficult task. For a moment the pleasure of such modern additions to her home drove out the fears that oppressed her.

In whichever direction her mind wandered, it brought her face to face with some anxiety. She tried not to think at all but it seemed impossible to have an empty head.

Pushing back a stray lock of peppered hair, she paid cursory attention to the cheeses dripping whey from the suspended straw baskets, but the thoughts were already back.

Harry, her second son, had been with the fleet now for over a year and she longed for news of him. Two village lads had been called to God in the past months, one with sickness and the other crushed beneath a mast. She avoided their mothers because she knew no words of comfort. She dreaded that before long other women would be avoiding her. It was a sin to admit it, but Harry was her favourite child. For that reason alone God might see fit to take him from her. She offered up a silent entreaty.

Rumours of war filled her with dread. To shut them out she concentrated on her first-born, Jed. She knew that behind her back folk said he was two apples short of a bushel and she felt for him with a mother's fiercely protective love. He would be happy enough if people didn't tease and fluster him. He needed time and patience and sometimes there was little enough of either.

At the same time she had to admit that when she and George were too old to work the farm, Jed would never be able to manage on his own. They held the land in lease for a period of three lives and Jed's would be the second. She could only hope that Lizzie would look after him and thoughts of her daughter too made her heart heavy.

Only last night she had been sewing by the fading light when George had raised the question of Lizzie's future. Since then she had gone over and over the conversation, looking for anything she might have said to change things.

'You know Silas Dore?' he had suddenly asked.

'Him at the fulling mill?'

'That's him. Anyhow, he's been made constable.'

'He'll beat them all to Jericho then,' she had replied, knowing only too well that Silas Dore was a harsh employer and a lecher into the bargain.

'Mebbe so, but I've been yarning to him and he's taken a shine to our Lizzie.'

Leah had put down her sewing and looked her husband in the face.

'What are you saying, George?'

'Nothing. Only that Silas is a comfortable-off chap and now he's constable he'll be pretty powerful hereabouts.'

'He's a cruel fellow to man and beast,' she had retorted. 'I wouldn't want none of mine trucked up with him.'

George was taking his boots off so that she could see only the top of his shaggy grey head. He dropped them on the stone floor and there had been a dull thud as the wooden studs made contact.

'He works all the land down beyond the bourne now. He's well respected at the church and he's been a widower for nigh on a year,' he had observed.

'He's heading on for fifty.'

'That's a good steady age.'

It had flashed through Leah's mind that the same applied to George, but she carried on: 'You aren't suggesting he should marry our Lizzie, are you?'

'Seems a goodly arrangement. She'll come off well if ever she be widowed and there's advantage to be had with use of the fulling mill.'

Leah had started to shake. 'You're no better than selling your daughter for gain,' she had shouted at him. 'I can't countenance it.'

There was a terrible silence before he had replied: 'Like it or not, Mother, I've told him yes.'

He had risen from his old wooden chair and climbed the narrow stairway to their bedroom, leaving her trembling in the darkening kitchen.

With a sigh she turned back to the cheeses and it was then that she felt the quickening inside. It was hardly even a feeling, the merest ripple in her belly, but she knew undeniably what it meant. Until now she had gone on hoping. Surely she was now at the end of her natural courses? But that and the sickness and the dragging tiredness had all pointed to the unthinkable and

16

now this, this stirring inside. Dear God, please don't let it be, she prayed, but she knew that this was one prayer that would remain unanswered.

At six on Sunday morning Silas Dore turned heavily in the goose-down mattress. He knew by the sun that it was past the time for him to be up, for he was due at the church at seven of the clock. As constable it was his duty to ensure that all the villagers observed their religious devotions.

The accursed maid had failed to wake him. He remembered then with misgiving that the night before he had forced her. She had struggled and cried and in the end he had struck her to subdue her. It had happened once before and on that occasion she had wept for days and he had been afraid that she might report him to the priest. He had bribed her with a kerchief and a groat, promising that it would not happen again. She had been sullen ever since, keeping well away from him, but last night he had had too much ale. It had been nearly two months and he justified it to himself because prolonged abstinence for a virile man such as himself was bad for the health. Anyway she was only a poorhouse slut.

He sat on the edge of the bed, yawning and scratching his naked torso. Blearily he rubbed his hands over his heavy jowls and down across his chest to his potbelly. Both his wives had died childless so, with the exception of the maid and the two hired lads who slept above the barn, he lived alone.

He realised with relief that the maid would be departing in a few weeks for the annual hiring, so if she happened to be with child it would not then be his problem. Now that he was constable he could not afford to have the finger of scandal pointed at him.

Remembering the conversation of yesterday with George Galpine, he smiled to himself as he heaved his bulk off the bed. Not much longer would he have to choose between forcing and abstention. Little Lizzie Galpine would soon be called upon by God Himself to do the things that he liked best and a legitimate heir might be forthcoming. It was beyond him why God should have cursed him with barren wives.

With this thought he dragged on his breeches and shirt and stumbled down the stairs, calling on the maid to be quick and

17

get ready for church. She was in the kitchen and he could see her swollen face and half-closed eye.

'You should do as you're told,' he said gruffly. 'You'd better tell them you walked into the doorpost.'

'I bain't be going!' she retorted, bursting into tears.

'Course you're going. They'll fine me tuppence if you don't attend and I'll stop it out of your wages.'

He pushed her and she scuttled back into her cubbyhole.

'Tidy yourself up,' he shouted at her hunched back. Swilling down a chunk of bacon with some ale, he set off across the green in the direction of the church.

Nearly all the village was present for the seven-o'clock service. Lizzie and her family stood in their accustomed pews, the men on one side of the aisle and the women and children on the other. Slowly the church filled.

Silas Dore, wearing an expression of pious devotion, turned to look at her as some of the little ones in front began to squabble. She shook their arms and blushed under his scrutiny.

She wore her regular Sunday kirtle, which she had helped to dye and sew. It was in a pleasing shade of harvest gold extracted from boiled onion skins. A tiny ribbon of pleats about her neck made her feel fashionable. In a pious moment and in order to avoid Silas Dore's gaze, she closed her eyes and prayed for forgiveness for her vanity and for divine guidance in her attempt to lead a pure and blameless life.

The service lasted for two hours. Eventually the congregation emerged, blinking and stretching, into the sunlight. The priest gave them all God's blessing and Lizzie expelled her breath in expectation of a breakfast of pottage, ale and meat.

Ahead by the churchyard gate, Silas Dore waited. Leah put her arm around Lizzie's shoulder and drew her aside.

'Marnin', George, ladies.' Silas raised his hat to them.

'Marnin', Silas, be you well?'

'Well indeed, George.' He stepped closer. 'And how's this little lady then?' His eyes were on Lizzie's breasts and she blushed, dropping a curtsy. 'Pretty as a picture,' he continued, not shifting his gaze.

'It's a disgrace! I don't agree to it,' Leah exploded. 'I want you to know, Silas Dore.'

'Shush!' Her husband nudged her with his elbow. The fuller frowned.

'What's this, George, a scold in your house?' Turning to Leah, he added: 'Take care, mistress, or you'll find yourself afore the justices and it'll be my duty to put ye in the ducking stool.'

Leah hurried away, chivying her daughter in front of her, leaving her husband gazing sheepishly at his neighbour.

'There's nothing to fret about,' he assured. 'She's worried about our nipper at sea.' In a lower voice he added: 'Nothing ain't been said to Lizzie yet so hold back for a week or two.'

'What's the matter, Ma?' Lizzie asked as they hurried across the green towards the cottage.

'Don't you fret, child, it's nothing I can't sort out,' the older woman assured.

Lizzie shrugged and promptly forgot the incident; she had far more interesting things to think about.

The weeks passed quickly for there was much to do before winter. Already it was dusk by eight of the clock and reluctantly the Galpine women had abandoned their after-supper parley with the other village wives for the confines of the kitchen.

As they gossiped they turned their spindles, making up the undyed wool for family use. Baskets of berries and fruit stood inside, ready for drying and dye making and winter wines.

May's departure was drawing near. Her father, showing little inclination to supervise her hiring, had persuaded George Galpine to take the girl along with him.

Each year George attended the Hiring Fair, not to find servants but more as an annual pilgrimage. The pretext was to sell the last of his fleeces but it usually turned into his last spree of the year, marked by an appropriate amount of drinking and spending.

More recently and in the light of past experience, Leah had taken to accompanying him, making her own goods to sell. He had protested at first but in the end the prospect of more money from Leah's cheeses and baskets had swayed his decision. These days he came back a sober and richer man.

With all this in mind, Lizzie sat with her mother stripping

nettle stalks to make sewing thread. When there was a lull in the conversation, she took the plunge.

'Tell us about what it's like in Newport,' she said.

She never tired of hearing about the town, which was the capital of the island and six miles away from their village of Caulbourne. The nearest she had got was the Summer Fair, held on the outskirts. Newport nestled at the mouth of the river that carried all the wool and timber, which was then shipped across to the mainland, and her own brother Harry had left from there on his journey to join the navy.

'Well, it's full of shops,' her mother started, warming immediately to the request. 'There's a great main street with tailors and glovemakers and cobblers and drapers and they all sell fine clothes like the Worsleys wear or the Earlismans.'

The Worsleys of Swaynson Manor and Earlismans of West Over were to be seen in their finery when they entered their private pews at the church on a Sunday or occasionally graced a village fête.

'Go on.' Lizzie's eyes shone in the flickering light. Her deft fingers automatically unravelled the stringy nettle stalks and she was oblivious to everything but her mother's words.

'Well, there's folks from all over the island, and down by the river there's great ships and strange men. I heard tell that they come from as far as London and Plymouth.'

Lizzie's heart was pounding. She knew everyone in Caulbourne by name and the thought of these foreigners had her palms tingling.

'May is going for hiring at the fair,' she finally announced, as calmly as she could manage.

'I know. I'm not surprised. They need the space, poor souls. And the money. Wilkie White has had no work since New Farm went over to sheep.' Leah poked the embers, adding a few twigs to give them more light. In a few moments they would all be retiring to bed.

Lizzie waited, afraid to ask her question in case the answer was no. Finally she blurted out: 'Can I go with Pa to take the cheeses?'

There was a pause before Leah replied. They both knew that it was her excuse to keep an eye on her husband. Lizzie felt her head pounding as she held her breath, fearing the reply.

With a sigh, her mother said: 'I don't see why not.' She added, almost to herself: 'Go and enjoy yourself, girl, for the time is short enough.'

Chapter Three

The barge was halfway across the Solent. A November wind keen as sheep shears cut into Mardi Appleby as she stood in the body of the vessel, her legs splayed to keep her balance. Around her a melee of sheep jostled and stumbled in their efforts to remain upright. In their panic they trampled over her bare toes but she was too cold to heed the pain.

As far as she could gauge she had placed herself in the middle of the vessel, for she knew from experience that if she could find the centre point the persistent bucketing would be less violent. By her reckoning she had now made this journey ten times. Of the five years before that, she had no clear recollection.

This was the first occasion that they had come so late in the year. Normally they crossed only once for the July fair, but now, a mere four months later, they were making the journey again. She shook off the sadness at the memory of the summer just past.

After leaving the island, the whole family had gone to Salisbury and there her mother and the little ones had fallen ill. She and her father had watched helplessly as one by one they had shivered and vomited their way into living skeletons before drawing their last exhausted breaths. None of her potions helped. The physician called by the constable had pronounced that they had eaten bad meat. On the occasion of their last family meal Mardi had been forbidden supper for some misdemeanour and her father supped as usual only on brandy. She remembered bitterly the dead chicken they had discovered in the hedge and the glee with which they had taken it to their camp.

Her mother and little brothers and sisters were buried in a pauper's grave and Jake and Mardi were banished from the town in case whatever it was that had taken their family was catching.

Afterwards they had wandered aimlessly in the New Forest and her father drank himself into a stupor which lasted for weeks before deciding to salvage what they could from the year.

Tonight was the eve of the Newport Hiring Fair and crossing to the island was their last-ditch effort to make some money before the cold made any form of work impossible.

Mardi shivered at the memory of that last visit. She had seen it all then in the cards but had not known what it meant.

She tried to blot out the other events, the near rape and her rescuer. At the thought of Will her spirits lifted and a tingle of anticipation greeted her. She wondered if he might be there next day and, glancing at her tattered kirtle, wished there was some way to transform herself.

Closing her rain-lashed eyes, she concentrated hard for some minutes, then relaxed. If he was not there tomorrow, then some when...

At the stern of the barge her father sat with the boatman. As Mardi glanced round she saw him lower his jar of brandy. His once handsome face was dissipated and his black hair clung wet and dishevelled across his cheek. Pulling his thick cloak tighter about him, he took another swig from the jar before passing the abrasive liquid across to the boatman.

Mardi huddled deeper into her own thin, shapeless shawl. Her heart sank as she realised that he would be drunk by the time they reached the Yar mouth.

'You've had enough of that,' she shouted but the wind carried her voice away.

Looking hopefully ahead she could make out the cluster of dwellings along the coast and the squat, forbidding presence of Yarmouth Castle blocking the route between the shore and the marshes. With luck they would be there within the hour. Once tied up, however, they would have to wait until dark before disembarking, for only those with permission from the Captain of the Island could cross the Solent. They had no such permission and Mardi knew her father would have bribed the boat-man with brandy.

Screwing up her bruised toes, she kicked out idly at the nearest sheep and was glad that her fellow travellers were not cattle or horses. These ewes were making the crossing before Advent to take advantage of the milder island weather, which would give their lambs a better chance of survival.

'Curse the sheep. Where's the soldiers?' she heard her father say for the third. time. He was given to repeating himself when drunk. Troop movements to the island were commonplace these days with the constant threat of Spanish attack, and travelling with soldiers would have meant easy pickings on the journey.

As she watched, Jake Appleby rolled back his sleeve and showed the large, festering sores on his arm to the boatman. The man shook his head and tutted but did not offer as much as a groat.

A particularly vicious blast of wind sent the barge bobbing like a leaf on a whirlpool. To add to her misery Mardi was now ankle-deep in water as waves washed over the sides. Surrep-titiously she moved to the side and, with a quick glance to make sure the boatman was not watching, she dropped some round white pebbles over the side and into the turbulent water.

'Still thyself, wind spirit'. Her lips moved as she formed the silent words and the waves became perceptibly calmer as the gale abated.

Finally coming ashore, she struggled with their belongings as Jake Appleby rocked blearily on unsteady legs. As a precaution she opened their wooden box and took out her most precious possession, secreting it inside her bodice. The shawl hid its telltale bulge between her tiny breasts.

'What you doin'?' Jake sounded aggressive, his words slurred.

'Just hiding my cards.'

He grunted, knowing that the pack was a certain money-spinner.

'Come on.' Mardi hoisted their load into her arms and, staggering under its weight, started out across the marshy expanse that skirted the port. They headed southeast in the direction of Newport. The man, empty-handed, stumbled and grumbled his way behind.

Having walked about five miles in the driving rain, they finally settled down to sleep in the great park behind Swaynson Manor. They found a hollow beneath the elm trees and were sheltered from the worst of the wind and rain. Jake was too sozzled to notice the weather but, with her cold fingers and stinging, chilblained toes, Mardi was a long time getting to sleep. To distract herself she rehearsed some of the spells she might be using when they reached the market next day.

At first light she dragged herself up, still clutching the damp shawl around her. Creeping through the wood, she collected some kindling. The twigs were damp but years of experience made this only a minor irritation. Her main concern was not to be discovered for as vagrants they could expect a beating at the very least. She had seen travellers branded through the gristle of the ear and in one case having their ears chopped off. She shuddered and rubbed her own small earlobes.

Wandering deeper into the forest, she came upon some beech trees and scrabbled in the leaf mould beneath to unearth a few now decaying husks. The nuts inside were still ripe and sweet and she grinned with satisfaction, for their only other food was a hunk of stale rye bread. As soon as the fire was blazing she prodded her father into wakefulness.

'Come on. Eat this.' Her voice was gruff as she pushed the meagre fare at him.

'I don't want it.'

'You must eat.' She nudged him again and he swore at her but forced down a few mouthfuls, washed down with the remainder of their ale.

'Come on, we'd best go.' Mardi pulled him to his feet. Loading herself with all their belongings, she turned to wait for him as he gazed unseeing into the gloom.

'Come on,' she said impatiently.

He continued to stare into space, finally saying: 'I miss your mother.'

Mardi was lost for words. Jake turned his once-fine amber eyes upon her. 'I really loved her,' he said.

The girl shrugged. Now that her father had started talking there was no stopping him.

'People calls us gippos,' he said, 'but it ain't true. There ain't no gippos in England no more. They've all been driven out. My father was an upright man.' He was warming to his story and with a sigh Mardi put her load down.

Drunken old fool, she thought, glaring at him. Aloud she said: 'If we don't get there soon, we'll be too late.' He continued to gaze into the distance.

'My father was born on the road. He was the leader of our troupe. They all had their own special skills.' He gave a little mirthless laugh. 'Some of them sold anything they could find, some told fortunes, some could juggle and dance and some was plain bullies. Me, now, I was gifted with the power to cure animals. That's how I met your mother.'

'I know.' Mardi, who had heard it all before, nodded distractedly. If they didn't get a move on, someone would discover them and anyway they'd be too late to get a good site. 'Come on,' she repeated, shoving him with her elbow, but he ignored her.

'Pretty as heaven she was,' he continued. 'Her father was that mad when I got her in child – that was you. He'd have liked to turn her out but your grandmother wouldn't let him.'

He was deep in thought, remembering. Knowing it was useless to say anything, the girl waited, kicking at the spot where their fire had been to make sure that it was out.

With a sigh, Jake continued: 'We was happy enough at first. I worked at the plough, looked after the animals. It was well enough but when you're born on the road there isn't a house that can hold you. I loved your mam but I couldn't just rot away in that village.'

Mardi remembered the arguments and her father coming home drunk. Suddenly, out of the blue, her grandfather had died and the land had been taken back by the lord for sheep. This was just the excuse Jake had been waiting for and soon Mardi, her mother and her newborn brother joined the growing bands of roving vagabonds. By then, though, the drink seemed to have taken over her father and he no longer made the potions for which he claimed he was famous. Instead he resorted to the practice of infecting himself with ratsbane and arsenic, thus causing festering ulcers on his forearms and in-

26

ducing the sympathy of the fairground crowds. It was lucrative but dangerous.

When she was a child she had thought him handsome as a god. Now as she looked at him she saw the shambling wreck of the man who had carried her shoulder-high through the lanes and highways of England.

'Come on,' she said again. 'Ain't no good grieving.'

Tears were running down his cheeks and to hide her sense of inadequacy she turned her back and started out towards the cart track that led in the direction of Newport. Glancing over her shoulder, she was relieved to see that he was following.

When they reached the highway she put down her load and sank down on the bank. A cart was approaching and she hoped that they would manage to get a lift.

'Going to the fair?' she shouted as it drew level.

A miserable-looking man with greedy eyes walked in front, followed by a large, dopey, oxlike youth who was leading the animal he resembled. On board two girls sat on top of a pile of fleeces, the one fat and grey-skinned, the other slim and with startling red hair. Mardi's heart gave a lurch as she recognized her. She was suddenly afraid and the playing cards flashed clearly before her.

Ignoring her, the farmer kept walking and Mardi's usual persuasiveness deserted her. In fact, a ride on this particular cart was the last thing that she wanted. She hoped that the girl had not seen her and remained where she was until the cart was out of sight.

Coming out of his stupor, Jake asked: 'What you doing, standing about?' With a sigh she picked up her load and struggled uneasily on towards their destination.

Chapter Four

The night before the Hiring Fair, Lizzie tossed restlessly on her straw mattress. It was still dark when she slipped out of the truckle bed. Although she was certain that she had not slept, she must have dozed at some time for her parents' bed was already empty.

She hurried into her kirtle. In the gloom she dressed her hair with clumsy, excited fingers and fastened it with a wooden pin fashioned by her brother Jed. He might not be very bright, she thought, but he was clever with his hands.

It was now four months since she had made her visit to the Summer Fair. The memory was still tinged with the disappointment of not seeing Will, but optimistically she was sure that he would certainly be at the Hiring.

Her brother Jed slept downstairs in the kitchen and as she came down she saw that his bed had already been stowed away.

'Where's Pa?' she asked him.

'Gone to fetch the wagon.'

Her father was borrowing the cart and ox from Silas Dore. She wondered why he was suddenly so friendly with the fuller, but dismissed the thought as more exciting things filled her head.

Going into the yard she unpenned the geese and chickens, her cold fingers fumbling with the wooden pins that held the coops. The birds blinked, stepping out cautiously into the half-light. She threw some scraps for them before hurrying back inside.

As she closed the latch she heard her father returning and Jed went out to help him load up with fleeces and cheeses, baskets and pies. Two boards were lashed to the top of the cart with hemp ropes for use as tables and when they had finished they came in, blowing on their fingers, to eat the hot soup before leaving at six.

Leah had packed them a basket of food. Mutton pies, cheese pasties and plum tarts were wrapped in cloths and squeezed into a corner of the cart. She fetched her brown woollen shawl and wrapped it around Lizzie's shoulders.

'Keep warm, girl,' she warned. 'And don't wander away from the stall. You know how to reckon the money?'

'Course I do, Mam.' Lizzie pecked her impatiently on the cheek and hurried out to join Jed and her father.

'You look out for vagabonds and cutpurses,' her mother called after them.

'Up you go, our Lizzie.' Jed hoisted her up on the cart and prodded the ox. The journey had begun.

At the end of the lane they stopped to collect May from the tumbledown shack that was her home. Her mother and little sisters clustered in the doorway; they were all crying. May came out, clutching her tiny bundle of belongings. Her face had a blotched, soggy look, pale in the light.

'Don't cry, May! Remember, this is an adventure,' Lizzie comforted, but her friend remained rigid.

'I'll never see 'em again,' she suddenly wailed, breaking into a fresh paroxysm of sobbing.

'Course you will.' Lizzie squeezed her arm. She felt disloyal but she could not ignore the excitement she felt. May's grief intruded into the most thrilling day of her life. 'Remember that Martin or Michael,' she encouraged. 'You'll be wed this time next year.' But her friend did not respond.

The road was bad but not impassable. Often by November the huge ruts were filled with water and every mile was an agony, but an inspector of highways had been appointed and, using gangs of men and women from the House of Correction, he had started repairs. Adults and children under his supervision collected rocks and pebbles, gradually levelling the surfaces, but even so George Galpine and his party several times hit a bad patch of road. The girls had to get down and push at the back of the cart to dislodge the wheels from the ruts.

Not far past Swaynson Lizzie noticed a young black-haired

girl and a swarthy-looking man loitering by the bank. They were surrounded by a collection of packs and parcels. It was the material of the girl's gown that Lizzie recognised first.

'See that girl? Can't we give her a lift?' she called to her father.

'Course not. They're a band o' vagrants. Like as not they'd cut our throats and rob us.'

As she watched, the girl stepped forwards and said something to Lizzie's father but he ignored her, calling on Jed to hurry up. Lizzie felt herself redden and glanced back as they drove past. She hoped the girl hadn't noticed her.

Slowly they made their way through the forest of Alvington and when they reached the steep chute at Carisbrooke it took all four of them to hold the back of the cart to stop it from running away. It was now fully daylight.

'Where be the castle?' asked May, coming out of her torpor.

'It's up there behind the trees,' Lizzie's father replied. 'You can't see it from here but from there they can see everything that's going on.'

May turned to Lizzie. 'P'r'aps Will'll be looking out and he'll see you coming,' she whispered.

'Shush!' Lizzie blushed, afraid that her father would hear.

As they began to descend the hill towards the town gate, the road became more crowded and soon the site of the Hiring Fair came into view. On the flat grassy expanse on the outskirts of the town, people were already erecting tents and rostrums to display their wares. Lizzie forgot May and the vagrants in her excitement.

George led the way to his accustomed corner and started to unload the cart.

'Come on, you gals, pay attention and remember what we're here for,' he scolded.

Obediently they set out the cheeses and pies, lavender bags and baskets and the homespun cloth for sale. From then on it was a question of waiting for customers and for the time of the hiring.

The event was due to start at eleven of the clock and as the time drew near George and Lizzie accompanied May across to the assembly of men, women and children waiting to be

30

employed. Only Jed remained behind to guard the unsold goods.

The hirelings stood in the centre of the field while would-be masters circled around, eyeing them up and down. The hopeful employees advertised their trades by holding up an appropriate symbol – a crook for a shepherd, a pail for a dairy maid and so forth. May was among the melee of unskilled workers. There was little work, and competition for jobs was fierce.

'Come on, gal.' George poked the girl as she stood, head bent, hugging her bundle to her chest. 'Try to look cheerful or they'll take ye for a lummock.'

'I don't want to go.' She turned beseechingly to Lizzie, looking for a reprieve.

'It's no good, May,' Lizzie pointed out. 'If you don't get a position you'll end up working for the parish, and you don't want that, do you? You'll get worse food than the swine and no hopes of meeting a nice chap and having a cottage of your own.'

May sagged in defeat.

A short, stocky farmer stopped nearby, regarding them with pale, piggy eyes.

'Can her cook?' he asked, eyeing Lizzie.

'She's not for hiring. 'Tis thissun.' George pushed May forwards.

The man walked around her and she gazed fixedly at the ground. He prodded her with his stick to make her move, then, going closer, squeezed her arm for signs of muscle.

'She's a good worker,' George offered.

The farmer sneezed, wiping his nose on the back of his hand and transferring the damp patch to his already filthy breeches. 'Can her lift heavy weights?' he asked.

'Aye, she's strong.'

As they talked, the man was turning May this way and that, raising her head and even looking into her mouth. She had surprisingly fine teeth. The girl stepped closer to Lizzie, shaking her head against the feared offer.

'I'll take her for ten shillin's a year tho' a gal ain't really worth it.'

'Fifteen shillings is the going rate,' George countered.

'Aye, but she'll be well fed along o' me.' He was now poking

31

May like a cow at market. Bending down, he lifted her skirt and looked at her solid legs and bare, chilblained feet. Finally he stood up and pushed his cap back on his head, scratching his neck and screwing his face up in indecision.

'Twelve an' sixpence.'

It was George who now hesitated. 'Will your wife keep an eye on her? She's only a bit of a gal.'

'Wife's dead. I need a general cook and house girl.' His eyes roamed hungrily over May's solid body.

'She's not going where there's no woman of the house.'

The farmer snorted and, taking another look at Lizzie, added: 'I'd pay fifteen shillin's for her.'

'No, thankee. She's spoken for.'

'Oo, he was awful,' May whimpered. 'Lizzie, I'm real scared.'

'There's no need to worry. Pa didn't let you go, did he?' Lizzie looked around for something to distract her friend. Everywhere there was bustle and activity. Suddenly her eyes caught sight of something.

'Look there!' She pointed to a beggar seated nearby on the ground, his thin body hunched, his dirty, skinny arm extended, the hand cupped to receive alms.

'For charity,' he repeated. 'For charity.' Rolling back his sleeve, he displayed a large, festering ulcer. 'I need food to heal my wounds.' He showed the arm to two passing matrons, who covered their noses at the stench and turned aside. 'Charity, mistress,' he called after them.

'Oh, the poor man!' said Lizzie, studying his still handsome face and the earring that gave him a curiously dashing look.

'Don't you believe it,' said her father. 'He ain't nothing but an old clapperdudgeon. They cheat honest folks by getting them wounds deliberate.'

'How?' Lizzie asked in surprise.

'They cut themselves and rub the wounds with ratsbane and arsenic,' her father replied.

'They don't!'

'They do, gal. Last few years has seen more and more folks taking to the roads. They get up to all kinds of devilry to earn a crust. I feel sorry for some of them, specially the littluns, but not a clapperdudgeon. They don't want to work. If they get

32

caught, though, it'll mean the stocks and a beating and if that don't stop 'em they'll string 'em up.'

'But if the wound doesn't heal, he'll die,' Lizzie pointed out.

'Don't you fret, child. They know just when to stop. He'll be richer than you'll ever be.'

'Get away from here.' The beggar scowled at George Galpine. 'I got a living to earn same as you.'

Lizzie and May instinctively stepped back and the man winked at them knowingly. The smell of brandy wafted towards them.

They were so engrossed that they did not notice a quartet of people who approached. At their centre was a young man in green velvet doublet and matching cape. On each arm he supported a young woman, both warmly wrapped in fine cloaks, the rich brocade of their skirts visible as they picked their way across the field. An older man brought up the rear, more modestly dressed in working breeches and a leather jerkin.

'This is entertaining,' one of the women was saying. 'Do you do this every year, John?'

The young man smiled indulgently. 'Somebody from the estate has to come and take on as many hands as are needed,' he replied with the air of one who was hard done by. Turning to the older man, he asked: 'What do we need now, Jack?'

''Tis nearly done, m'lord. Another scullery maid and we'll be well served.'

The young man was eyeing Lizzie speculatively and she stepped back behind her father to escape the limelight.

'Good day, fellow.' The man addressed as 'm'lord' spoke to George. With a glance at Jack, his estate bailiff, he asked: 'Is this young maid for hire?'

'No, sir, 'tis thissun.' Again George pushed May forwards.

Lizzie nudged her and hastily whispered: 'Smile, May. They're from Swaynson. If you go there you'll be nearly home.'

The manor of Swaynson was barely a mile from the village and nearly all the surrounding land belonged to the estate.

May stumbled forwards, bobbed a curtsy and flushed scarlet. Her chapped hands kneaded her skirt and she was trembling.

33

The bailiff came to take a closer look at her, asking her questions. Lizzie could not hear her mumbled replies.

'I don't know,' he said doubtfully, looking at George, whom he had known all his life. 'Her skin don't look too good.'

'She's the best anybody could find!' It was Lizzie who stepped forward, unable to help herself. 'She works that hard and she's honest and ...' Realising what she had done, she stuttered to a halt, her cheeks blazing. The young man burst out laughing.

'What a loyal friend you are,' he said and, turning to his manager, added: 'Well, Jack? She comes well recommended.' He laughed again.

'She ain't bad,' the older man conceded. 'She's Wilkie White's gal. He's a good sort though he ain't worked for over a year.'

'Then shall we take her?'

'Begging your pardon, sir, but how much?' George lowered his eyes in embarrassment.

'Fifteen shillings is the going rate,' the bailiff answered.

'Then I think that'll be satisfactory.'

The details were settled while Lizzie and May glanced covertly at each other.

'Oh, Lizzie, I don't want to go!' May started to cry again.

'It's all right, May. You're going to a good place. Why, we'll even see you sometimes of a Sunday.'

Although the manor had its own chapel, all the household came to the village church on special days.

Lizzie hugged her friend and, on a generous impulse, took her mother's shawl and wrapped it around May's shoulders.

'God be with you,' she said. Her chest constricted with emotion as the girl reluctantly went to join the other hirelings destined for Swaynson.

Her father and the bailiff were still talking so Lizzie started back in search of Jed, her arms chilly without the shawl's comforting presence. She thought that this was the saddest day of her life. Ever since she could remember, May had been there. As children they had minded the geese together or scared the birds away from the precious crops of rye and barley and helped to round up the sheep from the downland. Together they had spun and sewn, gathered berries from the autumn hedgerows, played games on holy days and made up stories to amuse each other. Now it was all finished, ended for ever. She sniffed back the tears as she walked blindly away from the hiring ring.

Round and about soldiers mingled with the crowd, enjoying a few hours leisure from duties at the castle. Their presence reminded Lizzie of the threatened invasion, and via Carisbrooke Castle her thoughts inevitably turned to Will. From the site of the fair she could see the castle clearly, high on its hill. It was barely half a mile away and the idea that Will was so close brought on the now familiar tingling sensation in the pit of her stomach.

Just then it was as if her thoughts and the outside world became fused. Inside her she could see Will's face and hear his voice and simultaneously someone was walking towards her, his voice and face identical. He stopped in front of her and raised his arm in greeting.

'Hello, Lizzie,' he said with a smile. 'Don't look so scared. It's only me, Will.'

Chapter Five

Lizzie must have looked confused, for the young man touched her arm and bent forwards to look into her eyes.

'Don't look so scared,' he said again. 'It's only me, Will. Are you all right?'

'Will! I was just . . .' She could not admit that she had been thinking about him.

'I got the afternoon off special,' he was saying. 'I had a feeling you might be here.'

She had forgotten the candour of his hazel eyes, his high cheekbones and prominent nose. As he opened his mouth she glimpsed the crooked lower tooth and savoured the sun's highlights on his beard.

'Well, don't I get a hello?' he asked. 'Aren't you pleased to see me?'

She nodded, not trusting her voice.

'Come on, this way. Let's walk.' Taking her arm, he led her towards the edge of the field and into the adjoining copse.

'Pa and Jed will be looking for me,' she warned.

'I saw Jed and said I'd take you round to see the sights.'

In silence she went with him. Her life had leaped from one state of being to another. One minute she had been wallowing in the pain of losing her friend and now she was transported to a state of pure elation. Will's hand burned a brand mark into her elbow as he guided her through the bracken.

'There's lots of soldiers,' she said to break the silence.

'Aye, nigh on a thousand and more expected. They reckon the Dons are coming and when they do we'll be ready for 'em.'

'Would you fight, Will?' she asked anxiously.

'Course I would if they land here.'

'You might be killed.' The invasion took on a sudden dreadful reality and she felt cold inside.

'So might any of us, Lizzie.' He turned her to face him. 'What sort of a man would I be if I didn't defend my homeland – and my girl?' He held her chin and gently kissed her on the lips. His mouth was sweet and firm and she closed her eyes to concentrate all the feeling in the smell and the touch of him. Pulling away, he smiled and held both her hands.

'You're a bonny girl, Lizzie. I think of you all the time.'

'I think of you too, Will.' She ought not to have said it but there seemed nothing now to fear in honesty. Guile was only for flirtations. This was love.

'When will you come back to the village?' she asked, half dreading the answer.

He shrugged. 'I don't know. My apprenticeship's up next year but there's no point in making plans with the war threatening.' He paused for a moment, then added: 'When I've finished my time, Sir George has offered me work up in London.'

'Would you go?' She was astonished to the point of gaping open-mouthed.

'I guess I would.' He looked away from her.

'But if you did that I wouldn't see you!'

He expelled his breath and squeezed her hands, which were still nestled in his. Then he turned to face her.

'It's hard to explain. My folks are ordinary islanders. There's none of them ever moved far.' He smiled as he continued: 'There's Granfer Gosden still living at Shorrel and minding the stable though he's nigh on eighty. I expect I would have been the same if my father hadn't took it into his head to join the navy. When he came back he told us about what it's like over there across the sea.' He nodded towards the north and then sighed as if the right words evaded him. Finally he added: 'I know I won't settle till I've been at least as far as London.'

She nodded, although she could not imagine how he could even consider leaving the island, let alone her.

'How long would you go for?' she heard herself asking.

He shrugged. 'Mebbe a year or two.'

'A year?' She felt numb with disappointment.

37

In a matter of minutes Will had come to her, only to be lost again. She had believed his kiss to be binding, a promise of marriage and a life together, and now the bond was as insubstantial as the cold wind that chilled her shoulders. She shivered.

'Where's your cape?' he asked in concern.

'I gave it to May. She's been hired. She's going to Swaynson.'

Tears threatened both for the loss of her friend and her lover, although she could not have separated the feelings of abandonment.

Will put his jerkin about her shoulders and held her close. Bending his head, he kissed her again and pressed her hard against his body. The pain of loss dissolved.

'Oh, Lizzie, I want you,' he murmured into her hair. 'There isn't a time when I don't think about you. I want you to know that as soon as my apprenticeship's up I'll be coming for you; just you wait and see.'

'But what about going to London?'

He raised his eyebrows in surprise. 'Well, don't you want to come with me?'

'Oh, yes!' Her heart began to beat faster and the perils of such a journey jostled with the slow realisation that he was asking her to marry him. She could not believe that he meant it.

'That's it, then. God willing, by Christmastide it should all be settled. I'll ask your pa proper then and soon as I'm released from my time we'll be wed.'

There were no words to convey her excitement, but a little laugh of pure delight escaped her. In response he pulled her close, kissing her face and neck, crushing her against his restless, virile body. Finally he broke away.

'Come on. I fear it's time we went.'

Taking his hand, she fought back the tears.

'Now then, don't cry,' he said. 'I want to make you happy, not sad. Come on, I'm going to buy you a keepsake.'

He led the way back into the field and around the stalls until they came upon a pedlar selling brooches and lace.

Lizzie stood close to him, shy and adoring, waiting to see what he would do. Leaning forwards, he picked up a silver clasp in the shape of a bow. Forming the knot in the centre were two stones shining deeply red, then black in the weak November sunshine. Turning to Lizzie, he said: 'Here, my love, this has to be for you. The stones shimmer like your hair and contrast with the green of your eyes.' Turning to the pedlar, he asked: 'How much?'

'It's part of a pair,' the man replied, unearthing an identical brooch.

'I only want the one.'

The man shrugged. 'They're a crown for the pair.'

Will took the second pin from the man's callused hand and looked at it. 'I don't want it.'

The pedlar's blank expression conveyed his indifference.

'A crown,' he repeated. 'They're real garnets and rubies, they are, the only pair like it in existence.'

Will was about to turn away but, seeing Lizzie's expression, he relented. 'Seeing as how you're so set on selling them both and I only need the one, I'll give ye a florin for the pair.'

He flung some coins down, ignoring the man's protests at the reduced price proffered, and, turning to Lizzie, pinned one of the clasps to her bodice. The touch of his fingers against her breast made her feel faint with ecstasy.

Smiling at her, he put the second clasp into his pouch. With his arm about her shoulders, he led her back past the fish stalls, past the leather workers, the singers and players, to the place where Jed was packing up the last of the unsold baskets.

'You been a long time,' he observed. 'Pa's gone to look for ye.'

Lizzie glanced at Will in alarm. She wondered if he would ask her father there and then for permission to marry her. At that moment George Galpine returned. Lizzie could smell the ale on his breath and he looked piqued. Recognising his dangerous mood, she gave her lover a warning look, willing him not to say anything.

'Where you been?' George asked gruffly. Looking at Will, he added: 'She's just a bit of a gal. Her reputation's not to be trifled with.'

Will remained affable. 'Don't you go misjudging me, George,' he said evenly. 'She wouldn't come to no harm with me.' He had removed his arm from around her shoulders and not gave her a fraternal smile.

'Well, we've got a long journey ahead. Thankee for minding

her,' the older man replied grudgingly, then to Lizzie: 'Come on, gal, we've wasted enough time.'

Lizzie looked longingly at Will as he stepped back.

'God's speed,' he wished them all. 'I'll see you in the future.'

As the others turned away, he winked at her and mouthed the words: 'Till Christmas.' There was the merest hint of a kiss on his lips. Then, with a wave, he turned on his heel and melted into the thinning crowd.

Chapter Six

Sir George Carey was enjoying a few moments' respite from his busy round of duties. From his vantage point in the hall of his nearly completed house, he gazed absently into the courtyard of Carisbrooke Castle. As Captain of the Island and with the curiosity of a natural leader of men, he watched an elderly retainer laboriously sweep leaves into a heap, only to see them ambushed by a playful easterly wind and scatter in all directions. Sir George was neither amused nor annoyed by what he saw, but he wondered why such ineptitudes were part of ordinary people's lives.

The courtyard was nearly deserted, which served to remind him that anyone who was not strictly needed had made excuses to go to the Hiring Fair.

In his hand he held a single sheet of vellum. Glancing down at it, he frowned and the world outside his window was dismissed. He had received similar messages before and the fact that this one again predicted the imminent arrival of the Spanish fleet did not unduly alarm him. What did concern him, however, was the knowledge that on previous occasions his replies had been mysteriously intercepted and relayed to the Spanish court. He knew this through the agency of a Spanish official who obligingly had a foot in both camps. Clearly there was a leak in the English communication system, but no one yet knew quite where. This message was from Medina Sidonia himself to the captains of other flagships in the Spanish fleet. If it was not a blind, it needed to be passed on and quickly.

Sir George had considered all the men he could possibly trust as emissaries, but in every case there was a distressing possi-

41

bility, however slight, that he might pick on the very traitor he was trying to avoid. It had then occurred to him that he should therefore pick someone who had no connection with either the court or the military.

Only recently he had heard from the Marquis of Winchester, at old Basing, about the work he was undertaking on his estate at Basing House, and Sir George reasoned that the offer of a good artisan to hurry the work along would not be viewed with suspicion. On the pretext of helping a fellow countryman he could send a reliable carpenter or mason to do a few weeks' work and at the same time instruct him to deliver a message which should not be intercepted. If it were then to be leaked at a later stage, he could be comparatively sure that the spy was not under his jurisdiction. It was a satisfactory solution.

As a first step he had consulted his foreman to establish who among the civil staff was the most conscientious and reliable worker. He had a shortlist of names but in most cases there seemed to be some impediment to employing them on this mission – they were too old, had family commitments or would simply lack the courage to undertake such a journey. Almost without exception none of his workforce had ever left the village, let alone the shores of the island.

He locked the message away in his cabinet and, glancing back out of the window, noticed that the old fellow was now in conversation with a strapping young chap whom he immediately recognised. Sir George's interest heightened and he watched the mime taking place below with increasing attention. This fortuitous arrival must be Fate indeed . . .

Will had hurried back to the castle in record time. He felt so elated by his meeting with Lizzie that he could hardly contain himself. He wanted to leap and shout just from the sheer joy of being alive, but he gave expression to his high spirits by whistling and jogging part the way, and kicking the odd pebble down the steep slope just to relieve the tension. His hand came to rest on the stone talisman hung about his neck and he thanked the Gipsy girl for bringing him luck.

He wondered if he should have asked for Lizzie's hand that afternoon, but George Galpine had been in no mood to listen sympathetically. On balance he felt he had been right to stick to his original plan. Old man Galpine was a greedy, grasping sort of chap but Will realised with satisfaction that he could play on this weakness by pointing out the lucrative future that would be his as a master mason. He did not doubt that George would see the value of such an asset in a son-in-law.

As he passed the guards at the gatehouse, he waved cheerily and made his way across the castle courtyard. He was confronted by old John Kent fighting a losing battle with a heap of leaves, and stopped to give the old man a hand.

'How are you, Grandfather?' he asked loudly. This was the title that every apprentice had given to this elderly retainer.

Old John grunted. 'You be in a high fettle, youngun.'

'Aye.' Will grinned. 'I've just asked the prettiest maid in Christendom to be my bride.'

Before the old man could answer, there was a sound from the upper floor of Sir George's residence. Looking up, Will saw the Captain of the Island leaning out of the casement.

'You. Mason!'

Me? Will pointed to himself in surprise. When Sir George nodded, he hastily removed his hat and rubbed his hand across his mouth as if to gird himself up in some way. In response to Sir George's beckoning hand, he hurried across the yard to the half-open door of the house. Sir George had already descended the stairs and stood waiting for him.

For a moment they faced each other in silence. Will's heart had started to thump audibly and he wondered whatever he could have done to make the captain himself send for him. It must be something very serious, for in the normal way of things Sir George would never deign to acknowledge the existence of such ordinary folk.

Finally Sir George spoke. 'How are you called?'

'Gosden, sir. William Gosden.' Will swallowed hard and looked the Captain straight in the eye. Will was the taller by several inches.

'Tell me, Gosden. Who are you?' Sir George asked with great seriousness.

'Sir?' Will was nonplussed.

'Well, I now know your name but that tells me very little. Who are you?'

After a pause, Will said: 'Well, I'm an apprentice, though

43

near the end of my time. I'm an island man ...' He shrugged and since there was no response he continued: 'I'm a God-fearing man and I hope to be a good craftsman and, well ... to lead a decent life.'

Sir George smiled briefly. 'You hope for a lot,' he observed. Serious again, he asked: 'But are you a good Englishman?'

'Sir?' Will looked at him blankly. Finally he said: 'What else would I be?'

Changing tack, Sir George asked: 'Are you a brave man, Gosden?'

Will shrugged. 'I'd die for what I believed to be right,' he said.

'You would?'

Will shifted from one foot to the other. Finally he said: 'What is it you're asking me, sir, or do you always speak in riddles?'

At this Sir George laughed. 'I see you have a sense of humour, young man. That is a good quality.' There was silence for a moment, then he continued: 'I'll be honest with you, Gosden, and that means I have to trust you.'

Will inclined his head. His lively eyes were alert and open to whatever his master might reveal.

'I have been making enquiries and you seem to be the only man who suits my purpose. I need someone who is good at his craft and who, at a day's notice, could be away from this island and heading for Basing House.'

Will did not know where Basing House was but he sifted the implications of this information.

'For what purpose?' he asked quietly.

'To the world in general it would be to help a friend of mine meet the deadline of some work. To you and me – and to no other living soul – it would be to take something to the Marquis of Winchester.'

As Will's eyes widened, Sir George added: 'It concerns the Spanish, Gosden. It may, just may, mark the beginning of what we all fear. I'm sure there is no need to tell you of its import-ance.' Seeing the young man's serious expression, he added: 'And you have to know that there are spies everywhere, even here. You should travel quick and straight and take absolutely no one into your confidence.' Leaning back against the table and stretching his back, he added: 'I have good reports about you. I hope they are not mistaken.'

'How long would I be away?' Will asked by way of acceptance.

'A few weeks. Any quicker and there would be suspicion. I want no one knowing that this . . . information was received. You will have to stay and work on Basing House until it makes sense to leave.'

'I would like to be back by Christmastide,' Will finally said, his face suddenly flushing with embarrassment. 'I have some important business.'

Sir George stiffened and his manner cooled perceptibly. 'There can be no business more important than the safety of this realm,' he warned. 'I hope I am not mistaken in trusting you.'

Will lowered his eyes. 'Forgive me, sir. I have today asked a maid to wed with me. It was simply my intention to confirm it with her father.'

Sir George nodded and his expression softened. 'Affairs of the heart,' he mused. 'She'll wait for you, Gosden, she'll wait.'

He stood up to show that the audience was at an end, but before he could turn away, Will asked: 'May I have permission to leave the castle?' A plan was forming in his mind.

Sir George nodded ponderously. 'You can find all you need to take with you here in the garrison,' he observed. 'And remember what I said about secrecy.' With a sudden smile, he added: 'Don't stay out drinking and whoring, you need to be fit at first light.'

Will returned his smile and, as he put his cap on, replied: 'Never you fear, sir, I'm practically a married man.'

The captain acknowledged the remark and, before he turned for the stairway to the gallery of his house, said: 'I'm glad to hear it. Now don't you forget, I want you off this island on the first tide.'

Chapter Seven

Will hurried back down towards the town in a daze. This was the most incredible day of his life. Within the space of an hour he had asked Lizzie to marry him and been given a mission of national importance to go to somewhere called Basing, which he gathered was across the sea. Sir George Carey was the most important person on the island and he, Will, was to see him again in person before daylight. In this way they would avoid prying eyes and then Sir George would give him all the details. Will's mind raced like a spinning top, flinging out unanswered questions in all directions.

He finally slowed his pace. By now he was nearly back in the town and he had not, as he had hoped, met George Galpine and his family along the way. He realised now that if they had left the fair soon after he did, then they would already be well on their way to Caulbourne, and a needle of disappointment deflated his excitement.

He stopped outside the Corn Market, deciding what to do. It would take him the best part of three hours to walk to Caulbourne and back and in any case, much as he would have liked to tell his news to Lizzie, he remembered Sir George's insistence on secrecy. Reluctantly he acknowledged that he should not share this momentous news with her. There was no doubt that she was trustworthy but the knowledge might put her in danger and he could not take that risk. He sighed and consoled himself with the thought that when he came back before Christmas he would impress her with all that he had seen and done.

Stepping into the White Hart, Will ordered some ale and marshalled his thoughts, but his mind was still a maze of exciting new prospects. There was one other feeling that impinged on his heightened state and that was a very basic hunger to relieve the sexual need that holding Lizzie had earlier engendered. Her body had been so soft and yielding and at this moment he would have given anything to relive that moment and to make her truly his.

He had been in the tavern for several minutes and his eyes were just adjusting to the smoky gloom when he saw her. There was no mistaking the tangle of black hair and that strange dress. As he watched, fascinated, the Gipsy girl from last summer's fair was running her fingers over the face of a chubby pink maid and telling her something that caused her to giggle and blush. Will found himself smiling as at the antics of a child.

The landlord of the tavern, suspecting that she was plying some illicit trade, pushed his way through the throng and started to hustle her towards the door. In response she swore at him and was summarily tipped out into the muck-strewn yard for her pains.

Without waiting to get a drink, Will followed. As he stepped into the mild, damp evening, he could just make out her expression, illuminated by the quivering rush lamp above the tavern door. She was brushing down her skirts and hurling abuse at no one in particular.

'Hello, Princess.' He was almost touching her before she saw him and he was amused to see her face flush. Hurriedly she smoothed her hair back and ran her hands over her bodice in the way he remembered.

Having recovered her composure, she tilted her head provocatively, and he noticed her even little teeth.

'I didn't think you'd be back so soon,' he remarked and saw her face cloud.

'My mam died. And the littluns.' She looked away, biting her lip. 'We've been to the Hiring. Pa thought we'd best get back to work before winter.'

'I'm sorry.' He squeezed her arm in sympathy and they started to wander in the direction of the archery butts. He gave no thought to why he was walking with her but it seemed the most natural thing in the world and she came willingly, glancing up at him as he spoke, her black eyes huge and glistening in the hazy light.

'When will you go back?' he asked.

She shrugged. 'Probably tonight. I can't get no sense out of Pa. He's always too drunk to think beyond the moment.'

'How will you spend the winter?' There was a fascination about the lifestyle of this vagrant girl.

She shrugged again. 'Probably in Salisbury or London.'

'You've been to London?' He was excited by the proximity of someone who had travelled so far and had to fight back the urge to tell her that he too would be leaving on the morning tide.

She continued: 'We usually do St Bartholomew's Fair.'

'What's it like up there, in London?'

She looked surprised at the question. 'Like everywhere. Folks are mostly greedy.'

By now they had crossed the butts and were nearing the river. It was growing colder and by unspoken consent they continued on into the haven of the copse. Once they were sheltered inside, he stopped and sank on to a fallen log to rest his aching feet. The girl sat down on the brittle, stunted grass, picking at it with her fingers.

Will didn't know what to make of her. He felt that she needed looking after, yet at the same time, for all her youth, she seemed to have some knowledge denied to ordinary folk like him and Lizzie.

Turning, she reached out towards him. 'Give me your hand.'

He held it out and she took it in both of hers, turning it palm upwards and tracing the lines with her small grubby fingers by the light of the hazy November moon. He shied away from admitting that her touch was like lightning. As he watched she frowned and he bent his head closer.

'What is it?' He grinned with the air of one who did not believe her powers, but at the sight of her expression his face sobered.

'You'll be crossing the sea very soon,' she forecast. 'It won't be as you imagine.' Looking up at him, she said: 'You've got a sweetheart but she won't be yours; not for many moons anyways. I can't see that far ahead.'

'Does it say anything about being rich – or having a beautiful black-haired mistress?' he teased and was surprised at the hostile flash of her eyes.

48

To make amends he reached out with his free hand and raised her chin. Her small face was streaked with dirt but her eyes were unfathomable and the desire to kiss her was suddenly more powerful than any feeling he had known. Very slowly his face moved closer to hers and he closed his eyes as their mouths made contact.

Her body smelt earthy and his senses reeled with desire. Gathering her in his arms he smothered her face and neck with kisses and lowered her into the smooth woodland grass. She did not resist him as he raised her skirts and lay astride her.

It took force to enter her body and he dimly heard her whimper of pain. When he had finished it seemed as if he was coming back from another world. Gradually the copse and the distant noises of the town broke into his consciousness.

Beneath him she was still. She flinched a little as he pulled away and the memory of her attack at the Summer Fair came back to him. 'Pa prizes my maidenhead,' she had said. Now he had taken it.

'I'm sorry if I hurt thee.' He teased the damp strands of hair away from her cheek. She did not reply and gently he bent and kissed the dark triangle of her body he had so brutally assaulted. She sat up.

'It doesn't matter, it had to happen.'

He felt suddenly uneasy, not knowing if she meant the loss of her virginity was inevitable or that by some strange destiny he had been marked out to deflower her.

Already he was ashamed of what he had done. She was little more than a child and he had used her. He didn't know what had possessed him.

'I have to get back.' He began to scramble into his breeches while she watched him with those unnerving black eyes. Fully clothed, he looked awkwardly down at her, not knowing what to say.

Finally he asked: 'Can't you stay over?'

She shrugged. 'No parish will have us. Our best hope is to lose ourselves in a town.'

'Can't you find work?' he asked. 'Proper work?'

'I've got proper work.' Defiantly she added: 'Don't you fret none about me.'

He sighed. 'I can't just go off and leave you.'

49

'Then why don't you stay?' She stood up and he sensed the hope in her, overlaid with the uncomfortable feeling that he was being manipulated.

He shook his head. 'I can't, I've got – things to do. But I feel responsible for you.'

Her mouth pouted and she kicked the grass with her naked brown toes. 'You don't have to. I'll survive without you.'

'I don't even know your name,' he said. He felt in his purse and found a shilling. Awkwardly he held it out and was quite unprepared for her reaction. Her face turned to thunder and she hit the coin angrily from his hand.

'Don't you treat me like a whore!' She withdrew from where he stood and clasped her arms about her shoulders, rocking as if holding in her fury.

'I'm not. I just don't want you to go without anything you need.'

'We've got all we need, Pa and me. We don't need the likes of you giving us charity.'

He sighed, trying to defuse the situation. 'You still haven't told me your name,' he repeated.

'It don't make no odds to you what I'm called.'

'If I didn't want to know I wouldn't ask.' He tried to touch her arm but she flinched away, still hunched and resentful.

'Please, Princess. Don't take on so.' Suddenly remembering something, he fished in his pouch and pulled out the garnet clasp.

'Here, I've got something for you. I've been carrying it round because I knew I'd see you some day.' He didn't know what had made him say it but, sensing her curiosity, he moved closer.

'See? It's got some stones in the middle and it flashes black as your eyes – and red as your temper.' He couldn't believe how easily the lie came to him.

She allowed him to pin the clasp to her bodice and as he did so he thought, I don't believe this is happening. It was as if his normal life had been suspended and replaced by this crazy dream. As his fingers touched her skin he was aware of her bony chest compared to the soft rise of Lizzie's breasts, and at the thought of his love he jerked back into the world he recognised.

The girl was looking down at the ground and he could see

that she was not mollified. He was totally out of his depth now and wanted only to get away.

'I'm truly sorry for what's happened but – well, I didn't force thee, did I?' he excused himself.

She turned to face him, her lower lip beginning to quiver. 'No, you didn't. I never said you did.'

With a sudden stamp of her foot she turned and flounced away, crashing heedlessly through the yellowing, moonlit bracken of the copse. He had the fleeting image of a wild faun.

Helplessly Will stood and watched until she was out of sight.

'Dear God, what have I done?' he asked himself and his heart sank. He had the certain feeling this was not the end of the story.

Chapter Eight

The journey back from the Hiring Fair to Caulbourne was long
and trying. The moon and the lantern barely illuminated the
hidden ruts. Many times Lizzie thought they would be stuck.
Still, as she bumped and jolted on the half-empty cart, her mind
drew her back to the afternoon's events and soon she was
oblivious to everything but the time she had spent in the copse
with Will.

As the night darkened into velvet blackness, the noises of the
forest began to distract her. Several times she thought she heard
horses and imagined vagabonds and footpads leaping out to
cut their throats. The money earned that day was wrapped in a
cloth and hidden in a basket at the back of the wagon. She
wondered if the Gipsy girl and her father were following them,
intent on robbery and murder. She had not seen anything of the
girl during the day and thought smugly that had she done so she
could have told her that her predictions had been wrong. She
and Will were already as good as man and wife. She fingered
her keepsake and lingered over the memory of his kiss.

Now there was undoubtedly a noise.

'I'm scared,' she whispered.

Jed laughed his loud, braying noise. ''Tis only deer,' he
chided, indicating the parkland to the north. ''Tis only chooky
pigs,' pointing to the oak woods to the south. 'You'm with Jed
now, Lizzie. I'm strong as a tree. I'll protect thee.' Pride and
pleasure sounded in his voice.

In the distance the lights of Swaynson Manor came into
view. A hundred candles challenged the night's black shield
and Lizzie thought to herself that May was down there some-

where. What would she be doing? Lizzie would have given a lot to be able to see her and find out what it was like in the great house, but most of all to tell her about her wonderful encounter with Will.

He loves me, she thought. He loves me and he's coming for me. She hugged her knees and rocked herself gently backwards and forwards, savouring the pleasure of this knowledge.

As the wagon finally rumbled to a halt outside the cottage, Leah came out to meet them. Dripping fog seemed suspended in the flickering candlelight and her face was grim. She gazed fixedly at her husband.

'May's gone to Swaynson,' Lizzie started, struggling down with a load of baskets. Leah squeezed her daughter's arm, a gesture that said 'Later, child', and kept her gaze steadfastly on George.

'Didn't do too bad,' he announced.

'Never mind about that. He's been round.'

'Who?'

'Him. Silas Dore. He says you've got it settled. He says he's fixed it with Parson.'

George avoided her eyes. 'Let me get this sorted out, woman. It's been a long haul.'

'Long haul?' she echoed. 'What do you think it'll be for Lizzie if she goes through with it?'

Lizzie, returning from the cottage, looked from one parent to the other.

'What's up?' she asked.

Neither of them answered. Finally her father turned to Jed.

'Take wagon back,' he ordered. Unquestioningly Jed led the tired animal away, and as soon as he was out of earshot George turned to face his wife.

'It's no good carrying on, woman,' he said. 'You should be pleased that she won't have nothing to worry about. She'll be well provided for.'

At first Lizzie thought that they were talking about May and could not understand her mother's anger. As the conversation continued, it dawned on her that it was something concerning herself. She felt a chill inside trying to imagine what she had done to cause the anger. Did they somehow know that she had kissed Will? Had she brought shame to the family?

53

By now her parents were shouting and she saw her father's hand go up as if to hit her mother.

'What is it?' she begged in panic.

Leah turned, her face distorted with fury. 'Your father's betrothed you. You're getting wed in three weeks,' she spat.

'Who to?' Lizzie's mind was suddenly blank. She began racing through the village boys but all the time a hopeful voice whispered 'Will'.

'It's Silas Dore.'

'Who?' Lizzie thought that she had misheard. Silas Dore was an old man, a smelly, leering old man.

'Silas Dore.' Her mother seemed lost for the right words. 'Your father thinks he's well set up and could help the family,' she continued without conviction.

Lizzie was shaking her head. 'I can't! I couldn't ever. Anyway, I'm spoken for.'

Both parents stared at her.

'What do you mean?' her father demanded.

Lizzie blushed and wished there was an escape. She said nothing.

'What's going on?' Her father stepped closer. Lizzie shook her head in confusion.

'What do you mean?' he repeated, shaking her.

'Will Gosden,' she whispered.

George tightened his grip. 'What you been up to?' His voice was dangerously low.

'Nothing. Nothing at all. Will loves me. And I love him.' She looked pleadingly across to her mother.

'Have you been up to nonsense?' George insisted.

'No! Will's not like that. He loves me.'

'Leave her, George.' Leah pushed him aside. 'Will's only a prentice,' she said quietly to her daughter. 'I don't see as how he can even think of marriage. Besides, things are bad with the farm at the moment and I'm . . .' She hesitated. 'There's a littlun on the way.'

Lizzie flushed, her eyes going involuntarily to her mother's belly. She could not see what this had to do with Silas Dore.

'Will'll be a master one day,' she began. 'If I wait –'

'We need help now,' George cut in. 'Silas ain't a bad chap.

54

He is constable and that's a goodly place you'll be getting. Just think, you'll be mistress of your own kitchen.'

Both women were silent.

'But I can't!' Lizzie finally wailed, tears trickling down her face.

'Can't don't come into it. It's settled and I won't hear another word.' With that George Galpine turned and strode into the cottage, leaving the women huddled together in the driving rain.

That night Lizzie lay rigid in the dark bedroom, trying to stifle her sobs. She felt like a leaf that had been plucked from the safety of its tree only to be buffeted by a storm.

In the big bed her father's snoring punctuated the silence. Her mother was so still that Lizzie guessed she too must be awake.

Her mind could not cope with the image of marrying Silas Dore. Along with the other village girls, she had discovered early in life that at the least opportunity he would get you alone and put his hands where no man should touch. She must have had a nightmare. Her parents would never allow him to do those things to her.

She remembered then the feeling of Will's body against hers and the magic of it and she knew that he would save her. As soon as he learned what was going on he would have it out with her father and then everything would be well. The problem was how to get a message to him. He was six miles away in the castle and she could never walk there and back in the day time without being missed. The only answer was to go at night. Resolving to set out the next evening as soon as it was dark, she fell into a disturbed sleep.

All the next day she worked silently. Her mother watched her, trying to make conversation, but it was stilted and unnatural and she finally abandoned the attempt. The subject of marriage was not mentioned.

Leah looked ill with her pregnancy. Lizzie wondered that she had not noticed before. This would be her mother's ninth, although only three of her children had survived. Sometimes lying in the dark Lizzie had listened to the grunts from her parents' bed and always pretended to be asleep. She wondered how her mother could allow such things to happen, for she was sure that she could not love her father. The idea of their copulation filled her with disgust and yet yesterday with Will she had not been able to resist the hard pressure against her belly. If you loved a man, then it must be different.

Mam was struggling with a bucket of water. She put it down and stretched, rubbing the small of her back. Immediately Lizzie felt guilty.

'Here, let me do that,' she said. She thought ruefully that Mam needed extra help now and peace of mind. It would be much easier for her if Lizzie could do as her father wished, she knew that, but the thought of Silas Dore with his foul breath and lascivious presence filled her with disgust.

The minutes seemed to crawl by, but at last the evening meal was over and it grew dark. One by one the members of the household retired to bed. It took an eternity before she was sure that her parents were finally asleep.

With great care she gathered her woollen blanket and eased herself off the mattress, halting at every step to check that all was well. With careful slowness she descended the stairway to the kitchen.

There was still a hint of warmth from the embers and stretched out in front of the fireplace Jed snored loudly. Lizzie found her precious shoes, wrapped the blanket around her and eased the door open. The click of the latch was deafening but Jed did not stir.

Outside, the difficulty of her task overcame her. She had only the haziest notion of the way and no light to guide her. As she stumbled up the lane to the road, the fear of vagabonds constricted her stomach muscles and her heart thundered. Within a few hundred yards she stepped into a deep rut, drenching herself to the knees. Her skirt clung cold and wet to her legs and only a fear that she might not find the way back kept her going.

Everywhere the trees menaced, hiding unknown terrors. She could have sworn that they were whispering to each other, warning that she was coming. She stayed for a while on the road but she felt so exposed that, steeling herself, she moved into the cover of the woods. This made the going even harder. The silence of the night was filled with activity. Twigs snapped, leaves rustled and the unbroken whispering crowded in on her. A sudden noise made her whimper with fear.

''Tis only the chooky pigs,' she told herself, echoing Jed's words, but he was not there now to protect her. Her eyes had grown accustomed to the darkness but still she could not see further than a few yards.

Suddenly somewhere out there she heard another sound, a deep groaning that froze her with fear.

'Oh, dear Lord, forgive me,' she prayed. 'I really don't mean to do wrong. Spare me, please!' Her blood was now pounding so loudly that she could hear nothing else. She held her breath until her lungs were bursting, trying to silence the cacophony inside her.

'Sweet Lord! Don't let it be the Spaniards! I'll serve Thee all my life if only you spare me now,' she whimpered to herself.

Ten yards ahead the undergrowth parted and a stag and two hinds stepped cautiously into the clearing, noses raised to detect any danger. Seeing them, Lizzie sagged with relief. Her movement startled them and they blundered across to a thicket. Simultaneously an owl screeched. Joining the blind panic of the woodland, Lizzie raced forwards, catching her foot in a tangle of brambles. Scrambling up, she fled back to the road and scurried in what she prayed was the right direction.

By some miracle she reached Carisbrooke as the first icy glimmer of light penetrated the sky. She had no idea how to reach the castle but followed the general direction through the narrow lanes of the village huddled at the bottom of the great hill.

Emerging from their tiny hovels, the early risers regarded her with suspicion. Ignoring them, she crossed the ford; emerging, her feet were deadened with the cold and the pain of her blisters numbed. She had lost one shoe in the mud and the other was tucked in the fold of her blanket.

In the increasing light she could see the road up to the castle and wearily began to climb towards it. Stopping exhausted in the shadow of some trees, she surveyed the huge grey citadel with its forbidding gatehouse. It was surrounded by a moat and around the ramparts guards kept a restless watch.

She did not know what to do next. Until now she had given no thought as to how to gain entry and find Will. Getting here had been her only concern. Now she felt so cold, tired and hungry that she would have given anything to be back at home. She sniffed back the tears, imagining her father's anger when he discovered that she was gone.

Before she knew what was happening, her arms were grabbed from behind. Her scream of terror was stifled as a hand clamped brutally over her mouth and her arms were pinioned to her sides by huge, encircling arms.

'What we got here then?' her unseen assailant asked.

'Lemme go! Help!' She had bitten his finger and now writhed desperately in his grasp.

'You little vixen!' He yanked her off her feet and sat astride her in the wet grass. Lizzie continued to struggle, for she knew her life depended on it, but his weight was squashing the breath out of her.

'You ain't no village girl,' he said now that he had her safely secured beneath him. 'So you can't be up to no good.'

She realised that he was a soldier, not a local man but one imported from the mainland, and this added to her fear.

'My betrothed's in the castle,' she cried.

'Yeah? And who might that be?' His expression was ambivalent, half ridicule, half lust, and she knew that she was in danger.

'I'm from Caulbourne. I'm spoken for by Will Gosden. He's a stonemason here at the castle. My pa's a farmer and I'm here with an urgent message.' Dire circumstances gave her the wit to invent whatever was necessary.

'Give us the message, then,' said her captor, grinning.

'It's not written down. It's in my head. I'm only to repeat it to the Captain.'

'The captain of the Guard?'

'No, Sir George himself.'

The soldier hesitated. 'Who are you?' he repeated.

'Elizabeth Galpine.'

'What's the message about, then?'

'The Spaniards.' Panic made her reckless.

'What do you know about the Spaniards?' he said disbelievingly.

'I can't say,' she repeated. 'Only to Sir George. Take me to him or you'll be in terrible trouble.'

For a moment he stared at her, then his grin broadened and he started to fumble with her skirt.

'Doubby diggy doo,' Lizzie cried desperately. 'That's Spanish, that is. I speak the lingo and I know something very important.'

The soldier hesitated again. By now the noise had attracted attention, so reluctantly he got up, pulling Lizzie with him, and dragged her across the drawbridge to the gatehouse.

There was a heated discussion. In spite of her dishevelled appearance, there was something about Lizzie that made the soldiers reluctant to dismiss her story totally. As they argued, she look desperately around, hoping that Will would miraculously appear.

Just as a messenger was to be despatched to the main building for instructions, a party of riders appeared and the soldiers hastened to attention.

''Tis Sir George,' someone whispered. 'Now you'll be in trouble.'

She gazed open-mouthed at the party. The finery of both horses and riders was unlike anything she had seen before. The horses were sleek and well fed, their coats shining like satin. As they were reined in, their bridles chinked with each restless step. The riders wore rich woollen cloaks intricately embroidered with what looked like gold thread and exotic feathers fluttered in their hats.

'What is amiss?' From the centre of the group, a man urged his horse forwards a few paces.

'Begging your pardon, sir, but we found this gal.'

Lizzie flushed scarlet as he surveyed her, ponderously twisting his neatly trimmed beard. She knew that this must be Sir George. He sat straight-backed and elegant in his saddle and she was ashamed of her muddy skirts and windswept hair falling brazenly from her cap.

She bobbed a curtsy, keeping her eyes lowered to the ground. Everyone knew that he was the most important man in the island. His grandmother and Queen Anne Boleyn had been sisters, which made him almost royalty.

'She says she's got a message 'bout the Dons, m'lord,' her captor volunteered. Sir George raised his eyebrows and appeared to reassess her.

'You know something about the Spanish, maid?' he asked her.

Lizzie shook her head.

'Then what is all this nonsense?' He looked from one to the other and the guards shuffled in silence.

'Well?' His eyes rested again on Lizzie. His fine, polished boot was level with her face and she smelled the perfume that he used to keep the stench of the castle at bay.

'My father's betrothed me to the village constable,' she finally started. 'I hate him. I'm already spoken for by Will Gosden.'

'Who, pray, is Will Gosden?' Sir George visibly stiffened and appeared perturbed so that Lizzie feared she may get Will into trouble but it was too late now.

'He's prenticed to the stonemason here at the castle. I need to see him.' She could not control her shivering.

Sir George conferred with one of his minions, then turned back to her.

'It seems that you are out of luck, girl. Gosden is no longer here.'

Lizzie stared at him in disbelief. 'But he must be!' she insisted.

Sir George's expression defied argument. It almost seemed as if he suspected some trickery. 'Where are you from?' he demanded curtly.

'Caulbourne, sir.' She was struggling with the disappointment.

'Ah.' He appeared to remember something, and more kindly he asked: 'How did you get here?'

'I walked.' She raised her eyes to look at him, willing him to have some solution.

'Why does your father wish you to marry this constable?' he asked.

Lizzie shrugged. 'He owns the fulling mill. Our mam's not well and the sheep are doing badly.'

Sir George considered, the corners of his mouth pulled down, his large brown eyes still assessing her.

'Well, I cannot condone your disobeying your parents,' he finally said. It sounded like a death sentence.

'Were you formally betrothed to this apprentice?' he continued.

She shook her head.

He sighed. 'Well, you're a resourceful girl, but you really must return home and fulfil your duty.'

'Sir, I cannot!' Despair made Lizzie bold.

'Enough!' The command was peremptory. 'You know little of this world, child. In all stations we sometimes have to undertake contracts we do not choose. If your family will benefit from this union, you should praise God for your father's wisdom.'

He turned and consulted again with his escorts, then turned back to the guard.

'There is a carriage leaving for Yarmouth shortly,' he said. 'Put this girl aboard and deliver her back to her family. Meanwhile take her to the kitchen and feed and warm her.'

With a nod to his assembly, he urged his horse forwards and the cavalcade rode off across the drawbridge and in the direction of the surrounding woodland.

Lizzie knew that she was defeated. Fate had prevented her from seeing Will. It was not possible that he could have left and yet why should Sir George lie? Clearly he was mistaken but she could not argue with him. She felt too tired and miserable to make sense of it and she could no longer pretend to herself that she could disregard her family's needs, especially Mam's. She sobbed quietly to herself as she was escorted across the courtyard, picking her way amid the soldiers' tents, the open fires and the rubble of building work.

In the kitchen she was given a bowl of onion soup and hot wheaten bread. Its warmth revived her enough to look around the huge room with its enormous blackened fireplace. It was as big as the village church but hot and bustling with activity. Whole sides of venison and boar were being roasted in the great chimney recess and from the open oven, the smell of delicious pasties filled the air.

No sooner had she finished than she was taken back to the waiting carriage and hoisted up beside the driver. She had never seen such a vehicle before. It was bigger than any wagon and painted shiny black with huge scrolls of gold along the sides. Thick leather straps and glinting buckles secured it to the axle

61

and it had proper doors with glass windows. Two black horses pranced impatiently in the traces, their coats as shiny as the paintwork.

Inside two beautiful ladies of the court had been helped aboard and wrapped around with blankets for their comfort. Outside it began to rain and Lizzie's blanket, now soaked, increased her chill.

'Tell Will Gosden I came. Please,' she begged the guards as they drove off into the foggy morning. She did not know if they heard.

Lizzie remembered little of the journey back. A cold knot in her stomach reached out to her limbs, creeping upwards until her head felt as if it had been snuffed out like a candle. With each jolt of the great carriage a pain shot through her temples and jarred her aching joints.

She was vaguely aware of the coachman speaking to her and yet she could not understand what he said. At some point she was lifted from the carriage. She could hear voices in the distance, her mother and father whispering, then shouting alternately from afar and then close by. Then there was the smell of Silas Dore.

'No!' she called, feeling that he was bending over her.

In the chaos Will was suddenly there, wearing a fine woollen cloak with intricate gold embroidery. He held her against him and then she was in a huge, hot kitchen preparing him a wonderful meal of venison and wheat bread. Will ... with a murmur of comfort she slipped into oblivion.

Chapter Nine

After Will had taken her, Mardi ran away, her feelings as tangled as her dusty black hair. After a while she realised that she was going in the wrong direction so she stopped and sat panting on a fallen tree trunk.

She was so confused that she did not know what to think about first. Things hadn't worked out at all as she had planned. She had concentrated all her thoughts into making him love her and instead he had used her. His heart had not been ensnared. Fear gripped her, for she had given him her greatest prize and it had not been enough.

As it was, she was sure that her own heart was broken. She allowed herself the luxury of tears, then despised her weakness. Getting up, she wandered aimlessly around, oblivious to the damp November chill. She had to admit that if this was love she had totally underestimated the suffering it caused. In future she would be more sympathetic to the maids who so often came to consult her.

With a sigh she started back the way she had come, reaching the clearing where she and Will had so recently lain. The crushed undergrowth bore witness to her undoing and the realisation that he did not love her brought the tears prickling afresh to her eyes. Clenching her fists, she pushed her bent forefinger into her mouth and sucked on it hard for comfort. Then, kneeling down in the place where they had lain, she closed her eyes, focusing on the memory.

She started to recite something she had learned in childhood, although until now its meaning had been lost on her.

The body of woman is a temple.
Whosoever desecrates its sanctity
Will be bound in servitude to the dweller therein
Being freed only by the separation of death.

As its significance dawned on her she knew that herein lay the answer. He might not know it yet but he was hers.

Her confidence restored, she got up and followed the route that Will had taken, emerging back into the open field. As if coming back from another age, she became aware that the fair was long since over. Only animal droppings and some abandoned sheep hurdles marked the frenzy of activity that had so recently taken place. Of her father there was no sign.

In a moment of panic she realised that everything they owned had disappeared too. She had abandoned her little tent and her precious potions at the tavern. Worse still, her playing cards had gone. She had won them on a visit to the island two years before from a sailor who had brought them back from France. Their potential in the telling of fortunes had been quickly apparent and their loss was a terrible blow. Pulling herself together, she cursed her stupidity and looked this way and that, wondering what best to do.

Making up her mind, she headed back into Newport and called at the alehouse. With luck, she would find Jake Appleby there, drawn by some irresistible force to spend any money he had earned that afternoon. She suddenly hated him for wasting all their money on his own destruction. Ducking inside, she was quickly aware that there was no sign of her father's slate-black head. As she was about to leave, she caught the tail end of a conversation going on near the door.

'So the constable took him away. They'll have marked him by now and sent him off downriver to get passage on anything going across.'

'Did you see his arm? That sore was enough to turn your stomach. I reckon he'll be dead inside a month.'

'Aye, from that or the brandy.'

The group of men did not notice her and she slipped back outside, her heart thumping. No doubt as usual her father had done something to draw attention to himself. They had been foolish to creep into the fairground that morning without

64

paying a toll. Without permission to trade and without belonging anywhere, they had taken too much of a risk. She shuddered to think that he might have been branded by now and the suggestion of his death left a sickness in her heart. For better or worse, he was all that she had left.

Making up her mind, she went on down through the centre of the town to the rivermouth, where a jumble of craft were moored. Some were larger vessels for carrying timber across to Porstmouth to be used for shipbuilding. An assortment of smaller boats, mostly used for wool and grain, nestled in the still water. It was high tide and she fancied they held their breath waiting for the tide to turn, when the outrush of water would set them straining at their leashes like so many restless hounds.

Most of the vessels seemed empty, but finally she found one with a man aboard. Calling out, she padded barefoot up the rickety gangplank.

'You leaving for Porstmouth?' she asked.

The man on board looked more like a bundle of rags. As he screwed up his eyes to see her more clearly, he dribbled between two tusklike yellow teeth.

'What do you want?' He emphasised the word 'you'. Encouraged by the glimmer of curiosity in his watery eyes, she went closer.

'I need a passage across to the mainland.'

He snorted dismissively. 'I don't carry livestock,' he replied.

Undeterred, Mardi came closer. 'I'd be willing to pay,' she offered, realising simultaneously that she had no money.

''Ow much?' She detected the greedy glint in his eyes.

'Something better than money.'

'Such as?'

'I can sell you a wind. Whenever you want you can command the wind to blow and it will take you anywhere you choose.'

He snorted again in disbelief.

'It's true. Just shut your eyes and I'll call it up.'

Grudgingly the man closed his eyes. Making a funnel with her hands, Mardi blew silently through the tunnel of her palms so that the air circled about the man's neck, causing his lank hair to lift.

He looked at her suspiciously.

65

'Well, I don't want none of your winds or nothing else. You'd best get away from here or you'll be in the stocks. Constable has been down with one fellow already.'

'What sort of fellow?' She dropped all pretence at being mysterious and was hanging on to his every word.

'Black-looking cove. Dark as you,' he added.

'Had they hurt him?'

He shrugged. 'How should I know? They flung his things in the river and sent him off on a barge heading out on the last tide.'

Mardi peered into the water as if she might see some of her precious belongings, but it was murky and impenetrable.

'When could I get across?' she asked.

'Not till morning. 'Ere.' He beckoned her to him. She took a few steps closer.

'I don't want no winds but I wouldn't mind a bit of – you know.' He made a grab for her wrist but she was too fast for him.

'Get off! You'd have to take me round the world before it would be worth that,' she retorted, leaping for the safety of the bank.

'I'd feed ye and ye could share me bunk,' he called hopefully.

Without bothering to reply, she hurried back the way she had come, thinking how she hated every man that had ever drawn breath.

She was tired and hungry and instinctively started back out in the direction of Yarmouth, where they had landed the evening before. It was some twelve miles' journey but she reckoned that she would be safer out in the woods than staying in town. As she walked, she began to think that perhaps she did not have to go back to the mainland after all. Now her pa was lost it would be easy to hide up, and she had heard the island was a warmer place to pass the winter months.

She was so preoccupied with her thoughts that she did not notice that her route was taking her further south than she intended. Instead of ending up near the Yar mouth, she found herself on what she later discovered was West Over Down.

Wandering cold and hungry in the bleak November gloom, she was about to find a bush under which she could curl up for the night when she noticed a shepherd's bothy. Creeping cautiously closer, she was relieved to find it empty and thankfully took sanctuary for the night. As she had done many times before, she staved off the worst of her hunger with handfuls of frost-brittle grass.

At first light she was better able to survey the landscape and discover where she was. To her satisfaction she realised that the hut seemed wind- and waterproof and she thought that it was as good a place as any to shelter for the winter.

She had no second thoughts about remaining on the island. It meant that she might see Will, and that was reason enough. By now her resentment at his treatment had subsided and she began to scheme how she could find him again. With nothing but what she stood up in, she could not make up a potion to draw him to her. That would have to come later. In the meantime she would concentrate hard on him. That way he would be unable to push her from his thoughts.

She did not try to define what it was that she wanted from him. It wasn't money or a house, for neither had any lure for her. Certainly it wasn't marriage. The married women she had come across seemed to lead lives of unrelieved drudgery. They had no time to please themselves and most of them had not moved more than a mile or two away from where they were born. No, she didn't want that. But she wanted him. Whether he would ever be her husband or even truly her lover made no difference. The only thing she knew for certain was that he had turned her from a child into a woman and for better or worse he had to be part of her life.

Chapter Ten

Although born only five miles from the sea, Will had never actually sailed across it. The voyage from the West Cow to Southampton was therefore a milestone in his life.

The sea was quite choppy and by the time they reached the mainland he had been soaked by spray, thoroughly chilled and felt sick. They had been bobbing around for what seemed like hours, for the wind had dropped without warning, and after a while he was sure that they were actually drifting back towards where they had started. By a combination of changing tack and using oars, however, the boat finally reached its destination and, with trembling legs and an overwhelming sense of relief, Will clambered ashore.

He stood miserably on the quayside, trying to remember Sir George's exact words. He was to find the Blue Anchor and enquire after other travellers making the journey towards London.

'You must remember that at any moment you may be ambushed,' the Captain had warned. 'For this reason you must ensure that you are always in company.'

Will doubted if anything on the mainland could be the same as on his own familiar island. Did they speak the same language? What were the houses like? How did people dress, how much did things cost? He was afraid of attracting attention as a stranger and shy of approaching potential travelling companions.

He watched another boat tie up alongside the Town Quay. Only two men came ashore and in considerable haste. They looked around them as if they had lost something or somebody and then, after a hasty consultation together, withdrew to the leeward side of a large warehouse, apparently waiting for something to happen. Spindleshanks and Lardychops, Will thought to himself, amused by their contrasting shapes.

With a sigh he picked up his pack and headed in what he hoped was the right direction. He walked as far as possible in the middle of the streets, glancing uneasily over his shoulder to make sure that he was not being followed, ever aware of the importance of the letter hidden inside his shirt. It was not to leave his person until he handed it himself to the Marquis of Winchester.

At the Blue Anchor he established that a coach together with three mounted merchants would be leaving at first light and it was agreed that he could travel as part of their company.

Following Sir George's precise instructions, he took a room for himself and hired a horse from the livery stable. He would have preferred to sleep in the barn with the livestock but that would have meant disobeying orders.

To his surprise, the food at the tavern was good. Sitting alone in a smoky alcove, he managed two whole doves, soaking the gravy up with coarse rye bread. It had been ten hours since he had eaten. The tavern also served strong, unfamiliar beer in pewter tankards. Halfway through the second measure his head began to feel muzzy, so reluctantly he left the drink and retired to the communal bedchamber on the upper floor. It seemed important to keep his wits about him.

He settled down to sleep with Sir George's letter still tucked into his shirt and his knife under the bolster in case of attack, but it was an uneventful, though disturbed, night.

As soon as he managed to put the present from his mind, he was swamped by memories of the previous evening when he had taken the Gipsy girl. The episode left him with nothing but regret. Most poignant was the knowledge that he had been disloyal to Lizzic, on the very day that he had offered himself as her faithful lover. It was a chilling contradiction and he had the feeling that some outside power was making him behave like a different man. On both occasions that he had seen the girl, he seemed to have been out of control.

Then on a practical level was the worry that she was probably pox-ridden, which was no more than he deserved. Hours

69

of sleepless self-reproach passed before he allowed himself the comfort of acknowledging that her virginity should after all guarantee that she was clean.

Knowing that he had violated her, however, brought another kind of guilt and he was angry with himself and with her for allowing it to happen. Every waking hour of the night was taken up with remorse.

As a result he was tired next day and the ride to Winchester proved long and trying. One of the merchants entertained them by reading from a book, but Will's mind was too distracted to pay much attention. He simply wanted the journey over, the letter delivered and to return to Carisbrooke, from where he could visit George Galpine and sort things out. Waiting until Christmas now seemed a mistake.

It was dark when they reached Winchester. On the way the coach had become stuck in a rut and when they had finally managed to release it, it had foundered again, this time breaking an axle. Will and the mounted men had ridden on ahead, leaving the coach passengers to shelter at the nearest inn.

While they had been hoisting the vehicle to safety, he had been almost certain that Spindleshanks and Lardychops had ridden by. Indeed, somebody had called out to them to come and help, but they had increased their pace and ridden on. Perhaps they had not heard and anyway in the gathering gloom he could not be sure that it was them.

The following morning it was raining as he moved off with another convoy of travellers. They were a subdued group, mostly clerks and legal men en route for the capital. Will had to leave them some distance from Basing House, since from there on their route took them in a different direction. He was not sorry to see them go.

Once he was alone, however, his responsibility weighed heavy on him. He followed the river Lodden until, breasting a gentle incline, the Marquis of Winchester's house came into view. At first Will did not recognise that he had actually arrived, for the house had more the appearance of a walled town, so vast was its circumference. A turreted jumble of red-brick buildings dominated the landscape, protected by a continuous curtain wall decorated with diapered brickwork. As he drew closer it was the main gatehouse that held his attention, a great tower probably some sixty feet high and with octagonal turrets at each corner. Any would-be attackers would soon discover that this was not a house but a fortress and not to be taken easily.

Will reined in the tired horse. From the shelter of some oak trees he surveyed the scene with misgivings. He very much doubted that the work he had done at Carisbrooke could ever be acceptable here. For a start, now he looked at it, the building was entirely of brick, although as he screwed up his eyes the better to see, he realised that there were stone quoins and mullions around the windows.

For a long while he was totally engrossed in the edifice before him, until a noise from nearby alerted him. His hand went to his dagger, but too late. At the same moment there was a rush of activity and somebody grabbed his leg. In a panic the horse reared and Will came crashing down on the rocky pathway. The breath was knocked out of him and immediately a hand was closing around his throat. Over his assailant's shoulder he saw with horror that a second man, whom he recognised as Lardychops, had raised his hand and the metallic blade of a dagger started its descent towards his chest.

Quickly Will flung himself aside, dragging Spindleshanks with him. Tearing loose, he scrambled to his feet, his own dagger now ready for action. The two attackers began to circle and he leaped back to prevent them from getting behind him.

As Spindleshanks lunged forwards, Lardychops rushed at him from the left. Sidestepping the first, Will swung his knife hard and true towards the other and with a sickening sound the blade pierced his rotund belly. The resultant scream was to haunt Will's dreams for months to come.

Lardychops sank to his knees and pulled impotently at the knife. Blood began to gush from his belly and he whimpered and cried like a stuck pig. The noise caused Spindleshanks to turn and race for the cover of the woodland. With his breath coming in great heaving gasps, Will watched as the injured man lurched forward, red frothing bubbles escaping from his lips, and pitched onto his face. He lay for several minutes twitching and gasping, but already his soul appeared to have left his body.

Will stood panting, closing his eyes to ward off the horrific sight. He fought to control his breathing and gradually his heart calmed. Lardychops was now deathly still.

Looking about him, Will saw the horse in among the trees. On legs like aspic he walked towards it, grabbing the trailing rein before the animal could take off. With relief he hauled himself into the saddle and calmed his racing mind. Concentrating on the gatehouse, he urged the horse on, rehearsing the set speech he was to repeat to ensure that the Marquis was made aware of his arrival.

'Halt! If you have lawful business here, speak without delay.'

Guards were posted on the bridge across the steep though dry moat. Their challenge caused Will to jerk to a halt.

'Your lord has need of a skilled man and my lord has pleased to send me to do his service.' Will's voice was hoarse with the tension.

The guards surveyed him and consulted together. They wore livery and Will noted with misgivings that apart from the fearsome-looking pikes they also had muskets at their belts.

'Where are you from?' the first one asked.

'Down south. Across the water.'

Apparently the answer was acceptable; the pikes were lowered to allow Will through the gate. He rode into the first of what seemed to be a series of courtyards, where a melee of working men and militia were rubbing shoulders.

He was ordered to dismount and as he did so he was aware that his jerkin was soaked with blood. Hastily he tried to hide it with his pack.

A groom was summoned to take the horse away. Now dismounted, Will felt doubly vulnerable and his hand moved unconsciously to check that the letter was still beneath his sodden jerkin.

Another servant in livery appeared across the courtyard and, without speaking, indicated to Will to follow. He was led through an archway and into another courtyard, then another, and finally up three steps, through a heavy oak door and into a receiving chamber. Left alone, he looked around, but his mind was too stunned to take in any detail of the tapestries and the embroidered horsehair cushions in the window recess, where he slumped down to recover. Through the tall, narrow window he glanced at the activity outside. It reminded him of Carisbrooke and a sudden homesickness overwhelmed him. He must have been bewitched to leave. He eased his shirt away from a graze sustained on his neck and discovered that the talisman was missing, ripped off during the fight. He shivered.

His reverie was broken by the sound of footsteps and seconds later the door opened and a man came in. He was not impressive to look at although he wore a rich brown cloak and fine leather boots, intricately embossed. His clothes gave him the air of unmistakable wealth and at that moment Will would have given a lot for the comfort of such garments.

'Carey's man?' The man's mouth was pinched and mean.

Will jumped to his feet and nodded, his mouth dry from tension.

'You have something for me? I am Winchester.'

'Sir.' Will fumbled in his jerkin and pulled out the letter. It was stained russet brown with blood. Will looked at the Marquis and said: 'There is a man lying dead in the woods out there. He attacked me. He and his companion followed me from the island. I recognized them.'

'I'll make sure that everything is seen to.' The Marquis spoke as if this was an everyday occurrence and Will was conscious of his trembling hands. 'I've never killed a man before,' he said.

Ignoring him, the Marquis broke the seal on the letter and unfolded the document, scanning it with a frown. With a sigh he folded it again.

'Right.' He turned to leave, but before he could close the door, Will asked:

'How soon can I leave, m'lord?'

The Marquis turned back and considered the question. 'There are no plans for you to leave,' he finally replied. 'Perhaps on the morrow or perhaps in six months. At some point I will need to communicate with your master. Until that time you must remain here.'

Chapter Eleven

Leah woke with a start and lay blinking in the darkness. Her dream had been so confused that she was left only with the feel of it and that was overwhelmingly of fear. Immediately her thoughts flew to Lizzie, who was now sleeping in Jed's bed downstairs in front of the fire. As quietly as she could she slipped out of bed and descended to the kitchen.

The fire was long since out and Lizzie lay still. For a terrible moment Leah thought that she must be dead, then the tiniest movement released her from the paralysing fear and she expelled her breath with relief.

She knelt beside the mattress, watching her daughter's pallid face. The girl was deeply asleep and the agues of the past week had mercifully passed.

Since Lizzie was brought back from Carisbrooke she had been on the verge of death. The realisation had struck despair into Leah, for her daughter was dearer to her, more precious than she had ever thought possible, and day and night she had sat by the girl, willing her to live. Finally George had intervened, and Widow Trykett was summoned to keep watch.

Widow Trykett was a good woman but old. Leah had been certain that only her own constant vigilance could save Lizzie from death.

'Bed, woman,' George had finally ordered and there had been no defying him.

In the darkening room, Leah's thoughts had raced crazily as she lay, too tired to sleep. 'Lord spare her,' she had repeated over and again in a compulsive litany. In the midst of her misery she had become aware of cramps in her belly and turned her mind to the unwanted burden within. The answer had suddenly been clear and she had started to pray aloud.

'Dear Lord, spare my daughter. If it pleases You to call one of mine to Your Presence, then take back this one inside. It can't make no different to You and I'll do anything if only my Lizzie can live.'

Bitterly she had thought of the girl's betrothal. In her heart she had resisted it as much as Lizzie, defied George, seen it as the worst thing that could happen, but now in this extreme situation she thought that the possibility of Lizzie being a bride was something she would rejoice to see, no matter who was chosen as her groom.

'I won't argue. I'll do anything you wish,' she had silently promised her maker.

That had been three nights ago. Now, sitting in the semi-darkness listening to the wind outside and the rhythm of her daughter's breathing, she suddenly remembered the essence of the dream that had awoken her.

God himself had been standing before her, asking which of her children he should take. He had looked carefully from one to the other. 'No, not Lizzie,' she had begged. 'Not Jed. Please, not Harry!' It was then that she had woken up.

Inside her the child moved and as she eased her position she was suddenly aware that Lizzie was awake. She reached out to touch her.

'How are you, child?' She tucked the blanket about her shoulders.

'A mite tired, Mam. I feel better.'

'Thank God.'

They were both silent while Leah fetched rosehip cordial and spooned a few drops into her daughter's dry mouth.

When she had taken all she wanted, Lizzie asked: 'What day is it?'

'It's Monday. You've been ill for more than a week.' After a pause she asked: 'Why did you run away?'

There was a long silence before Lizzie finally answered.

'I didn't. I went to see Will. To tell him about...' She did not use the words. When her mother made no comment, she continued: 'Has he come?'

75

Leah shook her head and watched helplessly as the tears brimmed from under her daughter's eyelids.

'You mustn't fret. Young men is that fickle. Things won't be as bad as you fear. Father's right that you'll be getting a goodly place and Silas – well, he's a bit of a rough customer but I'm sure there's good in him.'

For a moment Leah saw the old spirit of rebellion in her daughter's expression but then she sagged back onto the mattress and closed her eyes.

When Leah was certain that she was asleep, she got painfully to her feet and made for the stairway. As her foot came to rest on the first step, her daughter said:

'If I am to marry Silas Dore, then it would have been best that I had died.'

The wedding of Silas Dore and Elizabeth Galpine took place at ten of the clock on the morning of 1 December 1587. The bride was still unwell but the church permitted no weddings between 2 December and 2 January without a costly special licence and Silas had been unwilling to wait.

'I ain't wasting money on a new maid,' he told George. 'The quicker we're wed, the quicker the chores'll get done.' Apart from the duties of the marriage bed, Lizzie would have work to do.

The first of December was a crisp, clear day and the church was full. Lizzie's best dress in its once pleasing shade of old gold now hung loosely on her and the colour made her pale skin look sallow. Her mother had refurbished the gown with new ribbons and buttons, but in spite of this the bride had none of the radiant beauty the congregation had hoped to see.

The groom in his Sunday best had washed his face and hands for the occasion. His hair was flattened with lavender water, which, mixed with the grease from his scalp, gave off a sickly scent. He stood sweating and anxious lest his bride might even at this last moment rebel and refuse to consent to the union.

At the altar the Reverend Cotton pontificated at length on the joys and duties of married couples and their ultimate submission to God's will. Kneeling before him, the bride silently asked the Holy Father: 'How can You do this to me?', but the worst pain was the knowledge that Will had not cared enough to come and save her.

At the appropriate point in the ceremony she answered the priest's response with the words 'I do consent' and a heavy door slammed shut on all her dreams.

A feast had been prepared at the fulling mill, Elizabeth Dore's new home, and while the village folk took advantage of this opportunity to gorge themselves, she sat listless by the fire.

Her parents were the last to leave. She could see that her father had had plenty of ale and as he came to take his farewell he puffed himself up like a pigeon, smug and satisfied with the success of this marriage settlement. He patted Lizzie awkwardly on the shoulder.

'Well done, gal.' He bent to kiss her cheek but did not meet her eyes.

When they were alone for a few moments, Leah squeezed her daughter's hand.

'I'm sorry it is not as you wish, child,' she said. 'But pray to God and bear it how you can.' She hesitated when Lizzie did not reply, but then continued: 'When I was betrothed to your father, I had no wish for it. We didn't have a proper ceremony like this. We just declared our intention and then I moved in with him.' She gave a little sigh. 'I used to cry myself to sleep many a night but I expect it has worked out for the best.'

Lizzie now looked directly at her and her expression said that there could be no happy outcome for this marriage.

Struggling to hold back her tears, Leah held her daughter close and kissed her cheek. Lizzie remained cold and stiff as if some spark of life had gone out of her.

As soon as the bride and groom were alone, Lizzie started to clear the table. Silas watched her as she moved about the room. He had consumed gallons of ale and his gut hurt. He wasn't sure if he could manage the steep stairs to the bedroom but on second thoughts it was warmer down here by the fire. As Lizzie passed, he grabbed her wrist and pulled her down on his lap.

'Give us a kiss,' he slurred, pulling her face closer to his. She tried to turn her head away. At her reluctance, a surge of anger engulfed him and he grabbed her hair, forcing his mouth over hers. She started to struggle then and, still holding her by the hair, he pulled back and stared into her face.

'Just you listen. You think you're high and mighty. You think you're too good for me, but you're my wife now.' He struggled up and reached into the recess by the fire.

'See this?' He drew out an evil-looking birch switch. 'I'm constable, I am. I've used this on plenty of maids what's broke the law. If you don't do as you're told I'll strip you naked and beat you till you beg for mercy!'

Once more his mouth was on hers and his sheer weight forced her down into the rushes on the floor.

'Thassit,' he panted, straddling her skinny body. 'Thassit, gal. I'm gonna make a woman of you.'

Lizzie felt the tearing pain, followed by a shuddering explosion from the sweating mound on top of her. With a groan he drew away and staggered to the corner, where he vomited profusely. Grunting, he sank back into the straw and was soon snoring loudly.

Painfully Lizzie got to her feet and looked with disgust at the drunken, sated figure.

'I hate you, Silas Dore,' she said aloud. 'I'll get even with you one of these days, just you see if I don't.'

Chapter Twelve

Over the next few weeks, Will remained haunted by the experience of killing a man and he longed only to return home and to see his love. Although the workforce were affable enough, he felt separated from them by an invisible barrier and respite came only by throwing himself into the work. Daily he looked out for some sign that he could leave but there was no indication that that time would ever come.

Christmastide loomed and he began to panic in case he should disappoint Lizzie by not being there to ask for her hand. Since his infidelity with the Gipsy girl he fully expected some retribution to befall him, although in what form he could not have said. It was merely a feeling that he no longer deserved the happiness he had once assumed would be his.

Finally, on 22 December, William Paulet, the Third Marquis of Winchester, took it upon himself to inspect the building work in progress. At the age of fifty-two he walked with a decided stoop and, according to Will's fellow artisans, recent events had taken their toll on his health. He had been both a commissioner at the trial and then Lord Steward at the funeral of the Queen of Scots. Will had heard many rumours about his new master, none of them charitable. It seemed that he had been harsh and unbending to the late queen and had actively enjoyed having a monarch, even a Scottish one, at his mercy. The macabre spectacle of Mary's death was recounted a thousand times, embroidered by those who had never witnessed it; it made good ghoulish entertainment during the long, cold evenings. Rumour also had it that the slaying of Winchester's not so beautiful wife would give him a new lease of life.

As he carried out his tour of inspection, the Marquis stopped here and there to give orders to his overseers. Will had been precariously hoisted onto a narrow ledge to add some finishing embellishments to a stone mullion supporting a new window, but with the arrival of their lord he was hastily lowered down.

The Marquis made a show of examining the stonework and frowned in apparent disapproval.

'Who is responsible for this?' he asked the foreman.

The man raised his eyebrows in surprise, for the work was generally regarded as excellent.

'Er, the island man, Gosden, m'lord.' His face had coloured and behind him Will was tense with indignation.

'Well, it does not please me. I no longer want this man working for me.'

'But ...' The summary dismissal left the overseer lost for words.

'No, buts. I'll see him at three of the clock and he can pack his tools and leave.'

Will was about to remonstrate when some sixth sense warned him not to do so. Instead he shrugged and began to gather up his big wooden club hammer and chisels. Without looking at his fellow labourers, he trudged off back towards the servants' quarters, aware of the discomfort and unspoken sympathy of those left behind.

At exactly three of the clock he was escorted into the lordly presence. The Marquis dismissed his valet and waited until he was sure that he was out of hearing, in the meantime surveying Will in his customary unsmiling manner. Finally he said: 'Right, Gosden, I want you to leave here without rousing suspicion as to the reason. I have let it be known that I suspect you of theft.'

As Will went to protest, he added: 'Do not fear, a true report of both your physical skills and your loyalty will go back to Carey; but, more important, there is another report which is for his eyes only. You will see that it is delivered without suspicion.'

Will nodded, now understanding, and accepted the message together with his own reference.

Once out in the world again, he drove his horse hard with no thought now to the danger of cut-throats or robbers. His only wish was to reach the Isle of Wight before the Christmas festivities were over. When the horse was fit to drop, he rested it in the forest near Lyndhurst, regretting that there was precious little on which it could graze. He vowed that it would be handsomely recompensed when he finally arrived at the castle, with the best oat mash he could make. For himself, his anxiety to get home left him with no wish for food.

When he reached Lymington, the sea was calm and the tide favourable so that the crossing took little more than two hours. He still had the special pass that Sir George had issued to him on his outward journey, and while on board was granted the courtesy of Christmas roasted goose and abundant goblets of sack by the captain. It was now 25 December.

At Yarmouth Will changed horses, giving explicit instructions for the care of his exhausted beast. Freshly mounted, he rode with almost indecent haste back to the garrison.

He did not learn what the letter he had carried contained, but Sir George, replete from a family dinner of considerable proportions, read it with a closely guarded expression on his sullen face. Putting it aside, he thanked Will for his loyalty and devotion to duty and bade him a happy Christmas.

'Sir, may I have permission to visit my village?' he asked when he realised that the audience was at an end.

Sir George thought for a moment, then said: 'Do I recall that you were seeking permission to wed?'

'Aye.' Will blushed.

The Captain said nothing for several moments and appeared to be contemplating some mystery, but finally he shrugged his shoulders and said:

'As from the morrow you have my permission to travel home for three days. I hope that all turns out as you would wish.'

It was a strange answer, but by a man bent on seeking out his bride it was accepted without question.

As Will was bowing his way out of the door, the Captain added: 'Do not forget the secret nature of your mission. It is best if you mention to no one that you have been outside the castle walls. That way you may be able to serve your country again.'

The next morning Will set off at first light to walk the six miles to Caulbourne. It was cold but he had too much on his mind to

81

be bothered by the elements. His first stop was at his father's cottage and he arrived at about seven of the clock with some time to spare before the morning service.

Will's father now looked every day of his fifty-one years. His time in the navy had taken its toll and the younger man thought grudgingly that the only gift his father had passed on to him was the wish to travel. It still burned in him like charcoal.

Dutifully he kissed the woman he called mother, his father's second wife, and acknowledged the presence of her three burly sons, all of whom were present for the Boxing Day feast.

Without asking, his stepmother poured him a jug of haw-berry wine, heating it with the iron poker that stood at the side of the fire. He sat on a stool near the blaze and tasted the warm, sweet liquid.

'How be you then?' The question was superfluous, for she had already began to tell him of all the happenings in the family and news of the village.

'Our Micah's Jane is delivered of a boy,' she announced.

Will nodded to his stepbrother and offered his congratulations.

'Old Peter White was called to his maker last Martinmas.'

Will made an appropriate noise of regret. When there was a pause in the conversation, he asked:

'How are the Galpines?'

'Well enough. That daft Jed's still about. Don't think he'll ever be much use to no one.'

Will was preparing himself to tell them of his decision to see George Galpine that day and ask for Lizzie's hand. He found it hard to say the words because it mattered so much. Instead he asked:

'What about their gal?' His eyes watered with the effort of stilling his racing blood.

'Hadn't you heard? She's wed.'

Will had been about to raise his jug to his lips but it remained suspended halfway. His heart began to thunder louder than a smith's hammer. He was struck dumb.

Apparently unaware of the impact of her news, his step-mother continued: 'Her father wed her to Silas Dore.' She gave a little chuckle. 'Wicked old devil, he is. Still, you can't blame the girl for getting her feet under his table. I heard he's worth a tidy sum.'

'I just remembered. I've got to go.' Will stood up, fighting to keep control.

'Where to? Will!'

He ignored the astonished faces around him and hurried out of the cottage, turning blindly back towards Carisbrooke. A fist hard as a cannon ball lodged in his belly.

As he walked, he told himself over and over that it couldn't be true and yet it was no more than he deserved. He had known he would have to pay for what he had done with the vagabond and this was it. Perhaps somehow Lizzie had learned of that encounter and hardened her heart against him. No. It was more likely that God was punishing him by forcing her into this unthinkable marriage with the uncouth bladder of lard who owned the fulling mill. Poor little Lizzie! What had his own weakness done to her?

The burden of responsibility was too great to bear and after a while Will reasoned that Lizzie could have refused to enter into the marriage contract, had she so chosen. However much pressure her father may have put on her, she could always have told him that she was already affianced. Indeed, she might even have hinted that she and Will were virtually man and wife, perhaps implied that a child was on the way. After all, she knew that he would stand by her, she only had to send word to the castle – only he hadn't been there.

In the emptiness of the wintry countryside he roared with the anguish of a lion.

In a vain bid for some other solution he asked himself if Lizzie could be as greedy as her father. The prospect of living at the mill and acting like a lady might just have been too great a temptation. Maybe he was a fool to think that just because he loved her so much she should feel the same loyalty to him.

He was immune to the flurry of snow that now blew into his face and down his collar. The only thing that could make life bearable now was to get back to the mainland at the first possible moment.

Cursing all women for their fickleness and cruelty, he hastened his pace and made bleakly for his lonely bed at the castle.

Chapter Thirteen

That winter was harsh and throughout the island men and livestock struggled just to stay alive. In Caulbourne village, young and old alike died from cold and starvation in spite of help from their neighbours, but at the fulling mill and in the Galpine cottage there was sufficient food and firewood to ensure that everyone survived.

In the weeks following Lizzie's marriage she wrapped herself in a protective, numbing cocoon, burying the horror of the wedding night deep within her, for in spite of her misery she knew that there was no escape.

If she ran home her father would return her immediately to Silas with abject apologies for her wickedness, and she shuddered to think of her husband's relish in punishing her disobedience. If she were to run far away, then sooner or later she would fall into the hands of the officials of that parish and be sent back to her own parish, so the outcome would be the same.

The alternative was to join one of the bands of roving vagabonds and survive by thieving and whoring, but her upbringing and fear of breaking the Commandments made this unacceptable. No matter how she looked at it, she was trapped, so outwardly she adopted an attitude of cold acquiescence towards her husband and shielded herself by simply pretending that he was not there.

In is turn, Silas awoke after his performance on the wedding night feeling both ill and sheepish. Lizzie aroused in him an emotion he had never before experienced – inadequacy. He wanted to be liked by the beautiful red-haired girl who was now his bride, and her lack of response galled him. Thereafter, lumbering into bed each night full of expectation for the pleasure to come, he would try to arouse her. When there was no response he would first plead and then bully.

'Come on,' he urged as she lay passive beneath his heaving bulk, but she showed no sign that she had heard. If she had put up some resistance he could have overpowered her, but her corpselike indifference baffled him and to his horror he found that against it he was impotent.

He could not fault her, in any other way, for she carried out her domestic duties efficiently and kept herself and the mill clean and wholesome, but his overwhelming need for sexual conquest in the marriage bed eluded him.

'You should be ashamed,' he accused. 'A man has needs and God made women for their pleasure. You always find some excuse to cheat me out of my comfort.'

Provoked to reply, Lizzie answered: 'I never deny you. It isn't my fault if you always pick the wrong time.'

Silas grumbled to himself and felt that he had been outwitted but he was never sure quite how.

Throughout the winter the island buzzed with rumours of invasion. The coastal forts and the castle were in a state of readiness and a series of beacons linked the island from west to east. Lizzie gleaned most of her information from Silas after his various visits to Newport. As constable he was often called to the courts and on his return he would invariably sit long over his meal, recounting what he had seen and heard. Any mention of Newport served to remind her of her last encounter with Will, and to keep her emotions under control she would listen abstractedly as she busied herself about the kitchen.

During Silas's absences she actively enjoyed the role of mistress of the mill house and slowly she was clearing the accumulation of litter and with it some of the stench that so offended her. When fine weather promised, she took the bed-linen to the stream and washed it. As much as anything she was afraid that when Silas went to town he might come into contact with a new outbreak of sweating sickness or some other disease that would endanger her family. To safeguard them she put a sprig of tansy in each of his shoes to ward off the plague. She had heard that cleanliness was the best defence and that Sir George had once ordered the burning of some cottages because of their filthy state. This was not to be the fate of her house – she had paid too dearly for it.

She hardly noticed the passing of the weeks, but as the winter drew to an end she fell into a daily routine of caring for her own domestic duties and overseeing the welfare of her family at Sheepwash cottage, for Leah's pregnancy was now far advanced.

'Pray God this will be my last,' Leah told her daughter on one of Lizzie's regular visits. 'There have been too many for my poor old carcass to bear.'

Lizzie nodded in sympathy; then, suddenly aware that her mother was regarding her quizzically, she flushed and turned to stir the stew pot. Undeterred, the older woman asked: 'No signs of you making me a grandmother yet, then?'

'No.' Her reply was taut and clipped, and Leah refrained from further questioning.

'Don't misunderstand me,' she continued when the silence became oppressive. 'A child is a great blessing but you find yourself full of fears – fears for them not being strong and straight, fears for the pestilences and fevers, fears they'll be mistreated or starve or be called by their maker just when you get to love them. It's hard,' she finished lamely.

Lizzie met her eyes then and took her mother's work-worn hand.

'I've been thinking,' she mused. 'Can you really love a child if you don't love its father?'

'Of course you can. A child has some of you in it. It comes helpless and innocent. Oh yes, you'd love it even if...'

'Even if it was Silas Dore's?' Lizzie finished for her, then added: 'Well, that won't never happen so it don't really matter.'

'You mean you and he don't never – ?' Her mother blurted it out, then stopped in embarrassment.

Lizzie shrugged. 'I wasn't talking about me,' she countered. 'I was thinking of you and Pa. You haven't ever really loved him, have you? Not really, I mean?'

Leah hesitated, rubbing her belly. 'I love him in a way,' she said. 'In his way he's provided for me and all of you. He ain't a bad man. I know he likes his drink but God didn't make no one perfect.' She punctuated each sentence with the rhythmic slicing of turnips and dropped them into the simmering liquid of the stew pot as her daughter looked on.

'He ain't a bad man,' she repeated.

'He sold me into slavery,' Lizzie replied. 'That's the worst thing a father could do.'

'Lizzie!' There was pain in Leah's eyes.

'I've prayed to be able to forgive them, both Pa and Silas, but I know I never shall.' She rose quickly from the settle by the fireplace and with a muttered farewell set back out for her prison at the mill.

On 11 March Lizzie was in the kitchen stripping reeds to make candle wicks when Jed arrived.

'Mam says you've to come,' he panted.

Lizzie needed no further explanation, for the baby was now due and as a married woman she was to help with the delivery, along with Widow Trykett.

Leaving Silas's dinner to keep warm in the hearth, she grabbed her shawl and hurried out with her brother. She looked out for Silas as they went along but there was no sign of him so she sent Jed back to find him, for the cottage was no place for a young man at a time like this.

Inside Sheepwash cottage Widow Trykett had placed clean rushes under Leah and was dosing her with a special concoction known only to herself, which was guaranteed to ease the pain and hasten the travail.

Lizzie was shocked at her mother's pallor.

'How is it, Mam?' she asked. Leah opened her eyes and shook her head.

''Tis bad this time,' she mumbled between breaths.

'What can I do?' Lizzie asked, feeling helpless.

'Hold her hand and will her to push,' Widow Trykett ordered. 'If thissun ain't out soon he'll never see the light of day.'

Lizzie gripped her mother's wrists and squeezed them encouragingly. Leah suddenly arched her back with pain and moaned. Her daughter looked for reassurance from the elderly neighbour but her face was grim as she watched for the child's head.

'If he don't come soon we'll have to hook him out,' she said quietly.

'Won't that damage him?'

'Surely, but 'tis that or lose your mam.'

Lizzie glanced back in anguish at Leah. 'Please, Mam, push him out,' she implored.

Leah opened her eyes again. Her hair was wet and a nerve in her neck throbbed wildly. Engulfed in another spasm, she moaned and summoned the energy to strain.

'He's coming!' the old lady encouraged. 'Pray to God, Leah, and push him out.'

Suddenly he was there – a tiny, puce, blood-stained rabbit, his little fists feebly clenched.

'It's a boy, Mam!' Tears started in Lizzie's eyes as she took him to warm by the fire before wrapping him in the waiting swaddling bands that would keep his arms and legs straight.

A surge of tenderness filled her as she watched his tiny mouth search the air for succour, but his cry was faint and Leah in her weakened state could barely raise her head to look at him.

It became clear over the next few hours that Leah had little milk coming in and there was no other woman in the village with milk to spare. Try as they might, the little one began to lose interest in suckling and lay mute in the box by the fire.

He was baptised John Edward, after his two grandfathers, but there was little joy in the ceremony. Leaving the church, the parishioners washed their hands as the service required of them and it seemed to Lizzie that they were also washing their hands of responsibility for this tiny scrap, now officially a member of God's congregation. Three days later they returned to bury him beside his other brothers and sisters who had not survived infancy.

Leah seemed too ill to care. She developed a harsh bubbling cough and could not find the energy to get out of bed. There was no one now to carry out the tasks of fetching water, milking, making butter and cheese, cleaning and cooking.

Where possible Lizzie helped out with roast bacon and baked bread, and before long she was working from first light until sundown to keep both houses running smoothly. The only blessing was that she was too busy to let the pain of Will's absence gnaw into her.

Falling exhausted into bed each night beside the detested body of her husband, she asked herself again and again where in God's plan such tragedies could belong?

Chapter Fourteen

For several weeks Mardi kept herself busy making the shepherd's bothy habitable. It was the simplest of dwellings, consisting of four walls made from dung and sheep hurdles and a hastily straw-thatched roof. The doorway was a bedraggled sheepskin secured with some wooden pegs and the floor the bare earth with the merest sprouting of chalk-shortened, light-deprived grass. To her relief she found that inside it remained dry in spite of the persistent, bone-chilling rain.

As she had predicted, now the sheep were back in the village for slaughter or to overwinter in the straw yards, there was no reason for anyone to come this way. With luck she could remain hidden until the spring.

Those first few weeks were difficult. For a start there was no water and she did not even possess a beaker in which she could collect enough for a single drink. Each time thirst drove her she was compelled to make a mile-long journey to the stream behind West Over Farm and this meant risking being seen. With aching blue fingers she would break the ice already forming at the point where the stream meandered and scoop up a handful of water. She longed for the taste of ale.

Fire was another problem for she had neither wood nor flint and her first few nights were of unrelieved misery. She also feared that any smoke may draw attention to her presence.

Once settled, she set out on a series of night-time raids which proved very lucrative. From the fulling mill she risked the presence of two slavering dogs to steal a bolt of rough kersey cloth. Creeping back in the half-light, hugging her heavy burden, she relished the luxury of at last having a blanket. The temperatures at night were below freezing.

At Sheepwash cottage she unearthed a pile of turnips and, using her skirt as a sack, carried as many as she could back to the bothy. She took the precaution of replacing them with pebbles, arranging a layer of turnips on top to delay the discovery of theft. She knew that if rumour spread that a thief was abroad, the constable would soon come looking for her. She refused to dwell on the knowledge that discovery could mean death.

Her best finds, however, came from West Over Farm, where the buttery held not only a leather pail but also a tinderbox. Hugging these treasures to her bony chest, she crept back home thinking that now she had everything she needed.

There was plenty of dead wood to be collected and the need for warmth overcame her fear of discovery. Already the traps formed from plaited grass and stems had started to yield up a harvest of coneys. Now that she could cook their meat she was confident that she would not starve. A proper knife would have been useful but it wasn't the first time she had struggled with a sharp stone. Always trying to look on the bright side, she thought that in addition to her meat supply the coney skins would make a few pence.

In one way things were little different from how they had always been. Cold and hunger were not new; in fact, they were a normal part of life. What was new was the gnawing loneliness. Before she had always travelled in a company of people. By day they had worked in pairs or groups and in the evenings there had been games and music to pass the time. It might have been cold, but there had always been someone to cuddle up to.

Once her mother died, this had changed. Mardi and her pa were treated like lepers. They had no one else and cuddling up to Jake was unthinkable. It had seemed lonely then, but, although she had hated the responsibility of looking after him, it had given her life a purpose. Now there was just Mardi. She realised that for days she had not spoken to a living soul, and called out to a sparrow just to make sure that her voice still worked. It jarred loudly in the empty landscape. The fact that the bird did not reply added to her isolation.

To make things worse, once she had provided for the most

basic needs there was nothing to strive for. She took to sleeping and waking when she felt like it and began to lose all sense of time. Her brain did not seem to function any more. Thoughts of her mother and father tormented her and it took all her will-power to keep control. Some activity was required.

In spite of the cold, unyielding earth, she set out to collect a variety of seeds, nuts and berries. From these she started to prepare love potions to sell as soon as she could safely go abroad. It didn't really matter what was in them. She mashed up acorns and ivy berries, earwigs and rabbit droppings, and wrapped the paste in wet dock leaves sealed with spittle. This helped to restore her sense of reality.

By now she knew that Christmastide was past. From time to time she had spied on the village and seen the revellers going from house to house, heard the cheers and laughter from West Over. At that moment she would have sold her soul for a taste of beef or goose or a sip of elderberry wine, but most of all the company of other human beings.

As Eastertide approached she grew increasingly uneasy. Surely soon the shepherd would be coming to inspect his bothy and make any repairs for the summer months, when he would use it as home. She started to have nightmares that he would turn up while she slept and discover her cache of stolen goods. Since Candlemas she had sworn almost weekly to leave, but then the thought of punishments for vagrancy and theft, both witnessed and rumoured, would drive her on for a few more days.

Thoughts of Will went round in her head so many times and in so many different ways that she was no longer even sure if he was real. If she were not to become a lunatic, it was time to set out to find him. She must make a spell so powerful that he could not resist it or else dose herself with something to make her immune to his magic. Either would be better than this foolish state of longing that she had before associated only with the village girls. She wondered if her mother had felt like this when giving up her village life and taking off with her father.

By now her dress was so stiffened by mud and continuous wear that it felt more like a suit of armour, and she knew that she would have to do something about it before she could let

Will see her again. No amount of magic would overcome the handicap of looking as she must do now.

With overwhelming relief she prepared to leave the bothy. Before doing so, she took the precaution of washing her face in the last of the icy water in her pail. It was her sole concession to improving her appearance. Being alone has made me weak in the head, she thought.

Reluctantly she had to leave her treasures behind, including the coney skins, for she realised now they were lethal evidence of her winter of poaching and thieving. Taking only the love potions, she skirted around Caulbourne and made her way along a footpath heading in the direction of Carisbrooke. To her left the manor of Swaynson came into view. Abruptly changing direction, she picked her way through the parkland and crouched under cover of a huge beech tree watching the house. It was the back that interested her.

After about an hour she saw a flurry of activity in the yard as several horses were led out and saddled. They were led around to the front of the house and after a while a group of thickly cloaked men and women emerged laughing and shouting to each other. The women were helped to mount and the men took the lead as they rode off at a trot in the direction that Mardi had just come. They passed near by her hiding place and she felt a glow of satisfaction now that they were out of the way.

After about ten minutes she made her way round to the back door and peered cautiously in through the narrow window. The kitchen appeared to be empty but then at the very edge of her vision she saw a young woman laboriously grinding what looked like salt or sugar. Making up her mind, she knocked on the door, prepared to run at the least sign of danger.

The door was opened by the girl she had seen. On close inspection she was remarkably plain, her face a benign moon beneath a floppy, well-worn cap. Her body was squat and shapeless and when confronted with Mardi she stuck her finger into her mouth in a gesture of helpless indecision.

'Are you the lady of the house?' Mardi asked. Her voice sounded loud and unnatural to her unaccustomed ears.

The girl shook her head. After a moment she said: 'I'm May White, I'm the scullery maid.'

Mardi nodded her head. 'Is the mistress home?' she ventured.

'No. They've all gone off. There's only us servants here. Shall I call the housekeeper or the reeve?'

'No. I'm sure you can help me.'

Mardi glanced quickly round to make sure that no one else was present, then continued: 'I've lost my position. My mistress died suddenly down Braydin way and I've been walking, looking for work.' As she talked, her confidence grew and she began to feel like her old self again.

May was looking anxious, as if some decision were needed from her which would alter the course of history.

'I don't know nothing,' she interrupted.

Mardi paused for a moment and said: 'There are two ways you could help me. First, as you'll see, I need to borrow a dress – only borrow,' she repeated as she saw the girl's panic. 'And second, I'm that hungered, a bowl of stew and a drink of ale would save my life.'

'I don't ...' May was chewing her fingers again in anguished indecision.

'You got a sweetheart?' Mardi asked, changing course quickly.

May shook her head. Mardi feigned surprise.

'I'd have thought a pretty girl like you would have boys queuing up to court you.'

At this May blushed and giggled. Knowing that she was on target, Mardi produced one of her potions from inside the bodice of her dress.

'You got anyone in mind you'd like?' she asked.

May looked sheepishly at the ground.

'One of the young men working here?' Mardi guessed.

May nodded.

'Well, I can do you a favour. See this little package? It's a love potion; very powerful. All you've got to do is sleep with it under your pillow for one night and as you go to sleep think of the boy you want. Next morning bury it under an oak tree and sure as sunshine before Michaelmas that boy'll be pining for you.'

May hid her face in embarrassment but Mardi knew that she was hooked.

'How much?' May asked.

'Half a crown.'

The girl's eyebrows shot up in horror. Mardi could see the dream disintegrating before her. Before May could say anything, she added:

'I don't really need money. A pretty dress and some vittles would do as well.'

May had her worried look again. 'I got some food,' she started. 'But I ain't got a pretty dress.'

'What about your mistress? She must have more dresses than she can count.'

'Oo, I couldn't! I'd get in such trouble.'

Mardi produced another little package.

'No, you wouldn't. Hide this under your lady's mattress where she won't find it and I guarantee she'll never even notice the dress has gone. It doesn't have to be one of her best ones,' she added as she saw May wavering.

Holding the package out, she indicated to May to take it. In confusion the maid accepted it, then scuttled out of sight. Mardi waited anxiously until eventually the girl returned, trailing a green, rather old-fashioned kirtle with wide sleeves and a low neckline.

'Mistress don't wear things like this no more. They've all got wide skirts and stomachers these days.' May shoved it at her, glancing over her shoulder like a hunted stag.

'What about the food?' Mardi grabbed the dress and waited impatiently while May scurried around fetching bread and cheese and a mug of beer.

'What's this?' asked Mardi after draining it down. The taste was strong and unfamiliar.

''Tis beer. They don't drink ale no more. 'Tis only for servants and children.'

Mardi wiped the froth from her lips and felt immediately heady.

'Here.' She handed May the love potion and repeated the instructions. Then, armed with the food and the dress and shouting a promise to return it, she started to run towards the safety of the woods.

Chapter Fifteen

The death of her little brother remained with Lizzie like a black, enveloping cloud. More than anything that had happened, it shook her faith in a beneficent God, and yet in spite of her distress she continued to pray nightly for deliverance from her situation. She convinced herself that if she suffered enough she would surely earn the reward of rescue by Will. It was her only hope.

One sunny morning in late spring she was preparing to take milk and bread up to her family when Silas came in unexpectedly. His face was more flushed than usual and he was carrying two dead rabbits bound together at the legs with twine.

'Where did you get those?' she asked, picking up the provisions so that she could leave quickly.

'Your brother.'

She stopped what she was doing and stared at him. 'What do you mean?'

'Your brother snared these on Mr Earlisman's land.' He came closer, watching her intently.

'How do you know?' Lizzie knew that the anxiety was plainly visible on her face but she could not hide it.

'Because I catched him coming out of the copse.'

Her hand flew to her bosom as the implications became clear to her. 'Does anyone else know?' she asked. There was now panic in her voice and she put the bread and milk down absently upon the table.

'No.'

'Thank the Lord. It's terrible hard for Pa and Jed with Mam being ill.'

Silas interrupted her. 'It's a crime and I'm constable.'

His words made her jerk as if she had been pricked. 'What are you going to do?' she said, any pretence at indifference now deserting her.

'Do my duty. Take him to the courts and then carry out the sentence.' He was watching for her reaction.

'You can't! He's my brother.' She stared at him in disbelief.

'The law's the law.' His gaze was now resting on her bosom, his small eyes bright and calculating.

'Not our Jed. Please, Silas. It'll kill our mam,' she begged.

He pulled her towards him, the rabbits hanging stiff and lifeless between them.

'What do you want me to do, then?' he asked, his body now pressing against hers.

'Let him go. Please!'

He put the rabbits aside and pulled her closer. 'That's asking a lot. I'd be risking disgrace if anyone found out.'

'They wouldn't. How could they? Jed wouldn't tell and I . . .'

'And what would you do, then?' The insinuation in his voice made her go cold.

'Anything,' she finally whispered, turning her head away and closing her eyes to block out the sight of him.

'Anything?'

She nodded.

'Not just now but whenever I asks?'

Her shoulders sagged in defeat and again she nodded.

'Right. Upstairs now then in case someone comes. And just remember what'll happen if you breaks your word.'

'We can't *now*,' she protested, the panic rising in her. 'It's a sin to do it in the day.'

By way of reply he shoved her hard, moving closer as she reluctantly mounted the stair ahead of him, his hand already fingering her groin.

In the room above he sank onto the edge of the high, hard bedframe and Lizzie stood stiffly, her head averted, waiting for the ordeal to come.

'Take your kirtle off.'

She glanced desperately at the stairwell but knew that there was no escape.

Undressed, she pressed her legs tight together and her arm covered her bosom to shield herself from his hungry eyes.

'Come 'ere.'

Reluctantly she moved closer, cowering at the thought of his touch. She gave a little gasp of anguish as he grabbed her, squeezing her buttocks. Her breasts were level with his face and breathing heavily he rubbed his stubbled chin across her chest, drawing hard on her nipples with his broken teeth. She braced her hands against his shoulders to ward him off, crying out now in her distress, but he paid no attention. Nipping and licking his way down across her belly he buried his face between her legs, exploring with his tongue. A groan of repugnance escaped her.

Raising his head, he looked up at her and started to struggle out of his breeches.

''Ere, take these off,' he commanded.

In defeat Lizzie hauled them down over his bulk and as she crouched to pull them off he pushed her face into his groin. She heaved in disgust but he held her fast by the hair and writhed with pleasure. She gagged but he pressed on relentlessly, finally pulling her up and spreadeagling her onto her belly, then plunging into her from behind. In her unwilling state there was only pain.

Finally sated, he pulled her onto her back.

'Just you remember,' he panted, his face an unhealthy puce colour from his exertions, 'God gave me authority over you. This is mine whenever I wants it.' He ran his fingers over the triangle of wet hair and Lizzie could not suppress a groan of shame and outrage.

'Now get dressed and we'll say our prayers – and you'd better pray to be a good wife.'

She got up stiffly, tugging her dress hastily over her head, trying not to let the sobs escape her. She was bruised and hurt and felt more disgraced than she had ever thought possible.

He had not finished with her yet. As she edged towards the stair he called her back.

'Give us a kiss.' Leadenly she turned back and he squeezed her hard, his yellowed tongue in her mouth. Then he grinned with satisfaction, pulled down the neck of her dress and sank his teeth into the gentle rise of her bosom. She cried out in pain and he smirked.

'That's my brand mark, see. Now you go down on your knees and pray as how you've conceived a son for me. I've had enough of your hoity-toity ways. If you don't get with child soon I'll have to punish you.'

Shaking, she sank down in an attitude of prayer. Silently she vowed:

'Dear God, if You don't revenge Yourself on him soon, then I surely will.'

The dislike she felt for her husband turned at that moment into a knot of concentrated hatred.

Descending the stairs, his appetite sated, Silas shoved the rabbits at her. ''Ere, take these coneys and cook them for dinner. Seeing as how they've cost me me honour, I reckon I deserve them.' And with a little grunt of satisfaction he left the house and returned to his work at the mill.

Lizzie worked out her spite and misery on the rabbits, chopping and tearing, skinning and finally boiling them in the skillet over the fire. She added onions and turnips, determined that there should be enough to feed her family as well. One way or the other she would salvage something from her ordeal.

Leaving the stew to simmer over the embers, she left the house to find Jed and put his mind at rest. Poor Jed! She knew him so well, his fears and his innocence. Her anger bubbled over again at the thought of Silas taunting him, threatening him with prison. He would be so afraid.

Stopping at the bourne, she washed her mouth in the cool crystal water, trying to eradicate the taste of Silas Dore, but he seemed to have permeated her very being.

Jed was not in any of his usual places. Finally she found him in the dairy, hoping to hide from the law.

'Oh, Lizzie, I done wrong!' he cried as soon as he saw her 'Silas is gonna take me to Newport and they'll hang me fer a thief!' Large tears joined the rivulet from his nose and he gazed helplessly at her with his sad, frightened child's eyes.

'No, he's not, Jed. It's all sorted out now. But you mustn't ever do that again. Next time no one'll be able to save you.'

'Are you sure?'

'Course I am. Now go and help Pa like you're supposed to and remember what I said.'

'Course I will, Lizzie.' He picked her up and hugged her bruised body, not noticing her flinch. Kissing her forehead, he bounded out into the yard, his fears dispelled.

With a sigh Lizzie looked round the familiar dairy. Mam's cheeses and preserves were still on the shelves but the scrubbed surfaces were no longer clean.

Taking two leather buckets, she walked to the end of the lane and filled them with water from the well. Once back inside she swilled down the shelves and the floor. As much as anything it was a symbolic cleansing for herself. She then swept the water out of the door with the large twig broom and replaced it in the corner. With a last look round and a sigh, she reluctantly left the sanctuary of the dairy and started back towards the hated confines of the mill.

Halfway down the lane Lizzie halted. She could not face going home, although most certainly Silas would not be there. Instead she sat on the bank in the gentle afternoon sun and wondered how she was going to survive. Until today she had been able to endure what was happening to her but now Silas had a new weapon to control her: she was at his mercy. The future seemed unbearable.

She gazed at the panorama of gently rolling wooded hills, the tops of the downs showing like bald pates on bearded men. There was so much peace around her and so much turbulence within.

Gazing down the lane, she noticed somebody approaching from the direction of the fulling mill. He was too far away to see clearly but she could see that he was young, tall and well built. Something about his carriage made her sit up.

'Dear Lord, I don't believe it!' As he approached, tears welled up in her eyes. For a moment she was certain that God had seen her suffering and indeed sent deliverance.

'Hello, Lizzie.' Will stopped a few yards away, a wry smile about his lips. His expression quickly changed to concern.

'You don't look well,' he said. 'You're that thin and pale. Doesn't marriage suit you?' The phrase had a bitter ring to it.

'Oh, Will!' She scrambled to her feet and flung herself into his

100

arms sobbing, her words incoherent. He soothed her like a child until her heaving subsided, then held her away from him.

'I thought we had an understanding,' he said quietly. 'Couldn't you wait to get your hands on some property?'

'No! I came to see you and you weren't there. You didn't even come and try to stop it!'

He continued to hold her at arm's length. 'When did you come?' He knew the answer already.

'As soon as I knew. I came to Carisbrooke to tell you Pa had betrothed me to Silas Dore. They said you weren't there. I left a message.'

She looked plaintively at him and he longed to be able to tell her about his mission to Basing House, but even now he knew that he must hold his tongue.

'I didn't get the message,' he said truthfully.

Lizzie clung to him, the anguish of the past months soothed miraculously away. As long as Will still cared for her, nothing mattered.

Sliding his hands under her thick hair, he cupped her face and kissed her tenderly on the lips. Her response was total.

Letting her go, he smiled tenderly. His eyes came to rest on her breast and he frowned.

'What in the Lord's name is that?'

She hastily pulled the bodice of her dress to try and hide the bite. 'It's nothing.'

'Did he do that? The evil devil! I'll kill him!'

'Will, no,' she begged, anxious to protect him from a foolish act. 'It's not all his fault. I've been cold to him, not let him ...' She blushed.

'Don't! I can't bear to think of it.' He held her again, seeking solace for his own jealousy. He knew now that this was God's punishment for his infidelity with the Gipsy girl and he cursed himself again.

Nearby the bank led up to the Holywood copse. By mutual unspoken consent they scrambled up out of sight and picked their way into a clearing. The ferns succumbed as they sank into a natural bed in the dappled hollow.

'I've wanted you ever since I first saw you,' he told her, taking both her hands in his. 'But I know I don't deserve you.'

101

'I've wanted you too.' She nestled into the comfort of his arms.

'You're a married woman,' he whispered into her hair.

'I'm Lizzie Galpine that loves you.'

His hand rested in her lap and he felt her stiffen and draw back.

'Don't you want to?' he asked quietly.

'I do but ...' She blushed, lowering her eyes.

'Is it because you're wed?'

'No.' She looked about her as if searching for the right words to appear in the foliage that surrounded them. Finally she whispered: 'It's because it hurts.'

Will let out his breath and gently cushioned her against him.

'It don't have to hurt, sweetheart. It's because he's ill-used you. I swear he'll never do that again. It's all my fault. I'll never forgive myself.'

Lizzie's eyes were closed as she stook sanctuary in his warmth and strength. After a while she could feel his groin stirring against her thigh. She opened her eyes and looked at him for reassurance.

'Don't be afraid,' he whispered. 'I won't do anything – not inside you. I'll just hold you gentle like this and lie against you.'

He was out of his breeches, smothering her face and shoulders with kisses, and she gave herself up to the joy of it. As he slid across her she felt a great surge of need for him and, gripping him tightly, she raised herself to receive him. Reassuring her with each kiss, he eased himself into her and the pleasure of their union brought a simultaneous cry of ecstasy.

For a while the peace was complete and they lay absorbing their own tranquillity. Neither of them dared break the spell by moving for there was little comfort in the world outside. In the background myriad birds sang and danced. Finally Will stretched and propped himself up on one elbow. With his free hand he traced the outline of Lizzie's face, smoothing strands of copper hair away from her cheek.

'You're beautiful,' he told her.

She opened her eyes and smiled at him, the colluding smile of lovers who have shared something wonderful beyond description. She offered her mouth to be kissed and he gently touched her lips, but already his face was troubled.

'What do we do now?'

'I don't know.'

She felt he must have some solution learned from the great world beyond the village. Here adultery meant a whipping or the stocks and public disgrace. She shuddered at the thought of what Silas would do to both of them if he found out. A sudden terror struck her as she realised that their real enemy was not her husband or the villagers or even the priest but God himself. These were His laws and for some reason it was He who had forced her into this marriage. Try as she might, there had been no way out. If she continued to defy Him, then He might exact His revenge by harming Will.

'No!' She railed at His omnipotence.

'Hush love, there's no cause to fear.' Will gathered her to him.

'But there is. There's no escape.' She began to sob against his shoulder. He had no answer but waited until her grief subsided, then wiped her tears with his fingers.

'You must always remember, Lizzie, that I love you, no matter what. The reason I came today was to tell you I'm going away. I was hurt when I learned about your wedding. It's no more than I deserve but I thought you didn't care and that was too painful to bear. I know now that you do and though I can't take you with me I'll be back some day and I'll be rich and powerful. No one's going to stop us then.'

Lizzie was shaking her head. 'It's no good. It's God's will I'm married to Silas. I don't know why but it's so.'

'It's God that gave us this love,' he countered. 'Nothing's stronger than that.'

She accepted his comfortable interpretation.

'Where will you go?' she finally asked.

'To London. Sir George has a place at Black Friars. He wants some work done and now I've finished my apprenticeship he's given me the chance. I'd have gone already but this scare about the Dons seems true. I've got to wait now till the threat of invasion is past.'

'Will you be able to come again?' she asked.

He shook his head. 'It's best that I don't. I'm putting you in danger just by being here and what we've got today is enough to help us through.'

103

'There'll be hundreds of maids in London. You might meet someone else,' she said.

'There's no one in the whole world I'd have instead of you. Don't you fret. I'm the one who should be jealous. You've got a husband and he's got rights over you.'

'Don't!' Lizzie shuddered at the memory.

Will sat upright and stretched in the dappled sunlight. 'Listen. No man's got a right to treat his wife like that. You tell him you're going to report him to the priest. That'll stop him. In his position he can't risk any scandals.'

Lizzie nodded. 'P'r'aps I could get some herbs to quiet him down,' she mused.

'You be careful. Don't you get mixed up in magic. It can ruin your life.' He spoke with such feeling that she gazed at him wide-eyed.

Seeing the tenderness return to his hazel eyes, she smiled. 'I won't,' she assured, but already she was thinking of the plants that made men drowsy.

'If you want me to I'll come and warn him,' Will offered.

'No. I'll be safe. Now I know you still care, nothing seems so bad.'

She suddenly realised that it was dusk and that hours must have passed.

'Dear Lord, I must get back!' She scrambled hastily to her feet.

'Aye.' Reluctantly he stood up and, taking her hand, led the way to the edge of the copse. In the twilight he stopped and turned her to face him.

'Remember, Lizzie, always, I love you. I'm yourn and you're mine. Nothing else matters. Pray for me and I promise I'll be back.'

They clung together and he kissed her once more before drawing away. Turning quickly, he strode down the lane and did not look back.

'Will!' The word froze on her lips and she stood gathering the comfort of his visit around her like a cloak.

Chapter Sixteen

After Will had left her, Lizzie stood a long while in a trance. As the evening sky darkened, her mind drifted back to reality and, remembering again the lateness of the hour, she started to run down the lane and across the yard to the mill, her heart pounding.

As she entered the kitchen, Silas was sitting in his wooden chair, scraping between his toes to remove pieces of dirt and straw.

'Where you been?' he asked aggressively.

'To see my family, make sure they're well.'

'Oh. So you knows, then.' He continued with his absorbing task.

'Know what?' she asked as casually as she could manage.

'About your brother.'

Lizzie began to relax and moved about the kitchen, picking up trenchers and bowls to be rinsed and put away. 'I've just seen him,' she answered. 'He's all right. He won't do that again.'

'Not him, t'other one in the navy.'

'Harry? What about him?'

'There's been some sort of mishap. He's been crushed. They've had to take his leg off.'

'Oh, dear God, no!' She sank back against the scrubbed table, feeling faint. 'Poor Harry!' She was near to tears, not being able to take it in. 'How do you know?' she asked, looking for some clue that might show it was not true.

'Message came with Richard Vannum on his way back from market. I was with George when it arrived.'

105

'What about Mam? Oh, dear Lord, it's awful!'

'I thought you'd just been to see her?' he asked suspiciously.

'It took so long to find Jed I didn't have time,' she lied.

'Then best get back there but don't stay, mind, I want you here.'

She didn't answer but ran out to retrace her steps. As she passed the copse, her heart called out to the spirit of Will that would now for ever be there, as if it had some power over the fates:

'Please make it right.'

At the cottage they all sat in numbed silence, Mam in George's chair and the rest squatting in the rushes.

'Oh, Lizzie, Harry's been hurt,' Jed cried.

'Yes, I've heard.' She hugged her brother, looking all the time at her mother, who began to weep.

'We didn't know nothing,' Leah finally said, sniffing back the tears.

'Are they sending him home?' Lizzie asked.

'We don't know.'

'I'll fashion him a crutch and a new leg,' Jed offered, his eyes bright with excitement.

'Most of them gets a fever.' Leah's voice was flat and hopeless. 'It needs a miracle to survive a thing like that.'

'Don't you know what happened?' Lizzie squatted down in the rushes with the rest of them.

'Parson read the message. We sent for you but you were nowhere to be found.'

Lizzie flushed.

'It said his leg was crushed against the harbour wall when the ship was getting ready to leave Portsmouth.'

'Poor Harry!' The idea sickened her.

'It's naught but tragedy,' Leah continued. 'First our little babby took, then me being sick and now this. It's almost as if God is punishing our house.'

'No, Mam, we've done nothing wrong.' Lizzie shivered, wondering if her infidelity with Will could have brought such swift retribution.

Her mother reminisced quietly about her second son, his headstrong ways, his dream of travelling the world like the lords Drake and Hawkins. Jed moved closer, listening wide-eyed, and Lizzie thought, Harry is a hero to him, a mysterious, dashing figure. It was now almost three years since he had left. She suddenly missed him with an almost physical longing, made worse by the fear that they might never see him again.

'We warned him but he wouldn't listen,' her mother was saying. 'One morning I came down and instead of being out with the sheep he was gone. He told one of the village lads to let us know as soon as he was far enough away.' She sighed. 'Always was headstrong.'

Realising that everyone was listening, she straightened her back and surveyed them all.

'Well, if he does come back, then he'll need looking after.' At the thought her lips turned up reflectively and a barely perceptible spark of determination flickered in her tired eyes.

Meanwhile the practicalities had to be sorted out. Lizzie established that the captain of Harry's ship had had him taken ashore to a lodging house and left money for his care. Clearly, though, he needed his family's loving attention if he was to recover, and an expedition would have to be mounted to go and fetch him. Fortunately there was still a little money left from the last Hiring Fair and George and Jed would have to take the wagon, find a ship and cross to Portsmouth. This would take several days and the stock would have to be looked after in their absence. Neither man had ever crossed the water and as the plan was worked out their anxiety grew more apparent.

'Go and see Parson,' Lizzie urged. 'He'll tell you what to do.' She wished that she could go herself but that was out of the question. All she could do was to prepare food for the journey and blankets and medicines to help poor Harry bear the ordeal. She shuddered at the thought of his suffering.

'I must go home,' she announced, remembering Silas's words. 'I'll ask Silas for the wagon and I'll be back in the morning with the things you need.'

Kissing her mother and brother goodbye, she retraced once more the steps that on her last journey had led her into the arms of Will.

When she arrived home, Silas was in bed and Lizzie breathed a sigh of relief. She would get up at first light and start cooking, but for the moment she crept into the pantry and poured herself a jug of ale, for she had neither eaten nor drunk since breakfast.

The remainder of the rabbit stew was on the table and she thought wryly that some good had come out of Jed's mishap, for he and his father would now have a nourishing meal to sustain them on their journey.

Thinking back on the day, it seemed the longest and most intense she had ever known. Both the best and the worst things imaginable had happened. She suddenly felt exhausted. As quietly as she could, she mounted the stairs. The moon shone full in through the tiny window that lighted the upper room and the ungainly outline of Silas was silhouetted in the bed. Lizzie pulled off her kirtle and with infinite care slipped into the small remaining space, praying that he would not awaken. He merely grunted and flung his arm across her. She lay in that unnatural posture for the rest of the night.

Reluctantly she dragged herself from the bed at first light, thankful that Silas continued to snore. Everything was ready by the time he came down to the kitchen, yawning and stretching his bulk.

She could only imagine what sort of condition Harry would be in and as a precaution prepared some poultices of hyssop and herb robert to be applied to his wounds. She would have to explain carefully to her father what to do, and again she wished that she could go herself to see that her brother was properly cared for.

Silas wandered aimlessly around the kitchen, then poured himself some ale and looked in the pot to see if breakfast was ready.

'Father needs to borrow the wagon,' Lizzie announced in her most matter-of-fact tone. She wrapped some bread in a cloth to keep it fresh for the journey.

'What for?'

'To go and fetch our Harry.'

Her husband grunted and sank into his chair. 'I don't like people using that ox. He's a sight too valuable. He's got the biggest horns in the village. I used to soak 'em in honey and now there's a yard's span between his poll.' He grunted again and, when Lizzie did not respond, he added: 'Anyway, I'll be needin' it back by Friday, I'm goin to town.'

Good, thought Lizzie. Aloud she said: 'Why don't you get a

horse? It would be easier than carting the wagon to and fro each time. Besides, it goes better with your standing.'

Silas said nothing but looked at her in surprise.

Everything was now ready so Lizzie served up the onion pottage for breakfast with a hunk of bread. Taking his knife, Silas cut a slice of bacon and ate noisily, licking his fingers as the soup dripped from the bread and over his hand. Lizzie put her shawl around her and lifted the basket.

'I'll hitch up the wagon then,' she announced.

He belched and got to his feet, wiping his hands on his breeches. 'Give us a kiss, then.'

Hiding her feelings, Lizzie pecked him on the cheek and restrained herself from flinching when he gave her breast a squeeze. His hand closed over the hard outline of the keepsake Will had given her. She always wore it pinned to the inside of her bodice.

'What's that?' he asked suspiciously.

'Nothing. Just a present I had years ago.'

'Who gived it to you?'

Lizzie felt herself blushing. 'Just someone in the family,' she stammered.

'Let's see.'

He held out his hand and with shaking fingers she unfastened the clasp and reluctantly handed it over.

He was looking at it calculatingly as it lay in the palm of his hand. 'Are they real stones?' he asked.

'Course not. It's only cheap but I like it.' She knew that her cheeks were blazing.

He seemed to stare at her for an eternity. Then, putting the brooch in his pouch, he said: 'If you want frippery, then I'll be the one to buy it.'

She dared not object.

'You look tired,' she said to distract him from further questioning.

'So I am. Having a young wife takes it out of me.' He chuckled and Lizzie managed a smile.

'You need a tonic,' she added, moving just out of his reach. He took a step closer.

'You getting to like it then?' He licked his lips.

'I'll make you a potion,' she replied, ignoring the insinuation

109

and thinking of the valerian that Mam had always sworn by to make her sleep.

Silas followed her to the door and began to pet her, but she sidled away.

'I must go, or Father and Jed'll be late and they need a good start.'

He let her go and nodded philosophically. 'See you're back early,' he called to her retreating back.

Lizzie brought the ox out of the byre and expertly harnessed it to the cart, then climbed aboard and clicked it into motion. Slowly it picked its way along the lane and down the gentle slope to the Sheepwash. Jed came out to meet her.

'Father's seen the Reverend Cotton, Lizzie. We've gotta look out for Amos Cheke. He's got a boat down Wootton Creek and for tuppence he'll take us across.'

'Good.' Lizzie took out the medicines and went in search of her father to explain their uses. When she had done so and George and Jed were finally aboard, she stood with Mam at the cottage door and waved them off.

'Pray God they do come back safe,' her mother said, fighting back the tears.

Lizzie squeezed her shoulder. 'I'll be here to help, Mam,' she assured her, then silently echoed the prayer: 'Bring them back safe – and Will too.'

When Silas came home for his supper that evening, Lizzie had a posset warming near the fire, liberally laced with honey and ginger and containing a good dose of valerian. As he sat in his chair, she forced a smile and said: 'Have some of this.'

'What is it?' He sniffed it suspiciously.

'It's that tonic I said about.' She watched with bated breath as he picked the beaker up and took another sniff before sampling it.

'Taste's good,' he announced and drained the rest back, wiping the frothy dregs onto his sleeve.

In order to give it time to work, Lizzie told him about the morning's events and her father's departure and consulted him about killing the big gander that had twice pecked her hard enough to draw blood.

'Where did it hurt you?' Silas asked.

110

'On my ankle'.

'Let's have a look.' He lifted her skirt and started to rub the red mark, his hand working its way up her leg.

'Not now,' she said, her voice tight with revulsion.

He struggled out of the chair and yawned. 'Come on, then, I'm ready for bed.'

'In a minute. You go on up.'

She busied herself as long as she reasonably could, then quietly ascended the stair and undressed, easing herself into bed. To her relief he was fast asleep and in the dark she smiled to herself.

After a while she got out again, tiptoed to the other side of the bed and, finding his trousers, fumbled until her hand closed over her brooch. Carefully she took it out and hid it under the edge of the mattress until such time as she could find a safer place. Getting back into bed, she soon fell asleep.

Chapter Seventeen

Will's apprenticeship was now officially complete but because of the scare of invasion he found himself in a kind of limbo. He continued to work as before, helping his old master, although he was in fact now a journeyman and entitled to proper wages. It did not bother him unduly. His main concern was to fill in the time until he could leave the island.

It was a week since he had visited Lizzie. As he worked, he prolonged the pleasure of the memory by daydreaming of making a fortune and building a big house like the one they had completed for Sir George in the grounds of Carisbrooke Castle. He saw himself dressed as finely as the Captain himself, and on his return to the island he would be immensely wealthy.

He visualised going to steal his love away to set her up in his own house. He would be too rich and powerful for anyone to challenge him and if Silas Dore were to protest he would shoot him in his fat belly with a firearm like the one Sir George often carried at his belt. He was ashamed of his foolishness, yet without these dreams the future seemed unbearable. He had to believe that some day it would turn out as he wished.

To relieve the boredom he volunteered to go down into Newport and fetch masonry nails and locks from the smithy. It was market day and if they sent one of the lads he would no doubt make a day of it.

Will's journey took him through the main street and as he approached he was aware of a commotion outside the tanneries. As far as he could make out, a crowd of women were attacking one of their kind. Nobody appeared to be concerned or think it necessary to intervene, although a crowd had gathered to watch the entertainment.

Drawing closer, he winced at the torrent of abuse passing from the group of women to their victim and back again. Apart from half a dozen local wives, all he could see was a muddy green garment and a writhing, screeching child on the garbage-strewn road.

'I'll curse ye all to Purgatory, just see if I don't!'

He recognised the voice immediately and the tangle of black hair held fast by one of the harridans. The rest of Mardi was hidden among the legs of her attackers as they reined blocks and kicks on her.

'What's going on?' Will accosted another onlooker.

'Little urchin. Been trying to sell spells. Conned these gals out of their thruppences.' He gave a little snigger. 'They're that mad, they've sent for the constable.' He stopped talking, distracted by the fact that Mardi's skirt was now up to her waist while she twisted and screamed like a dervish.

Will did not stop to think. Wading in, he pushed the Newport wives aside and grabbed Mardi by the scruff of her dress. She was still clawing and swearing as he set her down on her feet. Recognising his strength, the women thought better of retaliation and stood in pairs muttering their contempt for the alien creature.

As Mardi's eyes came to rest on her rescuer's face, she froze into a startled, disbelieving statue. Will had the feeling that if he let go of her she would fall over.

'What're you doing here?' he asked. The episode in the copse was cast aside as he looked at this dirty, skinny child of the road.

'Nothing. I was trying to earn some money honest and these old crows poked their great beaks in.'

'She took thruppence off my gal for a bundle of old leaves, saying it was a love spell,' one of the attackers volunteered. 'She ain't got no abode. She ain't from round here. She ain't even an islander. She needs whipping and sending back where she came from.'

'Good wives, she's only a child.' Will's voice was appeasing, reasonable. Feeling in his purse, he drew out some coins intended for the purchase of the nails.

'If anyone has been robbed I'll make amends. I'll see that the child is taken away and properly cared for.'

Mardi scowled at him. The women, sensing a profit to be made, crowded forward to receive compensation for the ills they and their daughters had suffered at the hands of the Gipsy.

Holding Mardi firmly by the wrist, Will led her back the way he had come, no longer having enough money to make his purchases.

'What do you think you're doing here?' he asked her again. 'Where's your pa?'

Mardi was stumbling along behind him, half trying to free her arm from his grasp and half struggling to keep pace with him. After a moment she said: 'Pa's gone. I've been here all winter.'

Will stopped and turned to face her. 'Where have you been living?'

She shrugged and gave him another evil scowl. He noted how thin she looked; her breasts had grown, but she had the distended belly of the underfed.

Turning aside, he stopped at a pie shop and bought her a pasty.

'You look starved, child. What the Devil am I to do with you?'

'Don't call me child!' I'm big enough to –' He shook her to shut her up, his face colouring.

'That's enough.' He jerked her on again, back in the direction of the castle. Her wrists felt like brittle twigs and as she began to flag he hoisted her on his shoulder like a sack of flour, ignoring the stares from passers-by.

As they neared the castle he set her down again and stretched his aching shoulders.

'What am I to do with you?' he repeated.

'You aren't wed yet, then?' She stood with her feet apart, her hands on her hips, swaying insolently from side to side. He suspected it was meant to be alluring.

'Do I look wed?' He chewed his lip thoughtfully and with a sigh announced: 'I'd best take you to my grandfather's. You can stay there safely and then we'll find you some work. The way you're going you'll end up dead from starvation or the rope.'

'I don't want to! Why can't I stay with you? I'd cook for you and ...' She moved closer so that she was touching him and he felt his pulses go haywire.

'Stop it, you little faggot! That isn't going to work so just behave. You need some good Christian teaching, you do.'

She was pouting again. Dragging her once more by the wrist, he marched her up towards the gatehouse.

'Now stay there.' He stopped a discreet distance away. 'I'm going to see my master and then I'll be back. If you aren't here I'll seek you out and give you a good beating.'

She looked at him from under her lashes, provocative, fierce and yet childlike, and suddenly he wanted to laugh.

'You're a torment to me,' he finished.

'I know.'

With embarrassment he explained to his master that something unforeseen had happened and that he needed time to visit Shorrel. The old man agreed and Will hurried back outside, hoping that the girl had not found any other ways of humiliating him.

He didn't know whether he was relieved or sorry to find that she was still sitting where he had left her.

'Come on!' He pulled her to her feet and set off in the direction of Shorrel. As they walked he began to lecture her on the sort of behaviour he would expect. She responded with a series of grunts and scoffing disbelief.

'You must realise that my granfer is an old man. He can't be putting up with any nonsense. As soon as I can I'm going to find a decent place to take you in and then you'll be on your own.'

'When you getting wed, then?' she interrupted.

'Who said I was getting wed?'

'I can see things, I can. Your sweetheart won't wed you. I told you that already.'

Will felt his anger rising as if in some way it was this doxy who had come between him and Lizzic. Swinging round on her, he said:

'Listen, you little witch. You've caused me enough trouble already. I'm getting wed sure enough, don't you concern yourself about that. If you've got any silly notions about interfering, you'd best get rid of them now.'

Mardi was looking up at him with unblinking eyes. He found them hypnotic and added in order to defend himself: 'I know a place where they take in fallen girls. I think I'll take you there and they'll teach you to be decent. You'll learn how to sew and cook and behave like a proper girl.' Seeing her amusement and apparent disdain, he continued: 'You stink. You're filthy and more like a midden than a girl. No man'd want to touch such a sewer. You disgust me.'

At this, Mardi wrenched her arm free. 'You'll be sorry you said that!' Her eyes were flashing with anger. 'One day you'll be sorry you didn't take me home with you. I know things you never dreamed of. I could make you rich if you like. You'd be rich enough to build your own house and have fine clothes. You could do what you wanted.'

The similarity to his daydreams alarmed him, but before he could say anything she added: 'Anyhow, I want to pee so just turn your back and keep walking.'

She stepped towards the bushes, already raising her skirt, and he hurriedly turned his back and walked ahead.

After several minutes he looked round but there was no sign of her. 'Ain't you finished yet?' he called out.

She did not answer. For a few moments he kicked his heels, then, with a sigh of irritation, turned back towards the bush where he had last seen her. She was nowhere in sight.

He searched around for several minutes, then realised that she had given him the slip.

'The little slattern!'

At that moment his hand came to rest on the purse at his waist and he discovered that the remainder of his money had gone. You fool! he thought, but unaccountably there was a knot of disappointment in his heart.

Chapter Eighteen

To Lizzie's relief the daily dose of tonic she now fed to Silas continued to have the desired effect. Within half an hour of swallowing it he was yawning and expressing the urgent need for his bed. For a whole week he showed no interest in anything other than sleep and she began to congratulate herself on her achievement.

From then on, worry about Harry's return was her foremost preoccupation. The expected week had already stretched to ten days and prayer seemed the only, if forlorn, hope.

On the eleventh day after George and Jed had left the village, Silas was away on the court's business. About midafternoon Lizzie heard the sound of hooves and rushed to the doorway in the hope that finally her brother was safely returned. Instead she saw Silas coming up the lane from Freshwater mounted on a horse. She hurried out to meet him.

'Where did you get that?' she asked.

'Down Afton way. They be in trouble there – ain't paid their dues. I took thissun in exchange for fulling their cloth but I don't know how they're gonna pay their other debts. I reckon they'll lose the farm.'

'Pour souls!' Lizzie was smoothing the horse's solid neck. He turned his head and nudged her, his white, whiskery muzzle soft against her shoulder.

'He's nice,' she said. 'What's he called?'

'Called? Nothin'.'

'Then can I give him a name?'

'If you likes.' Silas walked to the side of the barn and relieved

117

himself. Lizzie rubbed her face against the horse's dun-coloured neck.

'He seems good-tempered; can I ride him?' she asked.

'No.'

Lizzie shrugged and pulled a face behind Silas's back. Aloud she said: 'Let's call him Farmer 'cause he comes from a farm.'

'Should be Fuller cause he's at the mill,' Silas replied, but Farmer it was.

He was stabled in a tiny disused outbuilding attached to the mill and when not in use turned out during the day with the milking flock. The rest of the sheep along with most of the village stock had been sheared and were now up on the downs fattening up for the autumn slaughter. They were so numerous that the panorama of gently rolling hills above the wooded valley appeared at a glance to be wholly white.

The gentle warmth of April melted into a dry and sunny May and concern was already widespread that with so little rain the harvests would be poor. In some places the water supply threatened to dry up. The village well, however, kept its level and the stream, although lower, still had sufficient water to turn the mill wheel before meandering on to serve the corn mill further down the valley.

When she could stop herself from worrying about Harry or longing for Will, Lizzie was almost content. She had quickly become friends with Farmer. With a brush made of withies, she liked to groom his dusty brown coat, teasing the knots out of his mane and tail. As she worked she told him about Will and her secret dreams. He appeared to listen, his neck lowered, his ears flickering backwards and forwards to catch the tone of her voice.

'You spend more time with that horse than with me,' Silas complained within the first week of his arrival.

Lizzie paid him no attention. She had just learned from Mistress Tawk that radish root and lettuce dampened men's desires, and made a note to add these to their regular diet whenever possible. The old lady confessed that she had been much bothered herself but now her Thomas was as placid as the gelded pigs. Unaware of his wife's thoughts, Silas kept taking his tonic, and continued to sleep almost before his head touched the pillow.

The next morning Silas rode into Newport for the court hearings. After each case had been heard, he was charged with the duty of ensuring that the punishment was carried out. He personally inflicted the recommended number of lashes on man, woman or child, and ensured that felons spent the correct amount of time in the pillory. It was also his job to escort waifs to the House of Correction and supervise an eviction or the repossession of goods in payment for overdue rents and debts and tithes.

Weighing up the situation, he would sometimes risk taking young female offenders into the bushes and for the price of half an hour's pleasure let them off a public beating, and when rents were owing he would sometimes offer to delay an eviction if the wife or daughter of the house was sufficiently pretty and willing.

He knew that nobody dared complain, for his malice would have brought far worse. As he saw it, it was one of the bonuses of the job and, his marriage having turned out to be a disappointment in that respect, he was entitled to satisfy his needs somewhere.

His term as constable, a yearly appointment, was drawing to an end. For most men it was an honour they would gladly forgo, taking them from their work and making them of necessity unpopular. It was also an appointment that could not be refused unless there was a very good reason. Silas had embraced it with zeal and regretted the opportunities that would be lost to him when he reverted to the role of simple fuller.

That afternoon Lizzie heard Farmer's hooves picking their way stolidly towards the mill. Taking her spindle with her, she stepped out into the glaring afternoon sun. To her surprise Silas was not alone. Behind him on Farmer's rump was a dirty bundle of clothes encasing what appeared to be the body of a child. Lizzie came closer.

'Who you got there?' she asked, surveying the dirty creature.

'Picked her up in Newport. We dunno who she is. Don't seem to belong to none of the parishes round here. They was going to put her in prison for vagrancy but I thought she could help you.'

Lizzie surveyed her new assistant with misgivings.

'She's filthy,' she said. 'I reckon she's alive with vermin.'

119

'Reckon she is. Fling her in the stream and burn that thing that's supposed to be her kirtle.'

The child sat rigid astride the horse, her eyes hidden in a tangle of dusty, matted hair. Silas shoved her off and she froze to the spot where she landed.

'Reckon she's a vagabond's brat what's been abandoned,' Silas said, letting Farmer drink from the stream. The girl seemed to be sinking into the ground.

'What's your name?' Lizzie asked, wondering how on earth such a bundle of bones could be of any help around the house.

There was no reply and Silas, taking the girl by the arm, dragged her across to the stream and started to pull off her filthy garment. She began to struggle and let out a series of ear-splitting screams. Silas cuffed her about the head but his wife intervened.

'Don't treat her like that. By the looks of her she's been beat enough already. Fetch me a pail and that soap I made and put some hot water in from the pot.'

Surprisingly, Silas went into the house and returned with the things she had asked for.

'We aren't going to hurt you,' Lizzie said, 'but you can't stay like that. You stink. Dunno what to do with her hair,' she added.

'Cut it off.'

From the state of it, that seemed the only answer. Silas went into the mill and returned with a pair of sheep shears, the twin iron blades crossing menacingly when squeezed shut.

''Ere. I'll hold her and you cut.' He grabbed the girl, who once again began to scream and kick, but his mountainous bulk soon overpowered her. Lizzie grabbed clumps of hair and sheared them off. The exposed scalp was scabbed and filthy and Lizzie forced the girl's head forwards to pour water over it before lathering it with the yellow tallow soap. Silas once more began to tear at her filthy dress but, sensing his mood, Lizzie pushed him away.

'You just leave her be. I'll manage that. Go and put Farmer away. I'll soon have her washed and she can wear my old kirtle.'

The girl now stared wildly from large black eyes in her streaked face. Only her short spiky hair was comparatively clean.

She appeared to find Lizzie in some way frightening and Lizzie had the feeling that she had seen her before but could not imagine where.

'Don't be afraid. I won't hurt thee,' she said kindly. 'Let's get this old thing off and I'll give you a new one.' She reached out to unfasten the material, which looked as if it might once have been green, but the girl shook her head and seemed ready to take flight. Lizzie grabbed her wrist.

'Don't try running away. He'll only catch you and then he'll really punish you. It's best to do as I say.'

As if acknowledging the logic of this, the girl slumped, though still glancing around for signs of Silas. Succumbing, she allowed Lizzie to peel off the filthy kirtle.

She stood with her back to Lizzie, naked by the stream, and her small bony frame was covered in sores and bruises. For a moment Lizzie remembered the clapperdudgeon at the Hiring Fair, but this was more a sign of neglect than deliberate disfigurement.

As the girl turned, Lizzie gave a gasp, for not only was she older than she had imagined by several years but she was also clearly with child. Her belly protruded unmistakably in the hollow of her skinny carcass.

Lizzie looked up quickly at her and met the challenging black eyes. It was then that she recognised her and shook her head in disbelief. Hearing Silas moving about in the barn, she hastily poured warm water over her, soaping her and taking care not to pull off the scabs or press the purple bruises. She then slipped her old kirtle over her new servant's head, turning back the cuffs and securing it around the middle with twine to prevent it from dragging along the ground. The telltale bulge was once again hidden.

'There. That's better,' she said aloud, surveying her handiwork.

Her thoughts were racing over what Silas would do when he learned of the girl's condition.

Mardi looked anxiously about for her abandoned kirtle. Seeing it by the stream, she grabbed it, fishing inside the bodice, where she unfastened something and held it protectively in her hand.

'What you got there?' Lizzie asked curiously.

'It's mine.' Mardi's expression defied further comment and Lizzie shrugged.

'Come inside and I'll give you some good fish pie,' she said, starting towards the mill.

Mardi followed close behind and was soon stuffing food into her mouth with the desperation of one who has not eaten for days. She downed a flagon of ale with equal speed and eyed the door as if gauging whether she could run off and get away with it. At that moment Silas returned and she moved behind Lizzie.

Silas ate his supper noisily, eyeing his latest acquisition.

'Don't know where she's going to sleep,' Lizzie said.

'Down here on the bench.'

'Don't you think she'll run off?'

'If she do, then I'll fetch her back and skelp her hide.' He shovelled the fish pie into his mouth with his knife, chomping away. 'Anyways, I'll put a fetter on her leg, then she can't go nowhere.'

'You can't do that. She ain't an animal.'

'She's only a flibbertigibbet.'

'She's just a child.' Lizzie flushed at the description. 'Please, Silas.'

Her husband shrugged. 'You gotta treat her firm or she'll give you trouble,' he advised. 'She knows I won't stand no nonsense – don't you?' He turned to the girl, who flashed him a hostile scowl.

'Her sort only understands the rod,' he continued, getting up to go back to the mill. As he went out, he added: 'You'd best set her to work, 'cause that's what she's here for.'

After he had gone, Lizzie looked round for something that Mardi could do. 'Can you spin?' she asked.

A barely discernible movement of the head implied that she might. Lizzie handed her the spindle and a fistful of the greasy grey fleece and after a pause Mardi began to pull it apart with her brown fingers so that the strands all lay in the same direction. She then deftly spun it onto the thread that hung from the spindle.

'That's good.' Lizzie started to clear the plates, dunking them in a bucket of water to get rid of the fishy juices. As she worked, she watched the girl out of the corner of her eye. Her heart was beating uncomfortably, for the girl stirred up memories of Will and the awful events that had followed her visit to the Summer Fair.

'You'll be quite safe here if you do as you're told,' she advised, needing the sound of her voice to reassure herself. 'Stick close to me and I'll make sure no one harms thee.'

There was silence. Mardi reached towards a pile of fleece in the corner and took some more. Lizzie nodded in satisfaction.

'What you called?' she finally asked. She waited before adding: 'I've got to know what to call you. There's no harm in saying your name.'

'Mardi.'

'Who?'

'Mardi.'

'That's a strange name. It don't sound Christian.'

The girl did not reply. By now Lizzie had finished stacking away the wooden trenchers and swilled out the pie dish.

'It's time to milk the ewes,' she announced. 'You'd best come with me.'

Mardi laid aside her spinning and followed Lizzie across the pasture. With a bucket and rope in one hand and a stool in the other, Lizzie cornered the nearest ewe. Expertly she tied her hind legs together and set about milking her. The familiar tasks kept her strange foreboding at bay.

'Can you do this?'

Mardi shrugged.

'Come and try, then.'

Holding the animal fast, Lizzie instructed her servant in how to draw the milk from the udder. Before long it shot in spurts into the wooden pail. One by one they caught and bound the sheep, milked them and finally herded them into a corner where they were secured with a wattle hurdle for the night. The two dogs, Tip and Tup, slept nearly under the hedge to keep prowlers at bay.

Mardi struggled under the weight of the pail, following her new mistress into the dairy.

'Now we set the milk to cool,' Lizzie instructed. 'Then tomorrow we can draw the cream off and make butter. With what's left we'll make cheese for market.'

They both stepped out of the dairy into the enveloping dusk and crossed the yard to the house.

'You'd best get to bed,' Lizzie advised, sensing the girl's fatigue. 'You sleep on the bench, but don't think of running away or he'll beat the living daylights out of you.' Staring curiously, she could not stop herself from asking: 'Where do you come from?'

When there was no reply, she continued: 'It's strange you should end up here. You told my fortune once.'

Her face coloured under the scrutiny of Mardi's unreadable black eyes.

She knows, Lizzie thought. She remembers. To cover her confusion, she asked: 'What are you going to do about the child?' but there was no response. 'Well, I don't know what my husband will say,' she finished lamely, but for the moment at least that could wait.

Left alone, Lizzie pondered on the day's events. Putting the coincidence aside, there was a certain satisfaction in having a servant. I'm almost a lady, she thought to herself, then felt ashamed for being so proud.

For the first time in many weeks she thought about May. May was a servant just like this one. She wondered if they were kind to her at Swaynson. She had been there for nearly six months now and they had not once encountered each other even at the church. Lizzie felt a sudden nostalgia for May and all the things that they had shared, and wondered what her friend would think when she learned that she was the mistress of her house and had a servant of her own.

Having dissuaded Silas from fettering Mardi, Lizzie found her trust rewarded, for in the morning the girl was still there, curled up in a nest of reeds. She had scraped up the floor covering and hollowed a niche, her dark eyes peering sleepily like those of a disturbed dormouse.

Getting up, she stretched, scratched and set to work. She immediately showed herself to be an excellent firemaker, having the expertise of one used to travelling the road with only damp twigs and grass to contend with. Under instruction she then made a posset with hot milk and beaten eggs. The girl licked her lips in anticipation, but it was left by the fire to keep warm, for there was other work to be done first.

Together they fetched the water, searched the barn for eggs, milked the sheep and let them loose into the meadow. While Lizzie attended to Farmer, Mardi chivied the oxen out into the early sun.

As they were finishing, Silas returned from the mill, accompanied by his two young hirelings. They all went inside and together stood around the table, heads bowed, hands clasped together as Silas said the morning prayers.

'Merciful God,' he intoned, his eyes tightly shut, his face raised towards the sky. 'We thank Thee for blessing our house and rewarding the diligence of its master. Look kindly upon Your servants, making them obedient and hard-working and grateful for the good treatment what they do receive here. Bless the wife of this house that she will always remember to do her duty to Yourself and Your humble servant. We pray for a blessing on our village and on the church and upon her gracious Majesty. May she soon find a husband worthy of an English queen. Amen.'

Watching Silas covertly under her lashes, Lizzie added her own silent prayer: 'And punish them two-faced devils who pretend to be good but ain't.'

Silas sat down in his large wooden chair at the head of the table, and the boys and Lizzie took the long wooden bench. There was no place for Mardi, so she stood until he handed her a piece of bread, which she took to the hearth, stuffing it into her mouth as she crouched on her haunches. Finishing in record time, she looked hopefully at Lizzie for more, but as her mistress went to cut her a piece of bacon, Silas's hand came down on hers.

'Don't go giving her good vittles. She'm used to eating anything she can find. Leftovers is quite good enough for her.'

Mardi watched as the posset was shared between Silas and Lizzie, the merest spoonful being given to the two boys, who were lawfully hired and therefore had to be fed. Lizzie sipped hers slowly, leaving some to give to the girl later.

After the men were gone, Mardi gulped the posset back, still hunched and resentful.

'I hate him,' she announced. It was only the second thing she had said since her arrival.

'You mustn't say that!' Lizzie knew that she had to take

125

control. 'I'll look after you but if you don't behave I'll have to beat you.'

She flushed at the very idea of beating this girl, and Mardi's hostile eyes surveyed her, weighing her up.

'I don't like to be cruel but I've got to keep order,' Lizzie added. Looking to the girl for some understanding, she said: 'I'm that worried about my folks. My brother's been injured and Pa and my other brother have gone to fetch him home.'

Mardi continued to regard her. Speaking almost as if she were not aware of doing so, she replied: 'Two more days and they'll be back.'

'How do you know?'

There was something about Mardi's tone that defied doubt and she did not bother to reply. Instead she picked up her spindle and, with the air of being the mistress herself, strode out into the early sunshine and sat by the stream, a tiny figure in too big a gown, but indisputably in charge of her destiny.

Chapter Nineteen

As Lizzie had both hoped and feared, Mardi's prediction came true and two days later George, Jed and Harry arrived back in the village. The journey had taken them two weeks and the family had despaired of ever seeing them again.

It was late afternoon and Lizzie was preparing to leave her mother to return to the mill when the distant rumble of cartwheels sounded above the bleating of the sheep and the persistent honking of the geese.

'It's them!' Both women were immediately out of the house and running to meet the wagon. Before it had stopped, Leah was aboard and had Harry in her arms.

'My precious boy,' she repeated, rocking him to her bosom. Looking down at his stump, she let out a wail.

'Get him indoors,' Lizzie ordered. A bed had been made up for him in the kitchen and he was carried in by Jed and laid on the straw mattress. Harry smiled weakly at his sister.

'I'm well enough,' he said, untruthfully.

Lizzie gazed in dismay at his haggard face and shrunken body. After the amputation his stump had been dipped in tar but his thigh was hot and swollen and he had repeated attacks of shivering. Lizzie fought back the nausea that threatened to engulf her and took his hand.

'What you need is some yarrow,' she said. 'You're fevered and we've got to get it down.' His pallor had now been replaced by flushing and a cold sweat on his brow.

Both women set to work to change the dirty dressings while Jed, already at the table, was ladling helpings of mutton into his trencher.

'I helped row the boat,' he boasted. 'They said if it weren't for me we wouldn't have got there.'

Neither woman answered but he continued to recount his adventures.

When the wound was dressed, mother and daughter looked at each other and shook their heads. They knew that Harry's recovery was in God's hands.

As they moved away, Lizzie said: 'Don't you fret, Mam, I'll be here,' but she wondered what Silas would have to say. Recently she had been too much away from home, according to him, and he never tired of telling her so.

At that moment George came in, having watered the oxen. Stiffly he sank into his chair.

''Twas touch and go,' he said. 'We couldn't find the place. 'Tis like a rat's hole over there. I'm glad we live where we does.'

Leah had now returned to Harry and was tempting him to drink sips of broth, but he turned his head away.

'Leave me be,' he murmured, slipping into a doze. Standing at his bedside, his mother bit her knuckles to keep back the tears.

'Sit down, wife, you'll wear yourself out.' George got out of his chair and shoved Leah into it. Wearily he joined Jed at the table and ate his long overdue meal.

When it was clear that Harry was sleeping, Lizzie got ready to go.

'I'd best get back,' she said. 'Silas'll be wanting his supper.'

She was feeling nervous, for when George had not returned by Friday, Silas had been very angry.

'When I married thee I didn't expect to have all your family's problems as well,' he had grumbled.

'It ain't my fault,' Lizzie had countered. Secretly she thought it served him right. He had continued to fume and now she wasn't there again when she was supposed to be.

Having taken the tired oxen back across the meadow, she was just bedding them down in the barn when the door opened and Silas came in. She could see from his face that he was in a dangerous mood.

'Where you been?' he asked belligerently.

'Our Harry's back. I've been helping Mam.' She went to slip past him but he grabbed her wrist.

'You need learning a lesson. Your place is 'ere with me.' She could smell that he had been drinking and his face was blotched and sweaty. Without warning he struck her a blow across the face.

'If I catch you across there again I'll take my birch to you. Now get inside and get my supper.' He gave her a shove that sent her sprawling to the ground, skinning her knees. With a sob she scrambled up and out of reach.

'If you lay a hand on me again I'll tell the priest!' she screamed at him.

He lunged at her but she was too quick.

'I'll tell him what you made me do – everything. It was a sin and you'll be shamed in public.'

He growled at her but she knew that the message had gone home. Wiping the tears on her sleeve, she hobbled across to the mill house.

When the meal was ready she set it in front of him and retired to the corner by the fire. He ate everything put before him and then sat back with a smile of satisfaction.

'Come 'ere,' he ordered, his tone now jovial.

She was in two minds whether to obey but decided to do so.

''Ere, come and sit on my knee.'

'You haven't had your tonic,' she hedged.

'Don't seem to be doing me no good. I'm tireder than ever.'

'That's 'cause it takes time to work.'

Ignoring him, she fetched the mixture and held it out. Taking it with one hand, he pulled her onto his knee with the other. She held her breath, wondering what he would do with the mixture, and to her relief he drained it back. She relaxed a little as he put the crock down, but then he started to fondle her.

'You'm a pretty little thing,' he said.

'Let me get you some ale.'

He held her back as she went to get up. 'I don't want none.'

'You've been that busy all day. You must be thirsty,' she insisted and eased herself away from him to pour a large measure from the jug. Taking it, he looked up smugly at her over the rim as he drained it back and again pulled her onto his knee. She endured his fumblings.

'Let's get upstairs,' he said thickly.

'Silas, about Harry.' She let him loosen her bodice. 'Mam

129

can't manage on her own. I'll have to go over and give her a hand.'

'Mmn.' He wasn't listening.

'May I go then?'

'I suppose so. Jus' you come on upstairs and we'll see.'

'You go on up. I just got one or two things to finish. I won't be long.'

He squashed her against him before lumbering up the stairs and she sank down by the hearth wondering how long she dared wait. Overhead she could hear the thumps and vibrations as he moved around. After a while they stopped and when she finally crept up the stairs he was snoring. With a sigh of relief she went back down to the kitchen and curled up near to her servant by the dying embers.

Next morning after breakfast she said: 'Thank you for letting me go over and help Mam. I'll be back in time for your meal, I promise.'

He looked at her suspiciously. 'I don't remember saying as how you could go.'

'You did. Last night. Don't you remember?'

He grunted. Swiftly she brushed her lips against his stubble and ran out, smiling to herself.

Harry was in a delirium for nearly a week. Day and night Leah or Lizzie sat with him, dripping honeyed almond milk between his lips, wiping his fevered limbs with damp cloths and packing the swollen upper leg with crushed comfrey leaves. The Reverend Cotton called daily to pray by his bedside and suddenly on the eighth day, Harry opened his eyes.

'I feel tired,' he murmured, accepting a few mouthfuls of rosehip tea; then he fell into a peaceful sleep. From that time his recovery seemed hopeful.

Silas continued to complain about Lizzie's absences until even George intervened.

'Where's your compassion, Silas? 'Tis her brother, after all,' he pointed out.

After that nothing more was said and Lizzie opted for night duties as long as she reasonably could.

Towards the end of the month there was no further excuse to stay away so she returned to the mill, carrying out her domestic

130

duties and feeding Silas his nightly drink, to which she now added some wormwood to aid his digestion. He slept like a baby.

In Lizzie's estimation Mardi was by now six or seven months pregnant. Clearly they could no longer pretend it was not happening and Silas would have to be told.

One day, after he had gone to the mill, she summoned her servant and broached the subject.

'When is your child due?' The question received the now familiar shrug of indifference, so Lizzie changed her tactics.

'Tell me about the father,' she urged. 'Was he someone you ... cared for?' Mardi continued to gaze stonily at the ground so Lizzie decided to try a more personal approach. 'Was he handsome?'

The girl looked up, meeting her eyes. There was something impossible to interpret in her expression.

'You would think so.'

'Well, tell me about him then.'

Mardi pouted and shrugged. 'Ain't nothing to tell. When he finds out he'll take me away and buy me a fine house.'

Ignoring the foolishness of the statement, Lizzie asked: 'So he doesn't know, then?'

'Not yet. There's no hurry.'

'Course there's a hurry. You should be properly wed.' She sighed, wondering how to communicate with this strange, wild girl. 'Listen, don't you want a house of your own and a husband?'

Mardi shrugged again. 'It makes no difference.'

With a sudden flash of insight, Lizzie asked: 'It ain't *his*, is it?'

'Whose?'

Lizzie found herself blushing. 'The master's,' she replied.

Mardi gave a laugh. 'D'you think I'd let a lump of dung like that touch me?' she challenged.

Lizzie sat back baffled. 'Well, why don't you say?' When nothing was forthcoming, she said: 'Well, I'll tell the master but I really don't know what he'll say. He may send you away.'

'No, he won't.' The words were uttered with such confidence that Lizzie could think of no reply. Dismissing Mardi, she watched in confusion as the girl went back to her work.

131

Lizzie went across to the dairy and continued to carry out her own tasks. She worked mechanically, for her mind was much preoccupied. She felt restless and sad and was not quite sure why. The death of her baby brother had affected her more than she had realised and even now tears threatened at the memory of his tiny, frail body and small, clutching hands. She felt afraid for her servant's child, wondering if it too would die almost before taking breath, but there was something more. The emptiness in her own womb left her feeling incomplete, purposeless, and without Will she knew that she would never be whole. Oblivious to the time and the place, she allowed the tears to run unchecked.

She was disturbed by a sudden commotion in the yard and, hastily wiping her eyes, hurried out to see what was happening. The first thing she saw was Silas holding Mardi by the neck of her kirtle and dragging her across the yard. The girl was struggling and screaming.

'What's going on?' Lizzie ran over and stopped just ahead of them.

'She's been a-thieving – look.' Silas held up a sheepskin jerkin and waved it at her.

'I ain't!' Mardi renewed her struggle and in response Silas kicked her with his solid leather boot.

'Stop it!' Lizzie was between them, trying to prise the girl away from him. He let go.

'Now what's been going on?' she asked again.

'Her's been thieving off Michael Young.'

'I ain't. He gave it to me.' Mardi's eyes were fierce as a dog fox's.

'Why?' Lizzie looked anxiously at her servant.

'It was a payment.'

Silas snorted. 'If you've been loose with the lads, I'll strip you naked and beat it out of you,' he threatened, his colour heightened.

Mardi ignored him, although her cheeks flushed, but she looked straight at Lizzie. 'I made him a potion,' she explained.

'What sort of potion?'

'A love potion.'

Silas sniffed again in disbelief. 'Doxy!' he muttered under his

132

breath. Aloud he said: 'If you've been mucking about with devilry, I'll take you to the pond and duck you.'

'It ain't magic. It's herbs and things. It works. I know lots of cures and potions.'

His response was to grab her again and start pulling the kirtle off her back.

'Silas, stop!'

'She's gotta be punished proper. I'll thrash her and you take the jerkin back.'

'No. She's my servant. I'll punish her and you take it back.' Lizzie held her ground.

'In that case, you beat her, but take her kirtle off so it don't get marked, and I'll watch to see you does it proper.' There was a hungry glint in his eyes and he licked his lips as if in anticipation of a treat.

'No. First of all I'll take her to the Youngs and find out what happened.'

'No need for that,' he protested.

'Yes, there is. If she stole it she deserves punishment, but that Michael Young's that daft, he might be as much to blame as her.'

Without waiting for him to answer, she dragged Mardi across the yard and up the road to the Youngs' cottage.

Shamefaced, Michael Young admitted that he was so smitten by Beth Vannum that he had indeed paid Mardi with the jerkin for a secret potion guaranteed to make his love reciprocated.

'See!' Mardi flashed her eyes at Lizzie.

'What's in the potion?' her mistress asked.

'I'm telling no one. It's a secret and if you beat me to death I'm not saying.'

Lizzie shrugged and handed back the jerkin, then led her maid back towards the mill.

'What you going to do then?' Mardi asked, trotting along beside her.

'I've not decided yet.'

'If you don't beat me, he will. He's a pig.'

'Shush! He's your master now and you mustn't talk about him like that.'

Mardi eyed her speculatively.

133

'If you like, I can give you a potion that'll make him dried up for ever, then he won't bother you no more.'

'What are you talking about?' Lizzie felt her face grow hot.

'Honeysuckle. Served up proper, it makes men seedless.'

'That'd be a sin.'

'I know what you're doing now.'

Lizzie turned her head away so that the girl should not see her scarlet cheeks.

'I don't know what you mean,' she mumbled.

'You're giving him something to stop him poking you at nights.'

Before Lizzie could deny it, Mardi continued: 'Don't blame you. So would I if I was wed to him.'

Fortunately, as soon as they got back a problem had arisen at the mill, so Lizzie was able to extract a quick promise from Mardi never to repeat her actions and leave it at that. By the time that evening came and Silas returned to the house, the incident had been forgotten.

The question of Mardi's condition still remained unresolved. Lizzie waited until the following evening before taking the plunge. As soon as Silas came in for the night, she sent Mardi off to see to the livestock and got him alone. After a few preliminary remarks, she said:

'I got something to tell you.'

'Yeah?'

Her heart was thumping because she did not want any trouble and she felt a genuine concern for the girl.

'It's about Mardi.'

'What's the little she cat been up to now?'

'Nothing. It's just that she's ... with child.'

Silas looked at her with his pale, piggy eyes. 'Took you a long time to realise, didn't it?' he replied.

'You know then?' Lizzie could not hide her astonishment.

'Course I knows. D'you think I'm stupid?' Eyeing her with his head on one side, he added: 'About time you was, too.'

Lizzie's face turned scarlet. 'P'r'aps I can't,' she mumbled. Seeing him frown, she added: 'Your other wives couldn't.'

'What you saying?' She could see the suspicion in his purple-lined face.

'Nothing. It's just that ...' She didn't know what to say.

134

'Well, just you stop thinking about the servant,' he said. 'It's time we tried harder. Just you get abed early tonight and we'll see what happens.' Heaving himself up, he left her sitting alone with the all too familiar knot of pain and fear.

Chapter Twenty

As the weeks passed, Lizzie's ordinary, everyday preoccupations were overshadowed by rumours of war. Unthinkable as it was, the Spanish fleet had finally left port and was making its way north.

According to the experts, the Isle of Wight was one of the most likely targets, and musters were now held almost daily to keep the military in a constant state of readiness. Even Jed was part of the citizen's army.

At four of the clock on the morning of Thursday 25 July, Lizzie awoke with a start to the sound of banging on the door. Leaping out of bed, she stumbled down the stairs in her chemise, which she had taken to wearing since, thanks to the tonic, Silas was invariably asleep when she came to bed each night. As she reached the door she was aware of another sound, the ringing of church bells, and for a moment she thought that it must be Sunday and that they had overslept.

'Who's there?' she called out.

''Tis me, Jed.'

Oh, my God, something's happened to Harry, she thought, unlatching the door, but as she opened it she could see that Jed was flushed and excited.

'Can't you hear the bells?' he asked. ''Tis happening. The Spanish is coming with their great ships to get us!'

Lizzie grabbed the doorpost to steady herself, for she felt momentarily faint.

'Come in,' she said. Taking a deep breath to right herself, she went to find her dress and waken Silas. In spite of the noise, he was still snoring.

'Silas, get up,' she said, shaking him. 'The Spaniards are on their way. They've sounded the warning.'

Looking out of the window, she could see the distant pall of smoke where a beacon had been lighted. Groggily Silas bestirred himself.

Already a stream of villagers were making their way to the coast up over West Over Down so that they could stand on the clifftop above Compton village and see what was happening. Those in good health and of sufficient youth were to muster at the church and collect their orders, ready to repel any stragglers who might land along the coast. The army had been on full alert since Monday.

Lizzie fetched a stout pole from the lean-to. In great haste she let the sheep out into the meadow to fend for themselves, thinking ruefully that the lambs would take all the milk intended for the cheese and butter. With a shiver she realized that by evening the whole village might be razed by marauding foreigners. I'll kill them, she thought, her blood pounding.

In spite of her protests, Mardi was ordered to stay behind. Leaving Jed to join the citizens' army at the church, Lizzie set off, her heart pounding, to meet up with the other women and children who were going to see the spectacle.

As they hastened along, speculation was rife. Marjorie Gier swore that the Spaniards were all cloven-footed, that being the true mark of the Devil, while Molly Wavell knew for certain that the men had nothing in their breeches but made babies through a spout in their belly holes. The laughter became more raucous as further incredible accounts of meetings with King Philip's invaders were invented.

'Not one of them's under two yards tall,' somebody called.

'They do sleep with their swords unsheathed and like as not run their women through when they do toss and turn.'

'That's how they've got nothing in their breeches,' someone added, and they doubled up with laughter.

Lizzie did not join in the merriment. She was remembering the tales that Harry had told her of sailors tortured and left to a hideous death, their limbs torn off and the wounds smeared with honey to attract stinging insects. She shuddered. This cannot be happening, she thought. In the distance they now heard cannonfire and the reality of the conflict sobered them.

137

For a terrible moment Lizzie visualised the devastation if the Spaniards should reach the village. She heard Leah's screams as she was put to the sword or ravished by these inhuman devils. She could not think about her own fate but gripped the pole more tightly and increased her pace.

She began to recite the Lord's Prayer. This war had to do with the evil Spaniards taking away their religion, so she knew that God must be on the English side.

When the group of women reached the highest point, the coastline became visible. The beach was seething with activity. To the east the six-o'clock sun was huge as a cartwheel, but all eyes were drawn out to sea where, rounding the headland from Freshwater, a flotilla of ships was clearly visible.

'Oh, Lizzie, be they ours?' asked Molly Wavell.

Lizzie did not know. Plumes of black smoke accompanied each thunderous bang.

'They'm galleons,' an old man told them. 'Look hard and you'll see the red crusader's crosses on the masts. Ours is the smaller ones. They bear the Queen's green and white.'

'Then God help us if ours are smaller. We'll surely be lost,' Lizzie said.

'Not so. They great bobbity things is only good for getting close and boarding,' the old man continued. 'Ours is sleek and fast and they shoot good and long. We'll see 'em off sure as honey be sweet.'

'Pray God you're right,' Lizzie replied.

The sky was infinite and cloudless, the sun already blazing down on the parched hills. In their haste many people had forgotten breakfast and neglected to have a drink. One by one the little ones started to whine as hunger and thirst tormented them. There was no sign that the Spaniards were getting closer or landing on the beaches, and the blackened convoy of vessels drifted slowly past.

The crowd waited in vain to see one of the great galleons burst into flame. With them, Lizzie longed to witness a mast come crashing down, sails blazing, the crew leaping for their lives into the waves and wading to the shore and to their deaths. If they did come ashore now, it would be a long way down the coast.

In spite of the deafening, sulphurous bombardment, they

could see no dramatic sinkings. When the realisation dawned on them that the Spaniards were on the run, a spontaneous cheer went up.

' 'Tain't over yet,' the old man warned. 'Them Dons is aiming for Spithead. If they can get round to the northern coast, then they might still manage it.' But the crowd were too full of the heady wine of victory to heed his words. As the opposing ships continued to drift out to sea, they began to slip away. There was less firing now and by the look of the sun it was well after nine of the clock. Pressing duties began to weigh heavy and Lizzie remembered that not only the stock but also the mill would be unattended. Turning back inland, she walked with Molly, only half listening to the constant babble.

'We beat 'em, didn't we, Lizzie?'

'Aye.'

'Why are we fighting 'em?'

'Because they want to take our land and make us Catholics.'

'Why's that then?'

'I don't know.'

Although now downhill, the journey back seemed longer and Lizzie felt hot and exhausted. After a while she said: 'You go on. I want to wait here a while.' With a little shrug of reproach, Molly waved goodbye and left her to sit and recover.

Will had been with Sir George Carey and the army ever since the alert had come on Monday. Because of his riding skills he had been allocated a horse and undergone some swift tuition in the use of a pistol. Thus mounted and armed, he felt like a different person.

With the local militia he had pitched camp on the High Down to keep watch and then passed several days peering out over the empty Channel. When nothing happened, the men became first restless and then lethargic. Finally, before first light on Thursday morning, the alarm went up.

With growing excitement Will witnessed the lighting of the first beacon and watched as the signal was picked up and passed on, making a ribbon of light towards the east as far as he could see.

Every man was now on alert, ready to make for the beaches and enter in hand-to-hand combat if the enemy landed. At the thought of it Will's throat was dry. He rememberd Lardychops – the thud of this blade against fat flesh, the pumping spout of red, and his gasp of disbelief. He thought wryly that the advent of the pistol would no doubt make the job easier.

As the first ship came into view, he, like every man from the garrison, was taut with anticipation. The tension was almost palpable. As he watched, one ship after another came over the hazy horizon until there were too many to count. Will had seen at least a hundred of the enemy and had lost reckoning of their own. The gunfire, at first a distant boom, became deafening and the order went up to leave their hilltop lookout and ride for the beaches.

His blood racing, Will set off at a gallop. Now that it was happening he wanted to be there. His expert horsemanship, learned at his grandfather's knee, had him far ahead of his companions and his only thought was to drive the invaders away and protect the island he loved so dearly from foreign trespass. At that moment he would have willingly died for the cause.

Reining in on the beach among the melee of sightseers, he waited impatiently, but minutes and then an hour or more passed and the flotilla continued to drift away. Finally he realised that there was to be no battle on island shores.

'You may go back to the castle,' an officer told him. 'We'll keep the regulars here but there's no reason for you to wait.'

With disappointment Will started to ride inland. His blood was up; not that he wanted to kill anyone but he needed some action.

As he rode, he daydreamed. Slowing for a moment, he made up his mind and changed direction, heading north towards Caulbourne. He reasoned to himself that there would be no harm in passing on news of the skirmish to his family, and it now seemed likely that he would be able to leave in a week or two so farewells would be in order.

Passing through a grove of fruit trees, he saw her. She was sitting in the shade, her arms hugging her knees. He knew that this was why he had come. He had known she would be there. I'm developing the sight, he thought, like the Gipsy, but he pushed the thought of Mardi away in the joy of seeing his love.

Hearing the sound of his horse, Lizzie looked up and leaped to her feet, first fear, then disbelief on her face. By now he was out of the saddle and facing her.

'Hello, Lizzie.'

'What are you doing here?' Her cheeks were a blaze of glorious pink.

'Looking for you. I had this feeling I'd see you if I came this way.'

She gave a little laugh of embarrassment or pleasure – he was not sure which.

Not taking his eyes from her, he added: 'Seems like the war's over, then.'

She nodded. 'Praise God there were no deaths.'

He agreed. Wrapping his horse's rein around a branch, he reached out and took her hand.

'Don't I get a proper hello, then?' he asked.

'Oh, Will!' She moved into his arms and pressed her body to him as if he might swallow her up. In turn he kissed her like a thirsty man finding sweet water.

'You said you wouldn't come no more,' she said when they drew apart.

'I know. It's madness and yet I can think of nothing else.'

After a moment, she asked: 'Does this mean you'll be leaving soon?'

Seeing the pain in her eyes, he said: 'Don't be afeared. The quicker I go, the quicker I'll make my fortune and be back for you.'

Her mouth quivered and he knew she could not believe the truth of what he said. Wanting it to be true, he added: 'I'm going to build a house for you. We'll raise our babbies there and live like lords till we're too old to cope on our own.'

She gave a watery smile. 'I've got a servant,' she said to steer the conversation to safer ground.

'You have?'

'A stray Silas brought home. A proper wild thing. She's with child.' She lowered her eyes and added: 'If I don't have no babbies of my own I could always adopt hers.'

Will felt suddenly uneasy. A vision of Mardi came to mind, but he knew that he was being unreasonable. Everywhere you looked these days there were homeless, abandoned women.

141

Turning back to his love, he bent to kiss her again. Oblivious to everything but each other, they sank to the cool ground and took their pleasure.

They lay a long while in their embrace, caressing and tending to each other in a single-minded state of reverence. As the tension and the need were washed away, they embraced as if absorbing some magical potion that would give them strength for the empty months ahead.

'You won't grieve, will you?' he asked after a while.

'No. I'll pray for you every day – many times a day.' Glancing around her, she added: 'It's best we go soon, before someone comes.'

He nodded, pulled her to her feet and held her close again.

'I give you my solemn promise my heart is yours for as long as I live,' he said.

'And mine yours.'

Mounting the horse and turning away from her, he had the feeling they had made an oath as binding as wedding vows.

Chapter Twenty-One

Lizzie walked back to the village in a dream. The taste and the smell of Will were like heaven on her body. The unexpectedness of his visit and the joy of their loving left her with a glorious optimism for the future. She knew now that however bad life might seem, Will could come at any moment and transform it. It might be weeks or months before she saw him again but the magic of this afternoon showed that everything was possible.

She stopped briefly at the Sheepwash to tell her family about the events at sea. Harry, sitting on a stool by the doorway, moved restlessly as he cross-questioned her for details.

'I should have been there,' he said bitterly. 'I can't spend the rest of my life just sitting here watching.'

Lizzie squeezed his shoulder, not knowing what to say. Her mood was so distracted that she felt she must get away before she betrayed herself.

'I'll come over tonight when Silas gets back,' she said, her voice strangely distorted. 'I'll tell you all the latest news then.'

'Be you unwell?' Leah asked, discerning her daughter's vagueness.

Lizzie nodded and kissed both her mother and Harry before continuing across the meadow to the mill house.

When she arrived she stood in the doorway looking in at the kitchen. There was no sign of Mardi and the fire was out, so she pulled up her sleeves and set about laying some kindling on top of the ashes. Taking a piece of flint and the bar in the hearth, she sparked them together until finally the bone-dry grass tinder began to smoulder. She blew on the small glimmering of heat until a tiny flame appeared; then, holding the now burning swathe of grass under the rushes and twigs, she coaxed the fire alight.

Going back outside towards the mill, she called her servant's name but there was no reply. She realised that nothing had been done that morning and felt a twinge of irritation. She would have to scold the girl for her laziness.

Silas did not return home until dark. The ships had by then long since gone and the Spanish Armada, nipped at the heels by their smaller English adversaries, had been unable to slip into the Solent and come ashore. Instead it had drifted on down the Channel, still pursued by the English navy. Five craft from the Isle of Wight were among the pursuers and those relatives who could had watched, praying for the safe return of their loved ones, until the fleet was nothing but a speck on the horizon.

Silas recounted these details to Lizzie as he sat in his chair waiting for his food. 'As far as we're concerned, it's all over. 'Ere, take these boots off.'

Lizzie bent down to remove them. His feet were swollen and she had to tug hard to prise them off.

'I'm hungry as a hunter,' he continued. 'Get us summat to eat quick. I must fill me belly.'

Taking his great wooden trencher, Lizzie cut a huge slice of tongue pie and poured him a tankard of beer. He ate noisily, each mouthful interspersed with more tales of the day.

'We seen Sir Francis Drake hisself on the deck of his ship,' he boasted. 'We knowed it was him 'cus Wayland Blore was with us and he used to serve with him.'

From what Lizzie had seen, she doubted if anyone was visible, let alone recognisable on any of the ships, but she said nothing.

'Dunno where the fleet's off to now but it won't be back this way,' he continued. Finishing his tongue pie, he started on a handful of the jumbly biscuits which Lizzie had shaped and boiled and flavoured with aniseed. Belching loudly, he loosened the strings of his straining breeches.

'Is everything attended to?' he asked his wife. Lizzie nodded, thinking that it was too late to go back to the cottage and pass on the latest news. Her annoyance with Mardi had changed during the afternoon to anxiety and now worry, and as darkness fell she desperately wanted to go and look for her.

Silas stood up and stretched.

'I needs me bed,' he said, coming up behind her as she scraped the leftovers into a dish for the pig. He slid his hands around her, cupping her breasts, and started to rock her against him.

'Don't!' she cried involuntarily, but he ignored her.

'Can't think how them gentry gets on,' he mused. 'All them women wearing they stomachers flattening their paps till they looks like a board. I likes my women to have nice rounded dugs like these.' He uncovered her breasts, massaging them with his callused hands.

'You haven't had your tonic,' she said in a tight voice.

'Don't think I needs it. I got better medicine in mind.'

She felt the panic rising.

'The skivvy's run away,' she said to distract him. He stopped what he was doing.

'When did she go?'

'Must have been this morning. I can't think why she would choose now. Her babby must be due.' As she said it, Lizzie had the certain feeling that this was the reason for Mardi's disappearance. Moving a safe distance away from Silas, she said:

'It ain't no good, we'll have to find her tonight. If she's gived birth out there, anything might happen.'

'Well, I ain't going looking for her.' Silas stretched. 'I'm off to bed and you'd best not be long. You can go and look if you likes, but don't come calling on me for help.'

As soon as he was up the ladder, Lizzie hurried out. She cursed herself for having waited so long, but fortunately the moon was full and she had no trouble in seeing her way. She wandered along the stream towards the corn mill and then back through the pastures, calling Mardi by name, but she was not to be found. Then, just as she was passing back through the orchard, she heard the unmistakable mewling of a baby.

'Mardi?' She stopped and located the sound, moving cautiously closer. There in a natural hollow under a cherry tree was Mardi and beside her on the ground a small blurred shape.

Bending down, Lizzie looked anxiously at them both. 'Be you all right?' she asked.

Mardi looked exhausted but she propped herself up on her elbows and nodded towards the newborn. 'It's a she,' she said.

'But are you well? Why did you run away?'

'Course I am. I didn't bear all the pain myself.'

'What do you mean?'

Mardi gave a little snort of impatience. 'Women don't conceive alone so they shouldn't suffer the travail alone either,' she said enigmatically. 'Anyway I didn't run away. I wasn't having my babby born under a roof. It's bad luck. The sun shone on her and the breeze touched her. She'll be blessed with health and wit.'

Lizzie picked the naked infant up from a nest of grass and leaves. 'She feels cold,' she admonished. 'We'd best take her indoors.'

Mardi scrambled up and followed Lizzie as she carried the child.

'What you going to call her?' she asked over her shoulder.

After a moment the girl said: 'Her name's Garnet.'

'I've never heard that before. Why did you choose it?'

'I didn't choose it. Our babes just come with their names. There is a reason.' Lizzie waited, but since Mardi did not explain, she hurried the girl inside and made them both comfortable. Mardi, obviously exhausted, submitted to Lizzie's ministrations without complaint. After she had drunk some ale she took the child to her small breast. As Lizzie looked on, her emotions ran riot. At that moment she longed for a child of her own with a savageness she would not have believed possible.

'Is she like her father?' she asked to forestall the anguish.

Those strange black eyes were on her and she felt again that there was a great but unknown significance in what Mardi was about to say. Falling back on the mattress, the servant sighed before answering: 'She'll be like her father all right. There's no doubt about that.'

After leaving Lizzie, Will rode for about ten minutes, then reined in his horse. He had had cramps in his belly all day and had put them down to the excitement of the invasion. While he had been with Lizzie they had disappeared and he thought sentimentally that he could have borne anything just to be in her presence. Now, however, they were back with a vengeance. He slid from the saddle and crouched down, hugging his stomach. The pains came in spasms, building up to a raging torment

146

and then fading. For about fifteen minutes this continued, increasing in intensity until it became one long agony and he felt that his insides were going to drop out. I'm dying, he thought. Panting with the effort to ward off his suffering, he crawled into the bushes and lay writhing. Of its own volition his body seemed to gather itself for one life or death struggle, and then the pains were gone as quickly as they had come. He fell into a tormented sleep filled with dreams of Lizzie. She was always just out of his reach. When he went to hold her he found instead that the Gipsy girl had taken her place.

Chapter Twenty-Two

Once it was certain that the Spanish Armada could not land, Will sought an audience with Sir George Carey. He needed permission to leave Carisbrooke Castle and set out for London. As he stood in the hallway of Sir George's house in the courtyard of the castle waiting for instructions, his emotions were a tangle of regret and excitement.

Standing inside the house that he himself had helped to build, he was now overawed by its grandeur. Around the walls hung bright tapestries and rugs, and a side chest so ample that a family could almost live in it was covered with pewter plate and dishes. On a beautifully carved table the silver salter gave out a gentle glow as the sun cast a diagonal corridor of light running from one of the bay windows to the opposite wall.

The planned journey to London had never been far from Will's mind. He wondered if once he reached the capital he would ever succeed in finding the route known as the Stronde, where Sir George's family lived in a house provided by the Queen herself.

With misgivings he feared that all London folk might be as remote and grand as the Captain of the Island. But if he stayed he was afraid that he would be unable to keep away from Lizzie Galpine – no, Lizzie Dore, that was what he must keep reminding himself.

With a start he realised that Sir George himself was descending the staircase. Wiping a nervous hand across his mouth, Will touched his forehead in acknowledgement of the Queen's second cousin and his palms began to sweat. He noticed that Sir George was limping and remembered that he had recently taken a fall from one of his stallions. Sir George had a passion for horses and a reputation for arrogance.

'You ride, don't you, Gosling?' he asked, not betraying by any sign that he recognised Will from their earlier encounters.

'Aye, my lord.' Will waited.

'Good. I am sending two mares up to London to Sir William Blount. I need someone reliable to travel with the groom. These horses are valuable and you will both be responsible for them.'

Will swallowed.

'My granfer was stable man at Wolverton, sir. I lived there as a nipper and I been riding horses all my life.'

'Good,' Sir George repeated. Going across to the window he surveyed the courtyard.

A trio of prisoners shackled together were entering the well house to tread the new wheel and bring up enough water for the day's needs. Already many of the troops billeted in preparation for the invasion had left for the mainland and there was an unaccustomed calm within the castle ramparts.

Over Sir George's shoulder Will could see his old master and two apprentices working on what used to be the chapel. He felt a pang of nostalgia for the good times they had shared.

'Right,' said Sir George, turning back. 'Now that you have served your time, I shall expect good work from you, and pay you accordingly. You will be under my foreman to start with but if you come up to expectation, you will soon enough work on your own. Make your way to the stud at Ningwood, where you will meet up with Danyel Jolliffe. He is the groom you will be travelling with. I am also sending two guards to protect the horses. They will have their own beasts so you can ride one of the mares, but remember her value.' Will nodded, feeling relief that someone else would now know the way.

Fishing in the purse that hung about his waist, Sir George produced a coin and held it out to Will.

'This is for your fare and lodgings. Do not lose it.'

Will took it, glancing surreptitiously to recognise a half-angel. His eyebrows shot up in surprise. He already had his last quarter day's pay, less the money he had spent on a night's ale for his friends, the cost of a leather pannier to carry his goods and half a crown he had given to Granfer Gosden when he went to take his farewell. He had never been so wealthy in his life.

149

The parting had been painful, for the old man was eaten up with the screws and Will feared that if he was away for too many moons they might not meet again this side of heaven. To hide his emotion he had joked about returning with a fortune. Secretly he hoped that he would return with his life.

He set out that afternoon to walk the seven miles to Ningwood. Amy, who worked in the kitchen, had slipped him a large pasty and a leather flask of ale.

'Ask no questions,' she whispered into his ear, rubbing her wrinkled cheek against his burnished beard. Will had hugged her, thinking how like a mother she had been to him and the other apprentices who had served their time at the castle. He rarely thought about his own mother now. She had died when he was a child.

Looking down at Amy, he suddenly kissed her and she bridled with pleasure.

'You'll come back a rich'un, I knows you will,' she prophesied.

'Then you'll be the first to share my good fortune,' he replied.

Hoisting his pannier over his shoulder, he gave her a final wave and strode out of the courtyard, across the bridge that spanned the moat and down the hill towards the village.

He had a choice of routes, but while needing to bear north he kept walking resolutely due west. Caulbourne lay straight ahead and it drew him like a magnet. Even when he reached the crossroad that would take him to Ningwood he went straight by so that he could pass the fulling mill and soak up the nearness of Lizzie one last time.

Peering cautiously through the trees, he could see down to the mill. The stream starved of rain made its way sluggishly under the wooden wheel and meandered back in the general direction he must take.

His hopes were rewarded: the door of the cottage opened and there was Lizzie. As he watched, she walked barefoot across to the stream, where she sat down and immersed her legs in the water. Her sleeves were rolled up and her neck bare, and to his amazement she was carrying a baby. He remembered then her servant and thought what a good woman she was. He had no doubt that she would show care and compassion to anyone less fortunate than herself.

For a heady moment he pretended that the child was hers – theirs – and imagined the joy such an event would bring to them both. He watched entranced as she cooed to the baby, periodically sipping the drink that she carried with her.

Will's heart thumped audibly and his knuckles, grasping a bough, were white with tension.

He didn't know for how long he stood there. After a while Lizzie withdrew her feet from the water and sat hugging the infant. He would have given anything to know her thoughts.

Her hair was escaping from her kerchief and he had to fight the desire to race to her, kiss her cool wet feet, tear off the kerchief and watch that glorious copper hair tumble to her waist. He longed to cup her small face in his hands and touch her cheeks, her eyelids, her forehead and her mouth with his own. At any moment, however, the fuller might appear and to put her at risk was unthinkable. At the thought of Silas Dore the jealousy seared through him. Just then, Lizzie stood up, stretched and with a visible sigh turned back and into the house.

Leadenly he moved away, each step taking him further from everything that he wanted in life. Angrily he wiped the tears that refused to stay buried within him and with grim resolution strode out towards the north.

Will was grateful to be making the journey to London in company. Knowing where to go and what to do was now a shared responsibility and the two guards armed with swords and crossbows had made the journey before.

Danyel Jolliffe, the groom, was a small leathery man not unlike the Granfer Gosden of Will's childhood, and it was a relief to let the older man make the decisions.

When Will had been a lad, it had been Granfer Gosden who had taught him all the country skills and of course how to ride and doctor horses. His own father had been too busy with his new brood to spare time for his own son. Will had continued to regard Caulbourne as his village but it was Shorrel he pictured whenever anybody mentioned home.

The news that his father had taken off without warning and signed up on a privateer going to the Indies had taken them all by surprise.

'Always was restless,' Granfer Gosden had said.

Will's visits to Caulbourne had stopped then and it was three years before his father returned, yellowed with fever but full of incredible tales that had infected his son with the urge to leave the island shores. Now here he was setting off on that journey.

At Yarmouth the horses were coaxed down a plank and into a barge for the Solent crossing. Being well bred and well fed, they were high-spirited and nervous, and before all four were aboard Will had received a kick on the thigh and a painful nip on the shoulder. The mare he was riding was bay with a long, slender body and strong legs. She had a white star on her face and this marked her out as of particular value. Will would have given all his money to have owned such a beauty. Her companion was almost identical and they were destined to be carriage horses as well as mounts for the Blount family.

With the unconscious skill of a lifetime's experience, Will held his mare's bridle and whispered to her, tickling her behind the ears and blowing on her muzzle to keep her calm as the barge rocked its way across. He had no time to pay attention to his own queasy stomach. The cool sea breeze was a positive pleasure after the scorching heat on land and Will shaded his eyes as the mainland of England became clearer.

Once ashore, they watered the horses and took a glass of ale at an inn before starting the northern trek. They were aiming to spend the first night at Winchester. By coincidence they chose the tavern where he had stayed on the second night of his journey to Basing. Will took care to give no indication that he had ever been this way before, pretending a curiosity that would have done an actor credit. Inside the building was low and blackened by candle smoke and wood from the fire. There was a pungent smell of stale beer and rancid fat and through an opening into the kitchen a woman served up dishes of mutton stew and venison.

The meals were delivered to the tables by a young girl, perhaps fourteen, with chubby pink arms and an arresting creamy bosom. She wore a low-cut bodice, now old-fashioned but having the effect of diverting the customers from the cost of the ale and stew.

In the stable Danyel Jolliffe insisted on supervising the bedding and feeding of the horses himself. Will helped him to rub down the dusty animals with a wodge of straw, check their hooves and see that the oats were fresh and the water clean. Having satisfied themselves that all was in order, they and the guards reserved rooms for the night. They were shown up to a small room with a sloping wooden floor and two beds. Will and Danyel were to share one and the two guards the other.

'Don't leave yer things unguarded,' Danyel warned. 'And make sure ye sleeps with yer heads on yer valuables.'

'That'll be tricky,' one of the guards rejoined, looking down at his groin. 'We ain't contortionists.' The laughter relieved Will's apprehension and together they went down to eat.

As they sat down on the long, narrow bench, the serving girl smiled slyly at him.

'Sheep or deer?' she asked, holding out two dishes.

'Er, deer.' He blushed. Bending over him to place the trencher on the table, she touched his shoulder with her breast. A ripple of desire raced through him and the girl looked at him knowingly.

After two tankards of ale he needed to relieve himself and went out into the yard. His nostrils wrinkled with distaste as he added to the already fetid smell; then he walked a few yards towards the river to breathe in some fresh air. The mass of the cathedral loomed larger than anything he had ever seen and a huge moon high in the blackness framed the building with yellow light.

Will raised his face and thought, I bet Lizzie's looking at that moon; then he wondered if there could really be only one.

As he turned back he came face to face with the serving girl.

'Pardon me.' He went to step aside but she moved in the same direction, eyeing him provocatively.

'You passing through?' she asked.

'Aye.'

'You lonely?'

For a moment Will did not catch her meaning.

She reached out and placed her hand on his groin. 'Give us a sixpence and I'll make ye feel summat you ain't never felt afore.'

She was massaging him through the fabric of his breeches and his desire bolted like a runaway horse. He swallowed, stifling a groan.

She lifted her skirt with one hand and removed the other from his crutch to hold it out, grubby palm upwards. 'Sixpence,' she repeated.

The blatant demand for payment broke the spell. She smelled unwashed and her hair was a greasy, indeterminate colour.

'Leave me be,' he snapped and pushed past her and back into the tavern.

'You been a long while,' Danyel observed. Will flushed and the older man noticed the maid come in, her face pink and sullen. He turned back to his young companion.

'Be careful, lad,' he warned. ''Tisn't only law-breaking men you gotta watch out for.'

Will spent a restless night. From the other bed came creaks and grunts as the guards shifted to find comfortable positions. Next to him Danyel snored rhythmically and lay still.

Will's groin ached and he longed to relieve himself but hadn't the courage to get up and leave the room. After what seemed like hours he fell into a troubled sleep.

He began to dream. He was meeting Lizzie in the wood. It was a sun-dappled afternoon and she reached out and touched him, lifting her skirt and pulling him close. As he went to hold her, he was aware that Silas was sitting on a fallen bough watching them. Jumping up, he and Silas started to struggle, and then suddenly they were at the mill. Silas gave him a mighty push and, overbalancing, he tumbled into the murky vat of fuller's earth. Coming up gasping for breath, he saw the huge hammers spring into action and he knew that at any second they would crush the life out of him. As they descended, he awoke with a jerk and a cry. In the half-light he thought he was wet from the mill water, but as he came to he felt only distress at the shameful release of his need. Burying his face in the pannier that served as a pillow, he prayed:

'Dear God, take away this torment and give me back the only woman I can ever love.'

Part II

August 1588 – May 1590

Chapter One

In the morning, stiff and tired, Will joined the others for breakfast before setting out on the next stage of their journey. They were now aiming for Basing village and once again the memories came flooding back. If all went according to plan, they hoped to reach London in four or five days.

There were no delays or disasters; Basing was followed by Windsor and they continued on towards the city itself. As they approached London, the road became congested with carts and carriages. Flocks of sheep and geese added to the chaos. Will thought to himself that even Newport on market day or the castle with its full garrison was nothing compared with this.

Stopping to ask the way from a carter, he caught his first glimpse of the river. It was alive with boats travelling in every direction.

'Is that the Thames?' he asked the carter.

'Course it is.' The man looked at him as if he were an idiot.

'I just arrived from the Isle o' Wight,' he explained.

The man shrugged and went on his way.

'Don't seem very friendly,' Will observed to Danyel.

'That's cause there's too many of them. They ain't got time for strangers.'

Will thought to himself it was a sad place that didn't let folk get to know each other, but he said nothing.

From now on their road ran parallel with the river. On their left the finest houses imaginable faced the other bank and their back entrances, past which they were travelling, lead into yards and stables. It was dusk when they finally stopped at one of these.

'Here we are,' one of the guards announced.

'Is this Somerset House?'

'Aye.'

Will stood gaping at the mansion. The size was breathtaking and he felt dwarfed as they stepped into the stable yard. They were directed first to the kitchen and then on to spend the night in the loft above the stables.

Will was too tense to sleep. The sound of carriages and revellers went on into the night and he lay awake trying to think of a way to get a message to Lizzie. Danyel was an obliging chap but he could hardly ask him to pass on word to the wife of the Caulbourne fuller. He could only hope that in the way that gossip spread, somebody might mention that the party travelling to London, which included Will Gosden, had arrived safely. For as long as he stayed in the city there would be no contact with Caulbourne unless Fate played one of her tricks, but this was too forlorn a hope to offer much comfort.

The noise hardly abated and he had to drag himself from the straw when the others got up at six. With genuine regret he said goodbye, for they were returning to the island that day. It was Saturday and he was now free until starting work on Monday morning.

The first thing was to find somewhere to stay. Carrying his pannier, he wandered out into the city. The roads seemed too narrow for all the traffic and overhead houses jutted out, each storey wider than the one below so that in some places there was barely a foot between the upper floors on each side. As a result the streets seemed dark even in the full sunshine.

After a prolonged drought, the dust was easily stirred by each passing traveller and damped down only by horse urine and the contents of slop buckets emptied from the windows above. Will learned quickly to keep to the outer edges.

Seeing a tavern on the next corner, he went inside.

'I'm looking for a room,' he told the innkeeper.

The man was burly and heavy-jowled. As he talked, he surveyed Will with hostile eyes.

'You got plenny o' money?'

'Enough.' Will eyed him warily and gripped his pannier tightly.

158

'It'll cost you fourpence a night or twopence sharing. Food is extra.'

'Sharing,' Will replied. He calculated that at this rate he would run out of money long before the first quarter day's pay fell due.

'How long?'

'Two nights, but I want to see the room first.'

The man shrugged and led the way up a narrow stairway. Pushing open a door he indicated a tiny, dark, evil-smelling cubbyhole. Inside an old man was sprawled on the only bed, his mouth open. From the doorway Will could smell his breath.

'No.' Shaking his head, he backed down the stairway and without another word stepped out into the crowded street.

His resolve was weakening. Everywhere seemed unfriendly, devoid of kindness. He longed for the familiarity of the island.

Walking until his feet ached, he called at another inn. It seemed brighter than the other, less dilapidated.

'How much is a room?' he asked.

'Sixpence,' the keeper replied. As Will hesitated, he added: 'Fourpence sharing.'

Will nodded. He was beginning to feel desperate. 'I'll take it – for one night.'

He paid the fourpence and another groat for a bowl of stew, then went up to the room. He was so tired that, using his pannier as a pillow, he fell asleep immediately, not even stirring when his roommate arrived.

The next day being Sunday, he set out in search of the nearest church. For the first time in his life he was praying totally among strangers and the knowledge left him feeling alone and homesick. As he came out of the church he was surprised to find people milling around the streets. It struck him that London must be a godless place, for at home everybody would have been at the service.

He was now free to go and explore. There was something about the city that soon set his blood racing – the bustle, the famous landmarks that were now within walking distance. Every few paces there was something to stop and admire.

Going to the river, he gazed up at the tall spire of St Paul's until his neck ached, and paying a penny he went to the top so that he could see right across the city. The grand houses of the

159

nobility were surrounded by a jumble of hovels, the narrow thread of the streets weaving a pattern as far as he could see. It was not possible to distinguish where the city walls ended, for a sprawl of shacks and tenements tumbled over the wall and away into the distance. Intersecting it ran the silver ribbon of the Thames.

When he had picked out Somerset House he descended and walked the short distance to the Tower. Here as everywhere building work was in progress and he lingered a long while. It was here that Sir George's great-aunt Queen Anne Boleyn had ended her days. The idea of killing a monarch and a woman was beyond his comprehension.

He was beginning to feel hot and tired, but before finding somewhere cheaper to rest for the night he thought he should locate the building site where he would start work next morning.

'Where's Black Friars?' he asked a pedlar who had set up his stall near the Tower.

''T ain't far. You can take a short cut through that alley.' He pointed to a narrow pathway between what looked like storehouses.

Nodding his thanks, Will stepped into the gloom. The path sloped steeply and his shoulders almost brushed the walls on each side. Halfway down there was a column of sunlight where another alleyway intersected his path.

As he approached it, everything happened at once. Suddenly he was surrounded by men. Almost before he could register that they were there, one had pinioned his arms behind him while a second grabbed his pannier and a third struck him a blow across the face, followed by a kick in the ribs that left him gasping for breath. He fell heavily against the wall as the men ran off down the alley and out of sight. For some moments he stayed where he was, pain and dizziness paralysing him, then he struggled to his feet, holding the wall for support, and gazed hopelessly down the now empty alley.

In near despair he realised that, with the exception of half a crown which he was carrying in a purse about his waist, all his belongings and savings had been in his pannier. He started back towards the Tower, thinking that the pedlar might well be involved but either way it wouldn't make any difference. He was now alone in London with nowhere to stay and half a crown between him and destitution. The only comfort was the knowledge that he had a job and, retracing his steps, he went in search of the Black Friars site.

Once he had found it, he climbed painfully through a hole in the surrounding palisade and surveyed the scene. The building work was already under way and he inspected the partly constructed scaffolding. Poplar and alder trunks had been set into barrels of packed earth and lashed together with bast ropes made from the bark of lime trees. He was relieved to see that the methods were familiar to him. Looking around, he noticed a makeshift lean-to and decided that he could shelter there for the night.

Desperately in need of food and drink, he left the site and went in search of something cheap to tide him over. For three farthings he bought a loaf of bread and a mug of beer, then, feeling exhausted by pain and shock, he returned to the site and made himself a niche in the lean-to, falling into a troubled sleep.

Twice he awoke thinking that he was being attacked and his bruised ribs kept him awake for much of the night. Before daybreak he dragged himself up and back through the hole in the palisade and waited in the morning chill for the workmen to arrive.

The overseer was instantly recognisable by his manner. Greyed by both age and stone dust, he appeared a uniform colour from hair to boots. As Will was preparing to approach him, he came over.

'You the country chap?'

'William Gosden.' Will bowed his head and swallowed hard.

'I'm Ned Mounthampton. I'm in charge of this job so you'll be answerable to me.' Looking closer at Will, he added: 'What you done to your face?'

'Just a little accident,' Will replied, not wishing to confess his naivety in allowing himself to be robbed.

'You had much experience?' the older man asked.

'I've served with a good master. I been working on Sir George Carey's house on the Isle of Wight.'

'Right. Come with me.' He led the way across the site to a group of his men.

161

'This 'ere's Will,' he announced. 'He says he's good at his job so he can show us how 'tis done in the country.'

Will looked up at the scaffolding. A young man about his own age was tightening the lashings by driving wooden wedges into them and two others were manhandling a wooden hurdle into place.

'Right, up you go,' said Mounthampton. 'I'll be keeping an eye on ye so just make sure ye give a good day's work.'

'I always do that, sir,' Will replied.

'You do?' The overseer grinned wryly.

Will shinned up the scaffolding, hiding the pain from his injured side, and balanced precariously on the hurdle. Below, a block of stone secured by a pair of huge iron tongs was manoeuvred into place. As one man turned the handle, the tongs tightened their grip and the stone was winched up and manhandled into place. Will took the brunt of the weight.

He worked steadily until nammet-time, only they didn't call it that. He realised unhappily that he had nothing to eat. Feeling embarrassed, he sat a little apart from the group of masons, carpenters and their boys while they supped their ale and tucked into fish pies, this being a Wednesday. The young man who had tightened the scaffolding noticed his predicament.

'Nothing for your break?' he asked.

'I come straight from where I stayed,' Will lied. He didn't mention that he had forgone breakfast too and that his stomach was churning.

''Ere, have some of this.' The lad held out a jagged piece of pie and his drinking flask. 'Share an' share, that's my motto.'

Gratefully Will took them, trying not to seem too desperate. The lad watched him as he ate, his striking blue eyes wide with curiosity.

'You come in a boat?' he asked.

'Yeah.'

'All the way?'

'No. I rode a horse up for my master.'

'What's it like on that island – where you lives?'

Will shrugged. 'It's quiet,' he answered eventually.

'I ain't never been out o' London. Don't think I want to neither.'

162

They were both silent for a while, then the young man asked: 'Where you living, then?'

Will hesitated. 'I ain't got a room yet,' he replied, then as an afterthought: 'I dunno where to look.'

His companion did not answer immediately. Finally he looked up.

'You can come home with me if you don't mind doubling up. It's up to you. It ain't much but my mum'll give you summat to eat and if you can pay towards it she'll be grateful.'

'I got money,' Will offered.

'Yeah, well, don't tell everyone.'

They sat in silence listening to the conversation around them and it was soon time to start work again.

'What's your name?' asked Will, getting up.

'Gilbert Bowyer. Me friends call me Bo.' He grinned. 'That's bootiful in French.'

He was shorter than Will, with sturdy legs and a broad chest. His light hair, although untrimmed, gave him an angelic appearance.

'Me grandad made longbows but there ain't much call for them now so that's why I took up carpentry.'

'You still serving your time?' asked Will.

'One year to go.'

By now they were back at work and the conversation ended.

Now that he had a friend, Will felt more cheerful and the day passed quickly. When work finished they set out through the maze of smelly lanes into Cheapside.

The house where the Bowyers lived had once been a handsome town residence but was now occupied by two other families. It looked forlorn as if it had a life of its own and had fallen on hard times.

As they entered, Will had the impression of a whole army of children gazing up at him. He later came to realise that there were five. From the smoky depths of the room a woman emerged, wiping her hands in her skirt. She looked tired and worn down by life.

'Ma, this 'ere's Will what's working with me. He ain't got nowhere to go so I said he could bunk up with us.'

The woman appeared too tired to register any emotion and Will nodded towards her in embarrassment.

'Ain't but a scrap o' halibut in the stew,' she said, looking at her son.

'Don't matter. Will says he'll pay.'

There was the faintest glimmer in her tired eyes and she nodded and turned back to the blackened depths of the room.

The little ones gathered around him before they were chivied away with affectionate pushes by their brother. Will was suddenly aware of someone else at the back of the room, an older girl, painfully thin and struggling with an armful of wood for the fire.

'Who's that?' he asked.

'That's Rose,' said Bo dismissively.

The girl lowered her eyes and hobbled over to join the old lady.

'She's your eldest sister?' Will enquired.

Bo shrugged. 'I don't think so. Afore he died, Pa brought her here. She helps Ma.' With a sly grin he added: 'Knowing Pa, she might be me sister after all.'

Will was still watching the girl. He felt an unaccountable pity for her. Her white, oval face contained the palest eyes, contrasting starkly with her black hair.

'What's wrong with her leg?' he asked.

'Dunno. It's always been like that.'

Will sighed, glancing after the girl, and turned to follow his friend up the ladder to the room above.

Looking around in the semidarkness, his heart sank. The room was bare except for piles of mattresses, blankets and what could only be described as rags. They seemed to be everywhere. The stale smell of human sweat permeated the air and Will thought to himself that he had never seen this sort of poverty before. He wished that he could leave but he could not repay the man's kindness with such an insult.

Going back downstairs, they waited in silence for the meagre supper to be dished up. Will was pushed to the front of the queue in spite of his protests and he was uncomfortably aware that he was usurping someone else's place as the others jostled behind him. The watery fish stew was ladled into a grimy wooden bowl and he ate quickly to make the dish available for someone else. It wasn't until later that he realised neither

Widow Bowyer nor the girl Rose had eaten, and with a pang of shame he thought that he must have taken their share.

In spite of the crush and the smell, he slept soundly. The girls shared a bed with their mother at one end of the room and the boys crowded towards the other end, a narrow gap between the bedding denoting the division. Nobody bothered to undress. When Bo shook him to get up the following morning, he felt curiously relaxed.

Coming downstairs they found a breakfast of sorts already laid out for them – two pieces of bread and some watery beer. Bo's nammet was already packed.

''Fraid you'll have to share again,' he said ruefully.

Will had the leather flask that Amy had given him when he left the castle, but he did not like to offer it to be filled in case they had nothing to spare. Instead he turned to Widow Bowyer and awkwardly offered her a sixpence for his keep.

'How many days will that last?' he asked.

She gazed at it hungrily. 'If you can give us one a week it'll keep us – I mean you – well fed,' she answered.

As a journeyman Will would be getting sixpence a day, but his first pay day was not until Michaelmas, eight weeks away. He wished that he had offered the widow less, for he now had only one and ten pence to his name.

The rest of the week passed uneventfully. After church on Sunday he continued his explorations, going as far as London Bridge. As a mason he considered the building problems. Gazing down into the waters, he watched the rapids as the flow was forced between the arches of the bridge, making little waterfalls. Halfway across, the whole centre section could be raised to let tall shipping by. It was truly ingenious.

His thoughts were interrupted by shouting and he turned to watch two carriages trying to pass on the narrow confines between the shops. There was much swearing and cracking of whips before the wheels were extricated.

Stopping to admire the ribbons and laces, canes and gloves in the multitude of shops on each side of the bridge, Will ambled across. He daydreamed about buying Lizzie one of the beautiful dresses displayed. It was in rich green velvet dripping with pearls and the colour would suit her perfectly. His reverie was shattered as he happened to glance up, for there, hanging on spikes at the end of the bridge, was a row of mouldering, disfigured heads. Unthinkingly he grabbed the arm of the nearest passer-by.

'What's that?' he asked, nodding in their direction.

''Ere! What's your meaning?' The man shook him off aggressively.

Will coloured. 'The heads up there,' he added.

'Traitors. Anyone executed at the Tower is hung up there as a warning. Don't you know nothing?'

Sobered by the discovery and embarrassed by the man's response, Will hastened to the other side and put the macabre scene from his mind as the expanse of Whitehall Palace came into view. He hoped he might see the Queen but he was unlucky. By now it was late afternoon. Seeing a crowd of people queuing to take a boat, he approached them.

'How much?' he asked the man in front.

'A penny.'

Reluctantly he retraced his steps and walked back, arriving at the place he now called 'home' in time for supper.

Recounting his adventures to Bo, he was aware of his friend's amusement.

'That ain't nothing,' he replied. 'If you want, I'll take you out and show you some real fun. We'll go down the Bear Garden. You can win a fortune gambling on the fights.' Suddenly grinning, he added: 'There's some of the prettiest doxies you can ever imagine and for a penny they'll let you ...' He leaned over and whispered into Will's ear.

Both men laughed but Will shook his head.

'I think I've seen enough for today,' he replied.

Turning round, he noticed Rose sitting by the hearth shelling eggs for the evening meal. As he looked around, her pale eyes were on him. Quickly she looked away and the prettiest pink flushed over her cheeks. By some strange alchemy Will flushed too.

Chapter Two

Mardi took the role of mother in her stride and was soon making plans to leave the mill and resume her itinerant way of life. It was already September, however, and remembering the winter in the bothy she had a change of heart and decided to stay where she was until the spring. For the time being the regular meals were welcome and when she concentrated hard she had the feeling that Will was a long way away and therefore not to be found.

Mardi watched curiously as her mistress appeared to become more and more obsessed with the baby. Other than feeding it, Lizzie had taken on all the duties of a mother, leaving Mardi free to wander in the woods and amuse herself. She had amassed a huge collection of plants and flowers for her potions. It was a very satisfactory arrangement.

Mardi quite liked the child, particularly the way in which it resembled Will with its similar colouring and deep-set hazel eyes. She promised herself that when the baby reached her tenth year she would give her the garnet brooch after which she was named and tell her about her conception. She saw herself as being rich by then and Will transformed into a duke or a lord.

She could not understand Lizzie's passion for cleaning and cuddling Garnet. It crossed her mind that it was time her mistress had a child of her own, although with that pig's offal for a husband it did not seem very likely.

Wandering in the woods, Mardi went over her first meeting with Lizzie at the Summer Fair and wondered how much her predictions had been ordained and how much they were of her own making. It seemed important, for if she had influenced the

167

future herself, then the child that now sucked at her breast might have grown instead in Lizzie's womb. She allowed a moment of compassion for her mistress's obvious hunger to conceive, but then decided that allowing Lizzie to care for Garnet was sufficient recompense.

She suddenly missed her playing cards, for with them she could have taken a look and seen what was to befall them. As it was, the outlook was blurred by this domesticity and the loyalty that Lizzie engendered. Once she was away from here it would all become clear.

Lizzie sat by the stream nursing her servant's child. Since Garnet's birth she had been convinced that Mardi had no idea how to look after a baby. Looking down at the child nestled in her arms, Lizzie felt a wave of warmth envelop her. This little girl, with her burnished brown, wispy hair and baby-blue eyes now changing to hazel, was much as she would have imagined a child of her own. In her dreams any baby of hers naturally favoured Will.

She rocked herself dreamily. A reflective smile spread over her face, ending with a little laugh of triumph. It was now seven weeks since she had lain with Will in the woods and she had two great prizes that no one could take away from her. She knew for certain that she was pregnant and she was equally certain that the child was Will's.

She had not yet hinted of her condition to anyone, wanting to enjoy it to the full herself before any complications could arise. She also savoured the irony of imagining Silas's pleasure, knowing that she had cuckolded him. He had never doubted that he could father a child in spite of the fact that his two wives had died childless, but Lizzie knew better. She remembered a great shaggy ram her father had once kept all summer. It was for ever mounting the ewes and charging anything in sight that might threaten its domination, but at lambing time not one ewe had given birth.

You're nothing but a dirty old seedless ram, she thought, nursing her satisfaction.

Her one anxiety was that for nearly three moons she had managed to avoid his advances. Once he learned of her condition it was certain that the dates would not tie up. She was

168

also relieved to realise that there was no action she now could take to remedy it. The idea of Silas touching her fell like a shadow on the brightest day.

Getting up, she went back into the mill house and laid the sleeping Garnet in her crib, then set to work to clean and pluck a chicken. She had wrung its neck that morning because it no longer laid. Taking the innards, she stepped outside into the fading sunshine, intending to feed them to the dogs. As she did so she almost walked into a woman. For a moment they stared at each other until recognition dawned.

'May!' Still clutching the giblets, Lizzie opened her arms in greeting, turning her face to kiss her old friend.

'Oh, Lizzie!' May placed her cheek against Lizzie's and it was clear that she was bottling up some worry.

'You go on in.' Lizzie crossed the yard and threw the giblets to the dogs chained at the barn door, then rinsed her hands in the stream before returning indoors.

'And how be you? We never saw you once,' she said, putting another log on the fire and drawing Silas's chair closer for her friend to sit down.

May sank back, her face working as she sought for the right words.

'Aren't you still hired?' Lizzie asked when nothing was forthcoming.

May shook her head, finally answering: 'There was some trouble about a kirtle. They couldn't prove nothing but they reckoned I stole it. Anyhows I can't go nowhere, I'm ...' She glanced at her belly.

'Oh, no!' Lizzie's heart lurched as she thought of the implications. 'Have you told your mam?'

May nodded. 'Father gave me a hiding. He told me to get out and stay as far away as possible. He still ain't got work and Mam's got another littlun.'

'Yes, I know.' It was May's seventh brother and there were five sisters besides. In spite of their grinding poverty they all managed to survive.

'What about the baby's father?' Lizzie asked.

May shook her head again. 'He cleaned the stables. He's left now.'

'You should have told him,' Lizzie insisted, handing her

169

friend a jug of ale, but she put it aside untasted. She was having trouble holding back the tears.

'I couldn't tell him. He used to come down the scullery sometimes teasing us girls and he made me feel silly when I wouldn't let him. He said he did it with all the others and how it was nice.' After a pause she added: 'He said nothing wouldn't happen.' She gave a huge sniff and wiped her nose on the back of her hand.

Lizzie looked pityingly at her friend and did not know what to say.

Noticing the crib, May's eyes opened wide. 'Is that yours?' she asked.

'No. It's my servant's.' Lizzie felt embarrassed at using the word.

'You kept her then even though she was...'

Sensing May's drift, Lizzie interrupted: 'Silas wouldn't consider no more bastards. He's not a charitable man.' Her face coloured at the brutal frankness and she fell silent, wondering what hope she could offer.

May suddenly blubbered: 'I'm that scared. I dunno what they'll do to me.'

'You should have told your master then,' Lizzie said. 'He'd have made him wed you.'

'Oo, I couldn't! Mr Worsley's that fine and proud. I couldn't never speak to him.' She sounded affronted at the very suggestion.

'Well, what about the priest?'

'No! I can't tell no one.'

'Well, they'll find out some time. Isn't there nowhere you can go?'

May shook her head, now crying soundlessly. 'I only knows you,' she sobbed. 'I heard you was wed. I thought as how ...' She could not put it into words.

Lizzie remained silent. She was glad that Silas was no longer constable, for if May was truly homeless and destitute she would certainly be sent to the poorhouse and it would have fallen to him to take her. She could not at that moment visualise him agreeing to let her stay with them. She racked her brains to think of anyone in the village who might take her friend in.

'How far you gone?' she asked to break the silence.

'Three months.'

'I am too,' Lizzie lied, adding a month to her dates.

'You are?' May was gazing at her belly in surprise. 'I thought as how Silas couldn't –' she started, then shut up.

'I'll tell thee what,' Lizzie said, ignoring her friend's remark, 'I'll go and see Mr Worsley and tell him. I'm sure he'll help you.'

'No. Please, Lizzie, you mustn't.'

Lizzie sighed. 'Well, you'd best stay here for tonight.' She wondered what Silas would say.

At that moment Mardi returned. Wishing to see Silas alone, Lizzie sent them both back outside to shut up the stock.

Tidying her thick hair under her white cap, she busied herself preparing the meal and moments later her husband came in.

'Be middling damp out now,' he announced, poking the fire with his boot.

'Aye. I've just had a visitor.' Lizzie took the lid off the black pot and prodded the chicken simmering inside. When he didn't comment, she continued: 'You remember May – Wilkie White's girl? She 'n me been friends for years.'

He still didn't answer so she added: 'She's in a spot of bother. She lost her place and she's got nowhere to go.'

'What's she come here for then?' he asked gruffly.

Lizzie hesitated. 'Her pa won't take her in. I thought just for tonight she could sleep here, you know, just kip down on the floor.'

'Did you? What's her like?'

'Nice. Ordinary. She's my best friend.'

He snorted. 'Where is this best friend then?'

'Helping Mardi shut up the stock.'

He said nothing. Passing him to put bread on the table, Lizzie glanced at his face, trying to assess his reaction. Reaching out, he pulled her to him and rubbed her belly. She managed a smile.

'I'll think on it,' he said, his hand now beneath her skirt. His eyes held hers and she tried not to show her revulsion.

'Best stop now. Someone will walk in at any moment,' she said in a barely controlled voice, her flesh trembling at the hated intrusion. He grinned, prolonging the contact until they heard the two girls coming back.

171

'If I does a good turn and lets your friend stay tonight, then mebbe you can do me one,' he said softly. There was no mistaking his meaning.

Without replying, she moved away. Blind panic crowded in on her. She had done this for Jed. Could she do the same for May? Her mind blacked out the answer.

The evening passed uneventfully. May ate with them and Mardi and the two hired boys waited until they had finished before taking their turn at the table. As bedtime neared, the nightmare of bedding with her husband enveloped her. Struggling to stay in control, she brought some rosehip tea for May and the tonic for Silas. She had doubled the dose.

'We need a bedtime drink,' she said, offering it to him, her hands shaking.

He took it without comment, his eyes on the visitor, and put it aside.

'Seeing as how ye're my wife's friend you can stay tonight,' he said. 'But after that we'll have to see. I'm not a rich man so I can't afford charity to all and sundry.'

May bowed her head and behind his back Lizzie gave him a look of disgust. 'Drink your tonic,' she said aloud, but he ignored her.

A straw pallet was fetched from the lean-to and placed in front of the fire for May to sleep on, and Silas took the candle signalling that it was time to retire. The tonic remained untasted. By now Lizzie's heart was thundering so fast that she could hardly hear what was being said.

Upstairs they undressed in silence. She shivered as she felt the cool linen against her skin. This new trembling disguised her other terrors.

Lumbering into bed beside her, Silas blew out the candle and worked his way down under the cover.

'You think I'm stupid, don't you?' he suddenly said into the darkness. 'That gal's in the family way.'

Lizzie was silent and he turned towards her.

Dear God, no! she prayed.

'You expecting me to let her stay?' he asked.

She hesitated before replying. 'She didn't tell no one at Swaynson about her condition.' Her voice sounded strangled and out of control. 'They might have helped her if she had. If

172

someone don't give her charity she'll end up in the poorhouse. Someone kind and unselfish,' she added.

As he pulled her closer, she said: 'I got something to tell you.' She pushed his hand away.

'What's so important then?'

'I'm going to have a babby.'

The news stopped him in his tracks. 'You sure?'

She nodded.

'Why, that's, that's . . .' He was stunned into silence. ''Ow far you gone?' he finally asked.

'Three moons.'

He nodded and she could feel his satisfaction.

'I knew as how you'd be fertile.' He closed in on her again but she pushed him away.

'No! You mustn't.'

'I'll just do it gentle.'

'No. I – I been bleeding a bit. We shouldn't take no risks.'

Silas let go reluctantly.

For a moment she relaxed, but suddenly he grabbed her wrist.

''Ere, give us your hand.' He placed it on his erection. There was no alternative. He continued to grip her and worked himself into a shuddering excitement, his seed finally bursting into her palm.

She turned her head away in disgust, vowing that as from tomorrow he would take his tonic, come what may. As he started to snore, she drew away and crept out of the bed to clean herself.

Lying as far apart from him as she could, she now had the privacy to escape the present and dream about Will and her baby. Its presence inside her was a miracle, a part of her love that no one could take away. In this knowledge she fell into an exhausted sleep.

The next day, being Sunday, they were all at church for the seven-o'clock service. Afterwards the village men remained on the green to play football. They divided into two unequal teams, one including Harry Galpine on his crutch. Men joined in or dropped out as they wished and the straw-filled pig's

173

bladder was belted up and down the village, the stream being one goal and the road the other.

'Stop our Harry,' Leah begged. 'They're that rough, they'll be the death of him.' But nobody died, although Thomas Urry had his eye blacked and Will Snudden could hardly walk for two days.

Silas had disappeared immediately after the service so Lizzie and May lingered watching the game. It was still in full swing when they made their way back to the mill house to prepare a meal.

About three hours later Silas returned, looking very pleased with himself. Settling into his chair, he ate his dinner with noisy relish and then sat back with a sigh.

'I've thought it all out and your friend can stay with Widow Trykett,' he announced.

'Oo, thankee!' A smile of relief spread across May's face.

Lizzie eyed her husband, assessing his motives.

'Widow Trykett receives the poor rate,' she observed. 'How's she going to be able to feed May?'

Silas hesitated, an expression of modesty on his face.

'Poor woman needs someone to fetch and carry,' he replied. 'So I, er, I'm giving her some money.'

'Oo, thankee.' May bobbed a curtsy and beamed at Lizzie.

'Get her moved in afore dark,' Silas added as he left the table, still wearing the pious expression Lizzie had grown to hate.

It did not take long to move May's belonging the few yards into Widow Trykett's cottage. It was tiny, just one room, and Lizzie gave May the straw mattress to place on the floor next to the old lady's bed and a blanket to cover her. She also took over a jug of ale since the old woman could no longer brew her own.

'I'll see thee soon,' she said, once her friend was settled, and then returned to the mill to finish stitching her new kirtle before it grew too dark to see.

Later that day, as soon as Silas and she were alone, she asked: 'Why you being so generous to May?'

He grinned, unable to hide his satisfaction.

'To tell the truth,' he said, 'I went to see Mr Worsley this morning. I told him what had happened under his roof. He was that upset, he made a settlement for the care of May. He's

174

charged me with looking after her and given enough to keep her for a year.'

'What did he give thee, then?'

Silas smirked. 'He gived me fifteen pounds and I've come to an arrangement with Widow Trykett.' He could not disguise his satisfaction.

'How much did you give her?' Lizzie demanded suspiciously.

'I said I'd give her three pounds each quarter day.' He grinned.

'You greedy rat! You're robbing Mr Worsley and Widow Trykett and May!' Lizzie leaped to her feet in disgust.

'No, I ain't. I'm just taking precautions. If ever they needs any more, I've got it.'

Lizzie snorted in derision. 'And who decides what they need?' she asked.

'Hold your tongue, woman, or I'll belt thee,' he retorted, but as far as she was concerned the point had been made.

The following morning, as Lizzie struggled to get out of bed, a wave of nausea overcame her. Retching, she fell back, her eyes closed, waiting for the torment to subside. Disturbed by her movements, Silas heaved himself up, grunting and puffing.

'You'd best stay there,' he said, levering himself off the bed. 'And don't get hauling they bolts of cloth around in the mill.'

Lizzie didn't answer but stayed gratefully where she was. Soon she could hear him whistling and humming to himself in the kitchen and a while later the familiar noises outside reached her as he prepared to start work. She listened to the water trickling peacefully through the water wheel, now disengaged from the machinery, but before long the great hammers started up, pounding and agitating the woollen cloth steeping in the huge vat of milky fuller's earth. At the end of each process she normally helped to heave it to the bank and spread it out to dry. It would then be shrunk and dressed, ready for dying and use. Today she felt only relief that she had been expressly forbidden to do the work.

The news of her pregnancy spread quickly, announced by the proud father-to-be.

'My wife's took badly,' he told the blacksmith. 'She's conceived and these early days go hard with her.'

'Got to get back home,' he informed the cartwright. 'My wife's having a babby. I gotta keep an eye on her, she's that foolhardy.'

The recipients of the news expressed surprise and offered congratulations to his face and sniggered behind his back. Silas's lechery was renowned and the idea that he had finally succeeded in fathering a child in his fiftieth year struck them as one of God's little jokes.

When Lizzie finally got up, she found the fire alight and freshly drawn water in the pails.

'Did you do this?' she asked Mardi, who was sitting cross-legged on the floor suckling Garnet.

'No. He did.' She pulled her familiar face when referring to Silas.

Kindnesses by Silas were unknown and they unnerved Lizzie. She wanted to hate him, and to justify her feelings she needed him to treat her badly, for how else could she be forgiven for loving Will?·

'Well, I'm having a child so you'll have to work harder now,' Lizzie announced.

To her surprise, Mardi went red and made some incoherent reply, then after a moment asked: 'How far you gone?'

Lizzie started to blush. 'Three months,' she lied.

Even before the words were out, Mardi said: 'Don't fret. The babby's going to be early.'

Lizzie could not meet her all-seeing eyes but, hiding her confusion, mumbled some excuse and set out across the meadow to the Sheepwash to tell her mother the news.

Leah was down in the pasture, picking watercress to flavour the soup she was preparing.

'Well, gal, it's another scorcher,' she said, surveying the September sun.

'Hello, our mam. You ain't doing too much, are you?' Lizzie took her arm and walked the few yards back to the cottage. Harry and Jed were nowhere to be seen.

'Where's our Harry?' she asked.

'Gone on his crutch to see the new cock bird Isaac Stallard's brought from town. It's supposed to be a champion fighter. I heard he paid a shilling for it. Men's got more money than sense.'

176

Lizzie nodded in agreement and accepted a posset that Mam had brewed that morning.

'I got some news,' she said after a few minutes.

Leah waited.

'I'm having a babby.'

'Oh, my dear!' Leah hugged her, stifling a sob. 'It's such good news and yet ...' She held her daughter at arm's length. 'I guessed you might be. You've been so pasty-faced.'

Lizzie remained silent. Hesitating for a moment, Leah added:

'I'm surprised as how Silas managed it after all these years.'

The girl's cheeks were suddenly scarlet. Her mother waited, eyebrows raised and when Lizzie said nothing, added:

''Taint his, is it?'

Lizzie shook her head. 'Don't tell no one, will you?' she pleaded.

'Course I won't. But if I think that, so will others.'

Lizzie sank onto Harry's bed.

'Have you been mucking about with a village lad?' Leah continued.

'No.'

Her mother waited but there was no further explanation so she added: 'Then may I ask who my grandchild is going to favour?'

'Will,' said Lizzie finally.

'Will who?'

'Will Gosden.'

'Ah.' Leah remembered. 'I ain't seen him hereabouts.'

'He ain't. He just come over once or twice.'

'Are you gonna tell him?'

Lizzie shook her head. 'He's gone away.'

'I see.' Leah took her daughter's hand. 'Least said then.' Lizzie nodded, her eyes downcast, memories of Will flooding in.

'What do Silas say?' her mother asked to distract her.

'He's pleased as a pup with two tails.'

'Good. Best leave it that way.'

Chapter Three

In spite of the Bowyers' kindness, Will resolved that when payday came he would find himself somewhere of his own to live, nothing grand but somewhere that would allow him some privacy. Even as a child at Granfer Gosden's he had been able to hide in the loft or out in the fields, but here there was nowhere that he could ever be alone. He mentioned this to Bo but his friend seemed surprised.

'Never been by meself,' he observed, and his tone implied that he didn't particularly want to either.

The one restraining factor, apart from the cost, was the knowledge that his sixpence was a vital part of the housekeeping. He wondered if he could make some compromise and pay to take some meals with the family but live elsewhere. He would never forget that in their own way they had been good to him.

By now it was moving towards winter and Will decided to postpone any thoughts of leaving until the spring. That way he would have the shared warmth in the upstairs room at nights and the company on the long dark evenings.

By giving an extra groat at Christmas, Will and Bo were able to buy a goose and a rabbit to feed them all during the festive time. Will also delighted in buying New Year's gifts for every member of the family. They were only little things, games and toys and sweetmeats, but the pleasure they brought would cheer up the household. From a pedlar he selected a kerchief for Widow Bowyer and a sturdy knife for Bo. He was about to start for home when he realised that he had nothing for the girl Rose.

Looking around, his eyes fell on a tiny brooch in the shape of a bow with the palest stone forming the knot in the centre. He picked it up, turning it over in his hand, and asked the price. The stone reminded him of Rose's pale eyes and with shame he remembered the garnet and ruby clasps. Now, here he was thinking how this would complement Rose. Yet he could honestly say he did not find Rose remotely comely or desire her except in so far as he very much had need of a woman. She was so thin and pale and not at all pretty or lively, not like Lizzie – or the other one, come to that.

With a shrug he produced a coin and held it out to the man. He had to buy the girl something so why should it not be a brooch? He doubted if anyone had ever given her a gift in her life. In his mind's eye he could see her limping about the cottage, her small shoulders hunched, hardly opening her mouth, a tiny impassive figure, and he knew that his feeling was only compassion. Pocketing the brooch, he put all thoughts of the girl from his mind and returned home.

Christmas passed uneventfully and, except for the grinding poverty of his surroundings, Will felt at ease in his new life. Of late, however, he had noticed that in spite of the extra four pence he gave to Mistress Bowyer, there was often insufficient wood or candles to cook and see by. Along with every other Londoner, he was aware that living costs were mounting almost daily.

A few days after returning to work from the Christmas festivities, he awoke in the early hours of morning to the sound of crying. It was a muted, hopeless sobbing and he strained his ears trying to recognise who it could be. After a while the girl, for girl it was, got up quietly and fumbled her way down the ladder to the lower room. Will waited for a moment and when no one else followed, he did so.

The hunched figure crouched near the blackened pile of ashes where the last fire had burned, as if trying to draw some heat from it by association. As he went to move forwards, she detected his presence and jumped awkwardly to her feet. It was Rose.

'Why do you weep?' he whispered.

She shook her head but tears still ran unchecked down her cheeks.

'What is it? Come on, you can surely tell me.'

Will took her arm and led her to the solitary bench that served as seating for all of them. She sank down dejectedly and cried. Just when he thought she was not going to reply, she said: 'I have to leave. Mistress can't afford to feed me any more. I take up too much room; I've got to go.'

'Where to?' Will bent closer and laid his hand on her shoulder.

She shook her head, still sniffing back the tears.

'I don't know. Perhaps they'll take me at the poorhouse.' She bit the side of her thumb to hold back her terror. 'I'm not much use,' she whispered. 'I can't work proper, not with my leg. I'm a burden to everyone.'

'Course you're not.' Will squeezed her arm and then stepped back, wondering what best to do. He felt an overwhelming pity for the girl, for he knew only too well how it felt not to belong.

'Don't you fret,' he told her. 'I'll talk to Mistress Bowyer when I return this evening. There's nothing to worry about; we'll work something out.'

Rose looked up at him gratefully and he winked at her, a gesture that was out of character but had the desired effect of bringing a watery smile to her thin, tear-streaked face. Gently he ushered her back up the stairs, then returned to the solitude of the living room wondering how best to help this poor, unloved waif. Apart from offering the Bowyers more money, he had no solution.

When morning came he felt tired, but before leaving for work he had a brief word with Mistress Bowyer. The widow was strangely adamant.

'She's got to go,' she said with finality. 'I'm not blaming the girl but there just ain't a place for her here any more.'

Will acknowledged that the younger ones were growing but he had the feeling that this was not the whole story. He waited but it seemed that the discussion was closed.

'Well, perhaps we can sort something out tonight,' he said as he left, but Mistress Bowyer merely grunted.

It had not taken Will long to establish his reputation as a good journeyman. His decorative work was much admired and when the job at Black Friars drew to an end he had been offered another one at Clark's Well. It meant at least six months' work and an unbelievable eight pence a day wages.

With all of this to contemplate, he called at the Bell Inn, where he now considered himself a regular, and supped a pint of beer. Sitting there, he returned to the problem of Rose's future. As far as he could see, if she left the Bowyer household, it meant either the poorhouse or the whorehouse, and neither of them offered her any sort of future worth living. If it was really a question of space, he would rather leave himself than let Rose be thrown to the wolves. When he got home he would put this to the widow.

He had arrived at the inn later than usual with Bo, but his friend had gone off with one of the doxies who frequented the inn.

'Come on, Will,' Bo had cajoled. 'It's only a bit of fun.'

Will had grinned but declined.

'Don't you like women?' Bo asked after a pause.

'Course I do, but I'm fussy.' Will had laughed, but in truth, while a part of him wanted to join in the fun, not think about anything other than the immediate gratification, something always stopped him. He didn't know if it was loyalty to Lizzie or the fact that it was fornication or the risk of catching the pox. Whatever the reason, he remained celibate and his unsatisfied need was the only scar on his otherwise smooth landscape.

While he was thinking, he caught a glimpse of a man half hidden by an archway. For a second he could have sworn that it was Hilton Kingswell from Yarmouth, whose barge had carried him across the Solent, but the next moment the man was obscured and Will told himself that he must have been mistaken. A second later, however, he was back in view and Will was on his feet and going across to him.

'Hilty?'

The visitor rose from the wooden bench. 'Will Gosden? Well, I'll be ...' They clapped each other on the shoulders, laughing at the coincidence.

'What you doing here?' asked Will.

'Come up on me boat, didn't I, with some timber. What about you?'

181

'I been here six months. I'm working, don't you remember?'

Hilton nodded. 'That's right. I took you across.'

The conversation followed predictable lines and Will bided his time until finally he asked:

'Any news of things down Caulbourne way?'

Hilton shook his head. 'Same as usual, I guess.'

'Do you ever see anything of the Galpines?' Will continued as casually as he could manage.

'I knows 'Erbert – him what's the wheelwright.'

'I was thinking of them down Sheepwash.' Will paid for more drinks and felt his mouth go dry.

'Is that George?'

'Aye.' His heart now deafened him.

'Their son lost his leg,' Hilton offered.

'I heard that. Er, what about their gal – Lizzie, was it?'

When Hilton looked blank, he added:

'Married to the fuller.'

'Ah, yeah. I know who you mean. Young, pretty girl and him old enough to be her father.'

Will's face blazed and he nodded.

'Her's in the family way, would you believe? That old goat was at Yarmouth not long ago. The way he goes on you'd think no one else had ever done it. Right old sod he is women, too.'

Will heard no more. The thought of Lizzie pregnant with Silas Dore's child made his body ache to the very fingertips.

'I've got to go,' he said abruptly.

'Right, Will.' Hilton blinked in surprise. 'Well, nice to see you,' but already the younger man had turned and was pushing his way to the door.

Outside he walked blindly.

It don't make no difference, he tried to tell himself, but his jealousy crucified him with pain. He turned into the Angel, where he ordered one drink and then another. The presence of the other customers intruded on his misery and he left, only to call at the next inn, then the next. Everywhere he could see Silas Dore's degenerate face.

'I'll kill him,' he said out loud, the world seeming suddenly blurred.

By the time he had left the next inn he was too drunk to find his way home. By sheer chance he stumbled down an alleyway and emerged almost opposite his lodgings.

Banging on the door, he fell in as it opened. Everyone with the exception of Rose was in bed and she peered at him with wide, frightened eyes. The last thing he remembered was the room spinning and a sudden nausea. Retching violently, he vomited over the floor and passed out.

It was Rose who cleaned up and dragged him away from the mess and into a corner, putting a log under his head and her shawl over him. When he awoke at first light with a thundering head and a pain in his belly, it was her that he first saw, hobbling around the table laying it for breakfast.

Struggling up, he groaned and sank back against the wall.

'Anything you want?' she asked quietly.

The memory of last night's news forced its way back into his mind and he closed his eyes. He had never felt more desolate. He seemed to sit motionless for hours but when he finally opened his eyes Rose was still there at the table. He called to her.

'Come here a minute.'

She limped across to him and stood staring down with her gentle, sad eyes.

'Come here,' he repeated and she bent down beside him. He reached out and took her hand, tracing the line of her small square fingers.

'Do you like me?' he asked, looking up at her.

Flushing, she lowered her eyes and he sensed rather than saw the nod of her head.

For a long time they were silent. Then, with a barely perceptible sigh, he said:

'You've got nowhere to go and I need to get away from here. Will you marry me?'

She did not reply but he saw that she was crying. Her silent, passive tears tore at his heart and he pulled her to him and rocked her against his chest.

'Don't cry, sweetheart,' he begged. 'I promise I'll take care of you better than anyone ever has before.' And, cradling her against his chest, he vowed never to allow Lizzie Dore into his thoughts again.

True to his word, he set about arranging their marriage and leased a tiny house not far away from the Bowyers. It was stone-built although tumbling down, and in his spare time Will set to work making it weatherproof and building over the earth floor. He even installed a chimney.

When Widow Bowyer learned of their wedding plans, she was moved to tears.

'You're a good man, Will. I know she's got her drawbacks, what with being crippled and all, but she's got a good nature and – well, if you're going to wed her, then you ought to know what there is to know. She was a foundling. Walter – he was my husband – found her when she was no more than eight. Just sitting in the gutter, she was. I think if he hadn't of brought her home she would have died. There's some as said it would have been better if she had, what with her handicap and all, but she's been a godsend to me.' She gave a mirthless little laugh. 'She ain't our flesh – well, anyone can see that – but I reckons she comes from good stock somewhere along the line. She ain't never said a word, though.'

Will listened abstractedly, nodding as and where necessary. He didn't regret his decision, spontaneous as it had been, but he wished he could feel a wild, tingling love for his bride-to-be. Perhaps it didn't matter. She would take away the ache that was always with him and she would look after his food and the house and just be there. The other one – he could not even allow himself to think of her name – she was somebody else's. She had been right when she said it was God's will. Who was he to challenge the Almighty – and yet? Perhaps it was God's will that he should take this pale girl to his bed and give her children, only they wouldn't have copper hair and green eyes. At the memory of Lizzie's colouring, he leaped to his feet, startling Mistress Bowyer, who stopped her monologue and went back to her chores.

When he broke the news to Bo, he was surprised at his friend's reaction.

'You serious?' he asked and his face flushed. Will wondered if he had had any serious intentions towards the girl himself. As far as he had observed, Bo either ignored her or was disparaging whenever he referred to her.

'You don't mind?' he asked.

184

'Course I don't.' He laughed but it lacked conviction and he still seemed ill at ease.

'As a matter of fact,' Will added, 'I was going to ask you to give her away. As head of the family. I suppose I need your consent.'

'I suppose you do.' Bo stretched, flexing his muscles. 'Well, if you're sure that's what you want . . .' He didn't finish but patted his friend on the shoulder.

'Right, our Will, so be it.'

Chapter Four

On the eve of Christmas 1588 a harsh frost enveloped Caulbourne village. The mill wheel was stilled as the stream froze and it remained so for weeks. It took Silas, the hired boys, Mardi and Lizzie all their time just to keep the stock alive.

During the summer Silas had eighty sheep grazing on the downland, but only twenty pregnant ewes remained to overwinter. The first lambs to be born died within hours from the cold, so Silas moved the rest of the ewes into the barn to give their offspring a fighting chance.

Breaking the ice on the bucket so that they could drink, he thought that the following summer he would allow his flock to run on the downs with his father-in-law's, thereby saving the services of a shepherd. He was also building a new loom and planned that that one-legged Harry should come and work for him in return for George's use of the mill. There was no point in having a lot of unnecessary relatives unless one got something out of them.

Through the doorway he surveyed the icy scene. The horse was out in the meadow, nickering for attention. Lizzie had made Farmer a coat out of an old bolt of cloth that had gone wrong. Silas shook his head at the thought of it. That woman gave the horse more attention than she ever gave to him. In a spiteful moment he wondered whether to sell it but it was too useful.

Lizzie's belly was now swelling and he congratulated himself on the prospect of his son. In fact, many a village bloke must envy him his mill and his pretty wife. The only trouble was that she still managed to avoid his advances by some means or other. During the day when he felt like it there was always somebody about and he was always whacked at night. He had stopped taking the tonic because he wasn't sure it didn't have the opposite effect, and after a few days he really thought he felt better, but Lizzie had persuaded him that it was full of herbs to help his screws and the wind, and he had to admit it did make him sleep well. He sighed.

One afternoon he had sent Mardi off to the mill to shift some old stuff and told her not come back until she was called. He had made plans to take Lizzie to bed but she had been that sulky, saying it was bad for the baby and wrong to waste God's good daylight in such a way. Saucy little minx! He had had a mind to beat her but in the end he had let her go, and by that night he had just dropped off as usual. It was a mystery.

Lizzie was out now somewhere visiting that mother of hers or her fat friend or some other old biddy in the village. She had a sight too much freedom. He glanced round at the boys struggling with the dripping bolts of cloth and then across at the house. The skivvy was over there now. He smirked to himself. That Mardi had filled out since she'd whelped, but she was too lippy and he'd had to lay a birch on her several times. He smiled at the memory of feeling her breasts when he had grabbed hold of her. She had tried to kick and bite, the little vixen, but he'd struck her a blow on the back where Lizzie wouldn't see it, just to remind her who was master.

Gauging the time to be about three of the clock, he guessed that Lizzie wouldn't be back for a while. Making up his mind, he gave the lads enough work to keep them busy, then made his way across the ruts to the house.

Mardi was grinding up malt ready for the next brewing as he walked in along with a vicious blast of wind. He strode across to the fireplace and held his numbed fingers over the warmth.

''Ere. Come and stoke this fire,' he called.

Mardi put the bowl and pestle down and picked up some logs from the hearth, placing them criss-cross over the burning fire. As she went to get up, Silas moved behind her.

'I wants to see under yer skirt,' he said into her ear, grabbing her and starting to pull up her dress.

'Get off or you'll be sorry!' she shrieked, struggling to get away from him. He tightened his arms about her and pushed

187

his knee under her legs so that she overbalanced. As she fell he pulled the skirt up to her waist, exposing the black triangle of her groin. His breathing came heavily as he poked his fingers inside, feeling the soft, pliant flesh. Holding her fast with one knee across her belly, he started to struggle out of his breeches, longing only for the pleasure of thrusting into her, but as he released his hold for a second a sharp pain in the calf of his leg made him jump back with shock. The girl had bitten him.

'You little trollop!' Before he could stop her she had struggled free and was on the other side of the table, her face contorted with rage.

'Don't you touch me, you stinking bag of wind!' she snarled. 'I know things that would make your blood freeze. If it wasn't for mistress I'd put a curse on this house.'

He made a lunge at her but she was too quick for him and was already by the door.

'You've done it now!' she spat. 'I swear you'll regret this. You think you're going to have your way with me while mistress is carrying. Well, you ain't. What's more, you ain't never going to have no children 'cause I'll curse your balls off.'

'Don't you threaten me, you she cat!' He blundered around the table just as the door opened and Lizzie stepped into the room.

'What's going on?' she asked, looking from one to the other.

Silas grabbed Mardi's arm.

'This ungrateful little heathen's been stealing,' he said. 'I'm going to give her what for.'

'What did she do?' Lizzie was looking at her servant as she spoke.

'Took money from me chest.'

'I didn't! You lying devil!' Mardi wriggled like a snake. 'He's been trying to ram me,' she shouted as he struck out and caught her a blow across the face.

'Stop it!' Lizzie grabbed his arm and hustled her way between them. 'You been bothering her?' she demanded.

'What do you take me for? Dirty little trollop like that? I gave her house room out o' Christian charity and this is the reward I get.' His outrage bubbled up and, pushing Lizzie aside, he began to shake the girl. Grabbing the birch from the alcove, he lashed out.

188

'That'll teach you to steal and lie,' he said, hitting her again. 'That'll teach ye to blacken my character!'

'Stop it!' Lizzie's face was scarlet with fury. 'I don't believe a word you're saying,' she shouted. 'I know you and your filthy ways. If you touch her ever again, I'll tell the priest.'

Mardi had struggled free and was easing the dress away from her stinging back.

The anger had blown itself out and Silas replaced his birch in the alcove with as much dignity as he could muster.

'You'd both better watch out,' he threatened, but it had no teeth. With a grunt he went out and back across the yard to the barn.

Left alone, the two women eyed each other uneasily. There was no suggestion of mistress and servant now, but rather two victims of a brutish tyrant.

'He'll be sorry,' Mardi finally said. 'I'll put a curse on him what he'll regret all his life.'

'No!' Lizzie shook her head at the impetuous folly.

'Don't you worry, mistress. I've fixed him.'

'You mustn't utter such things. It's madness.'

Mardi merely smiled. 'It's the truth,' she insisted.

'No,' her mistress repeated, but her voice lacked conviction and both of them knew that they would rejoice to see him rot.

Chapter Five

By Easter Will had made his wedding plans. He knew that it would have been easier to make a public declaration and simply move in with Rose, but he felt he needed a personal and public contract with God to ensure the binding nature of their union.

He bought a fancy doublet for himself and a new dress and a lace bonnet for Rose. After the wedding day they would be able to wear them regularly to church, and he was aware that in the city fashion was very much a part of life. He had realised soon after his arrival that Bo, although only an apprentice and coming from a very poor family, spent all his money on fine apparel. This weakness brought him an equal amount of teasing and criticism from those at work, but he seemed indifferent to their opinions. Will felt that it was none of his business, although he could never imagine being such a peacock himself. The old habits of saving and making do were with him for life.

Since their betrothal, his relationship with Rose had barely changed. He had made no sexual overtures to her and they continued to sleep as before, the whole family segregated into two groups in the upper room. His appetite for the wedding night grew daily.

The ceremony at the local church was simple. Rose was led to the church by two of the Bowyer brothers and the rest of the family were there as witnesses. Standing at her side, Will made his responses to the priest and had the feeling that he was bolting himself into a cage from which there was no escape.

Afterwards the whole family came back to see the new house. Rose, now Mistress Gosden, served up the sweetmeats and honeyed cinnamon cakes with the same humility that she had always shown as a skivvy.

'A long and happy life,' Bo toasted them, raising his beaker of elderflower wine.

'Happy life,' came the chorus.

'Thank'ee all. We'll be happy enough, won't we?' Will put his arm around his bride and squeezed her shoulders. She remained passively at his side, her eyes lowered.

'Right, then, us'll be getting along.' Bo chivied the family together. Will noticed that his eyes were on Rose but she did not look up.

'Go at it, mate.' At the door Bo punched the bridegroom on the shoulder. 'I'll think of you when I'm at the Bell tonight.'

'You go careful. You'll get in trouble one o' these days,' Will chided, but his friend merely grinned.

Once they were alone there was an awkward silence.

'Right,' said Will to break the tension. Rose went to move away but he caught her arm.

'Give us a kiss then, Mistress Gosden.' His voice was unsteady, partly from the wine, partly from anticipation.

'I'd best clear up first,' she said, her voice barely audible.

'No. I'll help in a minute.' He raised her face and touched his lips gently against hers. Her body was tense and she was shaking.

'Don't be afraid,' he said into her hair. 'I'm your husband. I'll look after you. I won't never hurt you.' She sagged against him and he kissed her forehead before letting her go.

They both kept themselves busy with unnecessary tasks until it was bedtime. Will poured out the rest of the wine and forced the girl to drink some.

'Help you relax,' he promised.

She sipped it demurely. There was no upstairs and their bed in the corner of the room loomed out of all proportion to its size.

'Come on and sit down.' Will took her hand and lead her across to it, dropping down and pulling her beside him. He could feel her reluctance.

His own need was such that he closed his mind to her resistance. Unfastening her cap, he loosened her hair and watched it tumble down her back. It was thick and very black

191

and he smoothed his hands down over it, thinking that it was really very beautiful. Moving his hands back again up under her hair, he started to undo the hooks of her dress. She arched herself against him and gave a little moan of fear.

'Hush, sweetheart. Don't you worry about nothing.' He unfastened the dress with clumsy fingers and eased it down. Her tiny breasts brought a surge of tenderness and he bent to kiss them. Feeling her anguish, he took both her hands in his.

'After the first time you'll get to like it,' he promised. 'It's natural, ain't it? Trust me and I'll make it easy for you.'

She suddenly began to struggle and scream. Instinctively he grabbed her arms and rolled onto her to keep her from striking out.

'Stoppit! I know it's your first time but you gotta go through with it.'

'No!' Her wail arrested his progress and he drew back. The ambiguity of her cry dawned on his fuddled brain.

'What do you mean by no?' he asked.

She was silent, her eyes closed, her head swaying from side to side with emotion. Finally she looked up at him and said:

'I ain't no maid. How could I be? You don't know what's been going on.'

Will took a moment to absorb what she had said.

'You mean you been ...' He didn't finish his sentence.

'I ain't been doing nothing. I didn't have no say, did I?'

'How come?' His fingers were biting into her wrists but she did not seem to feel the pain.

'You don't know nothing.' She sounded disillusioned, exhausted. 'For a while I thought you understood but you don't.'

'Understood what? What are you telling me?'

When she did not answer, he continued: 'You been going with someone else? Who? Who is it?'

She shrugged.

'Why do you think old man Bowyer took me in?' Her bitterness shook him. 'Mistress was in the family way again. He used to make me sleep on the outside so as he could touch me, then later ...'

Will's hatred for the dead man came bubbling up. He grabbed his bride and held her close.

'Don't think on it,' he said tersely. 'He's been gone two years. 'Tweren't your fault.'

Determinedly Rose freed herself and held him away. 'It didn't stop when he died,' she said bitterly.

'I don't understand.' For a moment Will thought that the ghost of old man Bowyer had come back to possess her.

'Why don't you think!' She was shaking with anger and he had never seen her like this before.

'You're Bo's friend. You know what he's like. Well, I'm not his sister so he couldn't see no reason why he shouldn't follow in his father's footsteps.'

'No!' Will turned away. 'I don't want to hear this. Tell me it ain't true!' He began to shake her.

'Don't you think I want it not to be true?' She was crying. 'What could I do about it? I thought about running away but the only way I could survive was by doing the same thing out in the city. At least where I was I had Mistress. She was good to me. I don't think she ever realised what was going on.'

Will pushed her aside and grabbed his boots.

'Where you going?' She was off the bed, still half naked, holding his arm to restrain him. He shook her off with such force that she stumbled back and without a glance he was out of the door and into the street.

All the time her words were pounding in his ears: 'He didn't see why he shouldn't follow in his father's footsteps.' The son of Satan! He stumbled into the Bell, then on to the round of taverns frequented by the man he had called friend. Not finding him, he finally arrived at the Bowyers' house.

A candle flickered inside and he thundered on the door before forcing it open.

'Bowyer! Where are you, you Devil's piss?'

Widow Bowyer stood by the table. Her hands shot to her breast in alarm.

'Will! Whatever be the matter?' Her fear changed to concern.

'Where is he?' Will demanded.

'Where's who?' She reached out to him but he was across the room and up the ladder. The children were huddled together, looking at him wide-eyed. Coming back down, he looked at the woman who had been so kind to him.

'Didn't you know?' he asked. 'Didn't you know your son was poking your skivvy – or did you think it didn't matter?'

'You must be mistaken.' Her distress was genuine.

''Tissent no mistake. Where do you think he is now – at prayer?' He knew by her face that she had suspected this. Suddenly it was clear why she had wanted Rose to go.

As he turned to leave, the door opened and there stood Gilbert Bowyer, blonde, bleary-eyed and sated with some doxy from the streets outside.

'I'll kill you!' Will leaped at him, landing a blow to his belly and another to his jaw. As Bo fell, his adversary's boots drove again and again into his ribs and groin. With a groan he rolled over and in one movement was back on his feet. The reddened eyes were now slanted, on guard.

'Stop it, you fool!' He sidestepped another blow.

'I'll kill you,' Will repeated through clenched teeth.

'Will, I'm sorry. I didn't think you'd take on so. When I realised you wanted her, it was too late. You knows my motto – share an' share ...' He tried a grin, a deprecating laugh, but in response Will's anger overflowed again.

'On God's honour, I swear I didn't touch her once I knew how you felt,' Bo said, fending off a volley of blows.

'Felt? How would you know how I felt? You use women like so much dirt.' They were circling each other, their eyes locked.

'Be sensible, man. I never done her no harm. If she'd have fallen for a babby, she could have gone on living here. 'Twouldn't have made no difference. Truly I never dreamed anyone'd want to marry her.'

The hatred subsided as Will thought of Roses's unloved face.

'You pig's shit!' He landed a final devastating blow on the chin of the man he had once called friend, then turned and stormed out of the house, running back towards his new home.

As he went in, Rose, now wearing her chemise, was at prayer at the side of the bed. He came up behind her and she opened her eyes, struggling to her feet with difficulty. The defeated expression on her face tore at him. Pulling her roughly to him, he began to kiss her.

'There's no need to fret,' he said, but the anger still stifled him. Pushing her back onto the marriage bed, he parted her legs

194

and emptied his venom into her. As he sobbed his hatred, her arms closed about his shoulders and she kissed his hair.

'Every woman I ever wanted has been sullied by some other man,' he said into the darkness, and then he fell asleep.

Chapter Six

Just when it seemed that spring would never come, the daffodils thrust their delicate yellow heads above ground like a defiant elfin army. A watery sun joined their ranks and gradually a green carpet replaced the dank, withered skeleton of last year's growth.

Leah, on her way to fetch water from the well, stopped to watch a blackbird gathering twigs for its nest. 'Tis a new year come at last, she thought gratefully.

She encountered young May White struggling with a bucket. She watched the girl with compassion for both her condition and her simple, uninspiring appearance. It was a sad fact that for poor, plain girls daydreams did not come true, but May was too young to know it.

'Good morning to you, May,' she greeted. 'You're looking well.'

May returned her greeting and asked after the rest of the Galpines.

'They're well, praise be to God. Even my Harry is on the mend,' Leah replied, hoisting the bucket over the parapet and letting it sink down to the water twenty feet below. 'Is Widow Trykett in good health?'

May had put her bucket down and leaned against the wall, easing her back. 'She seems that tired,' she answered. 'She keeps complaining of her chest and a heaviness in her arm.'

'I'm sorry to hear it.' Leah thought that although the old lady had been kind to May, there was little enough in a one-roomed cottage to help the long, lonely days to pass. The girl looked very near her time and Leah wondered sadly how the baby would fare.

'You all set for your delivery?' she asked.

'Aye. Widow Trykett will see to I. I bain't afraid.' After a moment May asked: 'Will you see to Lizzie?'

As Leah acknowledged that she would, it dawned on her that this girl needed her own mother's support at such a time. She gave her a little pat on the arm.

'If you need any more help, I'll always come,' she offered.

May nodded her head, letting out a sigh, and picked up her bucket. 'Thank you, mistress.' She made her farewell.

Leah watched sadly as the girl struggled back towards the widow's cottage, her ankles swollen like puddings, panting under the weight of her load. In her turn the older woman sighed and to cheer herself thought about Lizzie and the new grandchild. Her girl was young and healthy and, give Silas his due, he had fed her well. If God were willing, it would be a safe delivery. Dark thoughts threatened again, for two young wives had died in childbed in the past year, but she would not even think of it.

Instead she wondered if Lizzie had settled on a name. No doubt a son would have to be Silas but a girl, why, a girl might even be Leah after her. With this pleasant thought she picked up her pail and made her way back to Sheepwash cottage.

Walking back from the barn that same morning, Lizzie felt the first pain, more of a niggle, really. She quickened her pace and changed direction to her mother's cottage. A knot of anxiety tightened in her belly. Straightening her back, she strode out towards Sheepwash, telling herself not to be so silly. Her time was not yet due, but Mardi's prediction seemed to be coming true.

She found Leah collecting up the firewood that Harry was chopping, balanced expertly on his one leg. They both stopped to greet her and in unspoken reply to her mother's raised eyebrows, Lizzie nodded her head. Leah threw the wood down and went inside for her shawl. Harry, realising that something was happening, looked at his sister questioningly.

'My time's here,' she said with a nervous grin.

He put his arm about her shoulders and hugged her. 'Then God bless you, Lizzie. Give us a nice nephew – or niece.'

She nodded. Her mother emerged hurriedly and the two of them headed for the mill, Lizzie leaning on Leah's arm. The house was empty. Forcing her to sit in the chair, Leah fetched a clean pile of reeds that had been saved for the occasion and spread them on the ground near the hearth.

Mardi, coming in from collecting the morning's eggs, asked; 'Can I stay?'

As no one made any comment, she sat herself cross-legged on the floor. Baby Garnet was seated away from the fire, playing with some reeds. Her mother picked her up absently when she started to grizzle. 'Best get up and walk,' she advised Lizzie, seeing her tense with a spasm of pain.

Seeing that all was well, Leah left them and made her way across to the mill to warn Silas of the imminent birth.

'You keep out of the kitchen,' she advised. 'We'll let you know as soon as there's any news. We're staying downstairs because it's warmer. You can carry her up to bed when the business is over.'

Silas swallowed, a nerve in his cheek throbbing visibly.

'Don't take long,' he replied gruffly. 'I want to see young Silas.'

'He'll come in his own good time,' answered his mother-in-law and went back to her task.

Lizzie was crouched down near the fire, her knees apart, straining with each wave of pain.

'Lord, it do hurt!' she gasped as her mother came in.

'Steady. Don't hurry him, he's got plenty o' time.'

'Who said 'twas a he?' she asked between pains.

Mardi held her hand and recounted the births of her brothers and sisters, all of which she had witnessed while they were travelling from fair to fair.

'It's near time to push now,' she said with authority, but Lizzie needed no bidding, for her body gathered its resources and willed the child into the world. A small dark head was followed by a streamlined body.

Hands held out to receive it, Leah raised her grandchild for its mother to see.

'There, my love, it's over. Look, you're right, it's a girl!'

198

Lizzie gave a sob of relief and joy.

'Oh, my little darling,' she repeated, smoothing the damp head.

Lying back in the straw, she let Leah and Mardi attend to the afterbirth and clean the child. Soon the baby, tightly encased in swaddling bands, was in her arms and she surveyed its wrinkled face with tenderness.

'She's just like her daddy,' she cooed with joy. Leah flashed her a warning look and Mardi smiled a secret smile which said there was little joy in the prospect of a baby resembling Silas Dore.

As soon as things were cleaned up and Lizzie was wrapped around with blankets, Leah went back to the mill to break the news to the new father.

He came hurrying out at her approach.

'Well?'

'It's all over.'

He expelled his breath. 'Where is he? Where's my son?'

' 'Tain't a son, 'tis a daughter.'

Leah was totally unprepared for his reaction. He jerked as if some physical force had hit him and gazed wildly at her.

'Don't you come that with me,' he growled. 'Where's my boy?'

'Silas! The babby's a girl, a fine healthy girl.'

He pushed Leah aside and raced to the house, bursting into the kitchen. Seeing Mardi crouched beside his wife, he grabbed her arm and jerked her to her feet.

'What have you done, you witch?' he shouted. 'Where's my boy?'

Mardi wailed in protest and from the floor Lizzie tried to struggle up to protect her precious child from being trampled. Turning to her, he clenched his fist.

'You've bin bewitched by this Devil-worshipper,' he screeched. 'That's not my child, 'tis a changeling.'

For a terrible moment Lizzie thought he was going to grab the baby and dash its brains out or put it on the fire. Her screams of terror were halted by an urgent thumping on the door.

'Is Mistress Galpine here?' asked Henry Gier, standing

199

breathlessly in the doorway and gazing in at the scene by the fire.

Leah stepped forward.

Seeing her, the man sagged with relief. 'You must come quick, missus,' he urged. 'Summat terrible's happened at Pitt cottage. Old lady Trykett's been took and that gal is on the floor. There's blood everywhere.'

Arriving at Pitt cottage, Leah found Goodwife Vannum in the kitchen and a sober-faced group of men and women outside.

'What's happened?' she asked, pushing her way inside.

Goodwife Vannum shook her head and nodded towards May lying in the dank straw. The cottage was cold and in the only chair Widow Trykett, head bent forward, was in her final sleep.

'Girl keeps asking for the old lady,' Goody Vannum said. 'Keeps telling her to wake up. I dunno what's going on but the babby's stuck and she ain't pushing.'

'How be you, May?' Leah fell to her knees and smoothed the girl's cold, damp forehead. She was panting like a dog and her eyes flickered in and out of consciousness. The two women looked at each other in dismay.

'Only one way,' Goody Vannum said. 'We'd best hook the babby out. It'll kill him but . . .'

Leah shook her head. ''Tis May,' she said softly. 'There ain't no saving her.' She surveyed the spreading pool of blood. 'If we can get the baby out whole, it might live.'

They continued to regard each other, not daring to admit what must be done.

Finally Leah went to the fireplace and picked up old lady Trykett's kitchen knife. Wiping the blade across her skirt, she steeled herself for the grisly task, her mouth dry, her heart thundering. May was gabbling incoherently and then fell silent, her breathing noisy and irregular.

'God forgive me,' Leah cried, bending over the girl, and ran the knife into her belly. One desperate scream rent the air and then there was a terrible silence.

Leah, her hands shaking, thought of the rabbit she had gutted that morning and delved for the child. Hastily she pulled the membranes away and wrapped her bloodstained shawl around the small, grey, flaccid body. In silence she held him out and Goody Vannum took the boy and thumped him hard across the back.

'Come on, child. Breathe in God's good air,' she pleaded.

Men and women crowded into the kitchen, aghast at what they had heard.

Suddenly a mewling from the bloody shawl drew all eyes.

'Praise God! He's breathing,' somebody said.

Leah, no longer able to hold on, let a wave of blackness engulf her and found release from the nightmare in a faint.

Those who had witnessed events at Pitt cottage were stunned by the double tragedy. The more rational pointed out that as two lives had ended, so two others had begun, an apt parallel when all things had an allotted space and time. Others were less phlegmatic.

As they were debating the significance of the events, Silas Dore arrived. Barging his way past the onlookers, he strode into the cottage and straight up to Mistress Vannum, who still held the new born child.

'Give us that. 'E's mine,' he demanded, wrenching the babe from her arms.

'What do you mean?' She flushed, hesitating to challenge him. His face was puce and sweat coursed down his temples and into the folds of his double chin.

'Thissun's mine,' he repeated.

Around him people looked at each other tellingly. After all his womanising, it seemed that Silas Dore had finally fathered not one but two offspring almost simultaneously.

Without further explanation or the merest glance at May, the girl he had surely wronged, he strode out, clutching his bundle, and headed towards the mill.

It was Mardi who helped Lizzie up the steep stairs and into bed and who placed a hot brick in the wicker basket to warm it before laying the baby girl safely in it.

Lizzie was restless and kept asking after May. On being told that there was no news, she demanded that her baby be handed to her so that she could reassure herself that it was safe.

201

'Master's brains is addled,' Mardi said, handing the little one over.

Lizzie felt her heart thumping unnaturally against her ribs. In spite of his uncouth violence, she had never been really afraid of Silas, but now she truly feared for the safety of her child. She wondered if this was the punishment she deserved for her infidelity and began to pray for forgiveness for having feelings that she could not control.

With a heavy heart she knew that she would have to play up to Silas, reassure him that the next child would certainly be a boy, though that meant succumbing to his sexual greed. Her mind rebelled but the safety of her daughter might depend on it. She began to cry silently.

Lapsing into an exhausted daydream she wondered about the child's name. Until that morning it had been young Silas and the very thought had sullied it. Now, being a girl, it was separate from him and this gave her great comfort. Her thoughts drifted to Will and she could see his face as if he were in the room. She remembered the day that he had first kissed her when they had stood in the copse near the fairground. That had been the most magical moment of her life. Afterwards he had taken her out and bought her the clasp that even now was pinned inside her chemise. 'Them stones are real rubies and garnets,' the man had said. She knew then what she had to call Will's daughter.

Her reverie was shattered by the sound of the door opening and Silas came bounding up the stairs. As he appeared through the opening into the bedroom, he held out a bundle towards her.

'Here he is. Here's our babby,' he panted. 'Take him and suckle him.'

Lizzie gazed thunderstruck at the parcel.

'What ...' she began.

'Her's bewitched your friend and the old woman,' he continued, looking at Mardi, his face purple with exertion. 'Your friend's dead but my boy's been saved. She swapped 'em round. Don't you see?'

Lizzie didn't. With baby Ruby in the crook of her arm, she struggled to take the proffered parcel. Seeing the small, pasty face partially obscured by the shawl, she let out a gasp of anguish as the realisation dawned on her.

'May's dead?' she whispered.

'Aye. That murderous imp has killed 'em both. She wants hanging. I'm gonna have her tried for witchcraft.'

He was now breathing so fast that he began to gulp to take in more air. A strange gurgling noise started in his throat and he staggered back, clawing at the air, before falling with a sickening thud onto the floor.

'Silas!' Lizzie tried to scramble from the bed, hurriedly laying the two babies side by side. As her feet touched the ground a wave of dizziness overcame her, but Mardi was already there.

'Back to bed, mistress,' she ordered. 'I'll see to him. You must take care of yourself. You've got two babbies to see to now.'

Chapter Seven

The same afternoon somebody was despatched from Caulbourne to Newport to fetch the physician. They finally
returned after dark.

Grimly by candlelight the physician examined the bodies of
Widow Trykett and May White, both cold and stiff at Pitt's
cottage. After careful consideration he announced that in his
opinion, the midwife had been right to save May's baby.
Clearly the girl had already been called to her maker and to
have delayed would have sent the child straight back to God
without the benefit of proving his worth upon this earth.

About Widow Trykett he was more ambivalent. Of course
she was an old lady and he had seen others slip away under
similar circumstances, but he found it strange that God should
have called her just when she was needed right here in the
cottage.

He was then escorted the few hundred yards to the fulling-
mill house and here the situation seemed very strange indeed.
The fuller Silas Dore had been dragged onto some straw near
the fire and there he lay on his back, his eyes staring, his mouth
distorted into an ugly snarl. He had messed himself and the
physician held a kerchief to his nose to avoid the stench as he
bent over him.

He gave orders to send out for a woman to come and clean
him up and then set about bleeding him. Without a word he
then climbed the stairs to the bedroom.

Lizzie was sitting up in bed, suckling the boy child Silas. Her
own Ruby was fed and asleep across her lap. Modestly she
shielded her breast while the baby continued to suck noisily.

'Well, mistress, it's a bad day,' said the physician. Lizzie began involuntarily to weep and the man put his hand on her shoulder.

'All is not lost, wife. He is still alive. Pray earnestly and if God wills it, then he will recover.'

Lizzie lowered her eyes. Her tears were not for the man downstairs but for May. Her visitor turned to the window, gazing out into the darkness.

'A disturbing business,' he continued, apparently to himself, then to Lizzie: 'Your husband looks sore troubled. I am uneasy about this case.'

When there was no reply, he added: 'Clearly he is suffering from a surfeit but in addition to that I wonder if he has not an enemy?' Turning to face her, he asked: 'Is there anyone who might have wished him ill?'

Lizzie thought that the number of people who detested Silas was endless but she merely shook her head, and he sighed.

'Then we shall have to wait and see,' he said. 'I will be back on the morrow to bleed him again. Meantime you must rest. Good night, mistress. Guard your little charges well.'

Lizzie fell into an exhausted sleep, only to be woken later by Mardi bringing her a bowl of broth.

'How is he?' she asked sleepily, indicating the room downstairs.

Mardi shrugged. 'Mistress Snudden's been over and we've washed him. He's disgusting.' She wrinkled her nose and spat on the floor.

'I don't understand it,' Lizzie mused. 'How come all this happened at the same time? It don't seem natural.'

Mardi shrugged again. 'That silly old fool kept on about the babbies. He must be daft. You was there. You know which one's yourn.'

Lizzie agreed. There was no doubt that Ruby was her child – and Will's – yet she continued to wonder about it all. She settled back to rest but her sleep was troubled by menacing dreams. In the morning she felt so pale and washed out that she simply stayed where she was, gazing into space, not even asking after the work or the mill.

As the days passed, Silas showed no change. He clearly understood what was going on about him but he could neither speak nor move. Once Lizzie was up and about, she reluctantly took charge of his care.

Sometimes Mardi would help her but whenever the servant came near the stricken man became agitated, making strange noises in his throat. Even Mistress Snudden remarked upon it. Finally Jed was sent for to help with the lifting and the heavy work and Mardi was instructed to keep away from her master, an order she complied with enthusiastically.

It was a busy week at the church. The two occupants of Pitt cottage were buried at some cost to the parish in a joint grave and the two new inhabitants of the mill were baptised. Much as she would have liked to give the boy a different name, Lizzie felt that it was best to leave well alone, so the congregation welcomed Ruby Dore and Silas White to their number.

It was April before Lizzie was really back on her feet again. The countryside was bursting into life. Tender buds, newborn lambs, nesting rooks were everywhere. She breathed it all in along with the clean, sharp air as she took the babies across the meadow to visit her mother on her first morning out.

Since the infant Silas had been so violently torn from his mother's womb, Leah had remained at home. The experience had left her shocked and in a permanently grey humour. She had not been to visit the mill and news of her had come to Lizzie with frustrating ambiguity only via Jed. Looking across at Sheepwash cottage, Lizzie now saw the door opening and her mother come hurrying across to meet her. She was dismayed to see her looking so thin and grey.

'Oh, Lizzie, I been that worried! It's such a joy to see you.' Leah took one of the human parcels resting on Lizzie's hips and peered beneath the cloth that hid its face.

'Which one be this?' she asked.

'That's Silas. Thanks be to you he's alive.'

'It's thanks to God,' her mother corrected, kissing his forehead, then handing him back. Wiping her hands nervously on her skirt, she reached for her first grandchild.

Lizzie watched the emotions flit over her mother's tired face. It was tears that finally overcame her, spilling down her cheeks as she regarded the baby girl.

'She's such a beauty,' she said, visibly fighting to keep control. 'I really think she favours you.'

'She don't favour Silas nohow,' her daughter observed dryly.

Leah raised her eyebrows. 'How is he?'

'Lively as a turnip. He just lies there doing nothing.'

Leah seemed to be choosing her next words carefully. 'Is it true that he's really this babby's father?' she finally asked, glancing at baby Silas, her voice low.

Lizzie shook her head. 'Course not. He was someone that May worked with down Swaynson. She told me so herself.'

'Then why was Silas so set on having him?'

Lizzie sighed, her eyes now troubled. It was her turn to struggle for the right words.

'I don't know. He took against Mardi. He got some silly notion in his head she was – you know, had powers.' She spoke as if mentioning it might cause something unnatural to happen.

Leah nodded, then, to ease the mood, asked: 'How you gonna manage?'

'We'll cope as long as Jed comes over.' Lizzie was relieved to get onto safer ground. 'I can manage everything else along with the boys and Mardi.'

They had now gone inside and over a glass of ale talked quietly while Lizzie suckled the two babies. The morning seemed to vanish and by the time she had finished it was past midday.

'Dear Lord, I must get back,' she said, gathering her charges up. 'Please come and visit, Mam, I get lonely over there.'

The older woman's face clouded. 'I can't go out yet awhiles.' she replied. 'Not till all this tragedy is put behind us.'

'You'll never put it behind you if you sit here brooding,' Lizzie admonished. 'Promise you'll come over soon?'

'Aye, soon,' Leah said, but there was little conviction in her voice.

They kissed in farewell and Lizzie stepped back out into the sunshine. As she strolled in the direction of home she felt curiously at peace, in tune with the springtime around her. The babes moved rhythmically on her hips and a sadness touched her as she thought how much poor May was missing. Involuntarily she gave the little boy a squeeze on behalf of his mother.

'Don't you worry,' she said to the invisible woman whose soul was somewhere out there. 'I'll look after him.'

As the mill house came into view, Lizzie noticed that the door was open. Mardi had been told to go and help the boys, so she had either forgotten about closing the door or was deliberately indifferent to the need to keep Silas warm. With a sigh Lizzie pushed it wider with her shoulder and stepped inside. It took her a moment to adjust to the gloom, but she was immediately aware that apart from the supine figure by the hearth there was somebody else.

As her eyes acclimatised to the darkness, she was confronted by a large, toadlike woman sitting in Silas's chair. Lizzie stared at the newcomer in surprise and, when she did not move, asked: 'Who are you?'

The woman looked her up and down with exaggerated slowness, her eyes resting on each infant in turn. Drawing in her breath, she then struggled to her feet, her eyes glinting maliciously.

'So you're the one as bamboozled him,' she said, her voice sharp and spiteful.

'What you on about?' Lizzie demanded, feeling suddenly fearful.

'You dunno who I am, do you? Well, you got me to answer to now,' the stranger said.

'What do you mean? Who are you?' Lizzie repeated.

'Agnes Downer.'

As Lizzie continued to look mystified, the woman added: 'I'm Silas's sister.'

Lizzie shrugged and put both babies in the improvised crib near the hearth. On the other side her husband lay immobile.

'I'm sorry as how your brother's took bad,' she said, her back to the woman. 'He never talked about you much so I'm afraid I never thought to let you know he was ill.'

Agnes Downer lived at Thorley, some three miles away, and this was the first time that Lizzie had seen her. She had not even come to the wedding.

Lizzie turned round to find her visitor still staring at her. She flushed uncomfortably and, suddenly remembering the open door, asked: 'Where's Mardi?'

At this the woman's eyes narrowed and she pursed her lips malevolently. 'She's run off but that'll do her no good. I've alerted the constable and the magistrate.'

Lizzie stared at her in alarm. 'What you talking about?' she asked.

'She's a witch. I've denounced her. It's just a matter of time afore they brings her back.'

Lizzie was so startled she could not take in all the implications. She grabbed the edge of the table for support, her eyes on the older woman like a mesmerised rabbit.

'I knows all about her changing the babbies.' Agnes Downer looked across at the crib. 'You shouldn't leave 'em together,' she warned. 'That changeling'll do him harm.'

Lizzie snorted impatiently, the spell broken. 'Don't talk nonsense. It's the babby girl that's mine – ours,' she corrected herself. 'The boy's mother was my friend who died.'

'Yes, I know all about that too. Don't you see how she killed the old woman so as she could make the change?'

'No!' Lizzie was shaking her head, but some strange things had happened that could not be explained. For a moment she remembered when she had discovered Silas and Mardi alone in the kitchen. The girl had openly cursed him and now he lay there stricken. She shivered. Ignoring the unwelcome visitor, she picked up both children and hurried out of the house and across to the mill.

'You seen Mardi?' she shouted to the boys over the noise of the hammers. They both shook their heads. She returned reluctantly to the house. As she walked inside, Agnes Downer was bent over her brother.

'. . . I'll see her's punished,' she was saying, and fear clutched at Lizzie's heart.

'It's all a mistake,' she said, busying herself by making up the fire. 'Mardi ain't a bad girl. She's been a great help to me. Besides, it was Silas who brought her here.'

Mistress Downer sniffed derisively. 'Can't you see she's got you bewitched?' she asked. 'You want to watch out or you'll end up with her.' The words were unmistakably as much a threat as a warning.

Fighting down the panic, Lizzie asked: 'When are you leaving?'

Folding her arms over her huge bosom, the fat woman settled herself more firmly in her brother's chair and her lips turned down in the semblance of a smile. Finally she replied:

'Not till they catches the witch.'

Mardi was discovered in a barn at Newbridge. She was taken directly to Newport and there held in the Bridewell until her case should be considered.

Once the news was around the village, people began to remember things. Michael Jolliffe realised that it was since Mardi had delivered some apples to his cottage that his cow had started to go dry. It was clear to him that the animal had been overlooked. Witches had their own reasons for spreading destruction.

Mistress Dyer remembered several times seeing a grey cat going in through the window at fulling-mill house. She was sure it only happened when Silas and Lizzie were out and it was clear that the witch was feeding her familiar and giving it instructions to create more havoc. A search was instituted for the cat but it could not be found.

As these tales filtered back to Lizzie, she became increasingly afraid. Every time she ventured out she was aware that people were staring at her and whispering behind her back. Finally, to escape the gossip, she took the babies across to her mother and decided to go out for a walk or, better still, a ride. Since the births she had had no time to visit Farmer and she knew that he must be missing her.

Hunching her shoulders against the keen wind, she crossed to the lean-to and opened the door. The horse lifted his head and she saw with horror how thin he had become. A wave of anger swept over her as she realised that everyone had neglected him during her confinement.

'You poor old thing!' Grabbing his forelock, she led him out into the yard and observed that he was badly lame.

'What they done to you?' she asked, bending to run her hand down his hock. He flinched away.

At that moment Jed came out of the mill and shambled across to her.

'What you done to Farmer?' Lizzie asked. 'Look at him.'

Jed gazed at the horse. 'I 'spect he's been hag-ridden,' he said philosophically.

'What d'you mean?'

210

''Tis what I heard. Horses is ridden by witches at night when we're all abed and it wears 'em out.'

'Don't say that!' She jerked Jed roughly by the sleeve and swung him round. He looked at her in surprise. Sighing, she said slowly: 'They're all saying Mardi is a witch. If you say things like that then they'll ...' She paused, not sure what would happen. 'They'll harm her,' she finished.

Jed nodded. 'I won't say nothin' then,' he promised.

She sighed again, for there was never a way to explain to her brother the subtleties of a situation. Instead she sent him to fetch some comfrey so that she could make a poultice for the horse's leg.

There was very little feed left but she gave him a small helping of hay and a few withered turnips, then walked back home. Down by the stream a group of boys were fishing with a piece of twisted grass. As she passed they fell silent, but as soon as she was a few yards away they began to whisper. She thought she heard the word 'witch'. Hurrying back indoors, she waited until dark before daring to go out again and fetch the children.

Those two days after Mardi had been taken were two of the worst of Lizzie's life. With only Silas and the babies for company, she felt herself weighed down with the responsibility of caring for them. The little ones seemed fretful and when one wasn't awake the other was. She suspected that her milk was no longer sufficient to feed them both, and fear for their health preoccupied much of her time. Her first thought was for Ruby, her own child, and yet she had a special responsibility for little Silas because of his mother's untimely death. He was a greedy baby, however, and she feared that he might be taking the very sustenance that Ruby needed to survive. Such thoughts chased each other in the recesses of her brain so that sleep became impossible.

In addition, the welfare of Garnet was now also her responsibility. Being nine months old, she was an active child and needed constant watching. She was also permanently hungry, and Lizzie was forced to give her cow's milk. It did not suit her digestion and she was for ever grizzling. Lizzie was soon at her wits' end.

Meanwhile, Silas lay downstairs like a great millstone and

211

his presence sickened her. During the daytime Jed was around to lift him and Mistress Snudden continued to come in, but at night she was alone with him and his unintelligible grunting noises reduced her to near hysteria. Sometimes when she went over to him his frightened, piggy eyes would stare up at her and she could only turn away. Yet she tried hard to be dutiful.

'D'you want a drink?' she would ask, knowing that he must be thirsty. Interpreting his grunts as yes, she had to steel herself to raise his head and drip a few mouthfuls between his lips. Most of it ran down his chin and into the straw.

Meanwhile his other end would be wet and soiled and she longed just to leave him but, as the Reverend Cotton had pointed out, sometimes unpleasant duties befell a wife.

'Take heart and thank God for this opportunity to serve Him,' he had advised.

Holding her breath, she would scrape away as much of the soiled bedding as she could, wipe his dirtied legs and buttocks with hay and push clean straw underneath, then hurry to the door to breathe in deep gulps of fresh air. Don't let this last too long, she prayed, gazing into the dark and tempting emptiness outside.

At times like this she missed Mardi. Just the presence of someone else in the house had made it bearable and Mardi's humour had always managed to lift her. Now the girl was in Newport and she had no idea what was happening to her.

She had gone to the church to ask for advice but the Reverend Cotton had been ambiguous.

'Even to acknowledge that your servant is a witch and to claim that she has magical powers is a sin,' he had warned, standing in the porch of the church, his fingers still touching in an attitude of prayer. 'All power comes from God.'

'Does that mean witches don't exist?' asked Lizzie in some confusion.

Appearing not to hear, he continued: 'If she has been performing evil, then she will be punished. And we must praise God for it.'

'But she ain't bad,' her mistress insisted. 'People's took against her 'cause she comes from across the sea.'

'You must have faith,' was the reply. 'God will protect the innocent in the same way that He will punish the guilty.'

212

Lizzie shook her head in confusion. 'I don't understand,' she persisted. 'What's gonna happen to Mardi?'

The minister looked at her in surprise before saying: 'Why, for certain she'll be hanged.'

Chapter Eight

In spite of the drama of his wedding night, Will soon discovered that Rose was an exemplary wife. All her attention was devoted to the home. She cooked and cleaned, was frugal with any money that came her way, did not spend time gossiping with the other women and never blasphemed or was coquettish with men. As his confidence in their union grew, he found her to be a good listener and a trustworthy confidante.

But his feelings blew hot and cold. Sometimes he called her his sweetheart, stopping to steal a kiss as she dished up their evening meal, opening his heart about problems at work or long-term ambitions. At other times he was morose, barely acknowledging her existence or uttering remarks aimed at reminding her of her past.

'Matthew Finch was in a lather today at work,' he said on one such evening. 'That woman he took to his bed has run off with a navy man.'

When Rose did not reply, he continued:

'That's the trouble, see, he didn't know nothing about her past till after they was wed. Turned out she wasn't pure.'

Rose continued to serve up the meal and then sat down, her eyes lowered. The shutters of pain had closed Will off and he felt harsh and remote. Pushing his plate aside, he left without a word for the tavern and did not return until late. By then Rose was in bed.

Slipping out of his breeches, he lay with his back to her, aching for the comfort of her body but most of all the solace of her love. He wanted her to take him in her arms but perversely he knew that if she moved to touch him he would upbraid her for being unseemly and displaying the loose morals he so often accused her of. If she continued to lay stiff and apart from him, however, he would curse her for not loving him as a dutiful wife should. He knew that it was unreasonable but he could not help himself.

He was sure that she was awake and thought that he could just take her. After all, she was his to do with as he chose. With a grunt he rolled over and ran his hand down her body. He felt her tense and, as his hand came to rest on her crippled leg, she flinched. He knew that the leg caused her pain and that she was ashamed of its withered appearance.

'What happened to it?' His voice was harsh in the darkness. She did not reply so he pulled the cover back and ran his hand over it again.

'I'm your husband. I got a right to know. You never tell me nothing about yourself.'

He knew that she was struggling for an answer.

'It's been like that since I was born,' she finally replied.

'Where was you born?'

Again there was a long silence. He was about to prod her into speaking when she added:

'My mother worked in a grand house. I think I was the master's. Anyhow, they let us stay in the kitchens.'

'What happened?' He was beginning to forget his anger now.

After a while she continued: 'Master was widowed when I was about six. I think he took Mother back into his bed then. Anyhow, they both fell sick with sweats and they died on the same day. I reckon there was a scandal, 'cause I was packed off as a skivvy to another house.'

'Go on,' he said when she hesitated.

'It was awful. The housekeeper was always beating me and my leg got real bad there. I don't remember much but they built a new house in the country and when they moved they just left me behind – I don't want to think about it.' Her voice shook.

'Tell me what happened next.' He was insistent, ignoring her pain.

'Nothing. I just lived in the streets. I got real sick and then one day old man Bowyer took me home.'

'What did he do to you?'

'Please, Will!' She started to cry. 'Please don't. I can't bear to think on it.'

He turned his back on her again. 'I got to know,' he said, hating himself but unable to stop. 'How many men have you had?'

'Only what you know. Please stop.'

He suddenly felt ashamed. He knew that he was making her suffer and for something that was not her fault. Indeed, he was tormenting her because someone else had misused her. In return she had offered him an unswerving loyalty and, he suspected, love.

Turning again in the bed, he reached across and pulled her to him. He wanted to say that he was sorry but the right words would not come so he caressed her and kissed her neck and shoulders over and over. For an age she lay stiff and mute and then with a sob she turned towards him, taking him in her arms and into her body. Thus released and cherished, he fell asleep.

The next morning she was already up and working before he stirred. Lying blearily in the bed, he watched her hobble across to the fire and stir the soup.

'Come here,' he called.

She started on realising that he was awake, and came across to the bed.

'Here, sit down.' He patted the coverlet and she did so, her eyes avoiding his face as her crippled leg impeded her movement. His eyes rested on her legs and, reaching out, he pulled up her skirt.

'No!' She tried to cover herself again.

'Forgive me.' He gently caressed the withered calf.

'You deserve better than this.' She was fighting back the tears.

'No. It's you what deserves better.' He bent forwards and kissed the leg. Her hand went out to rest on his head, now cradled in her lap.

'Old Bowyer said it was God's punishment on me,' she said quietly. 'He said that was why he was punishing me too.'

'It was him what deserved punishment,' Will replied savagely. 'And me too. I'm no better. I've wronged you.' He sat up and took both her hands in his.

216

'Forgive me.' He said again, 'I'll make it up to you if you tell me what you want most.'

For a long while she was silent. Then, looking directly at him with her pale, sad eyes, she answered:

'I want you to love me.'

By way of reply he pressed her face against his shoulder.

'Course I do,' he answered and rocked her against him so that she should not read the truth in his eyes.

The weeks drifted into months and Will turned his thoughts to their future. He worked hard and saved his money until he could afford to find a bigger place with an upstairs and a yard big enough to keep a milking ewe and some chickens. He could not get used to the idea that all food was purchased from the market. At home they had always been self-sufficient, merely swapping their surplus for goods that some neighbour could supply. The market was for special occasions, buying little luxuries. He realised that if ever his money ran out in London, they would surely starve. As a result, even having his own milk and eggs made him feel safer.

He tried to be a good and dutiful husband to Rose and in most ways he succeeded, but what he could not give to her was the spontaneous passion he still felt for Lizzie. As soon as he allowed his mind to wander, Lizzie would be there in the forefront of his dreams, free and willing and solely his. It intruded on his every waking moment.

Making love at night, the memory of Lizzie was always between them. Each time he relived her instinctive response to his own passion that afternoon in the copse and on the day of the Armada, the mutual joy they had found in each other. By comparison Rose was a timid, acquiescent mouse.

He had no idea if his wife found pleasure in the act of love. He suspected that she succumbed for fear of losing him and he was aware only of her relief when he cuddled her to him afterwards.

'What do you feel?' he would ask, lying in the darkness.

There was always a delay before she put her thoughts into words.

'I feel happy,' she would reply.

217

'Do you?' He sounded doubtful, then persisted. 'What do you feel when I touch you?'

'... I don't know.' He could hardly hear her.

'You must know. Does it feel good to you or do I frighten you or what?'

When she did not reply, he asked:

'Why did you marry me?'

'Because I love you.'

He snorted and turned his back on her.

Finally she asked: 'Why did you marry me?'

The question took him by surprise, but with the merest hesitation he answered: 'Because you was there.'

He knew that she had started to cry now, soundlessly, and he fought between compassion and irritation.

'What are you afraid of?' he finally asked.

'I'm afraid to disappoint you. To lose you.'

With a sigh he cuddled her and she seemed to melt into his body as if trying to become a physical part of him. He guessed that was the only way that she would ever feel really safe.

Sadly he admitted to himself that instead of being fulfilled by this marriage, he felt only emptiness. He had hoped to find a refuge but it was in fact a cage. There were no bars but he could never run away.

'Go to sleep,' he said gruffly. 'I wed you, didn't I? I'll always be here.'

Passing through the market on the way home each day, Will always stopped to watch the fruit sellers, Gipsies and pedlars. Each word and gesture was an entertainment. Here it was commonplace but at home on the island it would have been a scene to marvel at. He wished that he could tell Lizzie about it. There he went again, thinking about her. It was wrong. He must stop.

Trying to concentrate on the present, he noticed some strange, knobbly vegetables on the nearest display.

'What's they?' he asked.

'Taters,' replied the stallholder.

Will picked one up. It was solid and heavy with a pocked brown skin.

'How do you cook them?' he asked idly.

218

'Boil 'em in a skillet.'

He bought one and took it home for Rose to cook. Inside it was white and feathery and didn't taste of much, but afterwards Rose found a piece that had fallen into the drip tray she used to catch the juices from the mutton on the hook above the fire. Tasting it, she held it out to Will to try. He wrinkled his nose but at her insistence took a nibble. It was better than anything he knew. Next day he returned to the market stall and bought some more.

'How do you grow them?' he asked.

'When there's flowers on the tops you just pulls 'em up and there they'll be,' the marketeer told him.

Will had grinned wryly, thinking that it was probably a joke, but nevertheless he dug up a small part of his yard, buried them in the ground and waited. Sure enough, after several months, fed with sheep droppings, watered with the rain caught in an old pail and warmed by the sun, the plants had pale, creamy tubers attached to the roots when he dug them up. From then on these became a regular part of their diet.

Chapter Nine

Lizzie was summoned to the court in June, two months after Mardi had been taken up. Together with Farmer Jolliffe whose cow had been overlooked, Mistress Dyer who had seen the cat, Mistress Vannum who had witnessed the birth of Silas White, and the Reverend Collins, Lizzie travelled the six miles to Newport.

Although Leah had played an important part in the happenings at Pitt cottage, she was granted leave to stay at home because of her poor health. Privately it was mooted that the witch had laid a spell on her. Publicly it was confirmed that, since Mistress Vannum had also been present, her testimony would suffice.

Lizzie left the three infants with her mother. In spite of Mardi's departure, Garnet did not show signs of missing her. She simply transferred all her affection to the woman who had already done more for her than her natural mother.

Feeding the children while she was away was the most immediate problem, but Lizzie had recently learned that Nell White, May's mother, still had milk aplenty following the birth of her youngest, who was now eighteen months. Mistress White agreed to visit Sheepwash cottage and suckle the babes during Lizzie's absence, which was something of a relief. Although little Silas was her first grandchild, she had shown little inclination to see him, agreeing only when Lizzie offered her the carcass of a duck that Jed had ensnared in a trap supposedly set for rats. Lizzie also suspected that part of her reason was to get a blow-by-blow account of the day's events when she returned from court.

Following the others into the audit house, Lizzie was so overawed by the formality that she could hardly draw breath. The seriousness of Mardi's situation now came home to her.

'What they going to do?' she whispered to the others, but no one seemed to know.

The first person she set eyes on was Agnes Downer and it was her testimony that opened the case. Listening aghast, Lizzie realised that for everyone present the guilt of her servant was already decided.

Mistress Downer was followed by the physician, who expressed his own fears about events at Caulbourne. The testimony of such an important man was another nail in Mardi's coffin.

One by one the others were asked to substantiate what they knew, and cases of sick cattle, unexplained headaches, barren sheep and curdled milk were laid at Mardi's door.

Mardi stood before the court, her hands tied behind her back, her eyes wild and frightened.

'They can't cry, you know,' Mistress Vannum whispered to Lizzie. ''Tis a well-known fact that witches never shed tears.'

'She ain't a witch,' Lizzie repeated, but with a sinking feeling she realised that she had no way to prove it.

There was some discussion among the court officials and then the clerk stepped forward.

'It has been decreed that she shall be tested,' he announced to all present. Every eye was upon him. Waiting for maximum impact, he continued: 'This woman shall be taken to the water and swum.'

'What does that mean?' Lizzie turned to the Reverend Cotton, who was sitting next to her.

'If a person belongs to Satan, then God's water, being pure, will not accept them,' he replied.

Lizzie shook her head, not understanding.

'That being the case, they will float,' he enlightened her.

'What if she be innocent?'

The minister smiled benignly. 'Then she will sink.'

For a few moments Lizzie considered what he had said, then turned back to him. 'I don't understand. If she sinks she'll be drownded.'

221

He shook his head. 'She'll be pulled from the water before that. It is all in God's hands.'

Lizzie found herself trembling. From the front of the courtroom Mardi began to scream as she was dragged towards the door. Catching sight of her mistress, she shouted:

'Save me! Tell 'em I'm innocent. Please!'

Lizzie covered her face with her hands, unable to bear her servant's distress. Mistress Dyer, sitting behind her, touched her on the shoulder sympathetically.

'She's enchanted you too,' she said with concern. 'But fear not, for God will protect you.'

They all filed from the courtroom and through the town towards Carisbrooke and the large pond at the foot of Castle Hill. As they paraded through the street they were joined by more and more townspeople. This was the first case of its kind in living memory and nobody wanted to miss the spectacle.

Mardi was laid on the ground and her big toes tied together with twine. Her hands were pulled behind her back and her thumbs tightly secured.

'Lemme go! Help!' she screamed.

A minister from Newport stepped forward and began to lead the crowd in prayer.

'Merciful God to whom everything is known, give us Your sign as to the guilt of this Thy subject,' he intoned.

The excitement was so great that the hubbub hardly died down while the prayer was being offered up. A rope was tied around Mardi's waist and she was hoisted up by two men and thrown bodily into the pond. Her screams were silenced by the inrush of water into her mouth. As she was struggling and writhing, the crowd watched, now silent. She tipped her head back and her body floated on the rippling water. A gasp of awe swept over the crowd. The men holding the rope tugged at it and as Mardi began to sink again she arched her back and managed to stay afloat. The crowd began to exclaim to each other.

'What does it mean?' someone shouted. 'Is she a witch or ain't she?'

The magistrate and the clerk, along with the minister of the church, had their heads together in conference. True, Mardi had gone under the water but then she had proceeded to float.

After much deliberation, the magistrate announced that the test had been inconclusive.

Terrified and shivering, Mardi was hauled ashore.

'Prick 'er, then,' somebody shouted. 'Look for the Devil's mark.'

There was more deliberation and then, clearing a space, it was decreed that they would hunt for the Devil's mark on Mardi's body.

In horror Lizzie watched as they stripped off the girl's dripping kirtle, laid her naked on the ground and began to search her body minutely for any abnormal lumps or warts. After a while someone was pushed forwards from the crowd, a greasy-haired, skeletal man dressed from head to foot in black.

''Ere, let him do it,' someone called. 'He's had experience.'

Reluctantly the searchers moved back to make room for the supposed expert. Behind him people were craning to see. Kneeling down, he began to look in Mardi's hair, inside her mouth, in the folds of her ears, then rubbed his hands down over her neck and shoulders, raising her arms to feel beneath. He paid particular attention to her breasts.

''Ow many nipples has she got?' came the call and a cheer went up from the men.

'Stop it! Please stop them.' Lizzie turned to the people about her, but they were oblivious to everything but the naked girl spreadeagled on the ground. Her legs were now being held apart while the self-appointed witch-finder was poking his fingers inside her. The crowd surged forwards again.

Turning her onto her face, he parted her buttocks and studied her closely.

'There's summat 'ere.' He pointed to a pimple on the rise of her behind.

'Prick it!' came the chorus.

A pin was produced and the now limp girl was subjected to the pin being stuck into her flesh. She gave a whimper, which was soon drowned in the wave of noise from the crowd. Withdrawing the pin, the examiners watched to see if blood oozed forth from the spot. It did not. Again the pin was pushed in, deeper this time, and again it came out dry. As they were considering the significance of this, two of Mardi's captors dragged her over onto her back and a flow of blood trickled from between her legs. The crowd gasped and moved back as one.

Seeing what was happening, Lizzie forced her way through the throng and, pushing the examiners away, bent over her servant, covering her with her own shawl. Mardi no longer appeared to know what was happening.

'You should be ashamed!' Lizzie screamed at the court officials, ignoring their exalted rank. 'She's nothing but a poor maid. It's yourselves you shame, not her.'

The magistrate, for whom things were now beginning to get out of hand, turned to face her.

'That blood does not count,' he said, his face flushing. 'We've pricked her according to the custom. She bears the Devil's mark and it does not bleed.' Looking into Lizzie's blazing face, he continued: 'It is now out of my hands. The girl must be sent to the next assizes.'

Chapter Ten

Mardi was to be transported to Winchester to await the next quarter's assizes and the witnesses from Caulbourne returned home. There was much speculation among them on the journey back; only Lizzie remained stunned and silent.

She had not been allowed to stay with her servant and did not even know if they had given her a dry gown before carting her off.

'I'll pray for you,' she had promised, leaving the girl her shawl. 'And I'll look after your little one till you come back.' It seemed small comfort. Mardi had been too dazed to respond but defiantly Lizzie kissed her, saying: 'God bless you,' loud enough for everyone around to hear.

Back at the mill there was little sense of peace. Every night she was tormented by nightmares and each morning she woke to remember that they were all true.

As the days became weeks, Silas grew thinner so that it was easier to move him, but in other ways things became worse. Large, putrefying sores appeared on his back and hips and he began to smell of rotting flesh. One morning, as she dutifully spooned some soup into his unresisting mouth, she noticed a single tear escape and trickle down his cheek.

'Witches can't cry,' she remembered and once again was in the grip of the nightmare. For the first time she felt pity for her husband.

Getting up, she made for the door, driven to get outside and away from the oppressive responsibilities. As she went to lift the latch, the door opened and her brother Harry was framed in the morning light. At the sight of him, Lizzie burst into tears.

225

'Now then, don't get upset,' he chided, slipping his arm about her shoulders.

Lizzie sniffed back her tears apologetically. 'I be that silly sometimes,' she said. 'But he does get me down.'

'How is he?' Harry ducked under the lintel of the door and hobbled across to sit in Silas's chair.

'He don't make no progress.'

'Well, he won't. Not if he's been cursed.' Harry took his sister's hand and she sank down beside him. 'Not unless her what laid the curse lifts it,' he finished.

'Do you really believe it's a curse?' she asked.

Harry shrugged. 'I know that such things happen. There was a feller on board ship who bought a wind from an old woman. When he used it to get back to port quicker than what the Almighty intended, it set up such a storm that the mast broke and killed a shipmate.' He paused for breath. 'Well, when he came ashore he was dismissed and he was that mad, he laid a curse on the ship. Sure as ninepence, on her next voyage she foundered and went down with all hands.'

Lizzie nodded, for she did not disbelieve it.

'If it was Mardi who laid the curse, could she put it right?' she asked hopefully.

'Course she could.'

'D'you think they'd let her go if she made amends?'

Harry sighed. 'She can't bring back the dead.'

Lizzie was silent as she thought of Widow Trykett and May. It dawned on her then that, much as she did not want Silas in this state, neither did she want him as he had been before. I wish he was dead, she thought and knew that she was as guilty as the Gipsy girl. She began to weep again.

'Come on now, our Lizzie.' Harry put his arms around her again. 'You gotta stop this. Remember, you still got the young-uns,' he comforted.

Both babies were in their third month and already there was a marked difference. What young Silas made up for in size he lacked in ability, and it was Ruby who cooed and laughed and responded to her mother's loving care. While Lizzie's love for her daughter was as instinctive and passionate as nature, she had tenderness and affection for the large, placid, motherless boy who was as good as her own.

With a sigh she looked at the third infant, now pulling herself up by Harry's leg. She felt her chest tighten with a peculiar mixture of love and fear.

There was something about little Garnet which reminded her all the time of Ruby. True, she was darker now, darker-skinned and her hair a deep brown, but the shape of her face and the hazel eyes were startlingly similar. With a shiver she hoped that this did not have anything to do with Mardi being a witch. If what they said was true, then perhaps she had influenced all the births. She remembered with misgivings that, as Mardi had predicted, her own Ruby had been born a month earlier than nature intended and yet she had shown none of the weakness of a child torn early from the womb.

Harry chucked Garnet under the chin and then picked her up, and Lizzie gathered both little ones to her.

'Could a baby be a witch?' she asked her brother.

'Not if it was baptised.'

She relaxed. 'You've made me feel better.'

He grinned at her. 'You worry too much,' he replied.

They left the cottage together and went their separate ways, Harry to Sheepwash and Lizzie and the children to Mistress White's. Twice a day she visited May's mother so that Silas could be suckled while Lizzie attended to her daughter. This way there was enough milk for both little ones and Garnet now had the sheep's milk, which luckily agreed with her better.

Mistress White was squat and pale-looking, much older than her forty years. It occurred to Lizzie that had May lived she would have grown to look remarkably like her mother. In fact, the cottage was peopled with an assortment of squat, pale children, with the exception of one lean, sandy boy, who was a source of mystery to both parents.

Having spent the day of the court appearance with her grandchild, Mistress White now seemed to have become very attached to him. As he hung on her breast, she clucked and cooed at him.

'It must be a blow to know your husband went astray,' she said conversationally.

Not fully understanding her meaning, Lizzie waited.

'Some men can't help it,' Nell White continued. 'Take my man now. He's never looked at another woman, I'll swear to

God. Then there's yourn with a pretty young wife and still he chased other girls.' She was shaking her head as at one of the mysteries of life.

Lizzie thought about the female offenders that Silas had had in his charge when he was constable and also wondered if his attentions to Mardi had been common knowledge. She realised that Nell was still talking.

'... the boy looks just like him.' She was turning young Silas's head to get a better look at his pudgy profile.

'Course my May was a sturdy girl. I can understand a man being drawn to her.'

For a moment Lizzie was stunned. 'Silas wasn't his father,' she blurted out.

Nell White looked affronted. 'Well, he said he was. He came and took him hisself.'

'I know.' Lizzie struggled for the right words. 'You got to believe me, though. Little Silas ain't his child. His father was someone May worked with. She told me herself.'

It was clear that the woman did not believe her. 'Then why did he want to have him?' she challenged.

'It's hard to explain. He thought someone had switched the babbies round and that – well, that they was muddled up,' she floundered.

'Who?'

'Who what?'

'Who switched them round?'

'No one. It was just that Silas – well, he took against Mardi and thought she swapped them over.'

'How?'

'I don't know.'

'By magic?'

Lizzie knew that she was getting deeper in the mire and Mistress White smiled with satisfaction.

'Then he knew she was a witch,' she stated.

'No! He was confused.'

Nell looked from one child to the other.

'Anyways, if this one's Silas's –' she looked pointedly at her grandson – 'then that one's ...'

'She's mine – ours.'

'She don't look like Silas.'

228

'She's more like my family.' Lizzie had now begun to tremble and Mistress White sniffed disbelievingly.

'You'd best be careful. If that child's a changeling she'll bring trouble.' She held the boy close to her. 'Perhaps you'd best leave him here with me,' she said.

'No! If – if you're right and he is Silas's son, then he belongs with his father at the mill.' Lizzie jumped to her feet and quickly gathered the babies up, hurrying to leave, but Nell had not finished yet.

'And what about the skivvy's brat?' Garnet was unconcernedly plucking at a piece of grass that had become attached to her dress.

'She's just a babe,' Lizzie replied, her voice unsteady. 'An innocent babe. No matter what her mother's done she's –'

'She and your maid look like peas in a pod. There's something ain't right there.'

Lizzie went to sweep her way past, but at the door Mistress White caught her arm.

'I be sorry, gal. I don't mean to offend ye but you gotta face the facts.'

Tearing herself away, Lizzie ran outside. A terrible fear weighed heavy on her and she instinctively cradled Ruby close. Garnet began to cry as she was dragged along hanging on to Lizzie's skirt. Looking down at the clear brown eyes and the high-cheekboned face, Lizzie no longer knew if she felt love, compassion or fear of this vagrant child.

Chapter Eleven

During the sixteen years of her life Mardi Appleby had suffered neglect, beatings and starvation, but never had she felt so cold as when she lay on the edge of the castle pond. Much of her body was caked in mud from the murky waters and it provided her only covering against the keen wind.

After the terrors of the icy water, the physical assault by her captors had left her paralysed with hatred. Dimly she was aware of Lizzie's voice but as she was dragged to her feet she thought that she had imagined it. The shawl now draped around her shoulders was, however, familiar.

Her dress lay nearby, trampled underfoot until it was a sodden, uniform clay brown. Somebody had the wit to pick it up but there was no way that the girl could be pushed back into it, so with only the shawl for protection, she was half dragged, half carried back to the prison.

Lying in the damp straw, her whole being was concentrated on trying to stop her chattering teeth. She hunched smaller and smaller in the hope of finding enough warmth to ease the chill in her belly. Finally a bowl of tepid stew was brought to her. It was too insipid for her even to guess at what it contained, but she drunk it gratefully just to get the taste of mud out of her mouth.

'Ain't you got no one to oversee you?' her gaoler asked.

Mardi shook her head. There was nobody in Newport to bring her food and clothes and to make her stay bearable.

'No money?' he added.

Again she shook her head. She was hunched into a little ball so that the shawl covered her entire body.

'Well, you'll only be here till tomorrow, then they're sending ye to Winchester. You'd best find someone there to look out to you.'

In the morning her kirtle was returned, still damp but with the worst of the mud washed out. She struggled into its clinging confines, feeling faint and exhausted.

She set out for Winchester with one other felon, an old woman who was little more than a bag of bones with milky eyes and a sunken, toothless mouth. She and Mardi were roped together at the waist and given into the charge of a guard.

He arrived mounted on a sturdy bay horse and proceeded to lead the way towards Yarmouth, his prisoners following on foot.

The old woman, having lost her stick after a few yards, hobbled with painful slowness, being alternately jerked by the rider in front and bumped into by Mardi at her rear. Before they had gone a quarter of a mile, she tripped and fell on the rocky, uneven pathway with a groan of agony.

'Are you hurt, Mother?' Mardi bent down beside her. The old lady was moaning, her hands clutching her hip.

'She can't walk,' Mardi shouted to the guard, who was attempting to hoist her upright by pulling on the rope. With an exasperated sigh he dismounted and came to investigate.

'Why don't you put her on your horse?' Mardi suggested. He gave her a dismissive look. He was a short, stocky man, not much taller than his young prisoner, his belly protruding over his belt and his face so bloated that his eyes seemed to be peering from two tunnels.

'Horses is fer guards,' he replied and started to heave the old woman off the ground. Ignoring her screams, he set her on her feet. Almost immediately she fell again, this time fainting. As there was now nothing else to do, he flung her over the horse's withers and set off at a trot so that Mardi had to run to keep up.

As they continued westwards, the wind came up and it began to rain. Stopping only to put on his cloak, the guard forced the pace, Mardi dragging behind in the icy wetness. They arrived at Yarmouth late in the afternoon and he made straight for the waterside.

He soon found the boat that was standing by to take them across, but there was bad news.

'Not today we won't,' the boatman said in answer to his

231

request. ''Tain't fit fer man nor beast out there. We'd best see what happens at first light.'

Cursing profusely, the guard dragged his weather-beaten entourage round to the castle that dominated the entry to the river Yar. On the landward side it was protected by a moat and they made their way across it, stopping at the entrance in the eastern wall. At the gate they were challenged. Fumbling in his jerkin, the guard finally produced a document. The sentry scrutinised it; it was clear that he could not read but he recognised the seal and allowed the visitors into the narrow passage inside the gate.

While their guard was escorted to see the officer in charge, Mardi was tethered along with the horse to a post. The old woman still lay like a scardycrow across the animal's shoulders. Slowly she slipped to the ground and lay unmoving at Mardi's feet.

She was about to touch her when the guard returned. Mardi was untethered and given into the custody of a gunner, who led her away. As they turned the corner, she glimpsed the guard shaking the old lady, but she did not move.

Mardi was led up the steps, along another passage and finally into a tiny room, where the door clanged behind her. It seemed the height of luxury, for there among the barrels and boxes were a mattress and a horsehair blanket. The floor was solid and the small, barred window which looked out across the Solent was glazed. For once there were no drips or drafts to torment her. Unhesitatingly she flung herself down on the mattress and pulled the blanket about her.

Her almost instantaneous sleep was disturbed by the arrival of the young gunner carrying a plate of hot venison and a mug of ale. Unable to help herself, she grabbed them both and ate and drank ravenously.

'You'm hungry.' The young soldier sat back on his haunches and watched her eat. 'What you done?' he asked after a while.

'Nothin'.' She chewed the last of the venison and wiped up the gravy with a hunk of bread.

'What they accusing you of, then?'

'Bewitchment.'

The young man said nothing but stood up, rubbing his hands against his breeches.

232

'Can't you witch yourself out of here?' he asked.

Mardi shrugged. He still stared at her and finally, as if making up his mind, he asked:

'Do you make love potions?'

The girl considered the question. 'For a price,' she answered.

'How much?'

'A shilling.'

'I ain't got that much.'

'What you got, then?'

'Fourpence.'

She thought carefully, then said: 'I'll take it, so long as you bring me some more vittles.'

He nodded enthusiastically.

'Right,' the girl said. 'Go and get me a pebble and some well water and ... and a spider.'

'Is that all?' He sounded doubtful.

She nodded. 'It's the magic that I say that makes it work.'

He hurried out and was soon back, looking nervously along the corridor before coming in and closing the door. Mardi smiled to herself.

'What's she called?' she asked.

'Who?'

'Her that you want to enchant.'

'Sarah.' He blushed. 'Sarah Liddell.'

Holding the pebble in her palms, Mardi raised it above her head and turned round solemnly three times, reciting an old poem her father had often told them when they were children.

'Round a way and down a way,
Such a girl as comes my way,
Kiss and bow and touch this stone,
And this'll make the girl my own.'

She dropped the stone into the bowl of water and, taking the now squashed spider, repeated: 'With my web I'll capture the heart of Sarah Liddell.' She dropped the spider in and stirred it with her finger. 'Now drink it,' she said to the soldier, holding out the concoction.

Reluctantly he took a sip of the liquid.

'You must drink it all.'

Shuddering, he obeyed.

'Where's the fourpence?' she asked, holding out her hand.

'You're sure it'll work?'

'Course it will.' She gave him a withering look and, standing on tiptoe, looked out of the window. The sea was lashing up against the castle wall and the wind howled eerily around the ramparts.

'Who you guardin' against?' she asked.

The soldier shrugged. 'The Frenchies, I s'pose,' he replied.

'You ever killed anyone?'

He shook his head.

'You used a pike?'

Again he shook his head.

Mardi was now so sleepy that she turned away from the young man and said: 'Pay up 'cause it's time you was gone.'

As if remembering where he was, he started and jumped to his feet. Dropping a coin into her hand, he hurried out of the powder room, hastily locking the door. She could hear him running along the passage.

Feeling pleased with herself, Mardi tucked the coin into the hem of her kirtle and flopped down on to the mattress. Within seconds she was asleep.

In the middle of the night she was aroused by the clanking of the lock. Before she could open her eyes, someone had a hand over her mouth. She froze.

'Don't you squawk or I'll fixe ye.'

She recognised the voice of the guard who had brought her from Newport. He was pulling back the blanket and climbing on top of her.

'Ged off!' As he loosened his hand over her mouth, she gripped his finger with her teeth.

'Yeouw!' He pulled back in pain.

Her eyes were now accustomed to the dark and she could make out his blubbery outline.

'You forget what I'm charged with,' she said with a calmness she did not feel.

Grabbing her shoulders, he pushed her onto her back. 'Shuddup and open your legs.'

'What's happened to the old woman?' She kept her legs tight

together and dug her elbows up into his ribs to keep his weight off her.

'Never you mind.' He tried to get his knee between hers but she continued:

'If you don't get off I'll tell 'em how you killed her.'

At this he stopped.

'They wouldn't believe you,' he finally answered.

'If I use my powers they'll believe me.'

She sensed his indecision and added: 'If you don't do as I say, I'll put a curse on you that no one can lift.'

She heard him gulp and knew that she was winning.

'I'll only ask one thing,' she said, pressing home her advantage.

'Whassat?'

'When we get to the other side you let me go.'

'I can't. If I does that I'll be punished.'

'If you don't I'll curse ye.'

'I'll tell 'em what you said. I'll say you've confessed.' There was triumph in his voice but it was short-lived.

'Even if you do I'll still put a curse on you.' She knew that his lust had subsided and wriggled out from under him. 'In fact,' she said, now free from his grasp, 'if you let me go I'll give you a spell to protect you, then they won't punish you.'

'What kind of spell?'

She hid her elation. 'All you got to do is get some well water, a pebble and a spider.'

'I dunno.' He hesitated.

To remove his doubts, she added: 'Remember what'll happen if I curse you. You'll die. Slowly.'

He moved for the door and hastened out.

'Bring 'em in the morning,' she called to his retreating back. 'It can't fail.'

Grinning to herself, she went back to bed and straight to sleep.

The next morning she went through the spellmaking ceremony, altering the incantation to suit the occasion. Retching and complaining, the guard drank down the potion and within the hour they were aboard the small boat and sailing with the wind towards the mainland.

235

The guard had left his horse at the castle and collected another as soon as they landed.

'Give us a ride,' Mardi demanded.

Grumbling, he hoisted her up in front of him. There was a growing warmth in the sun and they set off in the direction of Winchester.

Mardi felt the excitement racing through her veins. In the year that she had lived at the fulling mill, she had tasted for the first time some security. Food was always forthcoming, she knew where she would lay her head each night and Lizzie had shown an interest in her. It had been good. If it hadn't been for that old devil the miller, she would probably never have wanted to leave, at least not until she had found Will. Curse him, she thought.

Now, riding along, she remembered the anticipation of travelling the roads, of using her wits to get food and money from gullible villagers. She had almost forgotten some of her skills – netting wild birds for the pot, clay-baking a hedge pig and sleeping in a huddle of children under the trees. The balmy weather filled her with nostalgia for those days.

She had no idea where her father might be, if he had survived. She concentrated hard and did not think that he was dead but he wasn't near enough to see in her mind. Anyway, it didn't matter. She knew that she would find him sooner or later. She could look after herself well enough, and fall in with any other bands of travellers whenever she chose.

Nearing Cadnum she suddenly said to the guard: 'Right, I'll get off here.' She could feel him wavering, so she added: 'If I say the word, that potion you drank will turn to poison instead of saving you.'

He reined in and she slithered to the ground.

'Just you ride on,' she said. 'Say I put a spell on you and you were turned to stone for an hour. Say you searched for me but I'd made myself invisible.'

He nodded unhappily.

Before going, she asked: 'You got a shilling?'

He shook his head.

'Well, give us a groat then.'

Reluctantly he produced the coin and threw it at her.

236

'Don't forget what I said,' she called, picking it up. She turned her back with a grin and strode out into the forest.

Chapter Twelve

Will now had all the qualifications he needed to set up as a master craftsman in his own right. He had lived in London for a year and a day, he had served his apprenticeship, he was now a freeholder and he was twenty-four years old. With some trepidation he decided to do so and was immediately offered more work at Clark's Well, his earnings leaping to forty pounds a year.

He was also now entitled to take on an apprentice. In doing so he would be committing himself to staying in London for seven more years and the realisation filled him with misgivings, but he went ahead. He could have taken on the son of a yeoman or the younger son from a merchant's household and received a handsome payment in return, but instead, feeling very public-spirited, he went to the poorhouse.

There he discussed with the overseer the merits of the children in his charge. These were indeed the lucky ones, for they had been taken in and offered food and shelter in return for earning their keep. The unlucky ones, such as Rose had once been, lived and died in the gutters.

'I don't want no scoundrel,' Will warned. 'My wife's not in the best o' health and I want someone I can trust.'

'Of course,' the overseer concurred, scratching his huge belly. 'There's thissun, for example.' He reached out and grabbed the ear of a tiny boy who happened to be passing.

Standing on tiptoe to avoid more pain, the lad was paraded in front of Will, his head tilted. He was dark and skinny and his eyes looked too large for his bony face.

'Thissun's bright. He knows his numbers and we've always

238

impressed on 'em the importance of being polite and obedient,' the overseer assured.

Will could feel the boy's pain and he reached out to put his hand on the child's shoulder, thereby encouraging the overseer to release his hold.

'What you called, son?' he asked.

'Ben, sir.'

Will feared that he might be about to make a costly mistake, for the lad was so undersized that he did not look capable of carrying out any physical work. Something about his expression reminded him of Rose.

'Well, boy, you don't look very strong.'

'I am, sir.' There was desperation in the reply.

'Can I have a look around?' Will asked to buy time.

'Of course. We looks after 'em like we was their own families.' The overseer was obsequious, bowing to let Will precede him along the narrow, smelly corridor.

At the end of the passage were two large dormitories, one for the boys and one for the girls. In each room straw was scattered across the floor for the fortunate children to sleep on. It fell to the older ones to change the bedding as and when necessary, which averaged once a month. From the stench Will thought the month must be up.

He was taken to the kitchen, a bare room with a few dusty shelves and a fire on which burned a single blackened pot containing what looked like dirty water.

'We have soup today,' the overseer enlightened him.

'Do the children have clean clothes?'

The man looked surprised and not a little indignant. 'We ain't got facilities for a lot of washing,' he replied. 'This is a charity, remember. We're dependent on good will. Mind you, we keep the vermin down.' He indicated the row of shaved heads.

'How many littluns you got here?' Will asked.

'Near on fifty. We keep 'em till they're eight maximum, by which time they've gotta be employed.'

'How old is he?' Will glanced down at the boy Ben, who was shuffling behind them.

''Ee's nine. That's Christian charity, see. I hadn't the heart to just fling 'im out. But he'll need to go real soon.'

239

With a sigh, Will said: 'I'll take him for a month to see how he gets on, but if he ain't no good, then after that you'll have to take him back.'

'Of course.' The overseer couldn't hide his satisfaction. 'That'll be a guinea.'

'A guinea? You mean you want money for me to take him off your hands?'

The overseer wiped his hand across his mouth and shifted from foot to foot.

''Tis customary. 'Tis us what's fed and kept him in good health. Otherwise you wouldn't get no work out of him. Strong as a horse, he is.' He poked the child in the chest.

With a snort of disapproval, Will found a coin and begrudgingly paid up. Much as he wanted to refuse, he could not bring himself to leave the boy behind.

They left without saying goodbye, Ben sheltering behind his new benefactor and trotting to keep up. He came as he was, for of course he had no possessions. Once they were well away from the poorhouse, Will slowed down and looked round at his new apprentice.

'Don't you worry, lad,' he said kindly. 'You be a good boy and try your best and I'll see you're looked after.'

Predictably, as soon as Rose set eyes on the child she took him into the warmth of the cottage and set about feeding and cleaning him.

'Poor little mite! It ain't right, no one should be treated like this.' She had taken Will's old shirt and was already cutting it down to fit the boy.

Watching her, Will felt the tenderness that was his most common emotion towards her. He wished that she could have a child of her own to strengthen their union, but so far this had not happened. He was surprised at how much he wanted a son to whom he could pass on his skills. Somehow a child would give their marriage a purpose, a reason for having taken place. He wondered if her poor health was the reason that she did not conceive. It was an easier burden than believing that this was the Almighty's way of showing his disapproval.

In spite of their improved diet, Rose remained thin and pale and sometimes in the night Will would hear her moan softly with the pain from her leg. He paid out for a physician to examine her, but he recommended leeching and prayers, neither of which seemed to help.

To purge his guilt for not loving her enough, Will bought Rose a green velvet dress decorated with pearls, but it was too big and did nothing to alleviate her pallor. Bitterly he could only visualise how perfectly it would have suited Lizzie and he hated himself for his dishonesty.

Apart from his yearning for Lizzie, his homesickness for the Isle of Wight was genuine. Sometimes he longed for the wide open spaces that had been on his doorstep. In London he had to walk a couple of miles before he came to the countryside and even then the villages were spreading outside the city wall. It struck him as an irony that he was helping to build the very places that he disapproved of. It was clear, however, that in spite of crown regulations forbidding the construction of any new houses, nothing was going to hold back the growth of the city.

Will set Ben to work the next day and, small as he was, the boy struggled to lift the great stone blocks until his master had to restrain him. All day he worked tirelessly, learning to dress the gritty grey surfaces, and Will felt confident that if he continued as he had started Ben was going to be an asset rather than the liability he had feared.

Will remembered his own early days at the castle. He too had been anxious to please, but he could see that in the boy's case the terror of being sent back to the poorhouse was driving him beyond his capabilities. In any event Rose would never allow him to part with the child.

'Slow down, lad,' he cautioned. 'No need to harm yourself.'

His own memories of his apprenticeship were happy ones, for his master had been kind. There and then he vowed that he would do his best for Ben and treat him as the son God had so far failed to give to him.

A week later Will fell sick with a fever. For two days he was unable to leave his bed and, lying there feeling weak and sweaty, he had plenty of time to think.

He realised that if he had died Lizzie would never have known what had happened to him and he vowed that somehow or other he must find a way to get word to her.

As soon as he felt well enough, he wrote a letter to the Reverend Cotton at Caulbourne asking for any news of Granfer Gosden. It was from this minister that as a child he had learned his letters. He did not know how the letter would be received and he carefully ignored the logic that reminded him that he should be writing to Shorrel where his grandfather lived.

The letter was short and at the end he wrote:

'It would greatly please me if you could pass on news of my wellbeing to those who have memory of me and tell them that I would welcome news of them in return.' He mentioned his own good health and fortune but not his marriage. As soon as he was fit again he delivered the letter with a shilling to a carter travelling to Southampton, with the request that he would pass it on to anyone crossing the water to the Isle of Wight.

If God was willing, one day Lizzie might hear his news and he hoped and prayed that she would find a way to respond.

Chapter Thirteen

The news of Mardi Appleby's escape took some weeks to filter back to Caulbourne village. It was generally received with disbelief and frustration. For the witnesses at her trial it meant not only the loss of their moment of glory but also forgoing a once-in-a-lifetime voyage across the sea to Winchester. Besides, it had been widely assumed that when Mardi was hanged her body would be brought back and displayed at the crossroads. Now they were also to be denied this novelty.

Only for Lizzie did the news bring relief. She offered up a prayer of thanks for her servant's deliverance. With the knowledge that the girl was now safe, most of her nightly terrors ceased and in spite of her responsibilities life seemed a little less desolate.

Silas's condition continued to deteriorate; that and Will's silence were the two great burdens she still had to bear. They seemed inexplicably linked.

The children thrived in the summer sun. Coming home from visiting her mother one scorching August afternoon, Lizzie was full of plans for taking on a kitchen maid so that she would have more time to devote to them. With this satisfying thought foremost in her mind, she stepped into the kitchen and set about making a broth. Ever since that dreadful day when Nell White had implied that Ruby was a changeling, she had stopped visiting her. Now Lizzie had so little milk herself that she had to feed all the youngsters on boiled barley with mutton finely ground to a paste and mixed with ewe's milk. At least it worked.

She had been inside the cottage for a little time before going to look at Silas. She realised with some guilt that he had been unattended for a long while and that he must be thirsty. On the morrow she would get Jed to carry him outside, for although he could neither move nor speak he seemed to enjoy lying in the sunshine. It wasn't entirely kindness on her part. While her husband was outside she was relieved of his oppressive company and it alleviated the sickening smell of his decay in the downstairs room.

So much had happened since the day he had been stricken that she no longer felt a grudge against him. In any case, part of her believed that it was God's punishment to afflict him thus. Perhaps it was also God's way of testing her. Whatever it was, the feeling of hatred had died and she was glad to let it go.

As she drew nearer, she noticed that Silas was very still.

'Silas?' She called his name and shook him by the shoulder. He felt strangely solid, and with a shock she realised that life had finally gone from him.

'Dear God.' Her shoulders relaxed as if a great weight had been lifted and she stood for a long while just staring at him. Finally she roused herself and ran across to the mill to send Jed for the priest.

'He's gone. He's gone.' The words echoed in her mind. In their wake crowded the hopes for the future that she dared not put into words.

The priest came at once. When prayers had been said and she had accepted his condolences, she despatched Jed with a message to Silas's sister. Much as she hated Agnes Downer, the right thing had to be done.

For the rest of the day she carried out her duties mechanically. At last, when the babes were asleep, she retired to the sanctuary of the upper room and began to unravel her tangled feelings.

Of course she would have to mourn Silas, but after that ... Mistress Gosden – the title came unbidden into her head. Lying tense in the dark she pressed her lips against her shoulder, imagining it was Will who touched her, and her fingers trailed over her unfulfilled body.

'Oh, Will, I want you!'

Sleep would not come. She had no idea where he was. He had said that he would be away for a year or two and it was now over a year since he had left. Surely he must come back soon just to see what was happening? Once he knew that she was free, there could be no obstacle to their union. Suddenly she felt sure that her dreams would come true. With this knowledge she fell into the sweetest sleep she could remember.

Silas Dore was laid to rest in the village churchyard, and afterwards the family and neighbours returned to the mill house to refresh themselves.

Although Lizzie was the chief mourner, she soon found that the attention was centred on the dead man's sister. Sitting in her brother's chair, Agnes Downer ate as much food as she could pack away, all the time surveying the other mourners. When she had finished eating, she sat back and sighed audibly.

'I wants to know what's going to happen about the mill.'

The statement caused all present to stop what they were doing and look in her direction. There was a pause before Harry Galpine said:

'Our Lizzie'll carry on running it.'

The mourners looked from him to Agnes Downer and back again. Agnes stuck out her chin and fixed her watery eyes on him.

'I'm not at all happy that it should pass out of the family,' she stated.

'It won't. Lizzie is his next of kin now and one day it'll pass to young Ruby.'

'Who?' The older woman was now playing for effect.

'Silas's daughter,' Harry said evenly, not taking the bait.

Standing just behind him, Lizzie felt her face go scarlet. She quickly picked her child up from where she had been happily playing on the floor.

'What are you trying to say?' she demanded, her body beginning to tremble. She suddenly feared that this would be the moment when the truth was finally revealed. Looking at Silas's sister she imagined the malicious pleasure the old woman would feel in having stored up such a revelation, and she fought to stay in control.

'Seems to me as if that Mardi weren't the only witch around here,' Mistress Downer said. 'Silas must have been tricked into marrying such a young flibbertigibbet in the first place.'

245

'You old crone!' Any intention to stay calm deserted Lizzie, who now completely lost her temper, leaning forwards, her eyes ablaze. 'He was an evil old devil. I'd have rather died than share his bed. It was him what bullied father into letting him marry me.'

She saw her father flush uncomfortably but turned back to face her accuser.

In the face of Lizzie's onslaught, Mistress Downer changed her tactics.

'I'm not saying as how you meant no harm,' she said placatingly. 'But you gotta admit there's something not right about them children.'

'What you saying, mistress?' It was Harry who intervened again.

'Can't you see? That gal bears no resemblance to me brother. Then there's the bastard. You all knows that Gipsy witch wanted to get her hands on this place. She planted the child, didn't she?' Looking at Ruby clasped in her mother's arms and Garnet at her knee, she continued: 'I know they're too young to be tested or anything, but mark my words, the time'll come when they'll start the Devil's work.'

'No!' Lizzie squeezed her child tighter until she started to protest and reached out to draw young Garnet closer. Only baby Silas played oblivious on the floor.

'You stop saying such wicked things,' she demanded. 'She's my daughter. I should know, I birthed her. She's my own blood – and his.' She glanced automatically towards the place where Silas had lain so long.

'Have you any proof of what you say?' It was the Reverend Cotton who intervened, looking directly at the accuser.

Agnes Downer coloured under the scrutiny of the minister of the church.

'No proof as such, sir, but mark my words, 'tis true.'

'What you think and what you know are two different things,' he warned.

Strengthened by his comments, Lizzie straightened her back and glared at her enemy.

'I want you to leave,' she said firmly. 'Don't you ever come back again and don't you blacken my daughter's name or I'll...'

'You'll what?' Agnes was on her feet, her chins thrust forwards, froggy eyes narrowed.

Harry put his arm about Lizzie's shoulders. 'That's enough,' he ordered and, turning to Mistress Downer: 'I know you're upset but she's right. I'll send for your horse and you'd best be off back where you came from.'

In the weeks that followed, Lizzie remained tense and anxious, expecting some disaster to strike her, but as nothing more was heard from Agnes Downer she began to put the incident out of her mind.

In September she caught a feverish cold. She had to drag herself out of bed on the Sunday morning and decided against going to church. Her eyes streaming, she stepped out into the early morning light to make sure that the two mill boys were up and ready for the service. As she turned back, it was to see her friend Molly coming across the yard.

'You're about early,' she sniffed.

'Yeah. I was ready for the service so I thought as how I'd call for thee.'

Lizzie hesitated. 'I wasn't going to go,' she started, but as Molly made no move to leave, Lizzie thought that really her first duty should be to God.

'Come on then.' Together they set out for the church.

The service seemed interminably long and Lizzie began to wish that she had not come. Her nose was blocked and around her the parishioners were shuffling, prior to the last prayer.

The Reverend Cotton cleared his throat, a mannerism that preceded all his announcements, and took something from his pocket.

'Ahem. I have received a letter from one of our parish sons,' he announced. 'It came by way of a military man travelling to Yarmouth.' Unfolding the parchment, he cleared his throat again and continued:

'It is from, ahem, William Gosden. I am sure that most of you will know him and be interested to hear news of him. He writes to enquire for news of his grandfather at Shorrel but he also says, ahem: "God has granted me good health and honoured me with prosperity. It would greatly please me if you would pass on news of my wellbeing to those who have memory of me and tell them that I would welcome news of them in return."' He folded the letter and smiled at his flock.

'I shall ride to Shorrel this week and then send news of his grandfather to this young man. If any of you wish to send news of yourselves, I shall be pleased to include it.' So saying, he led the last prayer of the morning.

A great knot of emotion formed in Lizzie's stomach and she was hardly aware of what was going on around her. For the first time since he left, there was a message from him. She was certain that it was intended for her alone. Her whole existence had depended on the belief that one day he would come and at last here was the first sign that it was more than a dream. She clasped her hands so tightly together to control their shaking that she left deep nail marks on her skin.

'Lizzie!' Molly was prodding her and whispering loudly. 'Be you sick?' she asked.

Lizzie shook her head. Her cheeks were burning and she had an insane desire to laugh out loud.

'You looks queer,' said Molly doubtfully.

Lizzie struggled to appear calm.

By now the congregation was filing out but still she remained where she was. 'You go on,' she said and, ignoring Molly's questioning look, bent her head in an attitude of prayer.

She waited until the Reverend Cotton was the last person in the church, then got up and walked hesitantly towards him.

'Mistress Dore?' He bowed his head and looked at her enquiringly. He was a short, skinny man with a long, pinched nose and thin, straight-fringed hair framing his bony face. For Lizzie and all the other young people of the village, he was the only minister that they had ever known. While he was very much part of their lives, he was also held in some awe both as the representative of God and as one who dined in the two great houses of the village.

Lizzie half curtsied, her wits now deserting her.

'Do you need help, mistress?' he asked.

She swallowed, her mouth suddenly too dry to allow speech.

'When you write to William Gosden,' she finally started.

The minister waited, his eyebrows raised.

'Please be sure to tell him that Silas Dore the fuller be dead.'

He nodded sympathetically. 'Anything else?' he asked.

248

Lizzie shook her head. She knew that her blazing cheeks were betraying her and she turned away, hastening for the door.

Tell him I love him, she screamed inside. Tell him to hurry back and wed me. Tell him I can't abide one more night without him. She almost ran for the safety of her kitchen, where she paced up and down, alternately hugging herself at the joy of his message and fighting down the longing for him.

She calculated that it would be several weeks before he got her message and came. Finally she set her mind on his arrival in time for Christmas.

She could visualise him standing across the yard, setting down his pack as he saw her and racing across to take her in his arms. He would be as finely dressed as Mr Earlisman or Mr Worsley. Perhaps he would have a horse, black and silky like Sir George's. He would kiss her so hard that it would knock the breath out of her and insist that they should go that day to call the banns so that they could wed as quickly as possible.

Then of course she would present him with his daughter. She imagined his surprise, the look of joy as he surveyed her beautiful brown hair and saw his own high cheekbones and hazel eyes looking back at him. The thought of the child's small compact body melted her mother's heart. This would be one moment that would stay with all three of them for the rest of their lives.

These days the children spent much of their time with their grandmother, for Lizzie was too busy to give them the care that they needed. They were over at the Sheepwash at this moment and, taking her spindle, she set off across the meadow to fetch them home.

As Lizzie opened the cottage door, Leah was spinning by the shaft of light from the narrow window. The children were on the floor near the fire and they scrambled up to meet her. She picked all three up and kissed their small eager faces, then set them down and joined her mother.

Both women worked companionably together, passing the time of day. As Leah spun, Garnet handed her strands of fleece while Ruby played with a spindle and little Silas banged on the floor with a stick.

'I hear Will Gosden's writ to the Reverend,' Leah remarked. It was a casual observation but she was watching her daughter.

'Mmn.' Lizzie lowered her head and worked faster.

A smile played around the older woman's lips. 'You still sweet on him?' she enquired.

After a pause, Lizzie nodded.

'D'you think as how he'll ever come back?'

Lizzie now raised her head to meet her mother's eyes. 'I know he will,' she said, smiling.

Her mother returned her smile and said: 'He'd best not be too long. There's plenny o' others has got their eye on thee.'

Lizzie shrugged. 'I can wait,' she replied, putting down her spindle. 'No one's going to come between us now.'

Chapter Fourteen

As soon as Mardi was sure that the guard had gone she sat down in the bracken deciding what to do next. She thought she should go back to the island and fetch Garnet, but a small child was a burden and Lizzie could be relied upon to look after her. If she crossed the Solent, moreover, there was the danger of recapture and anyway the child would be more useful when she was grown.

Having made up her mind, she looked around to get her bearings and started out towards London. She wasn't sure of the date but hoped she may arrive in time for St Bartholomew's Fair. With luck she would then make enough to see her through the winter.

Mardi hitched a lift from a drover. As the cart rumbled along she told him he would soon be rich and successful with women. It seemed a fair payment but she could see that he had plans to put his success into practice that night, so as soon as they stopped she beat a retreat. It was easy enough to find another lift.

Next morning she fell in with a group of soldiers marching to London. Tagging along behind, she started to flirt with them collectively, and as they trudged along she selected her target.

The lieutenant was a straight-backed, fair-haired young man of obvious means. Keeping pace with his mount, Mardi was pleased to find his eyes straying to her and after a mile or two he invited her to ride behind him on his horse.

'Where you going?' she asked, holding him lightly around the waist.

'First London and then the Low Countries.' After a while he added: 'If you have no plans you could come too.'

'Why do you go?'

He gave her a self-satisfied glance. 'To fight the Spanish.'

'I haven't got a licence,' she forestalled him wondering if there would be any danger.

'No need for you to worry about that. I'd make arrangements for you.'

Mardi weighed up the wisdom of such a move. She had no doubt that she would be smuggled out and earn her passage as a whore, but the prospect did not dismay her. Since the birth of her child she had grown increasingly hungry for sex, although only on her own terms. She studied the lieutenant again and found him not displeasing. When the silence had lasted for several moments, he added:

'We'll be headed for Tilbury on the 26th. I'll be in the Nag's Head the night before. If you want an adventure, then meet me there.'

'What date is it today?' she asked, not committing herself.

'The 19th.'

Mardi smiled, for that meant there were still four days until the fair started.

'Maybe,' she said in answer to his offer.

Arriving in London, he bought her a meal but then had to report to his senior officers. Before he departed, Mardi allowed him an embrace in payment; then, with a half promise to meet him, she left to join the throng around Chepe Side.

Wandering the city, she helped herself to some cherries and cheese from a stall and used the cherry pips as the basis for insect repellent to sell at the fair. Wrapped in wormwood it had an interesting aroma and she held it under her nose to drive away the stench of pigs being driven to the slaughterer's at the corner of the street.

Using anything else to hand, she made a selection of potions and hid them in a deserted lean-to near West Smith Field ready for sale at the start of the fair. With a few tucked into the bodice of her kirtle, she then made her way to the grander houses along the river.

Here she sidled in across the courtyard and went around to

the kitchen. At the first one she was greeted by two fierce dogs and a bucket of water, but at the second she was luckier.

The maid who answered her knock had an anxious, pale face and intuitively Mardi said: 'You need a draught to bring on miscarriage.'

The maid's hand flew to her mouth and her face was transfixed with fear. She glanced down at her belly as if not believing that her condition could already show.

'No one knows,' Mardi said, hiding her triumph. 'It won't cost you nothing but a decent gown and some shoes.'

The maid had started to shake her head, but Mardi pressed on: 'It ain't no place for a husbandless woman on the streets.'

The maid swallowed hard and closed the door, leaving Mardi standing in the yard. She was not sure whether the girl was coming back but waited hopefully.

Just as she was about to give up, the door opened again and there she stood, hugging a rich red velvet dress with a panel of deep-burgundy brocade. Mardi's eyebrow's shot up at the grandeur. The girl also produced a pair of fine red satin shoes and two petticoats.

'Here, take 'em quick and give me the cure,' she begged.

Mardi accepted the clothes and produced one of her packages. It contained motherwort and sheep dung. As an extra precaution she placed her hand on the girl's belly and closed her eyes, wishing long and hard.

'There. It's all done. Drink this down in water and jump up and down until the first man walks into sight. After that you'll bleed.'

The girl nodded gratefully and scuttled back inside with her treasure. Clutching her own treasures, Mardi made a hasty retreat.

Now that her clothes were so fine she decided to do something about the rest of her. Once it was dark she went to the nearest tavern and crept into the back yard. There was a bucket of water standing by the well, and no one was about. She pulled off her filthy kirtle and poured half the contents of the bucket over her head, starting as the cold liquid coursed over her. Energetically she rubbed her body and head with sprigs of rosemary gathered on the way to London, then rinsed herself with the rest of the water. Dripping and shivering in the cool night, she dried herself as best she could with the inside of her old kirtle and tried on her new gown.

She grinned in the darkness, for it seemed as if tailor-made for her and to her delight the shoes also fitted. Being unused to covering her feet, however, she took them off again. If they served no other purpose, she could always sell them, but their shiny red smoothness was too great a pleasure to sacrifice for a while.

The weather was set fair and for the next few days Mardi amused herself around the streets, sleeping in the lean-to each night. She was saving all her energies for St Bartholomew's Eve.

The morning of 23 August dawned warm and dry and Mardi was at the fairground before daylight. She had no tent to pitch but practised her arts on the early traders and pedlars who, like her, had arrived to sell their wares. The fair was intended for the sale of cloth but cattle and horses, pewter and leather merchants made up a large part of the assembly. What really drew the crowds, however, was the maze of exhibitions and stalls, quack doctors and minstrels who for three days entertained and bemused the townsfolk.

Mardi's mixtures were selling well but her best earner was her palm reading. It never ceased to amaze her how gullible nontravellers were. At the same time she was often astonished when some inner knowledge arrived out of nowhere. Sometimes it frightened her.

The first day went well. On the second afternoon she was in the process of convincing two lads that they would win a sucking pig if only they paid her a farthing each to learn which lottery numbers to choose, when she saw him. He had his back to her but there was no mistaking his carriage and the familiar movements of his body. She had seen them so often in her mind's eye. He half turned and her belly somersaulted with desire.

Will was watching some fire-eaters, his head slightly tilted, his mouth curved up in a half-amused, half-disbelieving smile. Abruptly Mardi abandoned the youths and stood transfixed, the tip of her tongue licking her lips. Hastily straightening her bodice and smoothing down her newly washed hair, she took the plunge.

'Let me tell your fortune,' she offered, moving in front of him.

He gave an impatient shake of his head, not wishing to be distracted from the fire-eaters; then, recognising her, his eyes widened as they came to rest on her face.

'Well I'll be – it's the princess.'

Mardi jutted out her chin and thrust out one gently rounded hip, resting her hand on it. 'You look well,' she said.

'So do you. Have you inherited a fortune?' He was taking in the richness of her clothing and the maturity of her figure that was the legacy of childbirth.

He then glanced awkwardly around and Mardi realised that the drab, pewter-haired woman standing next to him was in his company. The group was completed by a very dark-haired youth.

'Er, this is my wife Rose and Ben – my apprentice.' He did not introduce Mardi.

Ignoring Rose, the girl looked at Ben and immediately felt uneasy. One of those unbidden feelings now enveloped her, for the boy had an aura of pain and violence that caused her to flinch.

'Be vigilant,' she found herself saying, but he merely smiled.

With an effort she cast aside the feeling of menace and allowed herself to look again at Will. To her mind he was perfect. He stood a head taller than she and his back was so broad and straight that it made her heart thunder just to gaze on him. His thick hair and neatly trimmed beard shone with wellbeing, but it was the steadfast honesty of his hazel-brown eyes that captivated her.

Pointedly, she said: 'You've got no children yet, then?'

She was aware that the woman Rose flushed and Will looked uncomfortable.

'Not yet,' he said noncommittally.

'You will have. I see two girls, much alike. Not this year or next but maybe the one after that. Some when.'

'Does that mean we'll have twins?' There was hope in Rose's voice but Mardi merely said: 'What is, is,' and kept her eyes on Will's face.

255

'Well ...' He looked awkwardly at her and she could see the flushing under his tanned skin. He took a step back but she did not move. Rose was looking from her husband to the stranger and back.

Ignoring her, Mardi said to him: 'I shall see you again.'

He nodded, trying to cover his confusion, and put his arm around Rose's shoulders.

'Well, we bid you farewell,' he said, at which Mardi smiled sardonically.

'Fare thee well,' she replied familiarly, and with a swish of her gown and a provocative flounce of her skirts she turned and walked away.

It was easy for her to follow him and once she knew where he lived she relaxed. Meeting him had cost her half a day's earnings but that did not matter.

Standing across from his home, she burned with the need for him. It was dark and she wondered if he was sating his appetite on that mouse of a woman he had called wife. That he should find satisfaction from such a broomstick was unthinkable and she huddled in a nearby doorway to keep a hungry vigil.

Next morning he emerged at first light and set off towards Black Friars. For a while she followed behind but, as soon as she was sure he would suspect nothing, she hurried around a back alley and cut across in front of him.

'The Lord has strange plans,' she said by way of greeting, feigning surprise at seeing him.

Clearly his surprise was genuine.

'Fancy us meeting like this,' he said. 'Or did you find me out?'

'Of course I didn't. I was on my way to the river.'

He slowed his pace and listened attentively as she told him of her near-trial and subsequent journey to London. The existence of her child remained her secret.

As she finished, she glanced up at him and added: 'Now Father's dead I've got no one. I find it hard to protect myself these days. The city is full of boys who would be bulls.' She allowed her hip to brush accidentally against his thigh and he pulled away as if scalded.

'Well, you must find safe lodgings and regular work,' he

advised. 'I could ask where I work if there's employment,' but already she was looking amused.

'I don't need housework. I can keep myself well enough. But I do need a man's ... protection.' She rubbed the back of her hand against his and he swung round in agitation.

'Look, it's no good. I'm wed. You need to find one of your own kind.'

'Yes? And what's that?' Her eyes flashed and he shook his head in confusion.

'A free man,' he said eventually. 'A free spirit.'

'My spirit ain't free. It's been chained to you since you took me.'

She clasped her fingers around his and he was now looking desperate.

'Don't think I don't want you, Princess. You're that beautiful. And wild as a kestrel, but I'm not for you.'

She kissed him then, reaching up and taking his face between her small hands. She was soft and yielding and her tongue sought out the inner reaches of his mouth. There in the street he pulled her hard against him as if longing to lose himself in her body.

'Tonight,' she murmured. 'I'll be in the Angel at eight of the clock.' She allowed her hand to drift gently down his body, her fingers lingering against his crotch, before moving away. She did not look back.

That evening Will started to shift a jumble of building rubble in the back yard.

'You must be tired, why don't you leave that?' Rose asked, but he mumbled something curt and threw himself into the task. As it began to get dark, he suddenly came into the cottage and said:

'I've got to go out. Something I must sort out. I promise I won't be long.'

He kissed Rose with fervour and she gave a little murmur of pleasure. He knew that she was watching him as he closed the door.

At the Angel, the first thing he saw was Mardi seated on a stool holding court to a group of young men. For an instant he thought of Bo and his jealousy erupted. At that moment she saw him and, sweeping past her admirers with disdain, came across to him, her cheeks flushed and her black eyes sparkling.

'You're looking for trouble behaving like that,' he said, at which she grinned.

'I've had to look after myself long enough to know what I'm about,' she replied. Taking his arm, she said: 'I've got a sort of place. It ain't much but we could have some privacy. Come and see.'

'I've only come to say I'm going to have a word with Sir George's housekeeper and see if they'll take you in. You got to be somewhere decent.'

As he talked, they were walking along the narrow streets in the direction of Mardi's lean-to. She kept up a running commentary which prevented him from having second thoughts. When they arrived, he looked at the ramshackle affair in disbelief.

'You don't sleep here?' he asked.

'Come on inside and look.'

Reluctantly he ducked inside. As his eyes grew accustomed to the gloom, he was astonished at the variety of belongings Mardi had somehow acquired. Her bed consisted of a goose-feather mattress and a rich brocade coverlet.

'Did you steal all this?' he asked with misgivings.

'Not steal. I earn most of what I have.' Seeing his face, she added: 'And not the way you think. I give you my word no one man has touched me since you –'

He touched her lips to silence her and she slid her arms around his waist, letting her head rest on his shoulder. With a sigh he smoothed her raven hair and absorbed the feel of her breasts against his chest.

'You torment my very soul,' he said.

Releasing her hold, she stepped back and calmly undid her gown, letting it fall to the ground. As she stepped out of it, he gave a little moan of desire and pulled her roughly to him.

Her passion kept pace with his own. The night before he had taken his wife but this coupling had another dimension. Three times in succession he entered her and lost himself in the pure feeling of pleasure; then, lying spent on top of her, he sighed.

'I've never known no one like you.'

258

'You won't neither.' She snuggled into him and he squeezed her hard.

'Now we've got to find you somewhere else to live and find some employment,' he started.

She pushed him away and sat up. 'Listen, I don't want your sort of work and I'm quite happy here.'

'But you can't live out a whole winter in this place.'

'I can if I choose.'

He could not understand her reasoning and after a few moments he changed tack, saying: 'It was cruel of you to tell Rose she would have two children. You know it ain't true.'

'I didn't say that. I said you would have two girls. I didn't say nothing about that wet rag birthing them.'

Will was now clearly annoyed. Mardi hugged her knees to her and let out a little sigh of exasperation.

'Why do you feel so guilty about me?' she asked. 'You don't own me. You don't make me do nothing I don't want to. If you want to go on living with a milksop like that, why should I care? You must just leave me to be myself.'

'That's enough!' He was getting dressed and Mardi lay back and watched him.

'Look, if you want to go on seeing me, then you got to be decent,' he insisted. 'I've got a responsibility towards you and I want to look after you but I can't have you running around like a trollop.'

With ice-cold disdain Mardi stood up. 'Don't you fret yourself about me, you prig,' she retorted. 'I won't embarrass you. I won't be here all winter.' Her mouth pouting and her back turned to him, she looked over her naked shoulder as she added: 'As from tomorrow I'm leaving for the Netherlands.'

259

Chapter Fifteen

Lizzie fed the flame of her dreams with intricately embroidered enactments of her reunion with Will. On each occasion she added a stitch here, a colour there, until it was a more familiar picture than the view from the cottage door.

But Christmas came and nothing happened. Miserably she began to invent reasons – the weather, impassable roads, ill health – and then to extend the deadline, but Eastertide and May Day, Lammas and Michaelmas passed and a second Christmastide, bitter as ashes, had to be endured.

As the New Year was welcomed into the village, she sat leadenly at home, watching the young ones play in the yard. She could not even find the energy to scold them for neglecting their duties.

As always, Garnet was in charge. Now nearing three years old, she was tall for her age and sturdy. At that moment her dark-brown hair was awry, her cap askew and she stood, hands on hips, ordering the younger ones to do her bidding. Even in winter her skin had the tawny shade that resembled Mardi's.

Toddling after her was Ruby. Lizzie saw again the startling resemblance between them. Ruby was as tall as the elder girl and had the same rich brown hair, though slightly tinged with red. It was their eyes that were so remarkable. Lizzie had always wanted to believe that Ruby's eyes favoured Will's but that was not really the case. She felt the familiar unease. In some way their resemblance was unnatural and she wished that Ruby were not so dependent on the Gipsy child. There was something about Garnet...

Young Silas was at that moment hiding behind a naked

hawthorn bush. He was clearly visible but did not seem to realise it. In spite of her gloom, Lizzie gave a little chuckle and shook her head at his naivety. In size he almost made two of the girls but sometimes she thought he hadn't a brain in his head. He was pale-skinned and solid, so like May, and again emotion tugged at her heart.

Turning back into the kitchen, she carried on with her work. With the help of Harry and Jed, life at the mill had been comfortable enough since Silas's death, but her heart, once so full of hope, had become increasingly heavy. She had been so confident that Will would come. Now she had to come to terms with the fact that perhaps he did not intend to do so.

At first it had obsessed her that the minister's letter might never have reached him and she agonised about how to send another message, but there seemed to be no way. In any case, if he really cared he would come just to find out how she was. Getting out of the chair, she sighed. No good fretting. It was all in the past. But if God willed it, then perhaps one day still...

As lambing started, the weather turned viciously cold. Lizzie sent the children across to stay with her mother so that she could give her full attention to the ewes. These days she and her brothers were weaving their own kersey cloth as well as fulling for the neighbourhood, and the summer past had seemed the right time to expand their flock. They needed a successful lambing.

On a frosty February Tuesday, she crossed the yard to the barn to help Jed with the lambs. Ice lay like white marble in the ruts and in spite of the watery sunshine the wind pierced her to the core.

'I'm shrammed,' she said, hugging herself and clapping her hands to her sides to beat some warmth into them.

'We got twins,' her brother announced proudly. 'Look, Lizzie, a li'l boy and a li'l gal. Like Silas and Ruby they be.'

She surveyed them with pleasure.

'Perhaps he'll make a good breeder,' she remarked, watching the sturdy male lamb butting his dam's belly.

'You oughta have more babbies.' It was an astute remark from Jed and it touched an unspoken longing in her heart. She looked up at him and her eyes started to water.

'I need a husband first,' she replied, squeezing his arm.

'You oughta wed then.'

'Who with?'

Before he could answer, their conversation was shattered as the barn door flew open and George Galpine rushed inside. 'Thank God I've found ye,' he gasped. 'Come quick, gal! Summat terrible's happened.' He gave a sob as his words tumbled out.

'Whatever is it?' Lizzie asked in alarm.

He shook his head and took her arm, pulling her towards the door. ''Tis terrible, terrible – yer poor mam!'

'What's happened to Mam?' Her voice rose in panic.

'No, 'tissent Mam. 'Tis young Silas. He's drowned.'

'No! I don't believe it!' With a wail she started to run, her father struggling to keep pace with her.

'Mam sent 'em outside,' he gasped. 'They went to the pond. The ice.'

She was running flat out over the waterlogged meadow, stumbling against the hardened ruts, then on past the stream and towards the village pond some fifty yards from Sheepwash cottage. Ruby came towards her, crying hysterically, and Lizzie swept her daughter into her arms, crushing the child and babbling words of reassurance. Garnet stood like stone, her arms clutched about her. She remained silent.

By the water's edge two cottagers from West Over Farm waited helplessly. One of them held the inert body of Silas White.

''Twas an accident, mistress,' he said. 'They was on the ice. It broke. The li'l gals was near the edge but this li'l chap was heavier. He just went straight down.' Both men shook their heads, pale and shocked by the tragedy.

Lizzie snatched up the wet, lifeless body and rocked him against her. Ruby, now at her feet, clutched at her skirt, still screaming.

'Where's my mother?' Lizzie finally asked, her voice tight with emotion.

'We've took her to the cottage. She's that cut up. Keeps saying 'tis her fault.'

Lizzie, the dead child in one arm, her daughter in the other and Garnet following a distance behind, walked in a daze to Sheepwash cottage. She found Leah sitting in the chair, staring vacantly ahead of her. Neither woman spoke, but somebody took Silas's body and as if driven by some invisible sign the two women moved silently into each other's arms, a cloak of mutual anguish enveloping them.

Lizzie finally straightened her back and held her mother at arm's length. 'You mustn't never blame yourself,' she said solemnly.

Leah heaved a great sob, fighting to get the words out. 'I was feeling that tired,' she started. 'I thought some fresh air would do 'em good, they was that lively ...' The irony of the words reduced her again to incoherent sobs. Lizzie held her fast, rocking her.

Poor little Silas, she thought. Like May, he would have expected little of this world and now he would never experience anything other than his all too brief babyhood. The thought of the dead child's grandmother, Nell White, came into her mind, and in her shadow the memory of her sister-in-law, Agnes Downer. She began to shake uncontrollably.

'This is a bad day,' she intoned, rocking backwards and forwards. 'Truly a bad day.'

Little Silas White was buried near to his mother. The rain fell in an unrelenting sheet as the mourners gathered around the graveside.

Nell White had to be helped away by two of her sons while Leah, her face shrouded, stood in mute misery. Only Lizzie, holding fast to Ruby and Garnet, was outwardly calm.

As they filed down the narrow path which led from the churchyard to the green beyond, Lizzie could hear Nell's voice, high-pitched and hysterical above the wind.

'I warned ye! I warned ye all! Those gals is cursed! This is just the beginning. Just you wait and see.' She then began to wail and shout her grandson's name, calling on his mother to take him up and guard him in Heaven above.

'Where's Silas?' Ruby's clear young voice cut across the windswept churchyard.

Tears streaming down her face, Lizzie picked her daughter up and shielded her from the White family as she passed them on the narrow path. Garnet walked at her side, head held high, seemingly immune to the anger around her. The Whites stared

263

accusingly and Lizzie began to run headlong like a hunted stag for the safety of the mill. Inside she began to tremble uncontrollably, blinded by her loss and the unrelenting fear for the future.

The next few days were a nightmare. She kept Ruby and Garnet by her at all times, whether she was working in the fields or the dairy or huddled in the great double bed she had once so reluctantly shared with her husband.

Everywhere they went she knew that people were talking about them, pointing them out, but when she finally confessed this to Harry, he merely said: 'People feels sorry for what's happened, Lizzie. They don't mean no harm.'

She nodded, wanting to believe him, and yet her anxiety persisted. The day soon came when her worst fears were confirmed.

One wet morning the children invented a new game of hide and seek and amused themselves by playing in the barn. It was a relief not to have them under her feet, so Lizzie took the opportunity to leave them with Jed and pop across to Sheepwash. There was no one at the cottage when she arrived, so she returned home straight away. As always, she felt a knot of unease when the little ones were not within sight.

The walk had taken barely ten minutes, but during that time she was pleased to note that the rain had ceased.

To her surprise, the barn was deserted. Going out into the frost-laden air, she called the children and her brother by name. When there was no reply, a fear borne of anxiety gripped her heart and she began to hurry on down the lane in the direction of the corn mill.

After she had gone about a hundred yards, she heard a loud braying noise and the sound of raised voices. She halted and moved forwards cautiously, rounding the bend where a rickety bridge crossed the stream, carrying the road on towards Freshwater. What she saw froze her to the spot.

The braying noise came from her brother Jed, who was tied to a tree. His protests went unheeded for nearby his captors, a group of village boys, were intent on another game.

Creeping forwards, taut as a statue, Lizzie was aware that their attention was focused on the mill race. Single words and gasps of excitement punctuated the air as they jostled for a better view of whatever entertained them.

It was as she took a step closer that Lizzie saw the two crumpled mounds of clothing on the ground, the green fustian of Garnet's kirtle and the russet of her daughter's gown.

'No!' Her cry was drowned in the babble of noise coming from the lads.

'Look! The biggun's floating! It's true, she's the Devil's spawn!'

Lizzie rushed forwards, pushing them aside, to stop aghast at the edge of the race. In the deep, freezing, murky water, the tiny forms of Garnet and Ruby struggled to escape. In response to their cries and flailing arms, the boys were prodding them back into the stream with stout poles.

Even as she watched, Ruby sank from view, only to emerge face down and lie unmoving on the water. Without hesitation Lizzie slithered down the steep, muddy bank and was immediately immersed in the heart-stopping chill of the stream. Her wildly flailing hand caught one of the poles and she wrenched it from the lad who had at that moment been poking Ruby under.

The buoyancy of the pole was just enough to keep her afloat, for she had no idea how to swim. Shouting on God to protect her, she grabbed Ruby by the hair and pulled her face from the cloying, mud-churned mire.

'Help me! Help!' she screamed in anguish at the boys, who regarded her with unblinking eyes.

'They're the Devil's spawn, mistress. Best to let them go,' one of them finally called.

As she struggled to hold Ruby afloat, Garnet had made her way over and was now holding on to her by the neck.

'I'm cold,' she wailed. Then, looking at the group of faces gazing down at them, she screeched: 'You get me out of here or I'll curse all your toes off. You won't be able to walk. And your fingers. You'll have hooves like a horse.'

The boys were looking from one to the other. Now that Lizzie was there they seemed to have lost their sense of purpose. The strident threat in Garnet's voice also seemed to weaken their resolve.

'Please. Pull us out,' Lizzie begged, her strength beginning to desert her.

There was some hasty discussion, then the ringleader announced: 'We'll pull you out, but the other ones, if we don't drown them now, they'll do us harm.'

'They won't. I swear before God they won't. You all know who I am. This is my daughter, she wouldn't harm a fly.'

Realising that they were unmoved, she added desperately: 'I promise if you save us now I'll send the girls far away so that they can't bring harm to you. I swear before God; on my own soul.'

Miraculously the promise seemed to satisfy them. Lizzie was hauled onto the bank and dumped in a shivering heap with the children. It was there that Harry found them.

He was all for sending for the constable and having the boys thrashed and perhaps pilloried.

'What they've done is near murder,' he fumed.

'No. It won't alter anything. I know what has to be done.' Lizzie lay wrapped round in blankets, thankful only that her daughter was still alive.

'What?' Harry demanded. 'What are you up to?'

After a while his sister took his hand and, framing the words with great care, replied: 'It's something I should have done a long time ago.'

She waited until it was dark and then, taking Ruby and Garnet by the hand, she went to visit her mother.

She had seen very little of her since the funeral, for Leah had become increasingly low. She refused to accept that she was not personally responsible for the tragedy that had befallen May White's child, and nothing anybody could say would change it. Looking at her now, Lizzie thought how old and thin she had become, and her heart ached for her mother.

'I'm going to market on Tuesday so I want you to look after the girls,' she announced, as soon as she was inside.

'I can't!' Leah was shaking her head.

'Yes, you can. You must. I must do something very important.'

'What?' her mother asked suspiciously.

After a pause, Lizzie repeated what she had said to her brother that afternoon: 'It's something I should have done a long time ago.'

The following morning the Reverend Cotton opened his door to be confronted by the widow Dore and her children.

'Mistress Dore, please step inside.' He looked ill at ease as if not knowing how to treat his bereaved visitor. His trite observations were clearly inadequate and Lizzie regarded him with a stern, uncompromising expression.

'How can I help you?' he asked.

'I need to write a letter,' she blurted out, aware of the blush spreading over her winter pallor.

'Ah. Well, if you wish me to write one for you...'

'No. I need some parchment. I can make my own quills and ink.'

He nodded his head. 'Well, I can certainly find you that.'

He turned to a chest against the wall and extracted a sheet of parchment. She took it with thanks.

'There's something else.' Her face was now unmistakably scarlet. 'I need an address. I need to write to Mr Gosden in London.'

'I see.' His curiosity was undoubtedly aroused but he returned to the chest without comment, rummaged around and produced a letter.

'Here is Mr Gosden's letter. You had best take it. If I can help in any way...'

'No, thank you. I know my letters. I'll manage.'

She half bowed towards him and, going to the door, stepped out into the cold morning without a backward glance.

That evening, as soon as the children were in bed, Lizzie lit another candle and, taking it nearer to the fire, prepared to write the first letter of her life.

Dear Will? Dear William? Dear Mr Gosden? Already here was a dilemma. She chewed the goose-feather pen and sighed. Bending forwards, she began painstakingly to write.

The letter took two hours to complete, yet it was very short. At the end she signed herself 'Your's respectfully, Lizabeth Dore, Widdow'. She carefully addressed it and with relief bound it with twine and laid it on the table, ready to take with her to Newport.

Leaving Garnet and Ruby at Sheepwash cottage, she set off at sunup on Farmer, intending to be back in time to help with the work, for there was always much to be done.

Farmer alternately walked and trotted until the six miles were covered. Lizzie did not go to the market. Instead, avoiding the people and livestock jostling in the main street, she picked her way down to the waterside. She approached the nearest boatman with her request.

'Do you know of anyone who takes messages to London?'

The man scratched his head and thought.

'Try ol' 'Enry Kingswell,' he suggested, indicating a boat further along the riverbank.

'Can you get a message to London?' she asked the old man on board.

'I might.'

'It's urgent.'

He scrutinised her and finally said: 'It'll cost a florin.'

Her eyebrows shot up but she made no comment.

'I must be sure it gets there,' she emphasised.

'It'll get there. I'm takin' two merchants across the water this very mornin'. They're bound for London. I'll ask 'em to see it's delivered.'

With a nod and a sigh she handed the letter to him, paid the money, and, remounting Farmer, set out straight away for Caulbourne.

A florin was a fortune to pay for a letter, but if it had the desired effect it would have been worth it.

Chapter Sixteen

It was a beautiful spring evening as Will knocked off from
work. The house they were building was coming along nicely
and every evening as he walked the mile and a half home he had
the satisfying feeling of a job well done.

Young Ben, about whom he had had such doubts as an
apprentice, had proved himself more willing and talented than
he would ever have thought possible. With Rose's loving attention and his own kind but firm guidance, the boy was becoming
a credit to them both.

He noticed on his way the fashion for building with bricks
and wondered how long it would last. He couldn't believe that a
brick house would be as durable as a stone one and the bright
colours seemed vulgar when compared with the restful, muted
tones of natural stone.

There was also a sudden rash of chimneys, some in bizarre
shapes, altering the skyline. As he took a short cut down an
alleyway he mused on the changes that he had seen during his
life. The alley was narrow and the sun rarely reached the
ground. Outside each small, dirty dwelling filth was piled high
in spite of the city proclamation that all rubbish should be
taken away and burned at least once a week. He avoided the
alley during the winter, not only because of the running channel
of sewage, but because no one bothered to light a candle to
show the way. Now, however it was daylight and he was
anxious to get home to a meal.

He was deep in thought when something distracted him, a
movement in a pile of dirty straw. He would have dismissed it
as rats but heard a strange, unidentifiable noise. Stopping and

moving nearer, he peered into the straw. In the midst lay a baby.

With an exclamation of amazement he lifted it out, holding it away from him as he surveyed its skinny, soiled body. Its eyes were closed and it made tiny clutching movements with its hands. Hastily putting down his nammet bag he took out the cloth that had held his dinnertime pasty and wrapped it around the child, then hurried for home.

Rose was crouched by the fire as he came in. She got up painfully and turned to greet him, stopping as she saw the expression on his face.

'Look what I found,' he said, holding out the child.

'Oh, dear God! The poor little soul!' She took it gently from him and laid it on the ground near the fire, removing the now soiled cloth. Taking some water from the pot on the fire, she cleaned the baby and wrapped him in her shawl, cooing to him gently.

Watching her, Will felt the familiar tenderness. He knew how much she longed for a child of her own and his eyes rested sadly on her small, dry breasts.

Picking up his thoughts, she looked up and said: 'I don't know how we can feed him.'

'Perhaps I could find a wet nurse,' he suggested.

She nodded. Meanwhile she took some warm milk and dipped a piece of rag into it, trying to drip it between the baby's lips. It offered a feeble protest.

Will realised with misgivings that it was probably too far gone but he said nothing.

After a while Rose asked: 'What shall we call him?' She was crooning softly to the child, her small fingers caressing his cheek.

'Best wait a while,' Will cautioned.

She looked up at him in alarm and then back to the child. 'Pray God he'll gain strength,' she replied urgently.

Rose sat up with the baby all night but as dawn broke the following morning it slipped silently away. Will woke to find her with tears coursing down her cheeks, distressed and defeated.

'I would have looked after him,' she sobbed. 'Why couldn't he be spared?'

270

Will did not know the answer.

'Hush, gal,' he said softly, putting his arms around her. 'It's not for us to understand such things.' Her head lay against his shoulder and gradually her grief eased. He thought how fortunate he was in having this tender girl as his companion. Drying her eyes with his fingers, he kissed her.

'One day we'll have a babby, mark my words,' he said with a confidence he did not feel, and gently but firmly took the child from her. On the way to work he called at the church and left the baby with the priest along with some money to bury it.

As he continued his journey he thought bitterly of the prediction that Mardi had made. Rose had spoken of it time and again, hanging on to the hope that one day she would have two daughters.

Mardi. He could still see her face ordering him away from that smelly hole where she had lived. He had gone to look for her a week later but the lean-to had been demolished.

Everywhere he looked there were bawds and vagabonds, dirty pathetic women, young and old, but not one of them had the magic of Mardi. It was wrong, dangerous, but he was under her spell.

In contrast the thought of Lizzie was still too painful to dwell on. Had God been kind to him, then he would never have lost her, but could he really blame God or merely his own stupidity?

He was distracted all day, cutting his finger on a chisel at work and not noticing when it started to rain. On the way home that evening he avoided the alleyway and stopped at the market to buy a linnet in a wooden cage.

As he went in, Rose was in her usual place preparing the meal. The clattering of the pot coincided with the click of the latch opening and she did not hear him. Creeping up behind her, he put the birdcage down at her side. She jumped in surprise.

'I didn't hear you,' she said. 'Oh, the pretty thing!' She lifted the cage and surveyed the linnet. 'Thankee.' She gave him a hug and a kiss on the cheek.

He was about to take her in his arms when her next words stopped him in his tracks.

'A messenger came by this afternoon. Look.' She pointed to the table where a rolled-up parchment lay.

Letting go of her, he went over and picked it up, his expression puzzled. Undoing the twine, he unfolded the letter and began to read the words with disbelief.

'Dear William Gosden,
I need to see you most urgent. I will be at Newport Market every Tuesday morning during May. I hope this does reach you.
    Your's respectfully,
Lizabeth Dore, Widdow'.

He continued to stare at the letter, suddenly aware that Rose was watching him.

'Bad news?' she asked in concern.

He swallowed hard, his mind racing through the possibilities.

'Is it your grandad?' she added.

He started to shake his head, then said: 'That's it. I – I ought to go and see him.'

He saw her anxiety and hated himself for the deceit, but he did not know what else to say.

'When you going?' she asked.

'I don't know yet.'

He lay awake for much of the night, thinking it all out. When he had first received the news that Silas Dore was dead, he could not believe his stupidity in having taken a wife. Somehow he had fought the temptation to run back to the island. Rose would not have known where to find him and Lizzie need never have known that he was already wed, but looking at his wife's careworn and adoring face he knew that he did not have the heart to do it. For months he fretted and fumed, then abandoned himself to the knowledge that he must remain where he was. Once he had made the decision it had been easier to bear, and as long as he did not think of Lizzie he found some sort of peace.

Suddenly she was back in his life again. On a practical level he was busy at work and now was a bad time to go away. It would also take at least ten days to get there and back, including travelling on the Sabbath or even two. He would need a good horse.

272

The only thing he did not question was that he had to go. It did not even occur to him that she had no claim over him. His feelings for her now were as potent as they had been when first he had watched her as a young girl scrambling about the village with her friends.

A gang of boys had been throwing stones at her brother Jed, calling him Ninny and Donkey-brain. At first Jed had shouted back but then he had started to cry as a stone hit him on the cheek. It was Lizzie, eyes blazing, hair tumbling from under her cap, who had leaped to his defence.

'You get off or I'll flatten you!' she had screamed.

When the boys had laughed she had rushed at the nearest one, pummelling him with her fists. Before he could retaliate, Will had stepped in, pulling the girl away to safety, using his superior height and strength to send the lads packing. By then Lizzie had started to cry with outrage at the injustice done to her simple-minded brother.

He had wanted her then, not with lust, not as a possession, but with an almost religious fervour. I am in love, he had thought in amazement.

Although he tried to deny it, nothing had changed and his love for her remained as tender and devastating as ever. I need to see you most urgent, she had written. He had to go.

Realising that Rose was awake beside him, he began to make love to her, not for his own pleasure but with a reverent concern for her needs, using all his skill and ingenuity to demonstrate his care. As he spilled his seed into her, he prayed that God would give her the child she so desperately wanted.

'Don't you worry none,' he murmured as they lay close. 'I'll be back as soon as I can and Ben will look after thee.'

'I know that,' she replied sleepily. 'I know you'll always come back to me, no matter what.'

273

Chapter Seventeen

On the first Tuesday in May Lizzie left the children with Leah and went to Newport market. There was so much turmoil in her head that she barely noticed the journey. She wore her best kirtle and bound her hair with great care beneath the small taffeta bonnet that Harry had given her as a New Year's gift. On her breast she pinned Will's brooch and she slipped a sprig of lavender into her bodice. Nothing that she wore had been given to her by Silas Dore and she thought to herself that, come what may, she was now her own mistress. The mill was hers, the sheep were hers. It should have made her happy but life was overshadowed by two great emotions: fear for her daughter and longing for the man who had fathered her. If all went well, today both of these cares might be miraculously transformed.

She kicked Farmer into a trot to relieve the mounting tension in her body. Two baskets of cheeses hung across his rump but they were merely an excuse for the journey.

As always, the market was busy. Trussed chickens, hobbled pigs, baskets of ducks, tethered oxen, all mingled with the throng of yeomen and housewives buying and selling wares.

The barber had set up his chair and as she passed he was pulling the tooth of a solid, bull-like youth, the lad's head held fast as he wrenched inside his mouth with a pair of pincers.

A bawdy basket was in the pillory as her punishment for being of no fixed abode and having loose morals. A group of children amused themselves by pelting her with balls of cattle dung. To Lizzie's surprise, somebody stopped her and asked to buy some cheese. She was too distracted even to display her wares.

274

The morning seemed to last for ever and as the crowd thinned and the alehouses became noisier she knew that he was not coming. Part of her felt relief. She feared that her vision of him was so unreal that it could only end in disaster. For all she knew he might have become fat and bald and all her tenderest dreams would be spoiled.

Consoling herself with this thought, she set back out for home. You are a foolish woman, she told herself. This scheme is harebrained. But only the knowledge that there was still next Tuesday, and another and another, kept despair at bay.

Nothing of any importance had happened at Caulbourne during her absence. As the days passed, Lizzie allowed herself again to dwell on the coming Tuesday. By the time it dawned, all her hopes and anxieties were once more paramount.

As before she dressed with care, left the children with Leah and made the journey on horseback. She carefully packed some goose eggs for sale and within half an hour they were all gone, leaving her with nothing to do but wander.

A humpty-backed man had found himself a space and was juggling. Stopping to watch, Lizzie wondered at his expertise and dropped a farthing into his cloak spread in front of him on the ground. He smiled at her, his face open and friendly, and she wondered why God had punished him with such a mis-shapen body. It was difficult to imagine him unclothed and as a lover, but two toddlers sitting on the edge of his cloak bore such a marked facial resemblance that clearly some woman had taken him into her bed.

'Hello, Lizzie.'

The voice behind her stopped her heart. Slowly she turned her whole body as if she were afraid that a quick movement would frighten him away. There he stood straight, broad-shouldered, his hair and beard shining, his hazel eyes resting steadily on her face.

'Hello, Will.' She gave a little laugh of embarrassment and he bowed his head.

'You look well,' he remarked.

She nodded.

He looked around at the bustle. 'Come on, let's get away from here.'

She noticed that he was leading a handsome chestnut horse and hurried to retrieve Farmer tethered to a nearby rail.

'Do you want to eat?' he asked.

She shook her head.

'A drink?'

She cast an eye at the crowded tavern and he added:

'I've got a bottle of wine in my pannier. We could ride out a little way and drink it in peace.'

She blushed as she agreed, and soon they were leaving Newport behind and heading for the woods above Carisbrooke village.

She felt as if she were play-acting. This setting and the stranger riding ahead of her were two fantastic creations. He sounded different, looked different and yet there was an intimacy born of dreaming in their response to each other. With each passing minute he seemed to dissolve into the familiar shape and sound of the man she had always loved. I shall wake up in a minute, she thought.

'You don't know how good it is to be back' he said, looking around. 'You can't imagine how I've missed – everything.'

She followed behind until, finding a glade among the oak trees, Will reined in and dismounted. He turned and helped her down, an unnecessary gesture for she was lithe as a deerhound, but his hands about her waist and the smell of him were such a joy that she almost laughed out loud.

Taking the bottle from his pannier, he spread his cloak on the grass and invited her to sit down. She did so, pulling her skirt tight about her knees and rocking dreamily as he joined her.

Will opened the bottle and offered it to her. She tasted it cautiously, liking the sweet, musky elderflower and drinking again. He in turn took a draught and wiped his lips on the back of his hand. He settled the bottle firmly upright between some tufts of grass and rested back on one elbow.

'You got my letter, then?' she said to cover her embarrassment.

'I did.' He raised his eyebrows questioningly.

'The Reverend read your letter out in church. I . . . asked him to let you know that Silas was dead.'

He made no response and for the first time she felt that all was not well. A tendril of unease touched her heart.

'Come on, then, tell me what's troubling thee,' he asked instead.

She gave a little shrug. 'It's a long story.'

After a pause he said: 'You had a child.' It was a flat statement and she nodded.

'Nine months after you ... visited me.'

Her face coloured and her heart gained momentum.

There was a long silence before he asked: 'What are you saying?'

She did not look at him. 'She's a girl, I called her Ruby – after the stones in my brooch.' She blushed and, glancing up, was unnerved by the disbelief on his face.

'She ain't Silas Dore's?' he asked, shaking his head.

'No.'

'Oh, my God!'

'What is it?' She reached out towards him but then dropped her hand. He was still shaking his head.

'I don't believe it,' he said.

No one knows, though if they saw you together...'

He did not appear to hear.

'I don't believe it,' he repeated.

'Will. I thought you'd be ... pleased.' There was fear now in her voice.

With a visible effort to shake off his shock, he looked at her.

'I don't deserve you, Lizzie,' he said. 'I ain't never really deserved you. I got it wrong all along the way.'

'I don't know what you mean.' She could not shake off the need to touch him and gently she ran her fingers along his cheekbone. Briefly he cradled his face against her hand, then with a sudden movement pulled away.

'You've got to know. I knew you had a child. When I heard I was that jealous, I...'

'Will! Whatever is it? It can't be that bad.' Her hand came to rest on his arm and the gesture caused him to close his eyes as if in some torment.

'Oh, it is,' he replied. 'It couldn't be worse. I couldn't bear the thought of him 'n you together, making a babby – so I took a wife.'

She made no reply. His words froze her. Only the rapid blinking of her eyes denoted that she had heard what he said.

277

'It's no good me pretending otherwise,' he added. 'I took some poor gal and cheated her because all my love belonged to you; and I cheated you because I gave some other woman my name.'

Still she said nothing, waiting in vain for him to tell her it was not true, but he merely said: 'I married out of my own pain, and in pity for the maid I took to bed. It can't help to say it, yet it's true. I think she'd have died otherwise.'

She did not ask him how, but her hands had knotted into small twisting fists in her lap.

'Why have you come?' she finally asked, her voice little more than a whisper.

Will turned to face her and there was pain in his eyes. 'I came because I couldn't stay away a day longer. Even without your letter I was always trying to find ways, then when I heard from you . . . I only knew that if you needed me, then I belonged here. I'm sorry, Lizzie. There ain't no words to say how sorry I am. You'd best tell me what's bothering you for if I can help in any way, I will.'

She turned away from him, her shoulders hunched with misery, struggling to keep calm. With an effort she started.

'It's a stupid story. Silas brought home a gal, a skivvy. Lots of things happened and she was accused of witchcraft. They said she'd stolen Silas's babby and put ours in its place. She looks just like you.' She was a long time gazing into the distance. 'Anyhow, the skivvy ran away but village folks still think Ruby is . . . is a changeling.'

She glanced up to see what he was thinking, but his face was impassive. Taking a deep breath, she went on: 'You recall my friend May? Well, she had a babby too, a bastard.' Lizzie flushed at the use of the word but continued her story. 'He was drownded as he played with Ruby. In the village they think she bewitched him – but she didn't, she didn't!' Will shook his head reassuringly, and haltingly she added: 'The village lads tried to swim her for a witch – they nearly killed her!' Closing her eyes as if to blot out the terrible memory, she finished: 'I've got to get her away from here or they'll try again, I know they will!'

She began to cry then and did not resist the haven of his arms.

'What do you want me to do?' he asked, cradling her against him.

'I had hoped you would take her away from here, somewhere safe.'

'Then I will.'

Pulling away, she gave him a look of contempt.

'Not now! D'you think I'd let some other woman punish her because she's your child? D'you think I'd let your other brats bully her and call her names!'

'Lizzie! There aren't any other brats. We ... there ain't been none.' He sighed. 'Rose isn't like that, neither. She'd be good to a child and love it.'

'Like a mother?' she finished for him.

They were both out of their depth, then almost to herself Lizzie murmured: 'You said you'd come back for me. I waited.'

Will bowed his head in defeat. 'I don't know what to do,' he confessed. 'You're all I ever wanted. Ever. I got no one but myself to blame for the mess I'm in now. I can't hurt Rose. She don't deserve it. Anyhow, I'd only be bringing you shame.'

Straightening his back, his hands resting on his knees, he announced: 'It'd make me proud to take the little maid back with me, but what are people in the village going to think? How're you going to explain where she's gone?'

Seizing on something practical, Lizzie answered: 'I'd planned for you to go and see the Reverend Cotton. I intend to explain it all to him. Everything. He won't approve but at least he'll bear witness to the fact that she hasn't just disappeared.' She swallowed hard and continued: 'After that, I wanted you to come to the mill after dark – and before dawn – to take her away.' At the thought of parting from her child, she began to rock.

'Lizzie!' He held her fast, cushioning her, bowing to her misery. When she finally seemed calmer, he said: 'I'm going to visit my granfer tonight. I'll call on the Reverend Cotton tomorrow evening and then I'll be over to the mill after dusk.'

Lizzie got leadenly to her feet and caught Farmer's trailing rein. As she went to mount him, Will pulled her back.

'Lizzie. I'm truly sorry. Please try to forgive me.'

Her body was limp, defeated, and she did not resist when he raised her head and kissed her. When he stopped, she turned away again and mounted the horse.

She urged him forwards a few paces, then turned. 'I forgot to

279

say, there's another child. She's not mine. We don't know who her father is. Her mother was the skivvy I told you about. She and Ruby are like sisters. They're both in danger so I want you to take her too. Please be like a father to them, treat them equal.' After a pause she added: 'Goodbye, Will,' and without looking back started on the lonely journey home.

Chapter Eighteen

Lizzie was so numbed by shock and misery that she remembered little of the journey home. She went straight to her parents' cottage to collect the children, trying desperately to hide her anguish.

'You don't look well,' her mother observed, but she brushed the remark aside, taking Ruby by the hand and gripping it so tightly that the child protested.

'Say goodbye to your grandmother. Proper,' she insisted.

The little girl climbed onto the old woman's knee and kissed her.

'I'll see thee soon,' Leah said.

'Kiss goodbye to Uncle Harry and Uncle Jed and go and find Granpa,' her mother continued.

Garnet, who was under the impression that this was her own family, did likewise. The formality of the farewells did not occur to anyone until afterwards.

That afternoon Lizzie visited the Reverend Cotton. Her heart began to beat as she wrapped on the door with her knuckles. It was opened by the minister himself.

'Mistress Dore.' He swallowed hard and his eyes took on the glazed appearance that Lizzie had come to notice whenever she faced him. For some reason she felt that her presence discomfited him and if anything it made her feel more nervous.

'I have to inform you that the children are going away,' she blurted out. The minister stared at her with unblinking eyes.

Lizzie took a deep breath and continued: 'You have to know. My daughter Ruby ain't Silas Dore's. Before I was forced to wed, I was secretly betrothed to William Gosden.' She found herself blushing at the mention of his name. 'Ruby's his,' she finished lamely.

As the minister continued to stare at her, she repeated: 'The children are going away, to Master Gosden. He's coming to see you himself.'

Reverend Cotton appeared to expect more, so she added: 'Folks round here think they're bewitched. It isn't safe for them.'

As he appeared so nonplussed, she finished: 'I want it to be known that they have gone to a patron across the water to be properly schooled.'

Finally the Reverend Cotton observed: 'You seem unwell, mistress. Have you asked God for help?'

Lizzie raised her arresting green eyes and composed her expression with slow deliberation before replying: 'Even God cannot help me now.'

The following evening, as Lizzie prepared Ruby for bed, she said: 'I have some exciting news. Your father's coming to see you.'

The little girl looked at her in surprise. 'My father you talk to in the copse sometimes?' she asked.

'That's right. He's coming here and he would like you to go with him on his horse and then on a boat across the water. Would you like that?'

The child nodded, her eyes shining.

'And Garnet?' she asked.

'Garnet too.'

'And you?'

Lizzie shook her head. 'I can't come.'

'Why not?'

'I've got to stay here and look after the mill.'

At that moment Garnet came in from the dairy and Ruby told her the news. 'We're going to see my father. He'll take us on the water in a boat.'

'He's my father, too,' Garnet replied.

'Is he, Mam?' Ruby looked to Lizzie for conformation and she felt a knot of unease in her belly as she said:

'Well, yes, in a kind of a way he will be your father too.'

282

Garnet nodded with satisfaction. 'I've been thinking,' she continued. 'You're not my mam, are you? Not my real mam?'

For a moment Lizzie did not know how to answer, but Garnet added:

'I've been thinking about my real mam today. She's coming to fetch me.'

'No! Your mam had to go away when you were little. She won't be back.'

'Begging your pardon,' said Garnet with authority, 'but she will.'

Ruby, having given the matter much thought, asked: 'When will we be coming back?'

'One day.'

'What day?'

Taking her child in her arms and fighting back the terror, Lizzie repeated: 'One day.'

She put both girls in her own bed and sat downstairs by the fire until, in spite of the excitement, sleep overcame them. She seemed to have been sitting there for ever but finally there was a knock at the door. When she opened it, Will stood there. He was so broad that he filled the doorway. In the candlelight she could see that his face was drawn, his eyes tired. Standing aside, she let him in to the room.

Putting down his bag, he looked around the kitchen. 'You got it nice here,' he said in a neutral voice.

She did not answer but poured him some ale.

'I've seen the priest. It's all taken care of.' He sat in Silas's chair, the shadows from the fire dancing across his face.

'Have you told the children?' he asked her.

She nodded. 'Do you want to see your daughter?'

He nodded.

She led the way up the steep stairs to her bedroom and there, dwarfed in the bed, lay the tousled girls. Gazing down on them, Lizzie felt the terrible truth hit home. Never again would they lie in her bed, in her house. She clasped her hand to her mouth to hold back the grief.

Turning to her, Will whispered: 'Which one is mine – ours?'

For a moment they looked so alike she wasn't even sure, and the cold gripped her, but pulling herself together she indicated Ruby, her head against Garnet's shoulder.

283

Reaching out, Will moved a lock of damp hair from his daughter's cheek. His tender expression tore at Lizzie's heart.

'She's beautiful.'

'They both are.'

He turned towards her, his eyes moist with emotion. 'Lizzie!'

'Don't!' But already he was kissing her, caressing her, and her body was drowning in the river of need for him. She clung to him, trying to lose herself in his very being, but as he went to lift her up, some cold terror took possession of her.

'No!' She struggled free and ran to the stairs, hurrying down into the safety of the kitchen.

After a moment he followed. As he came in, she was sitting by the hearth, fighting to keep her feelings under control.

'You can sleep there,' she said, pointing to the pallet. Her voice was terse and brittle.

'Lizzie, we must talk.' Will sank down on his haunches close to her.

'What about?'

'The future. Their future.'

'That's in your hands now. I'll trust you to do what's right.' Looking away, she added: 'I only ask that you let me know how they are.'

'I'll send a message.'

She nodded, her hands clasped together to hide their trembling. 'It's late. I'd best get to bed.' She rose and moved towards the stairs, her outward calmness defying him to protest, but he followed her.

'Lizzie. Stay down here. Please. We've only got tonight.' He took hold of her hand and pulled her gently towards him. She could not bear the pain in his eyes.

'No!'

As his arms closed about her, she began to beat her fists against him, sobbing out her despair. She took refuge now in anger.

'Leave me be, you traitor! I don't want no more bastards!' She spat the word and he let her go.

'Lizzie, don't!'

She ran to her room and closed the door behind her. Great churning sobs stifled her. Downstairs she could hear him moving about and she strained her ears, longing for him to come and force his way in. In the face of such devastating loneliness, the rights and wrongs no longer mattered. After a while, however, there was silence.

Time and again she nearly opened the door, nearly descended the stairs and went to him. Pride and anger were costly virtues when she might never see him again. But the minutes passed and the longer she waited, the more difficult it was to take the first step. Finally, when she felt too exhausted to listen any longer, she fell onto the bed and cradled the children for what she knew must be the last time ever.

In the morning Ruby was awake early and down the stairs to inspect the mysterious man who was her father. As Lizzie came down, they were lighting the fire together, a father and daughter sharing the everyday things of life. Once again the pain threatened to overwhelm her but she captured the memory for a time when she could bear to think of it. Garnet still slept and for the moment she left her where she was.

Lizzie went through the motions of preparing breakfast, although her hands shook so badly she could barely hold the trenchers. The ale spilled as she placed it on the table.

At that moment Garnet appeared and was pulled across the room by the younger child to see the visitor.

'We're going soon and it isn't even light,' said Ruby with enthusiasm.

The children sat down to eat while Will, refusing food, went out to see to the horse.

As each moment passed, Lizzie fought the rising hysteria. She could not let them go. Nothing on earth could separate her from her child and yet she could not let her stay either. If they were to be safe, she had to make the biggest sacrifice of her life. A moan of pure torment escaped her lips.

'What's wrong, Mam?' Ruby eyed her curiously.

She managed to say: 'Why, nothing.'

She realised that Will had come back into the room and was staring at her, his own distress apparent. For a moment he stood helplessly, then he stepped forwards and pulled her roughly into his arms.

'I can't go,' he whispered, his face against her hair. 'It's no use.'

'You must!' She pushed him away and turned her back, hugging her arms about her. After a moment she was aware that he had taken both children and left the room. She listened in mute despair as he talked to them quietly, reassuring them and finally eliciting giggles and positive squeals of pleasure as he lifted them astride the horse.

'Lizzie.' He was back in the doorway but she did not move.

'Go,' she said, and after a moment he withdrew. She heard him speak to the horse and click her into motion.

'Goodbye, Mam, see you soon.' The girls chorused their farewells as they rode across the yard. She knew that in their young minds they had no inkling of the reality of this departure. By suppertime they would be looking to come back home, and the thought of their distress made her race for the door.

'No!' Her wail had an inhuman desperation, but they were already too far away to hear and disappearing into the trees that skirted the stream.

Giving way to her grief, Lizzie fell to her knees and began scraping handfuls of earth from the floor, throwing it over herself in some primitive gesture of appeasement to the God who had punished her so.

Later that day, Lizzie went to Sheepwash cottage and told her mother what she had done.

'Lizzie! How could you?' Leah stared at her aghast.

'It's for their protection. No one must know. We're saying they've gone to a gentleman's house across the water to be properly schooled.'

She spoke without emotion and Leah continued to stare at her in disbelief. 'Have you no feelings?' she finally asked.

Lizzie shook her head. 'No, I haven't.' It was almost as if somebody else spoke instead of her.

Her mother shook her head in disbelief. 'But what about Will? Didn't he want you to go with him?' As she spoke, she saw her daughter's expression harden.

'What he wants is no concern of mine,' she replied. As if forgetting where she was, Lizzie turned and wandered out of the cottage and in the direction of Holywood copse.

'God help us all,' her mother wailed. 'I fear the Devil has taken my poor girl's mind.'

At the church service on Sunday the Reverend Cotton announced the departure of little Mistress Dore and her companion to be reared as young ladies.

While some whispered that they were too young to be sent away and that Lizzie was too full of airs and graces, most agreed that the village would be a safer place without them.

Chapter Nineteen

The children set out happily enough with their new-found father, but before long they started to cry for their mother and nothing that Will could do or say would distract or comfort them.

They were terrified by the rocking of the boat, buffeted as they were for two hours on the choppy water. Will's attention was stretched to the limit trying to cope with both children and the frightened horse. When they finally got ashore, Ruby screamed and kicked, shouting for her mother at the top of her voice, while Garnet assumed a pose of sulky accusation. He was loath to take them into an inn for fear that somebody would accuse him of stealing them, but finally, in the moist evening gloom, they fell into an exhausted sleep on his shoulders and he was able to take a room where they slept through the night cradled in his arms.

He himself lay sleepless in the dark, still too stunned by events to take in their true meaning. He blamed himself for everything and yet some things had been outside his control. He could not have prevented Lizzie's marriage because the nature of his mission to Basing had been too sudden and secret to allow any diversions on his own behalf. But he had not had to marry Rose. That had been of his own volition and now she stood between him and the woman he loved. Poor Rose! She loved him. He had taken her out of pity and to hide away from the truth, but the truth had not been what it seemed. Lizzie's child was his. It was paradoxically the best and the worst thing that could have happened to him.

288

The next day both the youngsters were morose, staring accusingly at him, and his heart ached for their unhappiness.

'You must be brave girls,' he told them. 'Mother would not wish you to be unhappy. She loves you.'

'I wanna go home. I want her, I want her,' Ruby started to sob.

'I want her too, sweetheart.' Will cuddled her, wondering how long this would last. He was tempted to take them back, but Lizzie's fears had been genuine enough and this kept him going.

Passing through Winchester, he tried to distract them both by pointing out sights in the bustling market. Garnet maintained an aloof but disapproving interest; Ruby remained dejected until her attention was caught by a white puppy rummaging in the filth.

'Dog!' She held out her hands. Will grabbed the small creature by the scruff of the neck, holding it up to her.

It wriggled and whimpered, then licked his hand with the pathetic look of one abandoned. Will thought that its expression was like that of his child.

'Do you want to keep it?' he asked.

'Yes!' The first spark of pleasure showed in her face and he sighed with relief.

'She's yours then. We'll take her to London and you can show her to Rose.'

The children looked at him questioningly and he added: 'She's my wife. She'll be your new mother.' Seeing Ruby's face begin to pucker, he added: 'Just till you go back to your own mam.'

She nodded philosophically and turned her attention to the pup, but Garnet continued to regard him with those strangely familiar hazel eyes. He thought to himself that in some ways she seemed older than he was, and the thought made him uneasy.

With her new-found companion, Ruby adapted quickly to her situation and they made swift progress. As they neared the city, Will began to wonder what he should tell Rose. His trust in her was absolute but he did not want to confess to anything that would cause her pain. He decided that while telling the truth about everything else, he would spare her the knowledge that he had any feeling left for Lizzie. After all, that had happened before he first went to London and the past must be forgotten. Forgotten. He closed his mind to the image of Lizzie standing stricken and abandoned in the kitchen.

With a sigh he decided to concentrate on Garnet and explain how she was a foundling child. In this way the reality of his own daughter might seem less intrusive.

They finally reached home after dusk. He tethered the horse in the tiny yard and gathered up his pack, both girls and the puppy. Opening the door, he went down the single step into their living room, but forgot to duck and hit his head on the beam.

Rose had on her best dress and the place was spotless. The fire burned welcomingly and the smell of food made his mouth water. He had an overwhelming feeling of peace here in this room.

'I knew you'd come today.' Rose started towards him, then stopped, surveying the quartet in amazement.

'Now what have you done?' She started to laugh. 'One week it's a babby and now its's some little orphans.'

She held out her arms and Ruby went willingly to her, the puppy wagging its tale and whimpering to follow. Garnet stood at Will's side, her eyes large as saucers.

'Oo, she's a sweetheart.' Rose was kissing Ruby and smoothing her thick, brown hair. Looking up, she held out her arms to Garnet and pulled her close. 'They've been well looked after – where did you find them?'

Before he could frame his answer, she continued:

'They'll be fine along of us. We'll raise them like our own.'

Setting the children down, she placed a pale hand on Will's arm and reached up to kiss him. He put his arms about her and hugged her.

'We'll just think of them as ours,' he said, evading her earlier question.

'You can see they're sisters,' she observed.

Will turned and threw some wood onto the fire. There was no doubt that Ruby was his child, even he could see the likeness, but Garnet must be some sort of changeling sent to haunt him. He looked at her suspiciously, but she was holding the puppy and her expression was benign. He tried to shake off his silly fears but the cloud of unease remained.

'What are their names?' Rose asked.

Will hesitated. 'What would you like to call them?'

Before Rose could answer, Garnet announced: 'My name is Garnet. I do not wish to change it.'

Will met Rose's eyes over their heads and she smiled. He returned the smile uneasily.

'I always favoured the name Ruth,' said Rose.

'Ruth and Garnet.' He looked pointedly at the older child and she lowered her eyes.

So it was that Ruby Dore became Ruth Gosden and Garnet remained herself.

Rose was now in her element. Although childless, she had had plenty of experience in caring for children in the Bowyer household and the girls responded cheerfully to the attention.

As they got ready for bed, Ruth suddenly asked: 'Is this our mother till we go back to mam?'

Will nodded and his face began to burn. He was aware that Rose was watching him.

'P'r'aps some day she'll see her real mother again,' he said noncommittally.

Rose looked doubtfully at him. 'I don't know how any woman could let her children go – specially to strangers,' she remarked.

He could think of no reply.

Later, when Ruth and Garnet slept and the puppy was curled up in a pile of straw by the fire, Rose poured him some ale and sat on his lap. It was unlike her to be so demonstrative. Generally she was reticent, accepting any attention he chose to give her with touching gratitude. Will fleetingly thought that the children were already giving her a new sense of worth.

Leaning back in the chair, he put his arm around her and kissed her on the forehead.

'Well, it's come true at last,' she murmured, snuggling closer to him.

'What has?'

'That Gipsy's telling. You remember? She said we'd have two girls and now we have.'

Again anxiety gripped him and he began to wish that he had not answered Lizzie's call. Rose was persistent.

291

'Do you know where their mother is?' She cupped his face with her cool hands and he avoided her pale eyes.

After some hesitation he said: 'They ain't sisters, but if necessary I could take them back where I found them.'

Rose gave a little sigh but made no comment. After a moment she said: 'I wouldn't want that.'

He wanted to tell her, 'Ruth's mine,' but the words would not come because his longing for Lizzie was gnawing at him like hunger.

At that moment Ben arrived home and Rose greeted him with the news. Will watched the lad's dark, intelligent face as he listened to Rose's story. He's grown, he thought. Not just in body but in confidence.

There was something extraordinary about Ben but Will could not pinpoint what it was. Something in his intensity and demeanour marked him out from the other young lads he met daily at work.

Grinning at Rose, Ben seated himself at the table and consumed the trencher of bread and meat that she placed before him. As he ate, he filled Will in with news of work on the house at Clark's Well.

When there was a gap in the conversation, Rose said: 'He's looked after me that well, like a son.' She laughed and added: 'I got three children now.'

Lying in bed, Will felt Rose turn tentatively towards him, her small hand resting on his chest. In the dark, tears suddenly formed in his eyes and coursed down his cheeks. Fighting them back, he turned and entered her frail, familiar body, easing his need. The ache in his heart remained.

Chapter Twenty

Lizzie had closed and bolted the mill-house door so that no one should see her. Outside she heard Jed rattling the handle and calling her name, but she ignored him. Her eyes were red and puffy and she was in no mood to offer explanations to her brother.

She knew that it was weak and useless to give in to her grief and yet for the moment she needed the release of tears to wash away the worst of her pain. She could only weep in privacy.

By now Will would be on the way to London, back to his wife. The fact that he had said he did not love her was small comfort. The woman had everything else that Lizzie held dear – his name, his presence and most of all his body beside her at night. Those brief moments in his arms had stirred up thoughts of what might have been, and she dwelt on the distant memory of those occasions when they had made love. It served only to make her frustrated body the more restless and unfulfilled.

She thought sadly that she had never shared her bed with him and now, through her own pride, it seemed that she never would. Perversely she regretted more than anything not having lain with him for that one night when he had been under her roof.

Thinking of Will was marginally less distressing than thinking of Ruby. The loss of her child left another kind of emptiness, a fearful concern for the wellbeing of a vulnerable girl who until now had relied on the love of her mother to protect her. That protection would no longer be there when Ruby needed it and Lizzie tortured herself with all kinds of horrors that might befall the girl. Of Garnet she thought only that, like her mother, she would know how to look after herself.

She must have dozed, for the next thing she knew there was a persistent knocking at the door. From the tone she knew that it was not Jed this time. Blinking to disperse the mists of sleep, she struggled to her feet, brushing down her crumpled skirts.

'Who's there?' she called, trying to sound calm.

''Tis me, Harry.'

She slid back the bolt and, without meeting her brother's eyes, stepped back to let him inside.

He said nothing but crossed the room and sank onto the solitary stool to rest his leg.

Finally he observed: 'Jed said you weren't to be found this morning.'

She shrugged in reply. When the silence became oppressive, Harry added:

'Have you heard the news? Old Nell White has died. In childbed. There's been a parish meeting and they're asking folks to take the nippers in.'

Lizzie felt a multitude of emotions, muted by her own personal pain. Little Silas's grandmother was no more and his young aunts and uncles would soon be scattered around the parish. She remembered the last child that Nell White had borne, another pale, solid boy.

'Mam wanted to offer a home to the youngest one,' Harry continued, 'but we said no. She isn't well enough to take on such a burden.'

Lizzie knew what he was trying to do, but in spite of herself she could not get May's family out of her mind. Through thick and thin they had somehow survived but now, with the death of the woman of the house, they were finally to be auctioned off like so many chattels.

'I can't,' she said to Harry.

'Can't what?'

'You know very well. I've sent the girls away. Why should I burden myself with some village foundling?'

'They were your friend's family. You used to go there often enough.'

Damn you, Harry, she thought. You know just how to twist the knife. Aloud she said: 'This is no place for a child.'

'They ain't all children. The bigger ones can work. You could get yourself another skivvy.'

'No!' The idea of having another Mardi in the house made her senses reel.

'Then a young lass; one you can train to help you about the place; or a lad to learn the fulling trade – seeing as how you seem set on not having any boys of your own.'

'Damn you, Harry!' She said it aloud this time, and in response he leaned back and surveyed her.

'What are your playing at, girl?' he asked. 'Are you set on being a lonely old crone? You're a widow woman, one with enough assets to attract every man within miles. Why don't you behave like any normal woman and take another man into your bed?'

'Because I don't want to!' She was becoming increasingly angry.

Standing up, Harry brushed some hay from his trousers and sighed.

'Well, I'll be leaving you then, seeing as how you're determined to live some sort of nun's life.' At the door he turned and added: 'Just don't let yourself regret it when you're too old for childbearing – and too wrinkled to attract a man under the covers.' He was out of the door before she could give vent to her anger.

After he had gone she sat down again and poured herself a large jug of ale. All the time the thought of the White children being split into parcels and sold off to the highest bidder raced round in her mind. If her Ruby was afraid, then how would those poor little ones feel?

Picking up her shawl, she wrapped it loosely over her shoulders and with a sigh set off in the direction of May's family home.

Two boys had gone as farm labourers and three girls to work in kitchens around the village. A childless couple had taken the youngest girl, which left the two youngest boys, Alfred and Sidney. Surveying them, Lizzie threw up her hands in a gesture of resignation.

'I'll take them both,' she told the overseer of the poor, who

295

had been on the point of carting them off to join their father at the House of Industry.

'Bless you, ma'am. They're fine little lads. They'll serve you well and God will see that you are rewarded.'

Would he? Lizzie doubted it. So far there had been little enough reward, but then she had wished her husband dead and been adulterous with another man. Perhaps it was no more than she deserved.

It dawned on her that this was another disturbing co-incidence. At the very time her own child had been leaving, these boys had been orphaned. This time she could not blame Mardi, but it made her wonder again whether her whole life was not already mapped out and whatever she did she would never escape her destiny. She shivered.

Coming out of her reverie, she found the two little ones staring up at her. Their eyes were large and anxious in simple, accepting little faces. At that moment her pity welled over and she bent to draw them both close.

'You know me,' she said to Alfred, the eldest. 'Me and your sister May was best friends. Don't grieve for your mam, she's gone to be with May now. You just come along with me and I'll see that you're looked after.'

Clutching both their hands, she glanced briefly at the overseer.

'Thank you, mistress.'

She bowed her head in acknowledgement as they left the hovel. This was it then. Her two girls had gone and now she had two boys – not bright boys with sparkling, intelligent eyes, but simple, lonely little boys who needed care. They reminded her suddenly of Jed. This was the way it was to be. She would work hard and do her duty by the orphans and ... She did not know what else would follow. Perhaps one day, if she fulfilled this duty well enough, God would relent and finally Will would be hers. Against all the odds, still the hope remained.

Part III

March 1595 – December 1598

Chapter One

The boat bobbed and buffeted its way across the North Sea and Mardi Appleby, making her return journey to England, was violently sick for the entire journey.

I hate boats, she thought, vowing that if she arrived alive she would never venture across the water again. Then she thought of the Isle of Wight and rephrased her promise.

She was not travelling with the lieutenant with whom she had made the outward journey. She had quickly tired of him and once she had found her feet it had been easy enough to take up with someone else. Latterly she had chosen another officer, who had both plenty of money and more spirit, and for the last few months she had stuck with him. He was now travelling home to his wife, which suited Mardi fine. Once she was back in England there were more important things to do.

She had to admit that at first she had barely thought of Garnet, but recently the child kept coming to mind, which probably meant that it was time to go and get her. There was plenty to teach her and a seven-year-old could be relied upon to be independent.

Another bout of vomiting distracted her. Lying back, cold and exhausted, on the wooden bench, she pulled her thick woollen cloak about her and tried to think of something pleasant to ease her suffering.

Will. She thought he must be old now, twenty-seven or twenty-eight. She wondered if his beard was grey and if he had lost his potency. The thought made her smile in spite of the sickness, for she knew plenty of cures for that. Apart from the medicines that could be swallowed, the best cure lay in her own hands. She had learned a lot while travelling with the military.

Will. Over the years she had found to her surprise that her hectic sexual encounters had not driven the thought of him away. She had lain with men of all types, rich and poor, young and old, handsome and ugly, but none of them had for long blotted out the memory of his face, the sound of his voice and the magic of his body. I must be bewitched, she thought, and accepted it as a natural phenomenon.

As soon as she was in London her first step would be to find him. She did not regret having driven him away and then going abroad. The expedition had been interesting and she had come back speaking fluent Dutch. In any case she could not have hung around in London while he clung to his boring marriage, but now she was hungry for him again and the thought of him sent ripples of desire through the aching muscles of her belly, strained as they were with the effort of vomiting.

Finally arriving in Tilbury, she slipped away from her officer without bothering to say goodbye and set out immediately to hitch a ride to the capital. Her heavy brocade dress clearly marked her out for what she was. Had she been travelling in the company of a family she could have been mistaken for a gentlewoman, but travelling alone she could only be one thing.

She had walked only a few hundred yards when a merchant reined in his horse and offered her the chance to ride pillion with him. She had no luggage other than money, carefully secured in the hem of her dress, so she accepted his offer with alacrity.

Stopping for the night at an inn in Maidstone, she paid for her board and lodging by sharing the merchant's bed and continued the journey next day, declining his offer of accommodation with a poor relative of his who could be relied upon to keep the news of her presence from the merchant's wife, she being a lady of some jealousy.

At Chepe Side she left her companion and made her way to the house where Will had last lived. Standing across the street, she surveyed the outside, but it gave her no indication of whether he was there. Concentrating hard, she then had the certain feeling that he was not and the disappointment settled

300

on her like a cloud. She continued to keep watch and after a while a slim, black-haired artisan stopped at the door.

As he was about to enter, she called out: 'One moment!' He turned and she felt suddenly afraid, immediately recognising the fear as that which had possessed her at St Bartholomew's Fair. The young boy had grown out of all recognition in the intervening five years.

Fighting it down, she said: 'I'm seeking Will Gosden. Do you know where he is?'

'He is my master.' The boy surveyed her with surprise, then added: 'I remember you. You were at the fair. You told my mistress she would have daughters.'

Mardi impatiently brushed his words aside. 'Where is Master Gosden?' she repeated.

'He ain't here. He's working away.'

Mardi hid her disappointment. 'When will he be back?'

Ben shrugged and Mardi knew that he resented her presence. Ignoring this, she asked: 'How long will he be?'

Ben shrugged again. 'A week. Or maybe two.'

Mardi thought that she could take advantage of the time to go and fetch Garnet.

She nodded, then found herself saying: 'Do you know you are in danger?'

'How?' His face had darkened and she thought he had the look of a zealot.

'Something you are thinking, doing. Take care.'

He bowed his head, a slight smile about his lips. 'I'll heed your warning,' he replied; then, as an afterthought: Did you wish to see my mistress?'

Mardi shook her head. 'She would not be pleased to see me,' she observed and took her leave.

Mardi went to an inn and soon found other travellers who were heading south. Paying for the use of a horse, she was pleased to be journeying in company. Money had never been her primary aim but it did have undoubted advantages.

At Winchester she fell in with a company of weavers bound for Southampton. The journey was uneventful, and arriving at the port she found a ship leaving within the hour for the Medina. Once she was on board, memories of her past cross-

301

ings crowded in on her and she wondered if her father could still be alive and travelling the fairs. She had barely thought of him in the past years but suddenly he was as clear as if he sat beside her. She shivered.

She replaced his image in her mind's eye with one of Garnet: short of stature, rich black hair and her father's eyes. More than that, she knew that the girl would have inherited her own Knowledge. Thinking hard, Mardi silently called: 'Think of me, child. Your mother is coming for you.'

As the boat changed tack, she wondered if the fuller had died. He must have done by now and her old mistress was probably remarried. But as the island coastline drew nearer, she had the sudden, vivid impression that Lizzie was not wed and that in some undefined way she was going to interfere with Mardi's plans to the point where she would be helpless to prevent it.

Mardi stopped briefly in Newport to hire a horse and see to her appearance. Now that she was a woman of substance, she was increasingly aware that her outward image gave her a status she had never before attained. With it came respect and power, and it seemed particularly important to impress her former mistress.

Having arranged things to her satisfaction, she rode straight to Caulbourne, arriving in the late afternoon. Her heart began to pound as she looked on the familiar buildings and the meadow and stream where she had once passed such a pleasant year.

She recognised Farmer grazing with a cow in the pasture. The cow was a new venture. She noted too that the thatch on the outbuildings was fresh and the yard swept. Things were clearly prospering, and yet there was an undefined air of gloom as if the soul had gone out of the place.

She reined in a discreet distance away to get a good look around, but her hoped-for glimpse of Garnet was not forthcoming. Indeed, she was suddenly certain that the girl was not there. Riding into the yard, she dismounted and hitched the horse to a post. The sound of her arrival had alerted the household, for both dogs started to bark and the door opened.

Mardi stared at Lizzie with some dismay. She was hunched

into her shawl in spite of the balmy spring sunshine and it seemed as if some spark had gone out of her. Mardi read immediately the loss in her eyes.

'You ain't wed yet, then,' she remarked by way of greeting. Ignoring this, Lizzie came closer.

'What are you doing here?' There was hostility in her voice. After a pause she added: 'You best be careful, they've got long memories round here.'

Mardi shrugged. 'I'm in no danger.' She surveyed Lizzie, then asked: 'Where's my daughter?'

At this, Lizzie's face tightened and she jutted out her chin defiantly. 'Thanks to you I had to send them both away. You and your witch's work!'

Mardi continued to stare and Lizzie added: 'We were all happy but then there was a tragedy. Little Silas drownded. Because of you, they thought my little maid was a witch – like yours. I've had to smuggle them away for their own protection. I won't never see my girl again.' She rubbed her hand across her forehead as if to staunch some pain, and Mardi stepped closer.

'Where are they?' she asked.

'It's no good you asking. You'd only go and cause trouble. I won't have Ruby put at risk. They're with . . . a friend. He'll see that they're both safe.'

'What friend?' Mardi's tone was challenging and Lizzie suddenly blushed.

Will. Mardi had always known that he was Ruby's father but until this moment she had not allowed herself to say it. It left her with a strangely numb feeling.

'You've sent them to your sweetheart,' she said.

'Just mind your own business.' Lizzie flushed defensively.

'It is my business if it involves Garnet.'

'Huh! She's no business of yours. What sort of mother have you ever been? You never bothered to come back or even send word. When you were here it was me who looked after her. She's as much mine as yours – they're like sisters.'

'Aye, they are.' Mardi pulled a rueful face. Looking at Lizzie, she sighed and asked: 'Are you going to invite me in?'

'No. You mean trouble. Just go and get on with your life and leave us in peace. I'm telling you, your gal is safe and well. You've got no right to ask for more than that.'

Mardi bowed her head. It was at that moment that she saw the clasp pinned to Lizzie's bodice and her eyes flew involuntarily to her own bosom. Following her gaze, Lizzie looked at the identical brooch and stared thunderstruck into the face of her visitor.

For a moment they were both silent, then Mardi said: 'It's true. He's Garnet's father. He tries to be good but he's weak. He can't help himself.'

Lizzie maintained a stunned silence, so Mardi continued: 'He wanted to wed you and be a perfect husband but things turned out different. He thinks he loves you,' she added generously.

'I don't believe you. You're making it all up. You're a witch. You've conjured up a brooch like mine the same way as you made your child look like mine.' Lizzie was shouting and Mardi could see that her hands were shaking.

She shrugged. 'If that's what you want to believe.' Stepping closer, she said: 'I know where he is. I'm going to see him.'

'You're making it up!'

Again Mardi shrugged and then, with the air of one who is being charitable to an imbecile, she said: 'I know you want him but don't get your hopes too high. He's tied himself to a pathetic drudge of a woman but that won't last for ever. When he's free he'll have to make a choice.'

Her face was now within inches of Lizzie's and with slow deliberation, she continued: 'I should warn you now that I don't give up easily. I've wanted him since the first day I set eyes on him – the first day I set eyes on you. Some things are written in the cards. I wouldn't give much for your chances.' So saying, she bowed with mock politeness and remounted the horse.

'I'll see you in Hell first!' There was such concentrated venom in Lizzie's voice that although Mardi deigned not to hear, for the first time in her life her confidence faltered.

Chapter Two

As spring gave way to summer, the weather remained bleak. Rain and biting cold ruined the harvest and a deadly murrain spread among the cattle.

If things were bad in the countryside, they were worse in the city. There was less and less in the markets and the cost of eggs rose to a penny each. Death by starvation became a daily occurrence and Will protected his chickens and his few crops, particularly his taters, by keeping Ruth's dog in the yard at all times.

Unrest continued to grow as people went hungry. Some blamed the working man for being too lazy. Many felt that it was God's punishment on a wicked people. Others said it was caused by inflation. Whatever the reason, things became steadily worse.

On the building site they discussed it at length but it was the young men just starting out who voiced their anger most vociferously.

Will had to work harder than ever to make ends meet. By and large he kept his fears to himself and took comfort in the knowledge that his wife was fulfilled in her role of mother. When he came home she invariably had some new tale about the exploits of her adopted daughters.

'They're that sharp. I thought I'd set them spinning and do you know, they can do it like they'd done it all their lives. I've never known younguns so quick to learn.'

'I expect someone had shown them how when they were little,' he started, then had a sudden vision of Lizzie bending over them, imparting all her skills. He quickly tried to blot it out.

'Well, I think they're bright as butter,' Rose insisted.

Ruth came over and sat on his knee, and he busied himself by making up a story. As her eyes began to close, he carried her to the little truckle bed and gently laid her down. Garnet, carrying her seven years with great dignity, stepped round him and pushed her way in beside the girl she called sister.

'Good night, Princess.' The choice of pet name took him by surprise and he recognised that no sooner had he been thinking of Lizzie than the other one invariably fought her way into his mind. It was a mystery but he was too tired to let it bother him, so he shrugged it off. Getting up stiffly, he yawned.

'I need my bed. I'm that tired,' he said to Rose.

'You work too hard.'

He grunted in agreement and, stretching his aching limbs, asked: 'Is Ben in yet?'

He saw Rose tense as she shook her head and he sighed.

'That boy needs taking in hand. He's out all hours. I don't know what he gets up to.'

'He's a good boy,' she said defensively.

At that moment the door opened and Ben came in. He nodded to Rose and looked uneasily at his master.

'Where you been?' Will's voice was gruff.

'Sorry if I'm late, master. We were talking.'

Will was aware of Rose's anxious face and fought down any rebuke, for he knew that she could not bear him to get angry. Instead he said: 'You mind what you're doing, lad. I don't mind you having fun but if you hang around the taverns you'll end up in trouble.'

'Not me, master. I got more important things to think about.' The boy looked directly at him and Will felt out of his depth. When he was fourteen he had only thought of having fun with his friends. This lad seemed to take the cares of the world upon his shoulders.

Since Ben's hair had grown it was black and curly and Will thought that he looked more like a Don or a Frenchie. He guessed that a visiting sailor had fathered him on some doxy down by the river. For this reason, he would never be a master craftsman in his own right even though his workmanship was more mature than that of most young men of his age. The guild would only recognise those who were English-born and not bastards.

Will thought that anyhow it didn't matter. He'd see the boy didn't suffer. He had no time for hating folks because they were different. He had felt different enough himself when he was a child. He just wished he could fathom the boy out.

'Well, mark what I tell thee,' he said. 'And best get to bed.'

Lying beside Rose, he was pondering on the apprentice when she suddenly asked him:

'Wouldn't you like to go back to your island to stay?'

The remark took him by surprise and he thought carefully before replying. 'Well, I miss it, yes, but there's more work here – and I got you.'

'I'd like to go there.' There was a dreamy quality to her voice.

Will grunted.

She nestled closer to him and murmured: 'Perhaps the girls would see their mother.'

Jerked into wakefulness, he replied: 'I told you, they don't have the same mother. Anyway, I couldn't go back. I got the apprentice.' Knowing how she felt about Ben, he expected that to be the end of the conversation, but she continued:

'He won't be with us for ever. When his time's served there won't be nothing to keep us here.'

'Hush, you'll wake the children,' he retorted, but her words stayed with him into the small hours.

Two days later Will came in from work earlier than usual, his face ashen.

'Will! Whatever is it?' Rose came to his side, her own face pale and anxious. He brushed past her and sank into his chair as if in a daze.

'I can't believe it,' he said at length. 'The boys. There's been a riot. Dozens o' prentices have been arrested.'

'Oh, my Lord! Where's Ben?' she asked immediately.

'I don't know. I tried to find him but it's chaos. They were protesting against the government and the soldiers were called in.'

'What shall we do?' Rose covered her mouth to hide her

dismay. As she came over to him, she noticed the bruising on the side of his face and gave a gasp of alarm.

'Whatever happened to you?'

'It's nothing.' He glanced up at her, then away again, not wishing to worry her further. Finally he said: 'The militia were beating lads wholesale, rounding them up like cattle. I don't give much chance for any that are arrested.'

'What did you do then?' She knelt beside him and gently touched his grazed cheek.

'I took on as many soldiers as I could, to give the lads a chance to get away.' He sighed. 'After a while some of my mates dragged me away. They were afraid of being arrested along with me so I had to beat a retreat.'

'They might come after you!'

Will shook his head. 'They've got too much to worry about without chasing after me.' Taking Rose's hands to reassure her, he said: 'A few years ago I was ready to die for this country, to keep the Dons at bay, yet now it seems that ordinary folks are in as much danger from their own kind. We're starving and when we protest we're flogged or strung up. The youngsters are right.'

'Please, Will, don't get in trouble,' she begged. 'I couldn't bear to lose you.'

He sighed from exhaustion but his only thought now was to find the boy he regarded as a son. 'I have to go out again,' he started. Seeing her frightened face, he promised: 'I'm only going to look for Ben. The fighting's over now so just you take care of the girls and pray for us both.'

Will scoured the city, calling at all five major prisons as well as the borough lockups, but there was no sign of Ben. Things were worse than he had feared. Altogether three hundred apprentices had taken part in the riot, overrunning the markets and selling the produce at what they considered to be a fair price. The five pence per pound demanded for butter was slashed to three pence and when the market clerk failed to regain control, the militia were called in and scores of rioters arrested.

It was on his second visit that Will finally located Ben at the Fleet Gaol. By bribing the guard he was allowed inside. The man led him down a dark, narrow corridor, the fetid smell choking him with each intake of breath. Underfoot the floor seemed slimy and a babble of cries and moans assaulted his ears. They finally stopped in front of a tiny cell, little more than a crevice, secured by a heavy oak door.

With seven other prisoners, Ben was confined inside. There was barely room to crouch down, let alone stretch out and sleep. One rotting wooden piss bucket was brimming over in the corner, and the straw beneath their feet was soaked with stale urine. Will choked at the smell.

Each prisoner was shackled and hunched. In a corner, one boy was shivering uncontrollably between bouts of vomiting. The eldest was barely into manhood.

Ben forced his way to the front, his face haggard, but there was a fiery zeal in his eyes.

'This is a bad business, son,' said Will. 'We must get you out of here.'

'We done what was right,' the boy replied.

'I'm sure you did but you've made your point and now we've got to get back to normal. When you seeing the magistrate?'

Ben shrugged. 'We could do with some vittles and some ale,' he said. 'There's people going down all around with gaol fever. I reckon we'll be lucky to get out alive.'

'Don't you fret. I'll sort something out.'

Will left but, try as he might, there seemed no way to find out what was going to happen. Finally he fetched food and drink, which seemed the only useful thing he could do at that moment.

By the time he returned to the gaol, there was a different guard and he had to bribe him to be allowed inside again.

The boy who had been sick was now huddled like a pile of discarded rags.

'This can't go on. I'll get him out,' Will insisted, but Ben regarded him impassively with his strange black eyes.

'It's too late. He's departed this life,' he said quietly. 'They don't take 'em out till morning.'

Will was at a loss. 'What do you think's going to happen?' he finally asked.

'I don't know. We're hoping for a release. Feelings are running pretty high and I don't think they'd dare hold us.'

I don't know this boy at all, Will thought to himself. Ben's calm confidence in the face of such extreme events left him humbled.

'Pray God you're right,' he answered. There was nothing else he could do, so he made a promise to return soon, then set out for work.

When he arrived there was already much discussion about the previous day's events; opinion was divided as to the rights and wrongs of the riot.

'That lad of yours is a wild one,' his fellow mason commented. 'From what I've heard he's been one of the ringleaders.'

Will shook his head. 'No. The lad ain't no troublemaker,' he replied, but he remembered how many nights Ben had been out and it was not because he was drinking and whoring. Suddenly he shivered.

When he arrived home that evening, Rose was frantic with worry. He kept his anxieties to himself and, beyond telling her that he had found Ben, who hoped to be released soon, he remained silent.

When he returned to the prison the next morning, it was to discover that the rioters had been moved, but nobody would tell him where they had been taken.

In desperation he visited the courts.

'I'm looking for Ben Fish,' he told the clerk. Fish was the name given to the boy as a baby when he had been found abandoned in the fish market.

The clerk consulted his ledgers. 'No person of that name here,' he replied. As Will was about to leave, he added: 'There was a Ben Gosden.'

'That's him!' He waited anxiously for news.

'Tried this morning. He was one of the blasphemers.'

'What do you mean?'

The man shrugged uncomfortably. 'He said it was not God who ordained the famine but Man's greed,' he replied.

'What's become of him?' Will was trying to read over the man's shoulder, so the clerk turned his back on him, covering the ledger with his arm.

'There were five of them,' he said. 'They showed no remorse. They were the ringleaders. They have been sentenced to execution.'

310

'Dear God!' Will felt himself go cold. 'When?'

'Soon. They are to be hanged – and drawn.'

'No!'

'They should have apologised, not talked treason. The government could not allow it.'

'Where is he? I must see him.'

'Newgate.'

Will stumbled blindly from the court and through the streets to Newgate Prison. He flung some coins to the guard, demanding to see Ben Gosden. Pocketing the money, the man took him inside.

The conditions were marginally better than in the Fleet; there was more space and a vent high up in the wall let in some fresh air and a little light.

Ben looked exhausted but was curiously calm.

'Don't fret yourself, master,' he said. 'We all got to die. I ain't afraid to meet my maker. I only done what was right.'

Will fought to stay calm. The horror of the ordeal facing the lad crowded in on him. He had witnessed such an execution once before. Following a crowd out of curiosity, he had watched as two men were paraded amid jeers and shouts from the spectators. As one felon was forced to watch, the second was hung up by the neck until his violent kicking and choking ceased. He was then lowered to the ground, revived and his belly was slit and his entrails paraded before his dying eyes. It was then the turn of the second, and Will could still remember his screams. He had turned in disgust from the blood lust of the crowd. Retribution he understood, but cruelty to man or beast was beyond his comprehension.

Now the nightmare he had witnessed was to happen to the boy he thought of as a son.

'I'm going to get you out of here,' he said.

'No! If we must die to make our point, then in God's hands be it.' There was no denying the strength of this young zealot, but his master intervened.

'I won't let you die, lad. I'll see the Queen herself if that's what it takes to get thee out of here.'

Ignoring the boy's protests, he left the prison and wandered the streets deep in thought. All the time he was headed in the direction of Whitehall Palace.

311

At the great gateway he stopped. Two of Her Majesty's guards turned from their conversation to challenge him.

'Who goes there?' asked one. 'What is your business?' The challenger was big and aggressive-looking, a large, evil pike half lowered towards Will.

'I must see the Queen.' Will looked the guard in the eyes and stood his ground.

'And who are you then to need an audience with the Queen?' The guard began to strut about in front of him, his manner taunting and offensive.

'I'm one of her subjects and I think I got a right,' Will replied, showing no sign of being intimidated by the veiled threat.

'So you might think but neither ways it don't make no difference, 'cause Her Majesty is away.'

'Then I must see someone else. Someone who can make decisions,' Will insisted.

In reply, both guards stepped closer. Their united action was undeniably menacing.

'Get away from here or we'll put you behind bars and lose the key,' one of them threatened.

'I ain't going till I've seen someone.'

In reply they moved swiftly, one grabbing Will from behind and other driving into him with his pikestaff. Will went to dodge away but the pike caught him across the ribs. The pain was immediate and violent. He tried to defend himself with his fists, lashing out at both men in turn, but they continued to beat him about the head and body until gradually everything became a scorching blur and he fell senseless to the ground.

When he finally came to, it was dark. Somehow he managed to get to his feet and drag himself home. As he fell in through the doorway, he was aware of Rose's stricken face.

'Don't fuss,' he said tersely. 'Just get me a drink and don't ask no questions.'

She hurried around tending to him, somehow holding back the questions. As she peeled off his shirt, she saw that his chest was a mass of purple weals.

'Dear God, what happened?' she implored.

'Nothing.'

As she helped him up to bed, he said: 'It's mortal bad news, but I'll tell thee all there is to know in the morning.'

312

The next day Will forced himself up and back to the prison. Hiding his injuries from Ben, he told the boy: 'I tried to see the Queen but she's away. Don't despair, though, 'cause I'll find some other means'.

Ben shook his head. 'I don't want you to,' he replied. 'Truly. I respect what you're trying to do but it ain't no use.'

'Then I'll come with you,' Will insisted, but again Ben refused. 'It's best you stay with the little maids and the mistress,' he said. 'They'll be that upset.'

There was nothing else to do. 'Is there anything you want?' Will finally asked.

Again the lad shook his head. 'It's best that you don't come no more.' Gazing steadily at his master, he added: 'You're a good man. If they were all like you there wouldn't be no riots.'

Will hugged the boy to him, his body shaking with emotion.

'Goodbye, lad. God bless you. I won't give up the fight till I've got you out of here.'

Ben smiled, disbelieving, and Will felt something die within him as he turned and left, making blindly for the sanctuary of his home.

Chapter Three

It took Mardi five days to reach London and the fact that she had not found Garnet pointed clearly to the course that she should now take. Once in the city she made her way to South Warke and to the gates of Paris Garden. Before setting out from her temporary lodgings, she spent two hours preparing herself, and she carried with her a letter of introduction from her officer.

Crossing the bridge over the moat surrounding the house, she stated her business to the guard who stood with pike at the ready by the entrance. After some minutes she was allowed inside. She was shown into a side room and through the leaded window could see the garden and, beyond that, the river.

In the garden, spaciously laid out with herbs and flowerbeds and bordered with neatly trimmed hedges, she noted a couple feeding the swans and a discreet distance away a second pair in deep conversation. They had the appearance of devoted lovers.

Her reverie was broken when the door opened and a woman of amazing appearance entered. Her dress was the most costly that Mardi could imagine, positively dripping with precious stones, and the woman appeared to be craning her neck in order to see over the deep and immensely intricate lace of her ruff. It was her face that held Mardi's attention, however, for it was coated with white lead, giving it the appearance of a finely polished mask. Only her small amethyst eyes and her tiny scarlet mouth broke the uniform colour. Her hair was handsomely bedecked with pearls holding her head dress in place. It was impossible to guess her age.

'You are?' Her voice had a cracked quality and Mardi,

normally not impressed by anyone, was immediately on her feet.

'Mardi Appleby, ma'am. I have a letter here.'

Although she could not read, Mardi was aware that the letter sang her praises and she had little doubt that she would be successful in her application for work.

The other woman scanned it and then looked her over. There was a shrewd arrogance in her eyes, a disregard for Mardi's possible sensitivity. With a circling motion of a jewelled finger she indicated that Mardi should turn. She did so, carrying herself with all the confidence she could muster, but she had never before felt so intimidated.

'You know my name?' the older woman asked.

'Dame Britannica, ma'am.'

'Dame Britannica Holland. If I decide to accept you, you will always refer to me by my full name.'

Mardi bowed her head submissively, peeping from under her brows to watch what her interviewer would do next.

'Anyone in my employ has to have many skills,' Dame Britannica Holland announced. 'The arts you claim are commonplace to many of your sex. My ladies must have dignity and culture. Can you sing? Or play the viol? Can you discourse on literature or dine with a lord? Do you know your manners?'

Mardi rapidly considered her skills and announced: 'I have a fine voice and I speak Dutch.'

'You do.' It was more of a statement than a question.

'I can also read the cards and see the road ahead in your hand.'

Dame Britannica raised her eyebrows. 'That is a novel skill in my establishment,' she conceded.

Mardi was beginning to feel more confident, so she straightened her back. 'If there are any skills I'm lacking, I am quick to learn,' she said. 'But the most important skills I have to my very fingertips.' She smiled knowingly and to her relief Dame Britannica allowed her mask to crack a fraction.

'Well, I will give you one opportunity. One only. I have a young man honouring me this evening. He is a younger son of a younger son, not the most elevated of my guests, but if you please him you may consider yourself in my temporary employ. I repeat, temporary. Time alone will show how far you can go.'

Mardi bowed her head again and Dame Britannica gazed impassively at her.

'You will need a new wardrobe,' she observed. 'A gentleman of breeding cannot be entertained in rags. There are gowns in many sizes in the dressing chamber. Once you are suitably attired, Betsy will explain to you what you may and may not do. Most importantly, you never disclose the names of your benefactors to anyone outside these walls.'

As Mardi nodded her head to show that she understood, Dame Britannica Holland added menacingly: 'Failure to observe this rule could find your cadaver in the sewer.'

Although Dame Britannica Holland expressed misgivings to Mardi's face about her uncouth manner, she was soon forced to acknowledge that there was some other quality in Mardi, a wild, provocative manner that attracted men to her. No matter how noble the patrons, they all seemed beguiled by the untamed demeanour of the newest arrival at London's most famous stew.

After the hardships of her childhood and the uncertainty of the Netherlands in a constant state of war, Mardi found the calm luxury of Paris Gardens like a glimpse into heaven. The work was certainly not arduous. To her surprise, some of her gentlemen did not even expect her to open her legs to them. She would recount episodes from her past to enchant her listeners. On occasion she was surrounded by a group of the noblest names in London, all hanging on to her every word. Her other pleasure was to read their hands and soon her predictions and character analyses were the talk of South Warke.

One afternoon in July, Mardi dressed more demurely than usual and made her way to Chepe Side. Will's cottage showed no sign of life and she stood uncertainly on the opposite side of the road, her usual confidence deserting her. Suddenly she was afraid of what Garnet might think. She wanted the girl's love and respect but had to admit to herself that she had done little enough to earn it.

For the first time ever she now had a position and money and, given the chance, she wanted to make it up to her daughter. Her other hope was that she could make some sort of private assignation with Will. She felt sure that now he was into maturity and touched by city life, the unrealistic ideals of their early encounters would have been cast aside. She remembered Rose's frail body and sighed. He must by now be bored to death with bundling such a rake each night.

As she was pondering, the cottage door opened and a child stepped out into the dusty lane. Mardi held her breath, her temples pounding. The child had rich brown hair and was straight-backed. She was calling back into the cottage to some-one hidden from view.

Garnet? Mardi feasted her eyes on her, wanting to touch her. As she watched, the girl tipped a pail of rubbish onto the pile at the corner of the street and walked back barefoot towards the house.

Mardi could not let her go. Hurrying across the road, narrowly missing a cart loaded with dung, she called:

'Are you Master Gosden's child?'

The girl stopped and looked unblinking at her.

'What's your name?' Mardi added impatiently.

'Ruth Gosden.' The girl half curtsied and showed her con-fusion by blushing.

'Ah.' Mardi hid her surprise and reached out, raising the girl's chin. She asked: 'Where is Garnet?' and was disturbed by the steady hazel eyes behind the reddish-brown lashes.

'She's helping Mam.'

'Get her.'

Ruth did not argue but went back inside. A moment later the door opened and Will stood facing her.

She was shocked by his appearance. He looked as if some terrible tragedy had befallen him and his shoulders were slumped as if an intolerable burden weighed him down.

'What ails thee?' she asked, forgetting where she was and the circumstances of her visit.

He did not answer immediately, although once or twice he opened his mouth as if to speak.

'Are you ill?' Mardi reached out and touched his arm, and the contact seemed to snap him out of his torpor.

'Not me. It's our apprentice, Ben. He's been taken up by the courts and his life's forfeit. They're going to hang him.' He closed his eyes and she could feel his pain.

'Can it not be stopped?' she asked.

Will shook his head. 'I tried to see Her Majesty but she's on a progress. I can't find a way to intercede for him.' Shaking his head, he added: 'The boy's that stubborn, he won't help himself.'

Mardi was thinking of her patrons. Surely among the noblemen who took their pleasure on her body there must be one who could be persuaded to intervene.

'I may be able to help,' she offered.

'You? How?' There was derision in his voice.

'You should know by now not to underestimate me,' she retorted. Changing the subject, she said: 'I hear you are now the father of girls.'

'How did you hear that?' He shook his head. 'I don't understand you. Have you really got some magic that makes you know the future?' Digesting what he himself had said, he then added: 'If so, can you see what is going to happen to Ben?'

Mardi felt a chill surround her and knew that his future looked bleak. She did not answer Will's question but instead asked: 'May I see the girls I conjured up for you?'

He shrugged, dipping back into the cottage to call both children to him. Her mouth dry, Mardi gazed for the first time in six years on her daughter.

Garnet was, if anything, slightly shorter than Ruth and her hair was now brown, which took Mardi by surprise – she had expected to see her own black locks – but like hers it was remarkably thick and wavy and Mardi observed that her child had honey-smooth skin that resembled her own. She swallowed hard. Garnet's flecked hazel eyes and her likeness to Ruth were the two things that most held her attention. She knew that they were sisters but how did Will explain their similarity?

'You're fortunate to have such daughters,' she remarked, resisting the urge to touch Garnet.

Will was looking at her searchingly. 'Tell me what you know,' he demanded. 'You know something about all this.'

'Me? How should I know?' She looked him calmly in the eye and he gazed helplessly back at her.

318

'Don't torment me. Tell me the truth.'

'The truth is that you loved a woman once and left her with your child,' Mardi replied enigmatically.

At that moment she was aware that Rose was standing behind him in the shadow of the tiny living room. Rose's face was a picture of misery and Mardi felt irritated by her vulnerability and willingness to suffer. She ignored her.

'I shall not call again,' she said directly to him. 'But should you wish to send word, I can be reached through Dame Britannica Holland.'

Will's eyebrows shot up in disbelief. 'You're working as a common whore,' he sneered.

'Not common, my dear. Certainly not common. If I can help your friend Ben, then I will, but do not hold out false hopes.'

Suddenly reaching out, she ran her hand down Garnet's cheek. 'Remember where I am, child,' she said quietly.

Turning her back on the stricken family, Mardi disappeared into the alleyway opposite.

Chapter Four

Mardi stretched languorously and turned her head to look at the man beside her. He had been in a mood when he had arrived, and gradually she had wheedled out of him that he had been snubbed. His daughter Elizabeth had been engaged to a nobleman, whose father had broken it off. From what Mardi could gather it was a question of money.

There was just sufficient light to make out Sir George Carey's features. He was running to fat and his petulant mouth was set in a hard, sulky line. Mardi sighed. She had to admit that as far as her patrons went, Sir George was one of the more amenable. Sitting up and leaning over him, she tugged at the curling beard on his cheek.

'Leave me.'

She hesitated for a moment, then began to stroke his chest. She saw his face relax so she set to work with slow, even strokes.

Some time later, when her head was snuggled into his shoulder, she said: 'Have you any unfulfilled dreams?'

He grunted in reply, so she continued: 'My greatest wish is to see Her Majesty.'

Sir George gave another grunt and, as Mardi started to speak again, he stretched and said: 'Am I to get no peace, woman? You're worse than a wife.'

In reply she kissed his nose and he sighed.

'Don't ask me to introduce you at court,' he warned. 'You may have half the Queen's courtiers around your thumb but you must never forget what you are.'

Mardi drew away from him. 'I wouldn't presume to embarrass the ladies of the court,' she retorted. 'Or, more properly, the gentlemen. I've seen inside enough of their breeches to know what babies they are.'

Sir George laughed then. 'You are a witch,' he teased. 'A veritable enchantress. I can't take you to the Palace but if you want to see the Queen, she will be at the landing stage on the morrow around noon. She is returning from her progress. I will of course be there to meet her.' As Mardi's scheming eyes surveyed him, he added: 'If, and only if, the opportunity presents itself, then I will draw her attention to one of her subjects. She likes to talk with the common people.'

Turning towards her and pushing her onto her back, he added: 'But you just be careful what you say. Mistress Holland will have you in the Thames if you disgrace her good name.'

On the morrow, dressed in her thickest cloak against the sudden northerly wind, Mardi waited at the front of the crowd for the royal barge to approach. A carpet had been lain along the path the Queen would take from the craft to the carriage that would carry her on the short distance to Whitehall Palace.

As the barge finally came into view, Mardi found that her hands were taut and she swallowed down the excitement. It was another half an hour before the vessel was secured along the bank, and then the minutes ticked away with no sign of an intended landing.

Finally a flurry of courtiers and servants scrambled over each other in their anxiety to see that all was as it should be. The guards who had been leaning on their pikes now pushed the gathering crowd back to keep the pathway clear. Mardi, at the front of the group, let her thigh rub against the buttocks of the guard who was obstructing her view. The man looked round sharply; then, seeing the well-dressed and amenable young woman at his side, he made room for her to see.

After an age and a fanfare of trumpets, noble ladies and gentlemen lined the immediate route and at last there she was. A spontaneous cheer went up and with the rest Mardi bowed low, then raised her head to look at the monarch.

To her surprise, the Queen at first reminded her of Dame Britannica in her make-up and clothing. From her crouched position Mardi was particularly aware of the golden buckles on Queen Elizabeth's neat little shoes. As she looked closer, she saw that the white mask of a face was deeply lined and that Her Majesty's teeth were crooked and yellow, yet the expression and demeanour of this long, thin-faced, wizened woman told Mardi instantly that she was the mightiest in the land and perhaps the world. She began to tremble.

It was then that Mardi saw Sir George. He was at the Queen's side, his head bowed deferentially as she was telling him something which he clearly found amusing. Sir George was smiling and nodding his head. He did not appear to be aware that Mardi was there.

As they drew level, however, he suddenly slowed his pace and the Queen looked round at him questioningly.

'Your good subjects are here as ever, Majesty, to wish you well,' he said, loud enough for those nearest to hear.

'Indeed, Cousin.' The Queen looked around and waved to her admirers. As her eyes rested momentarily on Mardi, she took her chance.

'Majesty, as a simple woman may I wish you well?' she called, aware of the tremor in her voice.

Queen Elizabeth turned. She sported a vivid red wig that made the ivory pallor of her face the more stark.

'You may indeed,' she replied and held her gloved hand out for Mardi to touch.

Heart pounding, Mardi let her lips brush against the huge jewelled ring on her sovereign's index finger.

'It's a pity you wear a glove, ma'am, or I could tell your fortune,' she heard herself say.

The guards had gathered closer and Mardi was aware that Sir George was staring at her warningly.

To everyone's relief, the Queen laughed. 'My fortune is in the hands of God,' she admonished, and was about to move on, but Mardi was not going to let her chance escape.

'Ma'am, I have heard that you are merciful. There are boys in the gaol awaiting execution for the foolishness of youth. There is such a dearth these days that they acted out of charity, not malice. I would pray you to forgive them.'

The Queen looked at Sir George Carey and the others about her. 'What is this?' she asked.

Mardi could not hear what was being said and she was almost fainting with her own temerity.

322

The Queen now looked back at her bowed figure and said: 'Those to whom you refer have not acted out of high spirits but to upturn the establishment of the state.' Addressing the crowd, she said: 'You all know that the welfare of my subjects is as dear to me as life. It is for this reason that we have been drawn into costly wars to protect our land. While we weep for the poor and the hungry, we have to put the greater good of our subjects first.'

Looking down at Mardi, she added: 'I am indeed a merciful woman and even now I would give thought to your request but it is too late. The executions took place this morning.' More kindly, she added: 'Had you spoken to me yesterday, it might have been different.'

Mardi slumped where she was and the procession moved on. She did not really care what happened to Will's apprentice; what mattered was how it affected Will himself. She longed to help him and win his respect and gratitude, but things had not worked out as planned.

As the procession moved away, she withdrew from the crowd and wandered in the direction of Chepe Side.

On the day of the executions Will stayed with his wife and shared her waking nightmare. The house was like a prison but they could not leave for it was outside in the city that the spectacle would be taking place. Each minute was an hour and the oppression was so great that he felt that he might go mad.

'I can't bear it!' cried Rose for the umpteenth time. She rocked herself in anguish as Ruby and Garnet looked on wide-eyed and stricken.

'Shush!' Will cradled all three against his chest. He knew with a terrible certainty that his wife was not strong enough to recover from such an ordeal as this. He mumbled words of consolation but they had no meaning.

Finally, when he was sure that the executions must be over, he said: 'We're going to leave here. I'm taking you all back to the island.'

'Oh, please! I can't bear to be here a minute longer. When can we go?' Rose was still holding on to him.

He sighed. 'We can't leave straight away. I've still got work to finish. But you can be sure we'll go as soon as it's humanly possible.'

Letting go of her, he turned to the two children and said: 'I'm going out now. Care for your mother, for she has suffered.'

'Where are you going?'

Rose's voice had an edge of panic in it, but he dismissed it, merely saying: 'I must go out. I have to be alone.'

Leaving the house, Will went to the Tabard, but talk was of the executions and he left without buying a drink. He felt as if his chest were constricted by great thongs squeezing the breath out of him, and he wandered this way and that trying to find some relief from his tormented thoughts. Finally he went into the White Hart and flung himself down on a bench in a corner. It was here that Mardi found him.

Silently she sat beside him and laid her small hand on his arm. He did not look up but the tears started to fall unrestrained down his cheeks.

'I tried,' she said. 'I saw the Queen but it was too late.'

Getting up, Mardi called a potboy to her, and before long they were shown to one of the better upper rooms. She led Will by the arm as if he were blind, and indeed he seemed unaware of anything about him.

Gently she pushed him onto the bed and, bending down, removed his boots. She then deftly undressed him. He did not resist. She poured him a large measure of brandy from the jug placed on the sideboard and he drained it back without comment. Pushing him onto the bed, she covered him before slipping out of her gown and shift and lying beneath the coverlet against the length of his body.

In the dark she held him in her arms, caressing him like a child, easing the pain and tension from his shoulders and down his back until he allowed himself to sob out his nightmare. When he was spent, she cradled him and sang as to an infant. He finally slept.

When he awoke some hours later, she changed naturally to the role of lover. His anger was foremost now and he took her savagely, venting his pain and fury on her acquiescent body. As his misery drained away, she eased her position and nibbled gently at his shoulder.

'It's all over now,' she said, breaking the silence.

'It won't ever be over. Not as long as I live.' After a while he added: 'There are them that don't see no wrong in such punishments but I can't be like them. Each man's suffering is mine and Ben was like my own flesh.'

Mardi, for whom every man had to think first of his own good, remained silent.

Will finally pulled away from her and lay on his back, staring at the first light of dawn.

'I'm going home,' he said. 'To the island. I ain't never belonged here.'

'Will you go alone?' she asked.

'Of course not. I'll take my family with me.'

'You don't have to. If you went back alone you could have what you wanted.'

She felt his tension as he asked: 'And what do I want, then?'

'To wed with the fuller's widow.'

'What makes you think that?'

'You always forget that I know everything,' she replied.

They both lay immersed in their own thoughts. After a long silence, she said: 'She's mine. Garnet's mine. I birthed her at the fuller's house.'

Will showed no signs of having heard. Reaching out, Mardi found his hand and squeezed it between her small fingers.

'I've always been afraid to believe it,' he finally replied. 'I didn't want the responsibility of you – you're too much for me.'

She sat up and bent over him, kissing his temple.

'And you're too good for me,' she countered. 'I won't never have no morals, not like you. You're such an honest man. It used to make me angry once but, God help me, I can't help loving you.'

Turning in bed, he took her again with the dreamlike passion he remembered from their first encounter. When he had finished, she asked him:

'You don't love your wife?'

'It depends what you mean by love. I wed her out of pity, yet she's been better to me than any man could hope for.'

'But it's the fuller's wife you really want, ain't it?'

His silence was answer enough.

'I shouldn't be here,' he suddenly said. 'I should be home comforting Rose.'

325

Mardi sat up and reached for her shift. As she pulled it over her head, she said: 'You'll be better able comfort her now that you've had comfort yourself.'

He suddenly squeezed her arm. 'You're amazing,' he said, holding her close.

Lying in his arms she had the strange feeling that this one night had encompassed all the emotion of a lifetime together.

As he was ready to leave, he asked: 'What do you want to do about Garnet? Do you want her to know who you are?'

'I don't know,' she replied. 'But when the time is right I'll send word.'

Seeing his face grow taut, she added: 'Don't fret. I won't cause you trouble.' Holding him close, she assured him: 'You should know by now that I always do the right thing.'

Chapter Five

'Is it true that you are a widow?'

The question took Mardi by surprise, coming as it did from Baron Hunsdon. The Baron, formerly Sir George Carey, had been elevated to the Lord Chancellorship on the death of his father and now spent most of his time in London.

Mardi did not reply immediately, wondering which answer would be most favourable. While she was making up her mind, Hunsdon added:

'Dame Britannica tells me that you have a daughter.'

'I do.' Warming to the subject, Mardi continued: 'She is exceedingly beautiful and bright. Because of my circumstances I have had to farm her out, but she is a credit to me.' Speculatively she added: 'It is my dearest wish to see her well connected. I wouldn't want her to end up like me.'

'Don't you like your work?' They were sitting in the Garden watching the swans and boats. Lord Hunsdon was smoking a pipe and generally taking his ease.

'Liking one's work and wishing it upon a child are two different thing,' she replied. 'Would you wish such a thing for your daughter?'

The Baron flashed her a warning scowl. 'Remember your place, girl. How dare you compare my family with your own?'

'I haven't got a family,' Mardi countered, unimpressed by his show of importance.

'Is your child old enough to work?' he asked, mollified.

'She's nearing eight.'

'Would it please you if I found her a place in my household?'

327

Mardi hid her surprise. 'It would be an honour,' she replied, bowing with exaggerated courtesy to him.

Lord Hunsdon smiled. 'There are too many whores in London,' he observed. 'And you are an imp, but if your child is as sharp as you are, Widow Appleby, then her skills should be directed into some respectable use.'

Mardi located Will in the Crown. It was the first time she had seen him since the day of the execution, and during that time she had made no effort to be in touch with her child.

Relying on her unerring sense of awareness, she was confident that Will was not yet ready to depart for the Isle of Wight.

She walked into the inn and without greeting sat down beside him. He hardly expressed surprise at seeing her but she noted that he looked healthier.

'How is my daughter?' she asked by way of introduction.

'Well enough. She doesn't want to leave the city but I'm planning on going as soon as spring comes.' Looking at Mardi, he said: 'If you wish to see her again, you'd best make up your mind soon.'

Mardi shrugged. 'I've been offered a place for her,' she observed.

'What sort of place?'

'In one of the best houses in London.'

'And what sort of house might that be, a stew?'

She flashed him an angry look. 'I would have thought even you did not have such a low opinion of me.'

He pulled a remorseful face and she continued: 'It's one of my patrons – a very important and respectable man. He's offered to find Garnet a place in his household. She'd learn skills like sewing and housecraft. It's true,' she added, seeing his disbelief.

He did not reply immediately, then with a sigh said: 'She's been a trouble to us of late. She's that strong-willed. To be honest, I've felt that she wouldn't be happy on the island. She sets Ruth a bad example, too.'

'Why do you call her Ruth?'

'It was Rose's choice. Garnet had a mind of her own.'

Mardi smiled with satisfaction. 'Why don't you let Garnet go? She must know your wife ain't her mother. Tell her the truth and I give you my word I'll look out to her. I . . . I really would like to do something for her and now the time is right.' She lowered her eyes with an exaggerated show of humility. 'If ever she's in bother, I'll send word and let you know, but my patron would see that she was strictly supervised.' She looked hopefully at him.

Will sighed. 'I don't know how Rose would take it.'

'Who wears the breeches in your house, you or the milksop?' Mardi asked provocatively, forgetting the image she was trying to project.

'I wear the breeches but I don't use my authority to hurt others,' he replied tartly.

'Well, you think about it,' she replied, getting up to go. 'But don't be too long or he may change his mind.'

Predictably Rose expressed both fear and distress at the idea of leaving one of her daughters behind.

'But do you know these people?' she asked anxiously. 'How can you be sure they would protect her?'

Will had not mentioned how he had come to find such an opportunity and Rose waited for an explanation.

'Please, Mother, let me go. It would be an adventure. I don't wish to leave London, truly I don't,' Garnet pleaded.

'Yes, let her go,' said Ruth with feeling. 'We'd get on much better without her.'

'Enough!' Will silenced them all. Turning first to Rose and then to his elder daughter, he said: 'I truly think that this is the way it should be.'

'But who would look after her? She'd be left with no family to care about her,' Rose repeated.

'You needn't fret yourselves. I shall find my true mother soon,' Garnet announced.

The three turned and looked at her with varying emotions.

'How can this be true?' asked Rose.

'You're making it up,' Ruth accused.

Will was silent but his face reddened.

'I just know my mother is nearby. I know lots of things. I always have.'

'You must not talk so.' Rose put her arm around the girl's shoulders. 'God sent you and Ruth to me and I cannot let you

329

go. I would miss you more than you can ever know. Besides, you came from the island where your father was born. It is right that you should go back there.'

'No!' Garnet stiffened and regarded her father. 'Tell them,' she said. 'Tell them my mother will come for me.'

In confusion, Will started: 'There is someone here – someone who would keep an eye out to her.'

'Who?' Rose and Ruth echoed.

'A ... a sort of relative.' He took refuge in his position as head of the family. 'You must leave it to me. I won't answer any more questions. When the time is right, I will take Garnet to meet her.'

Seeing the protest on his wife's lips, he added: 'Enough, woman. Remember you promised to obey.'

Before she could challenge him, he walked out of the room with an air of indisputable authority, but as he closed the door he wondered once more if he were not acting under a spell.

Mardi had instructions to deliver her child to the house in Clark's Well. Waiting for Will and the girl to arrive, she was in a lather of anxiety. Never before had she felt so afraid. It was as if her entire life was on display to be judged by the unknown girl who was her daughter. She suddenly feared that a greater, divine judgement might intervene and cause her child to disown her. At that moment Garnet's approval meant everything.

Suddenly they were there, rounding the corner, and she started towards them.

'Hello, Mother.' Garnet spoke up clearly and curtsied, her hazel-brown eyes lowered as a sign of respect.

'You've told her,' said Mardi, the relief spreading over her.

'No.' Will was looking perplexed.

'I always knew you'd come,' the child continued. 'I want to be like you.'

Mardi for once was at a loss for words. After a moment she clasped the girl in her arms.

'You are truly my daughter,' she said. 'I can see a great future for you and one day we will travel far together.'

Garnet nodded and Will had the familiar feeling of being excluded from some secret knowledge which both mother and child possessed but which eluded him.

He in turn put his arms around his daughter and kissed her on the forehead. 'Remember everything I've told you,' he said, trying to hide his emotion. 'If you need me I'll be at Shorrel village on the Isle of Wight.'

Garnet nodded and pecked him on the cheek, but already she was drawn into the orbit of her mother.

Placing herself between her daughter and the man who had fathered her, Mardi forced him to look into her eyes. 'When do you plan to leave?' she asked.

'Shortly.'

When she did not comment, he added: 'I suppose this is farewell, then.'

'Do you wish it to be?'

He appeared to be looking for the right words. Finally shrugging, he said: 'God does not allow a man to have three wives. If he did, then I could take care of you all.'

Mardi gave a snort. 'That would suit you, wouldn't it? Having three women to do your bidding.' She moved closer and tilted her head so that she looked down her nose at him. 'Do you seriously believe I'd share you with those two?'

'You would expect me to share you with half the upstarts in London,' he countered.

She gave a little smile, acknowledging the logic of his remark.

'I tell you what,' she said with the air of one who was offering a bargain too good to be refused. 'I'm a rich woman. Why don't you let that poor little weasel have the house and your savings? If you see that she's well cared for, you need have no guilt. Then we could share the things that have been denied to us.' Seeing that he was about to object, she quickly added: 'You've given her nigh on seven years of your life. You've served your apprenticeship there. It's my turn now. Dedicate the next seven years to me. I'll guarantee you will never wish to be released from your bondage.'

'You know I can't. I swore before God to stay with her until I die.'

'Or she does,' she added slowly.

He looked at her warily. 'Don't you do anything to bring that about,' he warned.

'You think I could?'

'I don't know. I only think that now we should say goodbye.'

331

Meeting his eyes, she smiled and reached for his hand. 'My dear Will, don't fret yourself. In spite of what you believe, I've never done a thing to hurt you. I do think you should realise by now, however, that where you and I are concerned there is no such word as goodbye.'

So saying, she reached up to kiss him and she felt his resistance weaken. As he pressed himself against her, perversely she pulled away and put her arm around her child, drawing her aside.

'God be with you, Will.' She looked back at him over her shoulder and the last he saw of them was heads drawn together, deep in conversation as they rounded the corner and out of sight.

Chapter Six

It took Will several more months to complete his work contract but his desire to leave London was undiminished. Now Garnet had gone he wanted to be away as soon as possible lest the lure of visiting his child would once more bring him under Mardi's spell.

Some days he felt he no longer had the willpower to resist, and the knowledge alarmed him. By then, however, it was winter and travelling was out of the question, so they had to mark time until the spring of 1596, when the roads were once more passable.

He did not seek his daughter out again to say goodbye in spite of Rose's accusing pleas.

'Should we not make sure that all is well with her?' she asked.

'No. I am sure that it is.'

'Then have you seen her?' There was suspicion in her voice.

'I haven't seen her. But I have faith in her ... relative to see that all is well.' Trying to appear reasonable, he added: 'If we see her now, we may unsettle her.'

'Then in that case she could still come with us.'

'No.' Once more he resorted to his position of power. 'Enough, woman. I have said all there is to say on the subject. Garnet is where she belongs and we leave tomorrow.'

The journey was not easy. Rose found it difficult to ride a horse and impossible to walk far with her crippled leg. Some days she looked so wan that Will feared for her survival.

Nor could they find good accommodation. In these days of so much trouble, townspeople were not welcome in the villages. They brought too many hazards – the sweats, the smallpox, the leprosy – and they depleted the meagre food supplies. In their turn the travellers were afraid for their valuables. Everything they owned was tied to a packhorse and Will's money was secured about his person. Ruffians were ever more desperate these days and he knew that many would cut their throats for a farthing.

They were reduced to sleeping in the open, hiding in a copse or a deserted barn, and Will remained always on guard. He vowed to himself that this would be the last journey he would ever make.

When they reached the coast, a boatman had to be bribed to take them across at an exorbitant fare, but nothing mattered beyond reaching the island shores. Once there, Will planned to take his family to Granfer Gosden's and build a new life.

As they boarded the boat, Ruth, who had been quiet for some time, suddenly said: 'I remember the boat from before.'

Will's heart jolted and he felt his face grow taut.

'You remember the crossing?' he asked unsteadily.

'I remember being with you and Garnet – and we both cried.'

'What else do you recall?' It was Rose who asked the question, her voice calm and encouraging.

Ruth smiled. 'I remember a beautiful lady.' Turning to her father, she said: 'Garnet says I have another mother too. Is it her that I remember?'

He was at a loss for words. They had not spoken of her past life since their arrival in London, for he could not bear the reminders and he had truly believed that it was better for them all if they put it behind them. Now he suspected that Ruth had been quietly waiting for the time when they would return.

'Do you believe what Garnet says?' he hedged, aware that Rose was watching him. Whatever he said now, he was sure to hurt someone.

'She said she was going to live with her mother and that mine was here, on this island.'

Still he did not confirm it. Instead he said: 'It was a long time ago.'

'But you are my real father?'

It was as much a statement as a question. He knew that Rose was still watching him. Before he could answer, her hand was on his arm.

334

'Don't fret,' she said, her voice unsteady. 'I've knowed all along. You only have to look at her – at both of them.'

He met her pale eyes.

'I didn't want to hurt thee,' he said.

'I know. Don't matter now.' She squeezed his hand. 'I feels sorry for her, losing her daughter – and all. As for Garnet, I guess she's found her mother too. She always seemed to know what was going to happen – like that Gipsy woman.' She looked at him pointedly, then added: 'But I've been the lucky one.'

Will nodded, his gratitude to Rose overwhelming him. He thought of Lizzie's sacrifice. If she was still alone, he did not know how he was going to stay away, but if she had remarried the knowledge would be equally painful. Whichever way he looked, there seemed to be no end to his guilt.

'I love you,' he said to Rose. It was the first time he had ever used the words to her and he meant it.

As they completed the last stage of their journey, Rose mounted on the horse, Will at its head and Ruth running in front with her dog, his wife suddenly said: 'I don't know what your granfer's going to think. There's me a cripple and barren. He'll say I'm a poor wife and a curse on you.'

'Shush!' Reining in the horse, Will turned to her. 'Don't you say that. You're my wife. Ruth's my daughter. That means she's our daughter – yours and mine. That's all Granfer needs to know.'

As she lowered her eyes, he added: 'You know what I'm saying?'

'That we're a proper family.'

'That's right. Just you, me and her.'

When the excitement of the journey was over and they were settled at Granfer Gosden's tiny cottage at Shorrel, Will told Rose the story of Ruth's birth and the subsequent suspicions that had fallen upon her and the vagrant child.

'It's that silly,' she objected. 'How could anyone think they were bewitched?'

Will nodded in agreement. 'Fact is they did, though. Some folks'll believe anything.'

There was a long silence before Rose added: 'You must have loved them very much.'

335

He knew that she meant Lizzie and Mardi. Did I love them both, he wondered? It was not the same thing at all. Mardi had been his temptation and Lizzie, why, Lizzie was his innocence, his ideal. He longed to journey back and find that unfulfilled dream.

Looking at Rose, he thought that she had been his salvation and he hugged her again.

'I'm not a promiscuous man,' he said, 'though it must look that way.'

'Are you going to take Ruth to see her mother?' Rose asked, her face cradled against his shoulder.

'No.' It cost him a lot to say it. 'If I take her back, all the rumours will start again. Besides, I can't let folk think that I'm her father, it might cause her mother trouble.' The oblique reference to Lizzie caused his hands to tingle.

Rose nodded, expelling her breath in obvious relief. She looked so frail and vulnerable, so dependent on his good will.

'If it makes you feel better, I give you my word that I won't see her neither,' he heard himself say. 'She thinks we're in London. It's best we leave it like that. When the child's more growed up, I'll think on it again.'

He did not register Rose's response because as he spoke he knew he was closing the door on all his wildest hopes. Turning his back on her, he strode out to nurse his loneliness in the empty countryside.

It did not take Will long to find work. As soon as they were settled he called at Carisbrooke Castle, and was happy to learn that Lord Hunsdon had plans for a major refortification of the castle. These were troubled days and the Spanish threat was still ever present. In the meantime there were odd jobs to be done and a man of Will's calibre was clearly worth holding on to. Will had sufficient money to be able to keep the horse so that he could now ride the four miles to work and back. The future looked secure.

Six weeks to the day after their arrival at Shorrel, Will came downstairs in the morning to find Granfer Gosden in his final sleep. He had clearly been taken peacefully as he lay abed, and Will was grateful for his easy departure, yet a sadness enveloped him, thinking of the old man's long life. He reckoned him to be well over eighty and was comforted to know that he had brought Ruth home in time to meet her great-grandfather. In its wake was the infinite sadness that the old man would never know that he had another great-grandchild.

Garnet. Will wondered if he would ever see her again.

Chapter Seven

After Granfer Gosden's funeral, Will sought permission from Mr Dingley of Wolverton Manor to remain at the cottage, and as soon as this was granted he set about enlarging it. In spite of his other disappointment, it was good to be making a secure home for Rose and the girl.

The summer months passed quickly. He was riding home from the castle one early September evening when he saw Ruth running to meet him.

'Oh, Pa! Mam's not well. She can't stand on her leg and she's abed,' his daughter gasped, stopping to get her breath. Bending down, he lifted her up in front of him and increased their pace.

Reaching the cottage, he hurried to his wife's side.

'Oh, Will, I'm that sorry. I can't walk. It's my leg. It's that painful. What a nuisance I must be!' Her face was whiter than ever and a fine dew of sweat covered her brow.

'You just stay there. I'll get a physician,' he said, and immediately set out again in search of help.

The physician, having examined Rose, came out into the evening sun, his face carefully composed.

'She has a fever,' he stated. 'And an inflammation of the leg.'

'Is it serious?' asked Will.

Ignoring the question, the man continued: 'The best treatment is rest. Regular doses of goat's milk have been known to be efficacious. I have given her a draught to induce sleep.'

'How long before she gets better?' Will persisted.

There was a pause before the physician replied.

'That is in God's hands.'

'Yes, but as a man of experience you must have some idea?'

338

The physician looked uncomfortably at him. 'These things take time.'

'How long?'

The man shrugged. 'Perhaps a year or two.'

'Are you saying she won't get better?' Will's voice was deceptively even.

'Again, that is in God's hands.'

The effects of the sleeping draught lasted for several hours. While Rose slept at his side, Will lay awake thinking the unthinkable. He began to doze from sheer exhaustion just as his wife awoke with a muted groan.

'Anything you need?' he asked, struggling to stay awake.

'No. You sleep and I'll wake you at sunup,' she said tonelessly.

In spite of her promise he remained awake, conscious of the warmth from her body and the shape of her small, skinny frame. The thought that he was about to lose this constant, unselfish woman chilled his being. However often he had imagined a different life for himself, the reality of a future without her was painful to contemplate.

Dragging himself from the bed, he went down the stairs and made the breakfast. He knew that the child had had a restless night and he left her to sleep until the last moment.

He made his final visit to the upper room before leaving for work.

'Wake up, gal, your mother needs you,' he said to Ruth, shaking her shoulder. She gazed at him unseeing for a moment, then, realising where she was, looked anxiously across at the bed.

'How's Mam?'

He shook his head. 'You be sure and take care of her. 'I'll be back as quick as I can tonight.'

Turning to his wife, he took both her hands, lying motionless against the coverlet, and gently squeezed them.

'You rest,' he cautioned. 'We'll soon have you fit.'

Her tired eyes met his and they both knew that it was a lie. Hastily he kissed her cheek and descended the stairs, wishing that it was time to come home.

He sought permission to finish early and on the way home

bought a goat from a farmstead at Bowcombe. It seemed a painfully slow journey, leading the animal along the bumpy road, and she stopped to investigate every bush and thistle. He did not like to risk bullying her for fear of stopping the flow of her health-giving milk, so he tugged and coaxed until they finally reached the village.

As soon as he was home he set about milking the goat himself and carried a bowl brimming with the frothy liquid into the house. The smell of food greeted him although the kitchen was empty. He could hear voices upstairs and in the bedroom he found his wife and daughter talking.

He surveyed their faces, thinking it was hard to imagine two women more different. His child was browned by the sun, her thick chestnut hair framing her oval face, her young body vibrant. In contrast her stepmother, wizened beyond her twenty-five years, lay back against the pillow, her face colourless, her eyes opaque, her hair a dull pewter against the bedlinen.

'How be my girls?' he asked jovially, bringing the milk to the bedside. 'See what I got?' He held it out to Rose. 'You sip this now and we'll soon have you fit.'

Obediently Rose drank a little but soon fell back. 'I ain't got no appetite,' she apologised. 'Perhaps in a bit I'll feel better.'

He nodded, hiding his concern, and went down with his daughter to eat his meal.

'Is Mam going to die?' Ruth blurted out the words, her supper untasted.

Will considered the question before saying: 'She's very sick but we must trust in God.'

She did not respond but lowered her head and he reached out to raise her chin, meeting the eyes that mirrored his own.

'We must be brave,' he said gently. 'We'll take care of her together and we'll always have each other.'

She moved to the comfort of his arms and he smoothed her hair, absently thinking of the ordeal that faced them all.

'Do you miss Garnet?' he suddenly asked.

Ruth shrugged. 'Sometimes I do, but sometimes she used to frighten me. I always felt she belonged somewhere else.' The girl hesitated. 'She understood things I didn't even know about. She seemed to see the future, as if she was only waiting for

340

something to happen – and it did.' Ruth looked to him for understanding and he nodded.

'Do you think Mam pines for her?' he added.

Again Ruth shook her head. 'I think Mam always knew Garnet was different, only lent to her really. Perhaps we both were.'

Meeting her eyes, he acknowledged what she was saying.

'Don't mourn,' he said. 'Having you both has been the greatest gift she could receive.'

Standing up, his daughter shook her head and replied: 'You're wrong. Having you was that.' Again they held each other close.

A pattern was now set for their daily lives. Each morning Will would drag himself to work too tired to notice the route. Leadenly he laboured through the interminably long days and on the ride back he would wonder constantly what he was going to find when he reached home. Each night he fell exhausted into bed but sleep would not come. Either Rose's pain intruded on him, try as she might to hide it, or if she slept herself he was too far gone to turn off to oblivion. It was a living hell.

Sometimes he fancied that Rose seemed a little better, but before long she would be weak and feverish and fear would once more clutch at his heart.

As the summer of 1597 drew to a close, Rose could no longer keep anything down, not even the goat's milk.

One evening as he made his nightly visit to her before eating his meal, she took his hand and motioned him to sit down on the bed.

'We must talk,' she said. It was an effort for her to speak but he did not try to stop her.

'It is time Ruth ... saw her mother.' She closed her eyes, summoning the energy to continue.

'I don't think now's the right time,' he started, the familiar pounding of his heart responding to the mention of Lizzie.

Rose lay back and looked at him.

'When I first met you I thought you were the most beautiful man I'd ever seen,' she started. Her speech was laboured as she struggled to breathe but her voice sounded dreamy. 'I hoped that one day you might kiss me.' She smiled at the distant

341

memory, then reached out to take his strong brown hand. 'How could I ever hope you'd ask me to wed you?'

'Hush, sweetheart.' He touched her mouth with his fingers, but she continued: 'What I'm trying to say is, it don't matter if you still want her.'

He swallowed hard and shook his head. 'I love you,' he said honestly.

'I know you do. And you're the best husband a woman could have, that kind and gentle. Don't alter the fact, though, do it? You must stop tormenting yourself and when I'm gone, go and find her.'

Again he shook his head. 'I can't. Besides, I expect she's wed.'

'Then you'd best find out – for Ruth's sake.'

She closed her eyes, exhaustion showing on her tormented face, and in reply he raised her small form from the bed and cradled her in his arms.

'I'll find out,' he murmured, kissing her dank hair. 'When the time's right.'

Chapter Eight

Rose Gosden died on Christmas Day 1597 and was laid to rest in the churchyard next to her husband's grandfather. In the crisp winter chill Will stared unseeing into the grave, holding his daughter by the hand. The few mourners present regarded him sadly, patting the newly widowed man wordlessly on the shoulder. Although he had brought an overner to the village instead of marrying a local girl, they had found Rose gentle and amiable and sympathised with his loss.

On the evening of the funeral Will and Ruth sat alone at the table. This had been their habit for many months but now the emptiness of the room upstairs was almost palpable.

'What's the first thing you remember?' Will asked his daughter in order to break the oppressive silence.

She thought for a while. 'The boat. And after that being in London.'

'You don't remember living nowhere else before then?'

Again she thought, twisting a wisp of her rich brown hair. 'I remember an old lady looking after me. I suppose she must have been my grandmother. Was she your mother or Mam's?'

Will chose his next words very carefully. 'I expect she was your mam's mother – your real mam.'

Will bowed his head as if in thought before meeting her eyes and continuing,

'When you were a babby, you lived here on the island with your real mam. Garnet was right. Her name was Elizabeth and she wasn't my wife but I was – am – your father.'

Ruth continued to regard him and he could not guess at what she was thinking.

'I loved her,' he said quietly. 'She loved me too but she was wed to someone else.'

'Was this before you met Mam?' she finally asked.

'Yeah. I went away to London and I didn't even know you was born. If I had ...' He stopped himself from pursuing that particular agony. 'Your mam – your real mam, that is – wanted to keep you but it wasn't possible. When you're really grown up I'll tell you about it but for now I want you to trust me when I say it was for your own safety.'

Ruth looked away from him. 'That's the beautiful lady I remember,' she said. 'Where is she now?'

'As far as I know she's at Caulbourne. I used to write and tell her how you were getting on but when we came back here I just left it. It seemed safer and it would have caused Mam – Rose, that is – pain.

'Why would it have caused Mam pain?' she asked.

'Because she couldn't have no children of her own. And she always knew I loved your real mam. I couldn't help it.'

'Do you still love her now?'

Will shrugged. 'I haven't seen her for more than seven years, but I still think of her a lot. Her husband died but she may be wed again. If she is, then it's best that I don't see her, but you – you got a right to meet her.

'What about Garnet?'

'What about her?'

'She said we were sisters.'

Will was struggling for the right words. 'You are,' he finally replied. 'Half-sisters. I'm Garnet's father too.'

'How?' When he did not reply she said: 'Did you love her mother as well?'

'I can't answer that because I don't understand it myself. Just say that it happened.'

Ruth nodded. 'What you going to do then?' she finally asked.

'I don't know. Wait a little. I must get things straight in my head first. I loved Mam,' he added. 'She was the best wife a man could have. She really cared for me.'

His daughter came to sit on his lap and he cuddled her as she began to cry.

'We made her happy, didn't we?' he consoled, rubbing his cheek against her shiny hair. 'She's gone to a better place now.

No pain in her leg. And she wouldn't want us to be unhappy, would she?'

'But I want her to be my real mam,' the child sobbed.

'She was. You and Garnet were the only children she had. It was she who said I should find your real mam when she was gone.'

Looking at her father, Ruth said: 'When I grow up I want to marry a man as handsome as you.'

Will rocked her to him. 'Marry a man who loves you,' he counselled. 'That's the best recipe for happiness there is.'

Now that he had told Ruth the truth, he felt a terrific sense of release. When it came to bedtime he took the child into the double bed with him and cradled her to sleep. He had only one more free day before he had to return to work and he wondered what to do with Ruth during his absences. He felt that he could not possibly leave her alone in this more than empty house and to take her to Caulbourne so suddenly, unannounced, was more than he could cope with. He decided instead to ask the neighbour if she could stay with her. The woman, who had five young children, was herself widowed and would no doubt be glad of the help. With this thought he fell into a dreamless sleep.

The next day he duly called on the neighbour and made arrangements for Ruth to stay. The woman had a tired, worn-out appearance. Her clothes and hair seemed dulled and washed out but there was an appraising spark in her shrewd blue eyes.

'We'll have a meal ready for you when you return,' she offered, and he realised with embarrassment that she was flirting with him. He felt old and tired and not remotely interested.

'Thanking you,' he replied. 'But I'd rather eat alone.' He was conscious of his brusque tone and added: 'I need to be by myself.'

'Of course, I understand. I know what it is to be bereaved.' She offered him some ale, which he declined, leaving as soon as he decently could. Her hungry eyes and the message coming from her body movements were unmistakable.

When he arrived at the castle it was to the sympathy and support of his workmates. He knew that they were making a special effort to bring him out of himself and he was grateful for their concern, but he wanted only to be left alone. Facing up to the inevitable, he put on a brave face and tried to work away his inner loneliness.

'You've had a hard time, lad,' his old master said. 'But you're still young. Things'll get better, just you wait and see.'

'Will they?' He smiled grimly before adding: 'Time will tell.'

As he worked he thought of all he had lost in the past years: his wife and his eldest daughter, the boy he called son, his grandfather, his provocative mistress; overshadowing it all was the longing for the woman he had truly loved and lost through his own stupidity. He sighed, chipped with sudden viciousness at the stone block before him, and repeated: 'Time will tell.'

Part IV

November 1595 –
January 1599

Chapter One

Lizzie sat as close to the fire as she dared and was grateful for the warmth. The day had been one of unrelieved, bone-chilling fog and even before the stock were secured for the night it had been too dark to see.

Extravagantly she piled more sticks onto the fire, both for heat and light. That evening she wanted to darn her stockings and also start knitting a pair of hose for her brother Harry for New Year.

It was no more than four of the clock but she was unlikely to see anyone now until Jed arrived the following day. The loneliness was more extreme because for tonight her two adopted boys had elected to stay with Jed at Sheepwash cottage. At the thought of them she smiled. They were good boys, without malice, and for some happy reason they regarded Jed as their hero. She was pleased for him.

There were only a few more days to the Hiring Fair and she had decided to take a servant to help with the housework. One outcome of her widowed state had been that she threw herself into her work with such intensity that there had been a resultant boom in the fulling business. Prosperity was pleasing, though her life was still lonely. It would be good to have another woman in the house. She had been sadly short of female company since the departure of the girls.

There, the thoughts were back again, try as she might to keep them at bay. In the long evening ahead she knew that she would go over again the saga of Will's visit and of Mardi's revelations.

Her thoughts were like a tapestry to which she kept adding

new threads as the picture unfolded. First there had been the bare canvas with her love for Will blazoned across its entire surface. At that time it had been uncomplicated in its purity, although she hadn't then known it, and only spoilt by the interference of her father.

Then the picture had been blurred by her marriage and Will's insistence on going away. If he had stayed, things might have been different.

Once she had got that picture straight in her mind, their child had brought bright threads to the landscape. Her thoughts shied away from the precious gift that had been lost.

With difficulty she made herself face up to the huge black clouds which had then obscured everything. The knowledge of Will's marriage had at the time been the greatest blow she could imagine. Then, after the departure of the girls, she doubted if she could ever have been more unhappy. As the weeks passed, however, she had begun to understand how he must have felt and even convinced herself that it was almost a compliment that his jealousy had been so extreme that he was forced to wed with the nearest woman in order to black out his pain.

She gave a little snort of derision as her thoughts moved on. Mardi! Trust Mardi to spoil everything. Even now she could not let herself believe that Mardi and Will had been lovers. If it was true, then the rest of her tapestry was a lie. Even when Lizzie was still a virgin, believing implicitly in his declarations of love, saving herself for him, he had been lying with the Gipsy. The venom of betrayal rose in her throat.

Nine months to the day separated the births of Garnet and Ruby. Then Ruby and Silas had been born at the very same minute. There must be some supernatural reason for all this. Lizzie fell back again on the consoling thought that it was Mardi, the witch, who had planned it all. How could she blame Will when he had been possessed? It was some small comfort.

Laying her sewing aside, Lizzie went up the rickety stairs to her bedroom and from under the bolster she produced two much fingered parchments, secured with fading ribbons. Taking them back to the fireside, she opened them and read the contents.

The first was dated 17 December 1592 and was very short.

350

Dear Mistress Dore,

This is to tell you that the children Ruby and Garnet are well and happy. They are larning their letters. News of you would be welcome to them and to your Servant.

Willyum Gosden

She sat long over the letter, trying to visualise them all. It had been written three years ago and in that time they would all have changed.

'News of you would be welcome,' he had said. Well she had news, news that he and Mardi had been lovers.

'I will see him shortly,' the Gipsy had said, and the searing jealousy enveloped Lizzie. No doubt by now Mardi would have laid a spell on his poor wife and stolen him away to live with her. She crushed the parchment in her hands.

The second document was dated a year later and was equally tantalising in its brevity.

... Your girl grows straight and tall. You would be prowd of her, as I am also. Things in this city are not good. The countryside is the true place to raise a family.

She did not know what he had been trying to say. Since then there had been silence and in bad moments she feared that something terrible had befallen them, but an inner sense told her that all must be well. She would know instinctively if anything bad had happened to her child.

With a sigh she suddenly threw the parchments onto the flames, where they curled and blackened. She resisted the temptation to grab them back, even at the last moment. It was no good clinging to the past, yet at that moment all the pain was back again, unabated by the passage of time. In sudden despair she feared that there would never be a time when she would be whole.

'You seems sad, our Lizzie,' said Jed when he came over to help at the mill the next morning.

'Just leave me be, Jed,' she replied shortly.

She was aware that he was watching her in his childlike, direct manner and deliberately ignored him.

'Is it 'cause Ruby and Garnet has gone to a gennleman's house?' he asked.

She wondered whom he had been talking to. 'That's it.'

'Then why don't you have them back?'

'Don't ask no more questions!'

He shrugged and went back to work, heaving the wet bolts of cloth around with the ease of a giant. Alfred and Sidney obligingly followed him around like shadows.

Later in the day she wandered aimlessly across to Sheepwash cottage, but Leah regarded her with silent reproach and there was nobody else that she could talk to. 'Where's the sense in sending your own flesh away and then taking in strangers?' her mother asked. It was the question that always came between them these days.

As Lizzie walked leadenly back to the mill, she remembered the many conversations she had shared with May in what now seemed like their idyllic childhood. May might have not understood the depth of Lizzie's passion but her friend's passive nature would at least have allowed Lizzie to spill it all out.

On top of everything else she knew that somehow she had been responsible for what had happened to Widow Trykett and May and also to young Silas. The burden of guilt weighed her down and only the penance of rearing May's brothers made her life purposeful. In a strange way she reasoned that perhaps the pain of losing Will, Ruby and Garnet might compensate to some degree for the ills that had befallen those around her. It was small comfort.

It was her brother Harry who finally came to her rescue. Harry's humour and his good looks had always been a source of comfort to her. She remembered that even as children her mother had always said they were alike. Because of his fine physique, the loss of his leg had seemed doubly profane, and yet his enforced stay at home had brought them closer together than at any time since their childhood.

Recently, however, Harry had been subdued and, coming out of her own torpor, Lizzie was driven to ask what troubled him. He was helping her to card some wool and as she asked her question he put the strands of fleece aside and turned to look at her.

'It's the usual thing that troubles men,' he replied with a wry grin. 'Women.'

352

Lizzie looked at him with interest. 'Any particular one?' she asked.

'Very particular. It's our cousin Bridget.'

The news took Lizzie by surprise, but she merely said: 'Does she care for thee?'

Harry shrugged. 'I don't know. Doesn't matter much anyhow. First she's my cousin and second her wouldn't want half a man.'

Lizzie snorted impatiently. 'Cousins have been known to wed,' she countered. 'And besides, there's a lot more than half of thee.' With a grin, she added: 'You still got the important bits.' It seemed like the first time that she had laughed for weeks.

Harry put his arm around her. 'And what about you?' he asked. 'You seem like a corpse these days.'

Lizzie let her head rest against his shoulder and was grateful for his maleness.

'I let my child go,' she finally answered. 'What could be worse than that?'

'Because of what they were saying about her?'

A wave of affection spread over her in gratitude for his intuition.

'Partly that,' she admitted.

'You should have let her stay. They couldn't prove nothing. It's all silly gossip.'

'Perhaps, but I didn't want her hurt.'

There was silence before Harry continued: 'It's more than that, ain't it? I know she ain't a changeling but I don't think she's Silas Dore's, neither.'

Lizzie shook her head and blushed. 'Don't make no odds,' she replied.

'D'you want to talk about it?' he asked.

Again she shook her head. 'Wouldn't do no good. He's wed.'

'So was you once.' Harry started to work rhythmically and she watched his strong deft hands, mesmerised by their movements.

'Mine was old,' she said. 'His is young. She'll probably outlive us both.'

After a while he asked: 'What about the other one, the vagrant's child?'

353

Lizzie felt her stomach tighten.

'What about her?' she asked.

'They're uncannily alike.'

She could not answer. All the time she had still been denying it.

Seeing her discomfort, Harry asked: 'Does he love you?'

It was then that tears started in her eyes. 'I always thought he did. I love him more'n God's earth. Perhaps that's why I'm being punished this way.'

Harry stopped work again and put his arms around her. 'Ain't nothing wrong with love,' he said. 'Just be true to it. I got a feeling it'll all come right in the end.'

She hugged him back in reply and allowed herself a glimmer of hope.

Chapter Two

As the weeks and months slipped by, Lizzie drove herself hard in an effort to put the past behind her. It was a relief to have a new maid in the house, for now in the evenings she could no longer give way to the sadness that sat permanently on her shoulder. The maid was a sensible girl and Lizzie felt it incumbent upon her to set a good example.

'You must not think of the past. At all,' she scolded herself as she baked a week's supply of bread for the household. Looking out of the window she could see in the distance the copse where Ruby had been conceived.

With a sigh she took a batch of loaves from the scorching recess of the oven. While the next lot were baking she would visit the church so that she could pray for the wellbeing of her child. Calling on Jane, the maid, to look out to the bread, she grabbed her shawl and set out across the green. This was one maternal thing that she could do and there was consolation in this small act of devotion.

Each day Lizzie divided her time between the large house that was her home and the modest cottage where she had grown up. Leah had never recovered from the violent death of May White and the departure of her only grandchild had reduced her to a state of melancholy. Her husband's reaction to her condition was to keep away as much as possible, which usually meant passing each spare moment in the alehouse. The once cheerful, bustling cottage was now burdened with the diverse ills of the family who had formerly seemed so united.

If things seemed bad at home, yet the mill and the Sheepwash thrived. By the end of the summer they were planning to take on more land and increase the joint flock, although, as Leah pointed out: 'There don't seem much point in having all this if there ain't no one to leave it to.' The lack of grandchildren was her most constant complaint.

In spite of Harry's hopes, Cousin Bridget announced her betrothal to a shepherd at Compton village. All the Galpine family were invited to the wedding and to the celebration afterwards on the green.

The ceremony took place on a balmy September morning and Lizzie, wearing a new gown, stayed close to Harry, aware of his pain. Everywhere she turned, however, her cousin Tom seemed to be at her side.

In spite of her protests, Tom dragged her to join the dancing. He was doing well these days, having followed his father into their wheelwright shop. Now that the old man was dead, Tom was his own master.

Tom did not favour the Galpine family, being thickset and pudgy-faced with light-brown, curly hair. As he took Lizzie's hand, she felt the sweat on his palm. He danced with clumsy exertion, his blue eyes never leaving her face.

'I must get back to Harry,' she said in an attempt to excuse herself, but he followed close behind.

Before they reached him, Tom asked: 'Why don't you come for a walk? Harry don't need you to mother him.'

Lizzie shrugged. 'He's in poor spirits,' she explained. 'He was fond of Bridget.'

'Was he?' Tom's hand was on her elbow. 'Pity he didn't say nothing then. Us Galpine's should stick together.' He squeezed her and she tried to move away but he still held on to her. From his awkward movements and his unfocused eyes she realised that he had drunk too much of the cowslip wine.

'It's a shame Bridget's going out Compton,' he continued. 'There's nothing there now but sheep. She'll be that lonely.' Stopping and turning to look at her, he added: 'But there's still you and me.'

Lizzie stared at him in surprise and he started to pull her away from the crowd.

'Come on. Come and walk with me. I got summat to say to thee.'

She shook her head but he did not release his hold so, not

wishing to draw attention to them, she allowed herself to be lead towards the churchyard and the copse beyond.

As soon as they were out of hearing, Tom turned her to face him. 'How about it, then?' he asked.

'How about what?' She was trying to hold him at bay.

'You 'n me getting wed.'

'You're drunk.'

'I ain't. Come on, say you will.'

'No! I don't want to wed.'

'You must do. You must miss – you know.' He pushed his groin closer to her and she shoved him hard as he winked at her.

'Huh! I don't miss nothing, having been wed to Silas Dore.'

'Don't you want no nippers then?' he asked, standing back a little.

Lizzie was shaking her head. 'Please, Tom, leave me be. I . . . I don't want nothing at the moment, save to be left alone.'

'In that case, I'll wait. Just give us a little kiss, though.' Ignoring her protests, he pressed his fleshy lips over hers. The contact caused him to writhe against her with desire.

'I said no!' She wriggled away and glared at him.

He raised his hands to appease her. 'But I'll wait. We'll make a good match, you and me.'

'No, we won't. You're wasting your time. I don't never want to wed again.'

'Your father thinks we should.'

At the mention of George, Lizzie's face blazed.

'It was him what made me marry Silas Dore. He's done me enough damage and I'm my own mistress now. I'll wed who I please!' she shouted at him.

'You do want to marry again then?' There was a foolish optimism on Tom's good-natured face.

'No! I don't know. Just leave me be.'

They walked back in silence and Lizzie sought out Harry for protection. Seeing her agitation, her brother raised his eyebrows

'Something wrong?' he asked.

'Yeah. It's that Tom. He's drunk and, you'll never guess, he asked me to wed him.'

'What did you say?' Harry leaned back and watched her with amusement.

'No, of course. He's creepy.'

'He ain't a bad sort,' her brother replied reasonably.

'You're not a woman. I hate men like that what mauls you.'

Her brother grinned and took her hand. 'Life just ain't fair,' he complained. 'I wish some woman would come and maul me.'

After Bridget's wedding Tom was a frequent caller at the fulling mill. Sober he was nicer than when drunk, but Lizzie had no wish to think of him as a suitor. She tried to discourage him but he shrugged off her indifference.

At Christmas he bought her a goose and for New Year he presented her with a pewter plate.

'It's very grand,' she said. 'But I can't accept gifts from you – it makes it look like we're betrothed.'

'We should be,' he replied, never losing an opportunity to press his suit. 'Why don't you say the word?'

Lizzie shrugged and he reached out to take her hand.

'Don't you like me?' he asked.

'It's not that.'

'Then what?'

Ignoring her resistance, he kissed her. She found no pleasure in the feel or the smell of him, and as soon as she decently could she pushed him away.

He was kind and dogged and she could not hurt him, but he held no attraction for her. Perversely his attentions stirred up a hunger, not for Tom, but for some unknown man who would come and satisfy her starved body.

'We're cousins,' she excused herself. ''Twould be best to find someone else.' But he shook his head.

'I don't want no one else,' he replied. 'I want you.'

Chapter Three

In July 1597 Lizzie reached her twenty-fifth birthday. Her body was still firm and her face unlined, but in spite of Tom's attentions she no longer believed that any man could want her. Drawing water from the well, she thought that if by some miracle Will should return to the village, he would find an old woman in the place of the young girl that he had left behind. She began to resign herself to a lonely old age.

Meanwhile, the yearning to see Ruby overwhelmed her, and every time she encountered a child of about the same age she could not help wondering how her daughter would compare. If they were to meet face to face she feared that they might not even recognise each other and, worse still, she did not know if the girl even remembered that she had once had another mother.

As always it was Harry who remarked on her distress.

'How come you're so sad?' he asked as they took their nammet to eat by the stream.

Lizzie shrugged. 'I can't stop thinking about the past. About what might have been.'

After a while Harry observed: 'To an outsider you would seem to be a very lucky woman. You have this mill and a healthy flock and you have good health and youth.'

'Youth?' echoed Lizzie, picking on the least contentious item. 'I feel old.'

'Then you're very foolish. You're wasting the present for the sake of things you can't change. If you really think your lover will never return, then you should wed and have more babbies. That way you could lay the ghosts that haunt you.'

When she didn't answer, he said: 'It was Will Gosden, wasn't it?'

'Yes.'

Harry sighed. 'Will's a nice chap but if he's wed, as you say, and living in London, then it really seems a lost cause.' Giving her shoulder a squeeze, he added: 'I hate to see you so empty and sad. Just think about what I've said.'

She made no comment but his thoughts stayed with her.

A few days later she stepped out into a bright August morning loaded with wet linen and started to hang it on the hedges to dry.

'Laces, silks, satins, mistress?' She jumped as her reverie was shattered by a husky male voice and she turned to find a pedlar coming across the yard. His voice had a foreign burr to it and he was very tanned, with black hair and a large gold ring in one ear. He stood not much taller than Lizzie and his eyes surveyed her with the easy confidence of a man used to attracting women.

'Nothing today, thanks be to you. I ain't buying trifles.' She wiped her damp hands in her kirtle and looked away because she knew that she was blushing.

Out of the corner of her eye she could see that he was grinning at her, a slow, appraising smile that made her flush even more.

'Then perhaps your husband would like to spoil his beautiful wife?' he suggested.

From his basket he produced a piece of lace and held it against her shoulder. She was very aware of the touch of his fingers.

'See how well this would suit your colouring?' He did not move the lace away and as it tickled her cheek a tingling sensation coursed through her.

'My husband's dead,' she replied candidly. 'I ain't got no need to make myself noticed.'

'If you've no man, then you've every need to make yourself as pretty as can be – not that anyone could be prettier than you.'

Lizzie tried to laugh as she moved away and then to be offended, but the strange, speckled eyes had set off a chain reaction like quicksilver running through her.

'I think you'd best go,' she said, backing towards the door.

He followed her for a few paces, then stood watching her.

'I'll be leaving this island on the morrow,' he observed. 'Tonight I could be making myself useful giving comfort to some lonely woman.' He grinned. 'There's nothing like the healing power o' love. It's God's good medicine. You look lonely – starved o' pleasure.'

'No!' Lizzie's face was scarlet, but it was mostly shame because his very presence made her want to melt against him.

'Why be afraid?' he teased. 'I wouldn't hurt you. On the contrary, I'd make you happier than you can remember.'

'You mustn't!'

The man shrugged. 'Well, that's a shame for both of us. These hands can do wonders.'

Gazing calmly at her, he ran his fingers down her cheek, past her neck and over her breast. She gave a sharp intake of breath.

'My name's Django and I'm skilled in the arts of love.' He laughed at her discomfiture.

Shaking her head, Lizzie backed into the kitchen and closed the door.

'Don't be afraid,' he called from outside. 'Leave the door unlatched tonight and I'll take thee to Paradise. I'll come after dark and leave before dawn. No one'll know save we two and it'll be a night you'll never forget.'

'I'm not alone here, I got a servant!' she shouted.

'Then I'll pleasure you both!'

She heard him laugh and her belly somersaulted with desire.

As it grew dark, Lizzie bolted the front door and then barricaded it with the table. The maid Jane had a bed in the weaving room. Lizzie lay tense and still in the great lonely bed, straining her ears for sounds. She feared that the man might force his way in and yet her body ached to be touched.

'Please, God, you done me enough harm,' she prayed. 'If you have any mercy, keep us both safe and please, take away this feeling.'

The man did not come but the feeling remained and she did not sleep that night.

'You're tetchy, our Lizzie,' said Harry when he came over to help with the weaving next day. She had been grumbling her way around the mill since dawn.

'You need to find yourself a man,' he observed, and she looked at him archly.

'And what about you? Don't you need a woman?'

'Sure I do.' He suddenly grinned his disarming smile. 'Reckon as how I've found one, too.'

'Who?' She forgot her indignation.

'Young Jane. Your skivvy.'

'But she's –' She spoke before she could stop herself.

'A skivvy?' He looked at her quizzically. 'Does that matter?'

Shamefaced, she shook her head. 'I suppose not. She seems a decent enough girl.'

'She's more than that. She's honest and virtuous. I know for a fact she'd risk dismissal before she did anything wrong.' He gave her an impish grin. 'I can't pretend as how I haven't tried to persuade her.' Serious again, he continued: 'I know she likes me for myself and that she wants to do things right.'

His sister made no comment. The girl seemed decent enough, it was true, but Lizzie was suspicious of her motives. Now things were going well for them all, Harry must seem a good catch. She had to admit that a part of her also felt jealous, for over the last year Harry had become her closest friend and confidant and she had no wish to have his attentions diverted elsewhere.

'You got plans to wed?' she asked.

'Could be.'

The plans came to fruition quicker than she expected, and a few weeks later the wedding of Harry and Jane took place in the village church. Any doubts that Lizzie had about the girl's intentions were quickly dispelled when she saw them together, but in their place she felt a hungry envy for the love and fulfilment they so clearly found in each other. To forestall her loneliness, she set to work with renewed vigour, taking on Jane's duties once more. Within two months her new sister-in-law confided that she was with child.

The experience with the pedlar, coupled with Harry's wedding, had a profound effect upon Lizzie. In the village two babies were born to women older than herself and a third woman had just married at the age of thirty. Lizzie had to acknowledge that her life was not necessarily over.

Tom bought her a fireside chair for New Year and she made him a doublet from their best cloth as a gift.

Catching her alone when he delivered the chair, he held her close and she did not resist the pressure of his body.

'You're that cruel, our Lizzie,' he said hoarsely. 'Won't you let me lie with you this once? I aches that bad.' She pulled away and his hands fell dejectedly to his sides.

'I'm sorry, Tom. Give me a bit longer.'

'What you waiting for?' he asked in exasperation.

'I must be sure.'

'Sure of what? You know I love you.'

'I know you do. I must be sure I'd be a good wife.'

'How you ever going to find out if you behave like a froze-up maid?' he challenged. With a sigh, he made ready to go. As he reached the door, he said: 'By Easter I think we should be wed. You'd best make up your mind 'cause I don't see no point in going on like this. I want you but I'm only human. I can't wait for ever. There's other maids what ain't so unwilling.' Putting on his hat, he left her to sort out the tangle of her emotions.

The force of his feelings caused her to waver and it occurred to her that if he had insisted on calling the banns that day, she might well have agreed. True to his nature, however, he had given way and allowed her a three months' grace. Three months. Anything might happen in that time and if not, then a secure future would still be hers. Dear Tom! She felt a wave of affection for him as she realized that, come what may, there was now a future of sorts to look forward to.

Chapter Four

Will worked hard during his first day back at the castle and when it was finally time to go home he was glad to escape the attention of his workmates and leave their sympathy behind.

As he rode along the winding lane he tried not to think about Rose, although her loss was like a great void in his heart. Best to concentrate on the child, he thought, make the future right for her. For tonight he could not think further than his recent loss but soon enough he would be able to look wider afield. The village of Caulbourne sprang immediately to mind.

It was dark when he arrived home. True to her word, the widow Gleed had a hot meal waiting for him and, true to his, he took it into the cottage with Ruth and ate it there, huddled over the fire.

In the long, dark evening they talked until sleep overcame them. Will told his daughter about his life as a boy in the village and at Caulbourne, about his parents, about the time they had spent in London and about Lizzie.

'You haven't even told me her name,' Ruth said as they got ready to go to the upper room.

'Lizabeth Dore. Least that was what she was when last I heard.'

She nodded as she slipped off her outer garment, preparing for sleep.

'Can I come in bed with you?' she asked.

'Best not. It ain't seemly for a young woman to sleep with her father.'

'Why not?'

Will hesitated. 'A man should only take his wife to bed with him,' he said.

'Why?'

'That's how God meant it.' He undressed himself and climbed into the bed he had so recently shared with Rose.

'Did you take my mother to bed with you?' Ruth asked.

He shook his head, wondering how to answer. 'When you're a grown woman you'll understand,' he said.

As he blew out the candle, the girl asked. 'Is it like the kine mating?'

'In some ways. But it's more than that. They don't know no love for each other. People should share more'n just mating.'

She grunted in reply and soon they both fell into their separate and lonely dreams.

The next morning it was very icy and as Will started work he wondered how long before they would be brought to a standstill by the threatened snow. The fortifications were nearly half completed but he sometimes felt that he had been working on them for ever and he longed for a change where he could use his finer skills. Still, it was a job and it had to be done. The increased use of artillery fire had made the old building vulnerable.

'Defence of the realm,' Sir George had called it on one of his inspections. 'He who holds the castle holds the island and he who holds the island holds the realm.'

Will's mind began to wander and, as so often in unguarded moments, he found himself thinking about Lizzie. Rose was barely in her grave and it was not without guilt that he allowed himself to relive the age-old hallowed vision of the Holywood copse with Lizzie, her breasts uncovered and her hair loose, amid the summer foliage. The long unsatisfied need stirred in him.

During Rose's illness he had refrained from more than holding her and these days he was hungry for some release. You're a fool, he told himself. One way or another you've got to find out if she's wed. If she is, you've got to find out how things stand for Ruth to see her, and if she ain't . . . Desire now coursed through him. This very Sunday he could be seeing her, hearing her voice, walking with her in the crystal-frosted lanes, holding her, entering her beautiful, willing body with all its comfort and pleasure.

He fought the feeling down and suddenly everything happened at once.

'Look out, Will!' The voice reached him simultaneously with the violent crushing blow as the great block of stone they were manoeuvring into place slipped and trapped him. The terrible pain was followed by all loss of feeling in his arm and he slumped forwards, held upright only by his trapped hand. Dimly he was aware of his workmates supporting him while a pulley was fetched to hoist the block up and release him. As his arm was set free, he slid to the ground, cold and sickness enveloping him.

'My God, he don't deserve that, not just losing his wife and all,' he heard someone say.

He looked at his senseless limb hanging awkwardly from the elbow. A piece of bone jutted through the skin and his fingers were crushed and bloody. Nausea overcame him as a first wave of raging agony stormed through the useless hand. He groaned. Around him men shook their heads.

A knitbone was sent for and, while his friends held him, the man pulled and manipulated the damaged hand into some semblance of its natural shape before securing it with wooden splints. Will passed out with the pain of the wrenched and damaged nerves.

He did not remember the journey home. Indeed, for the next few days he was half in and half out of this world. Sometimes he saw Ruth's anxious face close to his and he tried to reassure her, but the next moment she seemed a long way away. He was also aware of the widow doing shameful things to him as if he were a babby and he tried to push her away but he didn't seem to have the strength to reach her.

On the fourth day he awoke to the same pain but at least he knew where he was. As he moved he let out an involuntary groan and within seconds Ruth was at his side.

'Pa? How are you feeling?' She took his good hand and he studied the young face, noting the smudges under her eyes.

'You ain't been sleeping proper,' he said.

'I been worried about you.'

'I'm well enough. It's just this damned arm.'

366

'It's bad. You'll have to lie there till it heals.'

'I can't. I got work to do.'

The girl sighed with exasperation. 'You can't work. You must just be patient,' she said.

Remembering the ghastly sight of his crushed hand, he wondered if he would ever work again, and a different kind of chill overcame him. Meanwhile the girl had fetched some soup and in spite of his protests started spooning it into his mouth.

'You just rest now,' she insisted.

He gave a little smile. 'You're just like your mother,' he replied, but he did not say which one.

Chapter Five

Tom's ultimatum greatly disturbed Lizzie. She had to admit that she had grown to depend on him, for he was always there. If he found someone else, she would be very lonely. Her head told her that most marriages were for convenience. With Tom she would have friendship and security and a man who would treat her well. There might even be children. But even as she thought of it, her heart told her there was still the crazy hope that one day Will might come and somehow everything would still be well.

The pros and cons went round in her head until she was totally confused. Finally pushing her thoughts aside, she decided on Tuesday to go to market just to get away from it all. It was late March and frosty but Farmer was sure-footed and fat from lack of exercise. They also now had a second horse, a pack animal bought for three pounds at the market, and Lizzie loaded him with produce to make the journey worth while.

As she rode, her thoughts drifted of their own volition to the empty space in her life which in God's pattern of things should include a husband and children. In the eight years since she had sent the girls away she had received only two letters from Will. She did not believe that anything bad had happened to Ruby, for she had always been certain she would know instinctively. It seemed more likely that Will as a married man had decided to cut himself off from her. However laudable his decision, she could not forgive him for abandoning her. It was just another example of his betrayal.

Then there was Mardi. Mardi would have no scruples about visiting him and perhaps even now he had left his wife and

368

taken up with her. At the thought, jealousy again engulfed Lizzie. She faced once more the fear that Mardi might now have taken on the role of mother to Ruby, and such a thought was unbearable. She steeled her heart to protect her from the pain. No more thinking about them. Ever. Remember Tom.

The market was quiet and there were no peepshows or jugglers to distract her. Although she had sold very little, she packed up early and with a heavy heart set back off for Caulbourne to ensure that she arrived home before dark. The outing had not had the desired effect of cheering her up; in fact, as she journeyed out of Newport, she felt more dejected than ever.

As she climbed the hill leading into Carisbrooke, she noticed a young girl at the side of the road holding a chestnut mare. The child was examining the animal's leg and as Lizzie slowed down she stood up and turned helplessly towards her.

'Scuse me, mistress, I don't know what to do,' she started. 'The horse is lame and I must get to Shorrel but I can't take her that far. She can hardly walk.'

Lizzie looked at the girl and was disturbed by the candid hazel eyes, but she told herself not to be so silly and slid from Farmer's back. She bent to examine the animal. The mare's fetlock was swollen and she refused to put her leg to the ground.

'You'd best take her to a stable and leave her,' she advised, avoiding the girl's eyes. 'It's not far to walk to Shorrel.'

'I don't mind walking. It's just that I don't know where to take the horse and I need to get back quick cause my pa's ill.'

Lizzie now looked at the girl again but could not admit what she saw.

'Come along with me and I'll see she's stabled,' she said, leading the way back into town.

Eagerly the girl fell into step beside her, coaxing the mare back down the hill.

'How old are you?' Lizzie asked conversationally.

'Nigh on nine.'

'Where's your mother?'

The girl lowered her eyes. 'Mam died at Christmas. Pa's had an accident and he can't work.'

'Oh, I'm sorry. What does he do?' She was looking out for the stable in the gathering gloom and only half listening for the answer.

'He's a master mason. He's that good, everyone admires his work.'

The knot in Lizzie's stomach twisted tighter and she looked at the girl again.

'What's your name?'

'Ruth.'

She felt a small thud of disappointment.

'You got any sisters?'

'No. There's only me now. To tell the truth, Mam couldn't have no children. I mean none of her own. Pa . . .' She stopped in confusion, still struggling to keep the mare moving. 'Pa loved someone else. Not that he didn't love Mam – his wife, that is. He's a good man,' she finished lamely.

By now they had reached the stables and Lizzie had to keep a grip on herself as she arranged with the ostler for the care of the horse. Her eyes kept returning to the girl's long, high-cheekboned face and the arresting hazel eyes. She was sure that they must hear her heart thumping.

They left the stable in silence. At the crossroads at the top of the hill, Lizzie halted and looked again at her companion.

'You'd best let me take you home,' she said.

'Oh, I couldn't put you to such trouble.'

Ignoring her reply, Lizzie handed her the rein of the packhorse and with a nod the girl leaped astride.

'What you been doing in Newport?' Lizzie asked above the muted rhythm of the horses' hooves. Any conversation was better than the tormenting thoughts that raced in her mind.

'I been selling cakes and pasties. Pa can't work and I know he's worried so I thought I'd surprise him and earn some money.'

Lizzie's heart went out to the child. 'You must love your pa,' she observed.

'Oh, I do!' Even in the fading light Lizzie could make out the intensity of her expression.

'What's your other name?' She had waited as long as she could bear before asking and now it felt as if the whole world had suddenly become silent. Every tree and bird were listening for the reply.

'Gosden. Ruth Gosden.'

370

Lizzie expelled her breath audibly. 'Are you Will Gosden's girl?' she asked.

'Yes. Do you know him?'

'I know him.' Lizzie fought the mounting hysteria. 'How long have you been on the island?'

There was a moment of palpable silence, then Ruth replied: 'I can't recall exactly. One or two years.'

'Years?' The disbelief in Lizzie's voice caused Ruth to stare at her.

'Yes. We came back when things got bad in London. Pa thought it was best for us here.'

Lizzie was grappling with a tangle of feelings. This was surely her child, her own daughter, on whom so many of her hopes and daydreams had centred. Yet now she could do or say nothing. She could not believe that they had been living just a few miles away and that Will had not even bothered to let her know. It was unbelievably callous. I'm a fool, she thought bitterly. Now I have to face it. He doesn't care at all. I've been living a lie all this time. She gave Farmer an uncharacteristic jab and set him cantering. Behind her Ruth did her best to keep up.

Grasping at the merest straw, Lizzie thought, Tom loves me. It was small comfort.

Ruth? Perhaps this isn't my daughter after all, Lizzie tried to tell herself. It is just a coincidence that there is another mason called Will and he has a child called Ruth. The name so like Ruby but not the same.

Tentatively she said: 'I heard tell that Will Gosden had two daughters.'

Ruth nodded her head. 'There's Garnet but she's gone to her mother in London.' She hesitated before adding: 'She's only my half-sister. Pa doesn't like to talk about it because we had different mothers.' She blushed and Lizzie was silent.

As they reached Shorrel she said curtly: 'Tell your pa where the horse is stabled. They'll look after her till she's collected.'

Her daughter was now level with her, glancing anxiously into her face. 'Won't you come in?' she offered. 'I'll give you some ale.'

Lizzie merely shook her head.

After a pause, Ruth continued: 'Pa's been real poorly lately. Sometimes I thought he was going to die – like Mam.' Gulping,

371

she added: 'I feel scared when I go out in case he's been called to God while I'm away.'

Looking at the child, Lizzie saw the terror in her eyes and her own pain and anger were cast aside. Reaching out, she touched her hand.

'I'll come in then,' she said, and her heart began to thump louder than a blacksmith's hammer.

She dismounted, tethered both horses with trembling hands and followed the child into the small cottage.

Chapter Six

Inside the cottage there was an air of desolation as if the heart had gone out of it and once again Lizzie's jealousy erupted.

'I'll just see if Pa's awake,' Ruth whispered, skipping up the stairs.

A moment later Lizzie heard his voice. She found herself creeping nearer just to get a glimpse of him.

Tiptoeing up the stairway, she peeped through the open door and managed to see the bed and the child sitting on the edge. The man's face was obscured but he held his daughter's hand. She listened as the girl was telling him about the kind wife who had brought her home.

'She says she knows you. Shall I ask her up?' she was saying.

'No. Not when I'm like this. Who is she?'

'Hello, Will.' Lizzie stepped forwards and watched as his head jerked towards her. He blinked several times as if not believing his eyes.

'Lizzie?'

'I found your daughter. I thought I'd best see her home.' There was tension in her voice and he nodded, still stunned by her presence.

'Er, go and fetch Mistress Dore some ale,' he said with a visible effort at normality. Gaping at them both, the child obediently left the room.

'Well, this is a surprise,' Lizzie continued, her voice taut with sarcasm. 'And me thinking you was in London.'

'Are you wed?' The question cut across her conversation.

'Does it matter?'

He was looking directly at her. 'Like hell it does.'

She took a step closer and he lowered his eyes.

'I stink,' he said in embarrassment. 'I been in this bed too long.'

Ignoring his remark, she came closer, taking in for the first time his pallor and the strained look about his eyes.

'I'm sorry as how you're laid up,' she said. 'Are you mending?'

He shrugged. 'This hand'll take a long time. I don't even know if it will.'

'I'm good with injured limbs. Let me see.' She reached out to touch him but he pulled away.

'Truth is,' he said, 'I'm finished. I won't work again. I must say it to someone and I can't worry the child.'

Lizzie remained silent but took hold of his hand and gently manipulated the immobile fingers. The contact with him caused her entire body to tremble.

'Are you wed?' he asked again.

She shook her head.

'Thank God.'

Letting go of him, she replied: 'I don't see it matters, seeing as how you been here all this time.'

He struggled up in the bed, wincing with pain.

'You must understand that as long as I was wed there was nothing I could do. When Rose died I wanted to rush over and find you but I feared you'd be wed again and ... I just couldn't face finding out that you had someone else.' He shrugged. 'I know it sounds weak but it mattered that much. Then, just when I made up my mind to come and find you, this happened.' He nodded towards his hand. 'It seems as if God don't never mean us to be together.'

'What about Garnet?' She was aware that her voice had a tremor in it.

'I ... left her in London.'

'Who with?'

He looked up at her. 'Her mother,' he said. 'You know, don't you?'

She nodded. 'I can't understand. How could you ever, with a wild thing like that?'

He shrugged. 'I guess it was because she was wild.' Seeing the pain on her face, he added: 'I only lay with her the once before I learned you were wed. I don't know what made me then. It was the day of the hiring and I wanted you so badly I was ...' He pulled a face. 'I truly think she bewitched me. I never loved her – not what I call love – yet when she was around I didn't seem to be myself.'

Remembering Mardi, Lizzie knew what he meant.

'It's in the past now,' she said quietly.

'I hope you're right. Lizzie, I never meant to hurt you. I must sound like a monster but apart from Mardi and Rose ...' He looked to her for understanding. 'Truly. I'd hardly dared hope to find you free again. There's so much I want to say to you.'

At that moment they heard Ruth on the stairway and both fell silent. Lizzie looked from her daughter to Will and he was looking across at her, his eyebrows raised.

'Shall I tell her or will you?' he started.

Before either of them could say anything, there was another movement on the stairs and a young woman appeared in the doorway, carrying a platter of hot food.

'Oo, I didn't know you had company,' she said, looking at Lizzie with hostile eyes. 'I've brought your food, Will.'

The widow from next door brought the plate to the bed and set it beside him, smoothing the covers and busying herself around the bed.

The corners of Lizzie's mouth dropped and hurt and shame swept over her.

'Yes, well, I can see that you didn't waste any time,' she said. Moving towards the stairs she added: 'I'll see myself out.'

'Lizzie!' Will reached out towards her but the pain in his arm halted him.

Without looking back, Lizzie made for the door. As she reached it, Ruth appeared at her side.

'Are you Lizabeth Dore of Caulbourne?' she asked.

Lizzie stopped. The girl's expression was unfathomable. 'That's who I am,' she replied, hardly knowing what she was saying. Turning to look directly at her daughter, she added: 'I live at the fulling mill. If ever you need me, you can come.'

Without giving the child a chance to reply, she walked out, untethered the horses, leaped astride Farmer and rode flat out towards the sanctuary of home.

She galloped wildly, her tears blinding her, oblivious to

everything but the pain and humiliation of the time at Will's cottage. Everything seemed to be obscured by jealousies – jealousy of the dead woman who had shared his life, jealousy of Mardi who had bewitched him, jealousy of the unnamed woman who was now cooking and caring for him and, for all she knew, sharing his bed. She hated him for hurting her so. But then there was the miracle of having found her daughter. The girl was everything she had dreamed of, both physically and in her polite but self-possessed manner. She wanted her back with a sudden, devastating hunger.

If Will had another woman, Ruby would once more be at the mercy of a heartless stepmother. Lizzie vowed there and then to go next day and fetch her home. If he was fool enough to tangle himself with every woman who was willing, that was his affair, but she was not having Ruby – no, Ruth – hurt. There was an advantage in the child's having a different name. If Lizzie were to take her back to Caulbourne, no one need suspect that this was her daughter Ruby Dore. She could introduce her as Ruth Gosden, the new dairymaid to replace Jane. She nodded grimly. This was what she would do.

As soon as she was indoors she lit the fire and huddled over its warmth, wrapping herself in a blanket for comfort. The day's events went round and round in her head until she was granted the mercy of release in sleep.

Inevitably, she began to dream. Will looked young and bronzed as through the years she had remembered him. The Will of that afternoon had been tired and dishevelled and there had been pain in his eyes. In her dream they were walking in the copse. He was asking her to marry him but she was saying that she could not because he was only half a man. She noticed then that he had a crutch and his leg was missing.

Waking with a start, Ruth's words came back to her. 'Pa's been that poorly, I thought he was going to die.' She began to weep, remembering the injured arm. She should have insisted on staying and treating it. Her pride seemed a small, pathetic thing and all she wanted was to go back to him, but she could not face the humiliation of finding him with the other woman. As that pain enveloped her anew, she clung to the thought of Tom's dogged loyalty and made a decision.

376

For several days she waited. It was now April and daily new tokens of spring appeared in the fields and hedgerows. Although she was preoccupied by the recent events, she could not but rejoice in the wonder of the changing seasons.

The rooks were at their most vocal as they repaired their clumsy twig nests in the giant elms behind the fulling mill. Lying in her bed, Lizzie listened to them and watched their tattered shadows as they flew past her window. Irrationally she fancied that as long as they were content, all would be well for her too. In spite of her hopes, Ruth had not come, and Lizzie had come to the conclusion that Will had forbidden her. This thought was the last goad that she needed to put her plan into action.

'I'm thinking of getting wed,' she said to Harry as she sat cross-legged on the floor of the weaving room, watching him at work. The movement of his deft hands pushing the shuttle between the strands of wool had a soothing, hypnotic effect.

'Who to?' He stopped and turned to look at her.

'Tom.'

When he made no comment, she added: 'He's waited that long. I reckon he'll be a good husband.'

'Why now?' Harry asked, back at work again.

She shrugged. 'Just seems the right time.'

'Yeah? Why's that, then?'

She did not answer and her heart jolted as he said:

'I hear Will Gosden's back. I heard tell he had an accident.'

'I know.' She experienced the familiar churning.

'Aren't you interested in him no more?' Harry's voice sounded matter-of-fact but as she continued to be silent he turned round again and waited for an answer.

'He's got someone else,' she muttered, sounding calmer than she would have believed possible.

'What makes you think that?'

She wished he would stop cross-examining her.

When she did not reply, he asked: 'What about your gal?'

She lowered her eyes. 'I've seen her. She's beautiful. I want her back. She can live with Tom'n me. He'll understand.'

'Will he?' Harry had abandoned all pretence at work. 'You don't love Tom, do you?' he asked.

'I'm fond of him,' she said defensively.

'You think that's enough?' He came to sit by her on the straw and rested his hand on her arm. 'Why are you so sure that Will don't care for you?'

Lizzie shrugged again and wished she could escape from his steady gaze.

'He seems strange. Cold. He's got a woman there cooking his meals. She looked very at home in his bedroom,' she added acidly.

When Harry made no comment, she said: 'He's damaged his hand that bad, he can't do nothing for himself.'

Harry let out a sigh. 'If he's hurt that bad, don't you think that would stop him from seeking you out?' he asked. 'From what I remember, he's a proud sort of chap. He wouldn't want to be a burden.'

'That's silly,' she retorted. 'Anyhow, it don't explain the woman. Besides, you're the one as said I should get wed. Tom's always been kind to me. I ... I'm just tired of being alone.'

'How do you know your gal'll leave her pa?' Harry asked, ignoring her comments.

'If he takes another wife, he won't miss her.'

'If you take a husband, you won't miss her neither.'

At this, Lizzie scrambled angrily to her feet.

'Why are you going on at me? It don't make no odds what you say 'cause I've made up my mind. Tom's coming on Friday and I'm going to tell him yes.'

Chapter Seven

Will lay morose and silent as Lizzie left the cottage and galloped away. He felt too exhausted by pain to fight any more. His food lay untouched and when Ruth came back to stare accusingly at him, he merely said: 'Leave me be.'

'That was my mam.' Her voice was tearful. With a visible effort he turned to look at her.

'I want you to think about something very careful,' he said. 'Yes, that is your mam. She's a real good woman and I'm sure she wants you. I think you should go and be with her.'

'Why?' There was panic in her voice and her lower lip began to tremble. Will longed to hug her to him but he merely answered: 'I reckon that's where you'll be best off.'

'Don't you want me, then?' Her face grew more desolate and he sighed.

'Course I do, but we must face facts. This hand ain't going to mend. I'll never be able to work at my craft again. That means there won't be no money. You saw your mam. She's doing well. You'd be best off with her.'

Ruth raised her eyes and glared at him. 'Don't you love her no more?' she accused.

He shook his head, searching for the right words. 'Course I love her but I've got nothing to offer her, have I?'

'We still got money.' Her voice was plaintive.

He took her hand and motioned her to sit on the bed.

'Not much we ain't, and it won't last for ever.'

'I can work – see? I sold some pasties at the market today.' She handed him the penny farthing she had earned.

He kissed her smooth forehead but continued: 'Sweetheart,

trust me. I want you to go and see her. You'll make her happy. She'll look after you proper, too.'

'No! I'm not going. I got to look after you.'

By way of reply he scrambled out of bed, ignoring the agony the movement caused in his arm.

'Where are you going?' she asked in alarm.

'To the castle. I'm going to get it sorted out. You must face the facts, gal. I'm finished.'

Somehow he struggled into his clothes, fighting off the waves of nausea that threatened to engulf him.

'How you going to get there?' she asked defiantly.

'On foot. I'll get the horse later.'

'I'm coming too.'

'No! I forbid it. You go round to Widow Gleed's and stay there till I get back. It might not be till tomorrow. Now just do as I say.'

He did not look at her for fear that her stricken face might make him relent.

He managed to keep going until he was out of sight of the village and then he sank down on a boulder by the side of the road. The pain coursing through his arm numbed his mind to everything else. The idea that he would be able to work at anything that was familiar to him seemed remote.

Apart from the skills that had rested in his two good hands, he possessed few resources. Neither the cottage nor the land was his. There was the horse, provided that she was now fit, the goat, a few geese and chickens, his tools and a box of taters he had saved to grow for the coming year. He had a wild idea that if he could grow enough he would be able to sell them, for they were quite unknown around the village, but that would take time and anyway country folks were slow to change. He also had four pounds.

Without Ruth he could survive on very little. If he had to, he could join the ranks of the roving beggars and live on his wits, or go to the mainland and get assistance from the guild. It was like a nightmare, planning such a future.

Lizzie wasn't wed. All this time he had hardly dared hope that she might have waited for him and now all that he had to offer her was his poverty. With a desolate sigh he dragged himself up and on towards Carisbrooke. Why am I doing this?

380

he thought, but he knew that he had to tell them once and for all that he would not be back and put any dream of a miracle out of his mind.

By the time Carisbrooke Castle came into view, it was dark. He forced himself to walk the last few hundred yards and leaned against the stone parapet, fighting off the nausea.

'Who's there?' Hearing a noise, the guards had come to investigate, daggers and crossbows at the ready. Recognising Will, they lowered their weapons.

'My Lord! Will, you don't look fit to be here,' said the leader of the watch.

Will swallowed hard and with a visible effort stood upright.

Bright lights shone from the house in the courtyard where he had once worked and where Sir George and his wife had lived with their daughter. Now that he was Baron Hunsdon he was rarely here, but clearly tonight he was paying a visit to the island to check on the fortifications.

At that moment the door of the house opened and several people came out into the night air, laughing and calling farewells. Among them Will recognised Mr Dingley of Wolverton, who owned his cottage. He looked rather the worse for wear. There was much hilarity and cheering as the visitors, all male, rode off on horseback.

Seeing them out into the night, Lord Hunsdon stopped to have a word with the guards. It was clear that he was feeling expansive, voluble and at a loose end.

'All in order?' he asked.

'Aye, m'lord.'

He suddenly noticed Will leaning against the wall for support.

'Gosling?'

'Gosden, m'lord.' Will tried to stand upright but slumped back again.

'What are you doing here, man? You do not look fit.' The Baron came closer.

'I've come to say that I won't be back to work no more.' Will felt a strange lessening of tension now that he had said it.

'Are you certain of that?' Hunsdon was now so close that Will could smell the brandy on his breath.

'Aye, sir. This hand's as useless as a lame dog.'

381

Hunsdon tilted his head to one side, considering Will.

'Come with me.' He preceded him across the courtyard to his home. Inside, the conflicting smells of the dishes that had been served up to his guests tantalised Will's nostrils.

'I'm sorry to hear this, Gosden.' The Baron turned and sat on the edge of the table, swinging his leg. He wore white hose and neat black shoes with silver buckles. His shirt had voluminous sleeves gathered at the cuff and around his neck he had an intricately patterned lace ruff. Will felt ashamed of his unkempt appearance. His employer was perfumed and Will hoped that the scent would disguise the smell of his own unwashed body.

'Sit down, Gosden. You look fit to fall.'

Gratefully he sank into one of the large, carved oak chairs, holding his arm and gently rocking it.

'Have you seen a physician?' Hunsdon asked.

'When first 'twas done. I can't move my fingers.'

His host poured two goblets of wine, handing one to his guest. Will took a gulp. It was unlike anything he had tasted before, rich and fruity. He suspected that the goblet was gold, and it had small shiny stones embedded around the base. After a few minutes the pain in his arm began to recede.

'Now, Gosden, if you cannot work, what will you do?'

'Perhaps leave the island. I plan to leave my daughter with – a relative.'

'Yes. You lost your wife recently, did you not? A sad business. The child must miss her.'

'She does. We both do.' He thought sadly for a moment how Rose would have fussed over him.

'You have been an asset in your work, Gosden. I would like to make some sort of arrangement for you.'

'No. Begging your pardon, sir, but I don't want charity. My little maid'll be all right along with her – relative – and I'll manage.'

'Nonsense, man. You're good with horses, are you not? I seem to remember that you have a creditable chestnut mare.'

'Aye. She's a good beast. I could sell her for several pounds.'

His host was shaking his head. 'Do not sell your assets,' he counselled. 'Why do you not breed from her?'

Will considered for a moment. 'I ain't got access to a good stallion,' he replied.

'I have.' Lord Hunsdon sat up and his eyes gleamed in the candlelight. 'In fact, I have a young horse I've been wondering what to do with. One of my stallions, much to my shame, broke loose and covered Isaac Colenutt's working mare. She is a good, solid animal. Anyway, Colenutt had no use for the colt so I bought him back. I was going to have him gelded and sold on, but there is something about his lines. I like him.'

Will was listening intently. A throb of excitement started in his veins.

'I've got some savings, I could buy him,' he started.

'Damn it, man, don't be so proud. I want to give him to you. You are the sort of man I respect. Horses are in demand these days. If you must spend your money, look out for a second mare and set the young devil to work.'

Will nodded his thanks but then his face become serious.

'There is one problem,' he said. 'The mare went lame. Ruth, my child, left her at a stable in Carisbrooke. I don't know how serious it is.'

The Baron poured more wine. His movements were now slow and deliberate and he seemed to have some difficulty in focusing on his guest.

'That is easily solved,' he replied. 'On the morrow I will send a man to investigate. If the mare is fit I will have her delivered to you – also the colt. There, another new enterprise is born.' He chuckled to himself.

Will was fighting to stay awake, but the excitement of this new venture seemed like the miracle he had denied was possible.

'I don't know how to thank you, sir,' he said.

'Make a success of it. I leave for London on the morrow, but if you send word to the castle it will reach me. I'll be interested in buying the first filly you get.'

'I will.'

Hunsdon hiccupped. 'Time for bed,' he observed, standing up unsteadily. Reaching the door, he realised that Will was still there and added: 'You sleep there by the fire. I'll send someone with some bedding.'

Through the doorway, Will could see him meandering up the stairway.

Alone with the remains of the banquet, he helped himself to

some of the meats still laid out on the great sideboard. This is a dream, he thought. I'll wake up in a minute. He poured himself some more wine and as he sipped it he was aware that someone had come in.

Carrying a quilt and dragging a bolster behind her, a young woman crossed the room to the fireplace. Ignoring him, she laid the bedding out and puffed up the bolster with a great show of exertion.

'God in Heaven!' Will shook his head in disbelief. Mardi Appleby stood up slowly and looked at him with her shrewd, appraising eyes.

'What in the Devil's name are you doing here?' he asked.

'I could ask you the same,' she replied coolly. 'Only I know the answer. I willed you to come.'

'But...'

She started to laugh at his discomposure.

'Poor Will! You'll never know what to expect next, will you?' Taking his good hand, she sank down on the sheepskin rug by his chair. 'There's no mystery. Hunsdon has been my patron for nigh on three years. It was he who took Garnet into his household.' Seeing his stunned expression, she added: 'I told my lord about my visits here and as he was coming I persuaded him to let me accompany him.'

He shook his head again and felt his cheeks colour. 'Lord Hunsdon, of all people? You are beyond belief!'

Mardi bowed her head, then looked up again to meet his eyes. For a long while they gazed at each other; then he sighed.

'I take it that you'll be otherwise engaged tonight?'

She raised an eyebrow. 'Is that your business? What about that wife you are always so faithful to?'

'Rose died.'

'I'm sorry.'

He acknowledged her words and for a while they were both silent.

'Let me read your palm,' she offered.

'No. I don't know what the future holds; I'd rather find out when it happens.'

Mardi shrugged. 'My lord has overindulged,' she finally observed. 'He isn't going to notice if he sleeps alone tonight.'

'Are you suggesting you sleep down here with me?'

'It's up to you to do the suggesting.' In a serious moment she cupped his face between her hands and reached up to kiss him. 'You stink,' she observed but, seeing his embarrassment, she kissed him again, pressing herself to him. 'You smell like a man.'

Will moved away. 'You pop up in my life like a grasshopper,' he said. 'One minute you aren't there and the next you are. Trouble is, the next you aren't again and we never settle anything.'

'What do you want to settle?'

He shrugged. 'You should know by now I need things cut and dried. I can't just take what's there with no thought to the morrow.'

'If you wanted it, I could be there all the time,' she said quietly. 'I know my way of life appals you but look where it has got me.' She flashed the rings on her fingers and ran her hands over the jewel-encrusted gown. Sighing, she added: 'The strange thing is, now I've got more wealth than you can imagine, I don't really care about it. I would give it all away for a man who didn't want to buy me.'

Will looked at the ground. 'I haven't got anything to offer any woman,' he observed.

'Is that your way of saying you don't want me?'

'When he did not answer, she added: 'If I lived with you, then so could Garnet. You'd have both your daughters under your roof again.'

The idea filled him with longing, but he found himself thinking about Lizzie, who had been sold to Silas Dore but would never sell herself to save her life.

'How is Garnet?' he asked instead.

'Well. She is still under Hunsdon's roof.'

'We're different,' he finally observed.

Mardi looked ruefully at him and shrugged. 'I've been offered employment of a different kind. When I was in the Netherlands I learned to speak the language. Now I have the chance to go and work in the ambassador's house. I would be useful to my country.'

'What are you going to do?'

She placed her hand on his shoulder and looked into his eyes. 'If you don't wish me to stay, then I shall take the chance.'

'And Garnet?'

'She'll come with me.'

'No!' He felt alarm at the very idea.

'Have no fear. You forget that she is my child. I am a survivor and so is she.'

Remembering the fiercely proud little girl, he lowered his head in defeat. 'You'll make sure she always knows where I am?' he asked.

'Of course. In any case she would know by instinct.'

Will nodded and Mardi moved back from him. 'Well, I had best find my way upstairs.' Turning to look at him, she added: 'You're the only man who has ever refused me.'

'Will I see you again?'

'I think not. It seems that our ways are truly parting.'

Stepping forwards again, she kissed him gently on the lips and he prolonged the exquisite feeling of her touch.

'Mardi.'

She drew back and placed her hand on his cheek. 'Goodbye, Will. Don't you ever forget me.'

'As if I could.'

Chapter Eight

Curled up in front of the fire, Will slept better than he had for months. When he awoke, it was to bright sunshine and a maid clearing the room.

'His lordship knows I'm here,' he said to the girl.

'He's up and gone. He said to give you breakfast.'

'Is anyone else here?' he asked awkwardly.

'If you mean his companion, she went with him.' The maid looked down her nose in disdain and Will did not meet her eyes.

He ate well and afterwards, still bathed in the exhilaration of last night, set out for home. The pain in his arm was still there but it was bearable now that he had some hope.

When he arrived at the cottage, Ruth ran out to meet him.

'Oh, Pa, I'm glad that you're safe.' She bobbed him an awkward curtsy and for a fleeting moment he saw her not as a child but as a young woman. The realisation filled him with a strange reverence.

Putting his arm around her shoulders, he walked with her into the house.

'I'm better than I've been in a long while, gal,' he said. 'Lord Hunsdon is going to fetch the mare and we're going into horse breeding. I need a few days to sort things out and then, God willing, it will all be well for us.'

'Does that mean I can stay with you?' she asked.

'Just be patient, child, I got lots to think about.'

He drank some ale and then went out into the garden, deciding where he was going to plant the taters. He made an attempt at digging the plot one-handed, but the violent pain that accompanied each wielding of the spade soon had him cursing.

'Pa, you're that stubborn! Let me.' Ruth took the wooden spade and he watched in frustration as she struggled to turn over the topsoil.

Patience, he counselled himself. This is the first step towards our future.

The mare did not arrive the next day or the next, and Will began to feel uneasy. If Hunsdon had forgotten, he would be sorely disappointed, but now that the idea had been planted he vowed that he would get hold of a stallion, come what may.

With Ruth's help he got the taters into the ground and planted his broad beans and radishes. They were just finishing when he heard the rumble of a cart and the sound of hooves. Looking out into the lane, he saw a wagon approaching with two horses tied on behind. He immediately recognised his mare and started out to meet them.

Beside the mare, tossing his head restlessly, was a black colt. At the sight of him Will felt a tingle of excitement. As soon as the wagon stopped he was round the back, running his hand over the animal's shoulders and down his long, strong legs. He understood the Baron's reluctance to cut him. The horse regarded him with intelligent black eyes and, dipping his head, nearly knocked him over.

'Whoa, boy,' he crooned, blowing on his muzzle.

Greeting the mare, he was relieved to see that her leg was healed. The carter had descended and came to join him.

'Liddle devil he is,' he said, indicating the colt. 'Full o' life. You'll have yer hands full there.'

Will smiled to himself, thinking of his useless arm. The statement was half true at least.

'I got a load of oats and some hay fer ye,' the man continued. 'The gaffer says you're to take it and no nonsense.'

Will grinned. He suddenly felt alive again. With the man's help he unloaded the fodder and got the two horses into the small barn that stood on his piece of land. He watched the youngster pace restlessly round and the animal's movements filled him with pleasure. After he had offered the carter some refreshment, he stood and stared long and hard at the beginnings of his breeding stock.

388

The next day was Friday and he was up before daybreak. Going out into the yard, he doused his head and body with water, rubbing himself with the soap he had bought for Ruth when the fair had last visited. It smelled of roses and as he lathered his head he was amused at his vanity. Gently he washed the injured hand. The skin felt numb and yet tender. His fingers bent a little from the top joints and there was some slight movement in his thumb. Ignoring the pain, he forced his fingers forwards to make a fist. I'll make 'em work if it kills me, he vowed.

Wet and naked he went back into the cottage and struggled into his best clothing, then roughly trimmed his hair and beard.

When Ruth came down, he had already caught and saddled the mare.

'Where you off?' she asked in surprise.

'Out.' He turned to her and raised her chin with his fingers so that her eyes met his.

'I want you to brush your hair real nice and put on your best gown because we're going out on business,' he said.

'Where to?'

He gave her his lopsided smile and pinched her cheek. 'Why, to see your mother.'

Chapter Nine

On Friday morning, as the first hint of light invaded he room, Lizzie lay in bed and thought, As from today my life will change.

She wondered what it would be like to share the mill house with Tom. There was no question in her mind of moving and it would be easy enough for Tom to continue with the wheelwright's shop. He had only to walk to the crossroads. With satisfaction she realised that their combined incomes would make them truly prosperous.

There would be snags and she had to admit that in some ways she had enjoyed the solitude of living alone. Since Silas's death she had made all the decisions in conjunction with Harry. Her father had been deliberately excluded, much to his indignation, but she knew that her own prosperity had rubbed off onto Sheepwash cottage. I haven't been a bad daughter, she told herself.

Lizzie stretched and thought how comforting it would be to let someone else do the worrying. She was sure that Tom and Harry would get on well enough and when she had Ruby back – or should she say Ruth? – it would be like reliving her own childhood, when she and Leah had shared all the family chores.

Getting up and lighting the fire, she took a pan of water and proceeded to wash herself. New day, new beginnings, she thought, rubbing the wet cloth under her arms. She put on her clean kirtle, which had been layered with rose petals and gillyflowers, and enjoyed the sweet smell released by her body warmth.

It was not long before she heard the sound of whistling,

followed by a knock on the door. It opened and Tom poked his head round. Although it was a working day, he had on his good clothes and his face looked shiny. Lizzie had not seen him for some weeks and had forgotten quite how plump he was.

'Would you like some beer?' she offered.

'Please.' He wiped his hand across his mouth and stood awkwardly by the door.

'Well, sit you down.'

He plonked himself in Silas's chair.

'You looks real beautiful,' he remarked. 'I've missed you.'

'I missed you too.' She handed him the ale.

'Enough?'

'Enough for what?'

'To marry me.'

Lizzie smiled at him. 'I got things to ask you first,' she said.

'Ask away then.'

'You know that I got a daughter?'

'Aye. You sent her off to a grand house.' He hesitated. 'If we has nippers I wouldn't have 'em sent away.'

'I had special reasons,' she replied. 'Anyhow, I'd like to have her back.'

He nodded his head in acquiescence.

'The only thing is, I'd rather people didn't know who she was.'

Tom frowned. 'Is it cause of that fuss over the witch?' he asked.

She nodded, trying to assess his reaction. 'I don't want no rumours stirred up again. I couldn't bear that.'

'No, but won't people know she's yourn? She might look like you.'

'She don't. She looks like her –' Lizzie stopped herself in time and avoided his eyes.

'You seen her, then?' he asked, not pursuing her answer.

'A while ago.'

'Well, 'tis up to you.' He reached out and took her cool hand in his damp ones.

'The boys will have to stay, too,' she continued.

'Of course. You are a good Christian woman, taking them in like that.'

Lizzie thought of all her failings. 'No, I'm not. I had no choice,' she said obliquely.

'Does that mean I can set the date, then?' he asked.

As he pulled her close to kiss her, they were both aware of the sound of horses' hooves and turned their heads towards the window.

'Who be that, then?' Tom asked.

Lizzie, already standing, moved towards the window. What she saw caused her to gasp, her hand flying to her throat.

'What is it?'

'Visitors.' She was transfixed by the sight of Will and Ruth astride the chestnut mare. As she watched, he handed the child down and slid to the ground, his right arm hanging awkwardly at his side.

Tom had now joined her at the window, putting his arm about her shoulders. She drew away from him so that they should not be seen together. Her heart was thundering and her mouth dry. She knew that Tom was watching but she had no control over the emotion that engulfed her.

As she watched, Will walked towards the door, Ruth's hand in his. He was thinner than she had ever seen him but still he looked proud and straight-backed. I love him, she thought.

Her hand shook as she opened the door. Father and daughter regarded her with steady, matching eyes. She reached out and squeezed the child's shoulder.

'This is a surprise.' She stepped back to let them in, aware of Tom standing behind her.

'My cousin Tom,' she said. 'This is Will Gosden and –'

'My daughter,' Will cut in to avoid confusion. His eyes did not leave Lizzie's face.

'I remembers you,' Tom replied. 'Went to London, didn't you?'

Will bowed his head in assent.

'Your little maid favours you,' Tom continued, then, turning to Lizzie, added: 'She must be about the same age as yourn?'

Lizzie nodded but could not speak.

As she brought some ale for Will and honeyed rosehip cordial for the child, Tom put his arm about her waist. She froze as Will observed them and could not meet his eyes.

'Lizzie 'n me's gettin' wed,' she heard Tom say.

There was silence before Will replied.

'Then you're a lucky man.' He drained his beer in one long swallow, placing the tankard carefully on the table.

'We'd best be leaving now,' he said to Ruth. His voice was cool.

'Don't go!' Lizzie, her face stricken, reached out her hand but he moved away, still holding the child by the arm. Ruth looked from one to the other.

'But Pa, I want to stay. I thought ...' The girl looked desperately at him.

'Hush, child. Now ain't the time.' Will pulled her away and with unnerving politeness bowed to them. Turning on his heel, he walked away. As if turned to stone, Lizzie listened as the mare broke into a brisk trot.

Tom was still watching her. 'What was that about?' he asked. She shook her head.

'Looks to me like he's sweet on you,' he observed.

At this she started to sob and he put his arms around her.

'No need to get upset, dearest, I'll look after you.' He started to kiss her and she struggled to get free.

'No! Tom, I'm sorry. I can't wed you. I don't love you. I love him.'

The words came out in anguished gasps and he let go of her as if she had stung him.

'How can you?' he demanded. 'He's bin away fer years.'

'I always have.'

His blue eyes flinched at the hurt and she looked at him, begging for understanding.

'You bin stringing me along?' he finally asked.

'No. I really like you. It's just that I can't help how I feel.'

'I see.' He pursed his lips. 'Right. I'll be goin' then. I won't be back to trouble you.'

'Tom!'

He made for the door, slamming it behind him. Lizzie, alone and despairing, sank back against the table and wept.

After a while her sobbing eased. Pulling herself together, she took her broom and swept the dust out into the yard, working out her pent-up feelings. From across the way she could hear the loom clanking rhythmically as Harry worked. Flinging the broom into a corner, she went out and across to see him.

393

Glancing up as she came in, he continued to work for a moment. Then, seeing her red eyes, he stopped and sat back on his stool.

'Summat wrong?' he asked.

'I must go out. Can you look after things? I don't know when I'll be back.'

He nodded. 'Where you going?'

She lowered her eyes. 'Shorrel.'

He surveyed her with a quizzical smile. 'You still planning to marry Cousin Tom?' he asked.

'No.'

'Good.'

It was afternoon when she arrived at Shorrel. The first person she saw was Ruth, driving some geese from behind the cottage towards the meadow. When the girl saw her she stopped in her tracks and blushed.

'Hello,' she greeted. 'Pa's out.'

Dismounting from Farmer, Lizzie wound his rein around a post and smiled awkwardly.

Opening the cottage door, Ruth asked: 'Won't you come inside? I been baking.'

Lizzie followed her and accepted a piece of bread and some cheese, for she had not eaten since dawn. As she ate, the girl regarded her solemnly. To break the silence, Lizzie said:

'There's so much I want to say to you. I don't know what you've been told but...'

'Pa's told me everything. I'm growed up, I understand.'

Lizzie smiled gratefully at her. 'I've always had a dream that one day we'd be together,' she confessed.

Ruth's eyes were large and serious. 'Just you and me – or you, me and Pa?' she demanded.

'The three of us,' her mother said truthfully.

'Why did you say you'd marry your cousin, then?'

Ruth looked at her suspiciously and her mother sighed as she sought for the right words.

'I've known him all my life. He's been real kind to me and in the end I got that lonely, I thought it would be better than being by myself. I don't expect you'll really understand but loneliness is a terrible thing.'

394

Ruth nodded as if indeed she did recognise the feelings. 'Pa loves you,' she said. 'He told me so.'

'When?'

'When Mam died. And yesterday.'

'Who was that woman looking after him when he was sick?' Lizzie blushed as she felt her jealousy exposed before the child.

'Widow Gleed. She lives next door. She's got five littluns and I help her sometimes.'

'Does Pa like her?'

'She likes him. He says she's looking for a breadwinner.'

Lizzie's heart lightened. 'If it was possible, would you come and live with me?' she asked.

Ruth hesitated. 'I'd like to but . . . I couldn't never leave Pa. I love him,' she added in barely a whisper.

Lizzie reached out and squeezed the girl's small brown hands.

'Oh, so do I, my love,' she replied.

Neither of them saw Will come in. Suddenly he was there standing in the doorway, looking at them.

'Pa – Ma's here.' Ruth jumped up and went to him, flushing at the use of her mother's title.

'So I see.'

Lizzie said nothing.

'How's the colt?' the child asked, holding on to his hand.

'He's fine.' Looking at Lizzie, he said: 'You'd best come and see.'

Gratefully she fell in beside him and he took her across to the barn where the black horse was tossing his handsome head.

'He's a beauty. What are you doing with him?' The awkwardness was gone now that they were on safer ground.

'I'm setting up a breeding stock. That's something I can do with one hand.'

She reached out and gently touched his injured fingers. 'Can you use them at all?'

He shook his head. 'The thumb moves a bit. I'll get by.'

'Will, I ain't marrying Tom. I never – you know, with him.' She blushed and looked away.

He raised his eyebrows questioningly. 'I don't know if that's any of my business, is it?'

She shrugged. 'I want it to be.'

He raised her chin and traced the line of her mouth with his thumb.

'I ain't sure this breeding business is going to work out,' he said noncommittally. 'Till I'm sure, I ain't got nothing to offer you.'

'You're a fool,' she heard herself say. 'You got yourself. I don't want no more.'

He bent to kiss her then and her body melted into his.

'Will, I can't go on. Not without you. Please don't be proud. I need you so much, you and our girl. Don't deny me that.' She was weeping quietly against his shoulder.

He rubbed his face into her hair. 'There are a lot of things haven't worked the way I intended,' he said.

'Did you love the others?'

He held her at arm's length and looked into her eyes. 'Lizzie, I've only ever loved you. I had feelings for them, yes, but you've always been my life's blood.'

She relaxed into his arms and let the peace claim her.

'There are things to sort out,' he warned.

'There's plenty of room for all of us at the mill.'

'Including the stallion?'

In reply she kissed him, holding his face between her hands, closing her eyes and finding his mouth with hers. His tongue was between her lips and she tasted his sweetness, knowing nothing but the hardness of his body along the length of hers.

'Don't go back tonight,' he said.

'I won't. I told Harry I might not be back. He knows where I am.'

He hugged her and smiled. 'In that case I'll have to wed thee then.'

Arm in arm they returned to the cottage and Lizzie offered to help her daughter prepare the evening meal. As she stirred the cooking pot, she thought; This is how I always dreamed it would be. Aloud she said to the girl: 'It looks like there'll be three of us after all.'

Ruth smiled shyly. 'Good. I really prayed for us all to be together. When are you going back to your own house?'

'Not tonight.'

'We ain't got a spare bed,' her daughter pointed out. 'I sleep down here and Pa's got the big bed upstairs.'

Holding Ruth's gaze, Lizzie said: 'Looks like I'll have to share his bed then.'

The girl coloured. 'Like you was his wife?' she asked.

Her mother nodded happily.

'Exactly like that.'

At eleven of the clock on a January morning in 1599 a group of people huddled together on the quay at Tilbury. At the centre of the group, two women held their thick woollen cloaks fast about them. The wind had finally dropped to a slicing breeze and they were waiting to board the *Princess Mary* bound for Ostend.

The captain of the vessel came down to escort the ladies aboard.

'I feared that the wind would last for ever,' he said by way of greeting. 'But clearly the elements have been gallant to two such beautiful ladies.'

The widow Appleby and her daughter Garnet bowed in unison and at the same time a secret smile touched both their lips.

'You need have no fear, captain, the crossing will be calm,' Mistress Appleby announced.

The captain bowed again. 'I am glad to hear it, ma'am.'

Mardi and Garnet consented to take an arm each and were escorted to two tiny cabins. In spite of her grand demeanour, the child now found it difficult to hide her amazement at the neat and compact arrangements in the rooms.

'See, Mam, such little beds! And lanterns to light the evenings.'

Mardi smiled indulgently, but already she was looking over the girl's shoulder at the captain.

'I trust it is to your liking,' he said, a quizzical smile about his lips. 'When we arrive at the port you will be escorted to your destination. I believe you are to stay in the ambassador's residence?'

Mardi did not confirm or deny it. While ostensibly over-seeing the welfare of the ambassador's children, she would have ample leisuretime to entertain the important gentlemen who called on the Queen's representative. Even lords and diplomats could be indiscreet in the company of a beautiful woman.

The captain's eyes roamed over Mardi's body and she raised a provocative eyebrow.

'As you see, I have the right equipment,' she replied. 'Now tell me, captain, which cabin should I favour?'

The captain laughed and suggested: 'If your little maid wishes to have the small cabin for herself, then you and I could keep each other company on the journey.'

Mardi acknowledged that the arrangement suited her well enough.

As soon as he was out of hearing, the child exclaimed: 'Mam! You ain't going to bed with the captain?' Garnet frowned her disapproval but Mardi merely smiled.

'You must appreciate, my child, that like all craftsmen, I have to practise my arts regularly lest I lose the skills that mark me out as an artist in my own right.'

'Oh, Mam! How can you tolerate such boors and turkey cocks?'

Putting her arm around her daughter, Mardi looked into the eyes that so resembled William Gosden's. She felt a moment of sadness but knew that given the choice of living in a cottage in a remote island village with Will or in one of the grandest houses on the continent without him, the latter was where she would choose to be. She had lost the battle for his heart but suddenly she knew that it had turned out right.

Squeezing the girl's arm, she said: 'One day, my child, all will be revealed to you. Until then, follow your Knowledge. You are blessed indeed with the Sight and if you use it well, nothing can ever go wrong.'

Author's Note

The parish register of All Saints Church in Calbourne on the Isle of Wight records that on 22 October 1599, William Gosden of Calbourne married Elizabeth, née Galpine. Their union was blessed with two children.

On 28 October 1600 their first-born son, John, was baptised in the village church, and a second son, William, on 3 April 1604.

Whatever else befell them is lost in the mists of time.

The names of many other characters in this story are authentic and contemporary although their personalities and experiences are pure invention.

Sir George Carey remained Captain of the Island until his death in 1603.

Mardi Appleby is a figment of the imagination.